AF621437

THE THREE RAVENS FOLK TALES

New tellings of half-forgotten stories from England's 39 Historic Counties

ELEANOR CONLON & MARTIN VAUX

The History Press

First published 2025

The History Press
97 St George's Place, Cheltenham,
Gloucestershire, GL50 3QB
www.thehistorypress.co.uk

Text © Eleanor Conlon & Martin Vaux, 2025
Illustrations and cover design © Olly James-Dare

The right of Eleanor Conlon & Martin Vaux to be identified as the Authors of this work has been asserted in accordance with the Copyright, Designs and Patents Act 1988.

All rights reserved. No part of this book may be reprinted or reproduced or utilised in any form or by any electronic, mechanical or other means, now known or hereafter invented, including photocopying and recording, or in any information storage or retrieval system, without the permission in writing from the Publishers.

British Library Cataloguing in Publication Data.
A catalogue record for this book is available from the British Library.

ISBN 978 1 80399 968 5

Typesetting and origination by The History Press
Printed and bound in Great Britain by TJ Books, Padstow, Cornwall.

MIX
Paper | Supporting responsible forestry
FSC® C013056

The History Press proudly supports
Trees for Life
www.treesforlife.org.uk

EU Authorised Representative: Easy Access System Europe
Mustamäe tee 50, 10621 Tallinn, Estonia
gpst.request@easproject.com

For storytellers everywhere,
whether big or small,
hairy or scaly, real or imagined,
and all things in between.

Contents

Foreword

By Jeremy Harte

There are many ways to tell a story. Start with 'A man walks into a bar' and your audience knows exactly what they'll get – strong plot, straightforward character, and no frilly stuff with atmosphere or scene-setting. A lot of English folk narrative is like that, or at least that's how it feels when you read the great county collections. Of course, some of the plain speaking may be accidental. When Victorian folklorists walked into bars, they weren't armed with a smartphone to interview the old fellow in the chimney seat, and there is only so much of a story that you can carry in your head from a single telling, even for a generation that had grown up memorising Latin verse and the Collect on Sundays.

When you read the oldest transcripts of English tradition, their style is usually terse. It's a pity, but then we are lucky to have the stories at all. There's never been a time when everyone was above average, and collectors were lucky to find an informant who could remember what happened and when, let alone pace the funny bits and add an occasional touch of pathos. That wouldn't matter if we could go back to the original storytellers, armed with proper recording equipment: but those days are gone. The canon of local legend in England has been closed now for a good hundred years. Folklore continues to thrive, twining through our lives and institutions like ivy in a thicket, but the specific folk genre of the local legendary tale came to an end not long after the last soldier returned from the Great War.

But that end was also a beginning, for the one constant in tradition is change. As Heraclitus so nearly put it, a man cannot step into the same bar twice. By the time it had become clear that no more new tales (or songs, or dances, or curious customs) were going to be garnered from elderly rustics – or whoever else counted as 'the folk' – a new living tradition of performance was already in place, folk in its style if not its lineage. The twilight days between the old native informant and the new craft storyteller were marked, as twilights so often are, by shadows and false outlines. Many excellent raconteurs gained a hearing by pretending to pass on something orally inherited when in fact they were putting spin on a piece they'd read or invented from the folk idiom. What mattered was re-establishing live narrative performance as an art on a par with music or dance or drama.

Good stories are many, while good storytellers are few. Eleanor and Martin are two of the best. The Three Ravens (I know there are only two of them, but this is an English tradition, right?) bring a questing intelligence to the great collections of lore and their stories are just as much fun whether you are hearing them for the first time or whether you're an obsessive who's been tracking Herne the Hunter since he first rode out. Local legend is a very loose category, a rummage bin into which past generations have thrown the third division of medieval heroes, old landmarks newly explained, and proofs of the supernatural which entertain more than they convince. It is so grounded in the real that it provokes the imagination: wave the wand of story and our familiar hill is revealed as the coils of a dragon. And there is no better way to hold an audience than local allusion. Why send a man into a pub when he can walk into the Admiral Benbow, the Prancing Pony or the Moon Under Water?

This is the appeal of legend, its combination of somewhere that could be nowhere else – the Downs, the Peak, the Fens – with narratives that have been floating around the world free as thistledown for the last few thousand years. These stories tangle up with each other, like a kitten's knitting. Until you begin to tell them, you cannot say what motif will bring in another, pulled by some magnetic attraction. Often in this collection the Ravens will begin with one canonical story and another will insist on being told as a prequel or sequel. That is a time-honoured practice: how do you think the Bible was built up, or the tale of Troy?

Old-style storytelling was not just terse, it was chronologically flattened. Everything happened in the indeterminate zone of once upon a time: sort of medieval (it has knights, dragons and castles) but modern at the same time. I suppose that tradition began when medieval *was* modern. To the credit of the Ravens, they have found new settings for old tales, from the contemporary memoir to the eighteenth-century found document, and tell them in different voices, from dialogue to first-person to the most challenging of all, a story told from the perspective of the supernatural.

Turn from one tale to another and appreciate their chameleon changes in style, presentation and atmosphere. The modern performative story is a sturdy hybrid between two stocks: traditional oral narrative and a modern literary sensibility. From one it derives plot, location and the aura of expectation that clothes 'king', 'gold' and 'witch'; from the other it has learnt to ask what people feel, and why. Suddenly weary of the din in the crowded streets, the man turned with a shrug through the first door that presented itself, and found himself alone in a cool, dusty mahogany-lined bar.

Literature has taught us to ask questions never contemplated in the original tale-types. In traditional narrative, Jack returns from his travels with golden coins, a noble horse and a princess: any princess will do, they are as interchangeable as the coins and have as little choice as the horse. There is a bright innocent egotism about this kind of tale which suits the world of childhood, but we are telling for adults. With unobtrusive art, the Ravens give the actors in their stories an inner life. What does a mermaid expect out of marriage? How does it feel when other people call you a witch?

They say stories are universal but this isn't true. A straight delivery from the *Golden Legend*, that great medieval collection of saints' lives which fixed 'legend' as the word for our particular genre of story, leaves a modern audience deeply uncomfortable. Its blood libel stories, like Little St. Hugh of Lincoln, can be read in the study but they cannot be told or sung. There is a moral complicity about live storytelling, though that doesn't exclude acts of violence – at least, not yet. The body count in traditional narrative would make a police procedural blush and this goes back to the first singers of epic, when a man rode into a mead-hall and burnt it down with everyone inside.

Three thousand years after the *Iliad*, songs of battle still have the power to thrill rather than shock. We are less violent than our ancestors but we will die just like them, which is why the ghost flits through traditional story, a reminder that while we know so much more than previous generations, we are as ignorant about the one inescapable thing. The Ravens have a fine spectrum of ghosts – grim, wicked, sad, even misunderstood. For things are not always as they seem and even monsters have their good points. Inside every fire-breathing dragon lies the pet it once was, and the crooked figure bending over a still body may be a healer, not a witch. A good story has the power to make us think about buried things; we absorb them as children but return to explore them as adults. We may have given up guarding our houses against sorcerers and fiends with mark and spell, but they are still there inside us and the only protective magic is wisdom and compassion.

The Ravens are wise birds but they are also evocative, stylish, dramatic and frequently hilarious. Don't let me keep you outside any longer. Walk in and they will serve you.

Jeremy Harte
2025

Introduction

Gather round the campfire and listen in…

It was Isaac Newton who, in writing to Robert Hooke in 1675, famously said, 'If I have seen further it is by standing on the shoulders of Giants'. In this, Newton, like many grand people, proved himself to be a dreadful liar. He never stood on the shoulders of a single giant, as far as anyone can tell, even though England is absolutely littered with them. Some are sleeping, some are dead, and some are very wisely keeping their heads down…

To us, the kinds of giants who have helped us see further are writers. Be they chroniclers, historians, traditional storytellers, novelists, short story writers, or any other noble spinner of tangled yarns – since we were both children, we have gobbled up stories in a manner many would find outright greedy and quite unpleasant to watch. To name them all would fill a book in itself. Still, our love of folk tales and old stories, many of which we've retold in all sorts of ways over the years, prompted us to launch our podcast, *Three Ravens*, in March 2023, and share our passion for them.

When we embarked on the project, we hoped we might find a listener or two who would be interested in the same tales we were. Tales of ghosts, monsters, heroes, and mermaids, the odd urban legend, and even odder true stories, some of which are scary, some of which are funny, and some of which are just downright strange.

Little did we expect quite so many people to join us every week, and as *Three Ravens* has grown and grown, we have been overjoyed to discover that the world is positively teeming with people eager to hear our tellings. But it's important to remember, the stories were there before us, and will be there after we're gone, too.

Rather than ravens, we have been a bit more like magpies, picking up shiny and interesting tales as told by others then rewriting them to pass on, in the same way people have been doing since giants weren't so shy and dragons were plentiful, and many ghosts were still living people all going about their business. Nonetheless, passing these stories on to you has provided us with a huge amount of joy and, likewise, the thousands of other people around the world who have downloaded episodes of the podcast, and the many who have shared their favourite stories with us. Although, we do all now have a responsibility to *keep* telling these tales in our own ways, whether at bedtimes, or around pub tables, or in paintings, songs, or other styles in which you feel they ought to be shared. Some might make a nice hat, for example.

As for our tellings, they are all designed to be read aloud to others, ideally with silly voices, but you can just as well read them silently in your head. And if there are bits you don't like about them, do feel you can change them and make them better, because stories are at their best when the teller twists them to make them fit into an odd-shaped hole in their day. That way, they can be keys and unlock passages through to special places. Like the past. Or the world of the fairies. Or that achey bit inside you, just above your tummy, where love lives.

In fact, for us, this collection of tales is a love letter to England. Each of the nation's thirty-nine counties is bristling with half-forgotten strangenesses, crumbling castles, and layers of mystery waiting for people to dig down into to find stories buried in the earth. Each of these stories was written during just our first lap of wandering, listening, digging, and learning, and since then we have written more, with much muddier fingers.

So, although not every tale here is perhaps the most famous a given county might have to offer, to us each one is a special treasure: the shiny thing we unearthed and polished up to share. As such, we hope you enjoy the ways they all shimmer and shine. And if you find yourself, for whatever reason, stood on a giant's shoulder, do consider passing these tales on to the people below. Who knows what they might do with them, but knowing people, it will probably be something really interesting.

In the meantime, though, we'll get out of the way and let the stories speak for themselves.

And remember, don't whistle until you're out of the woods…

With love,
Eleanor & Martin

I

The Bottled Curse

A Bedfordshire Tale

Over 200 'witch bottles' have been discovered in Britain, buried in the ground, tucked up chimneys and bricked into walls. Witch bottles are associated with apotropaic magic and often contain pins, hair, nail clippings, and other viscera, fabric, and small personal items. The majority date from the sixteenth and seventeenth centuries.

I had been interested in the idea since researching witch bottles and bellarmines, and I wanted to bring into this story the folk belief that the spirit of a malicious practitioner of magic could be trapped within a bottle. However, the tale of Sally, the witch of Dunstable, was not an ancient Bedfordshire folk tale at all. It was invented by the headmaster of the local school in 1875. His name was Mr Wire, and he was apparently attempting to shame the vicar into tidying up the churchyard. Wire was so taken with the idea that he wrote an eighty-one-verse poem about it. The poem was incredibly popular but put an end to his career as headmaster.

I also wanted to tie in the local legend about Five Knolls, the barrow graves on Dunstable Downs. It was thought to be a supernatural place, where the Devil might appear to witches in the form of a cat.

EC

For most of us, chaos is a negative thing, an absence of law and order. But there are some who consider chaos to be a gift, a state from which creative thought can grow.

One such person was a witch named Sally, who lived a great many years ago in the town of Dunstable. Sally thrived on mess and disorder, and her ramshackle cottage was always in a complete state of disarray. There were piles of books and papers which threatened to cascade over and crush unsuspecting visitors. There were half-eaten cakes mouldering on platters and mouldy cheeses providing a feast for the mice. There were sticky rinds in the basins and bathtubs, and the windows were so filthy that Sally could barely see out.

She was a great collector of all sorts of things, from birds' feathers to fancy hats, copper pots to patty pans, and she liked nothing more than to have everything she had ever collected all around her, all at once. She also had a habit of picking up new hobbies all the time and not continuing with them, so a trail of evidence of her interests was scattered all around her. There was knitting in the bedrooms and painting up the stairs, and a full half of Sally's kitchen was devoted to a set-up she had devised for brewing her own beer.

I've mentioned that Sally was a witch, and she was actually quite a good one, although the mess in her house meant it was sometimes difficult for her to lay her hands on exactly the right ingredients for a love potion or a good luck charm. It was quite common for anybody who needed her services to have to wait for a good long while, trying not to drink the sweet tea offered to them in a dirty cup, while Sally rummaged around in cupboards which spilled their contents onto the floor, her frizzy grey hair flying everywhere, and eventually located the thing she was looking for in an unlikely place, like the coal scuttle or under the lid of the harpsichord. Nobody knew how Sally had got her hands on a harpsichord, but whenever she played it, her long ragged nails scraping against the yellowing keys, they soon knew that it was extremely out of tune.

Despite her eccentricities, Sally did manage to help the people of Dunstable with their little problems, so they kept coming to visit her. There was nobody like Sally for brewing teas to get rid of unwanted boils, babies, or birthmarks, or turning thorns and scraps of ribbon into amulets. She was good for a gossip, too, and most people left her house feeling satisfied with their visit, if slightly in need of a full body wash.

Sally did have one enemy in Dunstable, though. The local vicar, Mr Pascoe, disliked everything about the scatter-brained witch. He was a man who favoured order and cleanliness, and he was often to be seen polishing the church door knobs or straightening the chalice for Holy Communion. Sally and her lifestyle, not to mention her magical proclivities, went against everything Mr Pascoe believed in.

If Sally was quite a good witch, then Mr Pascoe was quite a good vicar. He took his job seriously and never lost an opportunity to spread the word of God to those he felt most needed it. And so, he forced himself to make monthly pilgrimages to see Sally, even though he hated being in her scruffy, cluttered house.

'Now look, Sally,' Mr Pascoe said, as he hovered nervously in the kitchen, not wanting to sit down on anything in case it stuck to his cassock. 'You really have got to come to church, you know. You've lived here for sixty years and more, and as far as anybody knows you've never been. The Queen doesn't like that sort of thing, and I have to report to the diocesan authorities. Won't you come this Sunday?'

'No, thank you, vicar,' said Sally, who was pottering about, absentmindedly stirring some evil-smelling liquid in a large pot, which she had vaguely claimed was rat poison. 'I'm far too busy.'

The vicar made his usual protests about being busy on a Sunday being a sin in the eyes of the Lord, but Sally wasn't really listening to him. He valiantly persisted, but Sally started loudly singing a rather rude ballad. It was difficult for the vicar not to hear some of the words, although he wasn't sure he actually understood all of them.

'Look, Sally,' he said at last, becoming very cross when Sally opened a cupboard and a small flock of blackbirds flew out and disturbed his carefully placed hat, 'you should address yourself to your immortal soul, and to this horrendous mess of a house. It's a shameful thing! Cleanliness is next to godliness, you know.'

Sally stopped singing, and her hand stilled as she stirred the pot.

'Are you calling my house messy, vicar?' she asked softly, in a tone which would have caused most people to take a step back.

'Well, it is,' said Mr Pascoe staunchly, in spite of the way Sally raised her copper ladle. Several drops of rat poison dripped from it on the floor and hissed where they fell.

'How dare you,' said Sally, who didn't consider her house to be disordered at all. 'Get out, and don't come back!' And she shook the ladle at him so ferociously that the vicar turned and fled, telling himself he had done his duty for another month.

Although Sally liked the way she lived, the vicar's words had upset her deeply. She thought about them all day, and the more she thought, the angrier she became. Hadn't she been doing her best to help the people of Dunstable, giving them exactly what they wanted and needed and never asking for any payment? She was doing a damn sight better than that pompous ass of a vicar. What did he ever do, except mutter prayers and obsessively tidy things up? It was unnatural, sweeping and scrubbing as much as he did, Sally thought. Somebody ought to teach him a lesson.

The more she thought about this idea, the more she became convinced that the person to teach the vicar a lesson was surely her.

Now, Sally had never been particularly malicious, but a person can be pushed too far. However, she knew that her skill with herbs and charms probably wasn't going to be enough to seriously inconvenience the vicar. She was going to need more power.

And so, at the next full moon, Sally put on one of her fancy hats and walked down to the Five Knolls, where it's said the ancient kings sleep. She made her way to the three bell-shaped barrows in the middle and she ran around them nine times widdershins. Then, rather out of puff, because she was pushing seventy-five years old, she squatted down and traced a magic circle in the soil.

No sooner had Sally closed the circle than out shot the Devil himself in a pillar of bright blue flame, whooping and cheering to be let loose out of Hell.

'Good evening, Devil,' said Sally politely, doffing her fancy hat. They had met before, of course, but it had been some time ago, when she had been a much younger woman. She hoped the Devil would still recognise her, especially with her clothes on.

'Hello, Sally,' said the Devil. To a being as ancient as he, Sally still looked exactly the same as the pretty young woman with a bird's nest of frizzy hair who had summoned him all those years ago. 'What brings you to summon me this fine moonlit night?'

'Well, Devil, I haven't asked much of you for all these years,' Sally said, 'but there's a small matter of a troublesome priest.'

'There usually is, sooner or later,' the Devil said, nodding wisely.

'In short, I need a bit of extra help,' said Sally.

'Not a problem,' said the Devil, who could be very helpful when he wanted to be. He felt a degree of fondness for Sally, as she often left him gifts of mummified cats and bottles of brandy, and in truth, he had a very similar attitude to mess and chaos, so they were well suited. 'I'll give you the power to make anybody who crosses you regret it.'

'Wonderful,' said Sally. 'I knew I could count on you.' And she shook hands with the Devil, thinking of all the ways she was going to make Mr Pascoe pay for insulting her. Blue flame shot from their clasped hands, and it flew so high that the few folk of Dunstable who were still awake at that hour mistook it for a shooting star.

Sally adjusted her fancy hat and started to make for home, but the Devil followed behind her.

'What are you doing?' asked Sally. 'Have you business in Dunstable, Devil?'

'I'm coming with you, of course,' said the Devil. 'I told you I would help, so here I am.'

'Hold your horses,' said Sally. 'You can't come with me looking like that. The priest already doesn't like me – he'll cause no end of a to-do if he sees *you*.'

The Devil looked down at his hairy goat legs and concluded that she was probably correct.

'Besides,' Sally said. 'The spare bed's got knitting on it, so there's nowhere for you to sleep.'

'That's not a problem,' said the Devil. 'I can curl up in the fireplace with the coals.'

'I don't think so,' said Sally. 'The postman always likes to sit by the fire when he comes, and I think he would be distressed to see you in there. Can't you do something about all – this?' she waved her hand, generally indicating the Devil's entire appearance.

'Oh, alright,' said the Devil, and in a shower of glittering blue sparks, he shrank himself down, yowling horribly all the while, until he was in the shape of a fat, shaggy tortoiseshell cat with glowing green eyes.

'Perfect,' said Sally, scooping up the cat and carrying it home with her.

From that day on, Sally and the Devil disguised as a cat were completely inseparable. Sally fed the cat bowls of milk with drops of fresh blood stirred into them and the cat slept on her chest at night and whispered things into her heart.

People who came to visit Sally began to notice a difference about her. Where before she had been good-natured, if a little scatty, she started to be irritable and say spiteful things. And her temper! Oh, it was fierce! If she suspected the slightest insult, she would lash out at the person responsible for it.

And strange things started to happen, too, whenever anybody crossed her.

The blacksmith asked for a love charm, but he didn't pay Sally quickly enough, so instead of becoming irresistible to the object of his desire, his face sprouted ugly, oozing pustules that Sally refused to help him remove.

The miller's wife asked for an elixir to help her have children, but she gossiped about Sally behind her back and called her a smelly old woman. News of it got back to Sally, and soon the miller's wife found herself giving birth to four goats instead of human children.

Word started to spread through Dunstable that Sally was a force to be feared, and when Mr Pascoe heard about it, he decided that enough was enough.

'Listen, Sally,' he said. 'I've been very patient with you for all these years, but you're causing real trouble now. If you don't stop at once, I'll have no choice but to call in the witchfinder.'

'You just try it,' Sally said, and the ends of her hair seemed to crackle with rage. She pointed a finger at Mr Pascoe, and behind her the tortoiseshell cat reared up on its hind legs and hissed and spat, and for just a moment Mr Pascoe could see the Devil there, as plain as the nose on his face.

But Mr Pascoe was determined, and despite his fussy ways he had courage enough. He summoned the witchfinder, who made his way up Sally's treacherous garden path and arrested her.

There was a trial, but it didn't take long, because it turned out that there was quite a lot of evidence against Sally, what with the goats and the pustules and all the other inconveniences.

Funnily enough, the tortoiseshell cat was nowhere to be seen. It had vanished into thin air the day Sally was arrested. I can only assume that the Devil had concluded that Sally's soul would be with him in his homeland soon and had gone back to make things good and warm for her.

Things were warm enough for her in Dunstable, for those were the days when witches were burned at the stake. The whole town turned out to see Sally, who was still spitting feathers with rage even as they lit the pile of wood below her. Mr Pascoe turned pale as she started to smoke, for she screamed a loud curse, vowing her revenge on the people of Dunstable and most especially the vicar. He was very relieved when Sally had been reduced to a pile of ash and went home thinking himself lucky that his troubles with her were finished.

Unfortunately, his relief didn't last long.

Strange things started to happen in the vicar's house and in the church. During Holy Communion, the chalice was suddenly lifted from Mr Pascoe's hands and the wine was tipped all over his head. The chafer dish was tossed from one end of the church to the other, scattering Communion wafers like falling snow. Hymn books were carried up to the rafters and dropped down in handfuls of pages, and foul smells wafted through the pews, making the congregation gag and cover their mouths.

After one particularly bad Sunday morning, Mr Pascoe was standing in the mess of his church, and he knew that it must be Sally's spirit exacting her revenge. Ever a proactive person, Mr Pascoe immediately wrote to the witchfinder, who wrote to his friend the exorcist.

The exorcist came down to Dunstable at once with his bag of equipment and Mr Pascoe watched as he solemnly conducted his ceremonies of candle, book and bell. Sally's spirit put up a good fight, but eventually the exorcist was able to annoy her into manifesting in the back corner of the church, near the font.

Mr Pascoe had a brief sighting of the furious ghost, its eyes blazing, smoke pouring from its ears, before the exorcist harnessed it and stuffed it into a bottle, which he hastily sealed with four layers of thick black candle wax.

'There you are,' said the exorcist, handing Mr Pascoe the bottled spirit, along with an extremely large bill.

Mr Pascoe didn't quite know what to do with Sally's spirit, but everybody advised him to bury the bottle deep in the grounds of the church to prevent Sally from ever rising again to cause trouble. So, that's exactly what he did, and he said any number of prayers over the site of its burial. He felt a little bit guilty, too, so he did say some prayers for Sally's immortal soul as well.

Although Sally's spirit never directly troubled Mr Pascoe again, that still wasn't quite the end of it. Slowly but surely, the churchyard started to show the effects of her influence. The fences fell down and the gravestones cracked. Poison ivy wound itself around the trees and crept over the ground. The grass grew long, concealing holes which liked nothing more than to twist people's ankles. The bones of the deceased began to poke up above the surface of the earth.

In short, the churchyard was soon just as much of a mess as the home of Sally, the Dunstable witch. But Mr Pascoe refused to dig up the spirit's bottle, for fear that Sally would get out again and terrorise him, and so the churchyard remains in a terrible state, getting worse with each passing year.

Perhaps one day a future vicar may tidy it up, and perhaps they may find a small, dirty bottle sealed with four layers of thick, black wax, and perhaps then Sally's spirit will roam free, causing chaos wherever she goes.

2

Herne the Hunter

A Berkshire Tale

A famous figure of English folklore, Herne the Hunter is mentioned by Shakespeare in The Merry Wives of Windsor *and in several other places, too. He is one of many ghostly wild huntsmen who haunt the nation's landscapes, sometimes with packs of dogs, including the likes of 'Old Crockern' in Devon, 'Gabriel's Ratchets' in Derbyshire and the North of England, and 'Eadric the Wild' in Shropshire and Hereford.*

Our first recorded Wild Hunt story comes to us from twelfth-century writer, Walter Map, in his De Nugis Curialium ('Of the Trifles of Courtiers'), *where the tale is of King Herla and set in Cambridgeshire. So the story goes, Herla rode into the Otherworld of the faeries and then out again, though once he had returned 300 years had passed.*

As for Herne specifically, he has stag's antlers and was – and still is – famously associated with an oak tree in Windsor Great Park. This tree has been felled and replanted several times and is held as significant to monarchs including Queen Victoria.

That the 'original' ancient Herne's Oak was felled during the reign of George III felt like too good a detail. After all, George III went mad, and it was under his reign that England lost the American War of Independence. This felt somehow significant. Hence my placing of this story in the mouth of Dr Robert Darling Willis, a real historical figure who had a complex personal life and treated the king alongside his father, Francis.

MV

Dearest Mary, how I crave to see you.

The shocks I have had to my heart and to my mind are the stuff from which some men never recover. Were it not for your love of me, I too may have lost grasp of my senses, as has he. But he is not mad, Mary. It is not what I thought. I have seen with my own eyes the truth of it. Our most noble king is no lunatic. Rather, he is haunted by a fiend most ancient and abhorred, afflicted with a curse I fear may never be lifted.

As you know, my father was the first in our family called to serve the king. That was in the year 1788, when I was still in pursuit of my fellowship at Gonville & Caius College. I was, at this time, intermittently employed as a physic in Grantham, working alongside my brother, John. He, being older, accompanied our father down from Lincolnshire to London, and there repaired to the White House at Kew Gardens under the strictest conditions of secrecy.

You know, my love, that the Willis family are not from an ancient or noble line and our fame and wealth, such as it is, is a direct result of the efforts of John and my father in the treatment of our king. For all the kingdom knew of the madness of King George III – nay, all the world knew of it – and so, those men who by their skill cured him of it, well, the world was open to them like a pearl revealed within an oyster.

I was at that time but twenty-eight years old, a decade from meeting you that fine summer's day. And now I know you are at home in Buckingham Street, with our angel Robert no doubt babbling on your lap. It is of great shame to me that I cannot be with you, and my heart burns to know the ignominy heaped upon men such as I, who wed though forbidden to do so.

As a Cambridge Fellow, I have duties to perform, and no greater duty than this which I have undertaken to do, and so we must remain apart and our love a secret. But I had always believed that once the king was well again, I could return to my duties as a father and as your beloved.

Alas! For what I have seen tonight chills me to the core and gives me the fear that I should never be able to return to your side, for our king's malaise is not of the mind but of the body politic.

Yet, how to treat this ailment? For I remember well Father's return to Bourne as a famous man with an annuity of £1,500. It was with these funds he opened Shillingthorpe Hall, his second sanitorium, following the model of Greatford Hall, his first success.

I should think you will never meet my father, for he is loath to travel now and is a sanguine fellow and formidable when formed of an opinion. It was my ardent hope that he would change his mind, but he is a man of iron intent, defined by his dedication to unambitious, all but artless, service of mankind.

His is a long shadow, and I but a Pygmy within it.

As a boy, I saw him treating those men and women all thought mad beyond mortal aide, all of whom he set to work on the lands of Greatford Hall. He put them to labouring as ploughmen, gardeners, threshers, thatchers – all attired in black coats with white waistcoats, black silk breeches and stockings. Each looked so neat against the russet earth and wide sky.

He even had the head of each bewigged, well powdered, neat and arranged, and it seemed a miracle that in that atmosphere of health and cheerfulness, he aided in the recovery of every person attached to that place.

Perhaps, Mary, you are unfamiliar with the ways of the asylums, but they are, for the most part, rotten places – little better than prison cells. Across this land, Christian souls are abandoned to gibber in their filth, but Father has always said, 'treat a soul as less than human and so their faculties will remain'.

His methods were in contrast to the likes of Baillie and Heberden, the first physicians to treat the king. Great men of their day, but they did burn the monarch's skin as if he were possessed by a demon, striking his person and restricting him within the confines of a straitening jacket.

The bleak nature of these treatments was hateful to my father, who instead set the king to work, of all things. So it was that His Majesty took to planting flowers in the great gardens at Kew, engaging in daily exercise and toil, with the companionship of my father and John.

This is how King George recovered. Yet now his illness has returned with threefold strength, and knowing its root cause, I fear there is little hope – though to say so may be treason.

You see, when John, who had accompanied our father at Kew, returned to the practice at Grantham, he was quiet on the matter of the king. I spent many an evening and a good deal of port wine in an effort to loosen his lips, but John is a faithful and trustworthy man, irrespective of the £650 he receives annually from the king as reward for his past labours.

When I would ask of him, his face would darken and he would say, 'Robert, speak not of it,' and I would know to let it be.

Only now, with father too old to travel, as you know well, it has fallen to John and me to attend His Majesty. And so, before we came here to Windsor, John finally abated and revealed to me the truth.

I remember his white face and bright blue eyes as he spoke, his hair already grey as wire. His nervous disposition caused his fingers to shake about his wineglass and he looked down as he spoke, as if ashamed.

'The trouble,' he told me, 'began in 1775, Robert. Much earlier than most know. For it was then that the king first saw him: the green rider, galloping through Windsor Park.'

It took a while for John to explain it fully, but it seemed the rider he alluded to was a phantasm seen only by His Majesty. A stag-headed man, he said, with antlers growing from his hoary skull, his skin covered with myriad mosses and lichen.

When John first told me of it, I laughed, thinking he was pulling my leg, but he shot back such a look of thunder that I knew I had transgressed upon his honour and that of the king, and I so begged forgiveness both of him and the king, and of the Lord, our saviour.

Thusly, I learned that the malaise began in earnest when, across the wide Atlantic sea, battles were raging at Lexington and Concord. Our American brothers had risen up against us and so, amidst this bad news, it was said the king first noticed the green rider about his palace at Windsor, thundering through the park on a horse of leaves and tree roots with eyes of coal-red flame.

There are legends of this place, Mary – of that rider – stretching back to the time of Queen Elizabeth and earlier still. It's said that on the threat of Spanish invasion, she saw him and called on Dr Dee, who also saw him and heard him, rattling his chains and leading hounds of pale blue fire about her forests. It's said that after he's seen, all the cattle hereabouts give not milk but blood, and for as long as there's been an England, when it's threatened the green rider will appear.

My father, being an ardent student of nature, thought these stories of the king's to be some form of delusion – a children's story heard by His Majesty as boy, twisted into a living fantasy.

So it was that, although the king was said to often speak to the rider, who he said came to his chambers, communicating to him in an endless, babbling stream of speech all through the night as well as the day, once repaired to Kew, away from the ancient forests of Windsor, the monarch made a recovery. My father was said to have convinced him, in time, that his talk of the green rider was but a product of an overactive mind.

With this knowledge, John and I attended His Majesty at his palace at Windsor, beginning our treatments last August. And though I came to that most grand of palaces with no doubt in my heart or my mind that His Majesty's tales of the green rider were but delusions, I have now learned better, and I must speak of it to someone.

John has sworn me to silence, and so that someone, my darling one, must be you.

You hold all my great secrets, the most sacred of all of which is our son, and though it is a burden, you must keep this one too, for as long as you live and ever after. And though you may think me mad, know, my love, that I am hale and well, but have seen such things as would shock a lesser man to death.

As I have told you before in prior missives, attending to His Majesty is not a task for all hours of the day. The king is in a weakened state and must spend some hours at rest. So, between John and I, it is not unknown for us to have spans of several hours in which to perambulate the woods and gardens surrounding the palace.

Even now, they are subject to countless improvements by none other than that great architect of our age, James Wyatt, whom I am yet to meet but one day hope to. It is a place of marvels to walk through, Mary. In recent years, it was the great work of Paul and Thomas Sandby to improve, with the Long Walk as laid out by Charles II flanked by elms planted by William of Orange. It was the Sandbys who expanded the lake at Virginia Water, adding a waterfall and the Obelisk Pond dedicated to the king's brother, the Duke of Cumberland as he was, God rest his soul.

It is a place of great tranquillity for the most part, and of great magnificence. In one area, there is a complete set of ruins built by ancient Romans – ruins the king himself had brought by ship from Tripolitania on Africa's Barbary Coast! I have walked amongst these ruins and touched them, and thought of the same sun shining on those stones that shone on Julius Caesar in the days of antiquity.

Greatest of all though, Mary, are the oaks. For in the great park at Windsor there are oaks that were planted in the days of King Offa and before. Trees that were acorns in the year of the birth of Christ.

Who might have guessed it would be one such oak that would ruin our king and wreak havoc upon his mind? For it was in the year 1796 that our doom was spelled by a team of men with axes. Men who felled the tree in which the green rider once slept.

I learned of it one night when, having laid the king abed, I went walking in the Little Park – which is not little, being over 600 acres.

I was strolling beneath a blanket of stars, pinprick bright amidst the shroud of night, when I heard a sound not unlike that of twigs snapping underfoot. But it was not twigs. It was the flints of a pistol clicking back into their place.

'Who goes there?' came a rough-sounding voice, unmistakably that of a Londoner who I thought must be a rogue or highwayman. 'State your name and purpose, or I shall shoot you in the name of the king.'

Well, I did state my name and my purpose, and learned that this fellow, of the name of Brown, was none other than a groundskeeper at work under the auspices of His Majesty. He told me that though the king had all the deer of the Great Park killed or chased off before even my father attended him, it was still the duty of Brown and men like him to patrol thereabouts in case of thieves or poachers.

'But I'll tell you now,' Brown said, 'you need not fear of poachers here. Only the unwise stalk this stretch of land at night, all round here know, elsewise Herne the Hunter will give chase and know them for his quarry!'

He scared me how he spoke, with a black-toothed smile. It was the first time I had heard the name, but I learned then from Brown of the history of Herne the Hunter and of the ancient oak in which the spirit of that forest used to dwell.

'Some say,' Brown told me, 'he was once a poacher, caught by King Henry, wrapped in chains and hanged upon that oak. Others say he was a cuckold, for wearing antlers is a punishment of old for those what cannot contain the lustings of their wives. But I know the truth, for I've seen him, and if he's not an ancient spirit of this land then I never lived. And since that oak came down, he's bound to nothing. He's free to ride, and does, you mark my words.'

I parted from Brown that night, shaken but resolved. I reported to John what I had learned, and he thought me a fool for believing Brown's stories. But I said to John – *warned* him – that if it were true and the king had cut down the oak in which the green rider dwelt, perhaps that was the cause of his worsened condition.

John made me swear I would not speak to His Majesty of it, and for a time I did not. But last night, which was a quiet evening, I did just that, saying to the king, 'Your Highness, tell me of Herne the Hunter.'

No sooner had I said the name than His Majesty turned as pale as snow, his mouth forming into a small, white-lipped circle, his words falling out of him like his voice was very far away. 'Tried to chase him off,' he told me. 'Had the deer shot. No more antlers. No more horns. No more drumming. No more drumming in the dark.'

I knew I had made an error, for then the king would not speak sensibly for many hours, rambling again of the dark drummings he had heard and of the green rider, his hounds, his horse of leaves and roots, and the language which echoed in his thoughts but that could not be understood.

In time, I had no choice but to treat him. I gave him a dosage of laudanum to make him sleep. And once he was calmed, I stormed from his apartments and went myself, my face hidden in shame, out into the Little Park. I pulled my cloak about me, cursing at myself and intending to find Brown and learn more of the ancient spirit in hope that I might do something to help His Majesty once and for all.

But the park… it is so big, Mary. And the trees are so high, and their foliage so abundant, that though I thought to cross one part quickly, ducking into the treeline and emerging near the site of the fallen oak, I became turned around and then sorely lost, wandering for what felt like hours.

I had time, on that walk, to think of a great deal.

I thought of you, Mary, and little Robert, and of my father, and the hopes I have as a man. For it is my will to lift mankind out of the darkness and better the lot of those thought mad and beyond repair. And my failure to do so for our king, the shame of it, saw me suddenly set to weeping, knelt in the tangled ferns of the forest floor.

I smelled him before I saw him.

It was as the smell after a thunderstorm, mixed with the wet and heady stink of peat. It made me start up, as if to stand, but then I froze in fear, hearing Brown's words in my mind. For if I moved, I feared he would consider me quarry and hunt me until his hounds tore me apart.

Oh, the hounds, Mary. You can't imagine them. Moving like a river, tumbling, surging, flowing in shimmering blue, like a glowing wave of blood. Though they howled and barked and scratched and leapt, they were silent as a tomb, moving through the trees and round about like floodwaters with ears and tails and teeth.

But his steed was not silent. Neither was it a horse, nor even much of a horse's shape. For though once there may have been the skeleton of a stallion beneath what it has since become, the animal is barely recognisable. Its hide is not leather or hair, but made up of a thousand, thousand leaves of birch and ash and alder, hazel, spruce and yew. Its mane is of holly, run through with berries red as blood. Through and about its mighty limbs run roots thick and thin, some delicate, spiralling like spiders' webs, and where its legs touch down flowers bloom and fade in seasons which last but an instant.

And atop that steed, in a saddle made of fungus grown wide and slick and yellow-grey with age, speckled with mushrooms and toadstools, masked in a haze of spores and pollen, rides Herne, the most ancient thing in all imagination. His garments looked like faerie clothes, sewn of moss and blackest fur, run through and threaded with silver and gold. All about him, he wore not chains but ancient leather straps, loaded with tools of flint and bone.

In one hand he bore a horn, cracked and split, as if hollowed from the head of an aurochs or some ancient, bull-like beast, black and shining terribly. His beard was long, made of tendrils of tree roots, grown blue and green with lichen of every kind.

And on his head was a skull – the skull of a great stag, white beneath the moon, antlers stretching wider than the span of an albatross, shooting from his head like captured sunbeams, vicious points of bleeding velvet, ragged, hanging, covered with bells which did not ring and signs on stones I could not read.

His eyes, Mary, were just as the king had said. Like coals, burning.

So were his steed's.

And though the vision of him is something I will never forget, it is the sound of his voice that haunts me. Like the breaking of stones beneath water or the splintering cracks of a sapling bent back far too far…

There was the wind at the edge of it, whistling through grass, weathering rocks, and the sound of it smelled somehow – his words stinking like a storm lashing a desert, making it grow with slimy things that walked and spoke his tongue and followed after him.

He turned to me and spoke, and I saw then the crown upon his head, made of twisted gold, and about his waist a girdle holding a sack.

As his steed moved by, grains spilled from that sack, ghostly white as moonbeams, landing on the forest floor and vanishing where they fell.

It was then, Mary, that I felt myself losing my mind.

So, though he spoke, the rushing, heady smell of his language drowning me, clattering and clicking, buffeting and breaking, I closed my eyes and prayed to God, and thought of the best thing I could in this world.

It was you I thought of, Mary. Of your love. And it was you, your face, in my mind, which made all his horrid words go quiet.

When I opened my eyes, he was gone. And I wandered many more hours, lost in those woods, until Brown found me and led me back to my apartment.

I don't know what to do now. Whatever must have trapped him, felling that oak has freed him and no force on Earth can contain him, of that I am sure.

For the king I can only do so much, for he is not mad, but knows the truth: that England is in crisis, and so long as this state remains, so he, Our Majesty, will not know peace.

Of all the things I can do, there is only one that I am sure is right, and that is to love you, Mary.

And I will do, all my days.

How I wish you were here to hold me.

How I fear that creature will return.

Oh, I must rest. Soon John will come and expect me to attend to my duties.

I love you now and always, Mary. May your face be the one I see when I dream.

Yours always,
Robert Darling Willis, M.D.

3

A Promise Kept

A Buckinghamshire Tale

Questions about life after death and the nature of the soul have always fascinated human beings.

This tale concerns a very specific visit to the Christopher Inn in Eton by a ghost intent on keeping a promise. Major George Sydenham and his friend Captain William Dyke, who were soldiers together in the reign of Charles II, often debated the existence of God and the immortality of the soul. They made a promise to each other that whoever died first would visit the other as a ghost. This is a reasonably straight telling of the contemporary account of this arrangement, although I've also included such classic ghost story tropes as the link between a spirit and an item they once owned and a warning to the remaining friend to mend their lifestyle before it is too late.

The Christopher Inn, a coaching inn dating back to the early sixteenth century, is now a boutique hotel. It can still be visited today, but, as far as we know, this particular ghost has never visited again.

EC

It was easy to forget the desperation of war, as we sat in the cosy parlour at the Christopher Inn in Eton, drinking brandy and reminiscing.

I was glad to see my Major again, as I always am. Although war with the Dutch was a memory now, and it was some time since either of us had seen active service, nothing brings men close like the immediacy of conflict, the terror and excitement of bombardment, of rapidly changing orders, of the knowledge that at any moment one friend might be lost, leaving a void in the other's life.

At that time, I thought that the person living with that empty space at his side might have been the Major, as I was wounded in the attack on the fort where we were stationed and though the wound proved to be superficial, I did not know that in the moment. I was caught in the shoulder by a bullet and would have been cut down as I lay in my own blood by the Dutchman who fired the shot. He stood teetering on the top of his ladder, levelling his musket at me, but in a moment, he was toppling backwards and falling to his death below as the Major drove his shining sword deep into the enemy's heart.

He had rushed to my side, and I remember how blue the sky was that day as he leaned over me, pressing his hands to my wound to staunch the blood, his arm supporting my weight. I opened my mouth to say farewell to him, thinking my life was about to ebb away, but he pressed his hands still harder to the flow of blood.

'Stay with me, William. Today is not the day your soul will go to God.'

Even as I slid between states of consciousness, I remember being unsure about that. The Major and I had often debated the existence of God and the immortality of the soul. It was a subject I had never been firm upon, and at that moment, lying on what I feared was my deathbed, I was even less sure. The existence of God was not something I could assert, and if He would want me was something even less certain.

The Major got me to the surgeon in time to extract the bullet, which fortunately had not pierced all the way through my shoulder, so I never found out one way or the other. Our friendship continued, greater than ever, strengthened by the bonds which can only be forged in the furnace of war.

Still, I was struck by how different a scene it was now, nestled in the warm back parlour at the Christopher, with freezing rain lashing the windows outside and a blazing fire inside. I was glad to see opposite me the familiar features of George Sydenham, my Major, the man who had saved my life. Even in peace, he had never lost his military bearing, unable to fully relax into a chair. But his blue eyes, the same colour as the sweltering July sky under which I had nearly died, were warm and kind.

We always met here, in the Christopher Inn at Eton. I had just delivered my son back to school here and was breaking the journey as I always did. I was happy to dally in Eton, not only because it gave me the opportunity of seeing the Major, but also of lingering before returning to my wife. Ours was not a happy home, and in truth, it often caused me to seek amusements elsewhere.

I had never been to the Major's home, which I knew was not far from the Christopher Inn. I knew he lived alone, but even so, there was an unspoken line there which neither of us dared cross. It would mean a change in our friendship, I think we both knew, and neither of us were willing to risk altering something which was so precious.

Besides, the inn was comfortable, and I was always happy to be with my Major, conversing and recalling old times as we always did. We were not old men, though we were perhaps starting to feel the years a little.

'Do you remember those conversations we used to have about life after death, and the existence of the soul?' said Major Sydenham, swirling his brandy about his glass.

'I do, well,' I said, thinking of the easy camaraderie of our days in the regiment and the many nights we had sat up late talking about those very things.

'I think of them often,' he said, 'and how I constantly tried to persuade you to change your mind.'

'And how you always failed,' I said, watching him take a slow sip. 'I cannot credit that there is anything after this earthly life but to lie in quiet until all is dust.'

'There is no way to convince you, William, and there never was.'

'Unless it can conclusively be proved to me, no,' I said.

A light came into the Major's eyes. 'Well, let us prove it to each other,' he said.

'What do you mean?'

'Let us make a promise,' he said. 'Whichever one of us dies first–'

'Which event is a great way off, I hope,' I said hurriedly, but he brushed past that and continued.

'Let us agree that he who dies first shall appear to the other, by any means necessary, and thus prove that there is more of human existence beyond death.'

'Appear – as a spectre?' I said incredulously.

'A spectre – a spirit – a soul – however you like to call it.'

I was extremely dubious. I believed in ghosts even less than I believed in a host of angels waiting to welcome me into their throng. But my Major seemed very serious.

'Very well,' I said, unable to deny him anything he wanted. 'Let us say that he must appear to the other at midnight – and as for the place – well, why not here? It is where we always meet, after all.'

'If you insist,' he said, but he was smiling, obviously pleased that I had been drawn into his scheme. 'Perhaps it should be some while after the funeral, though, to allow enough time for whatever may come. Shall we say three nights?'

I did not care to talk of funerals, so swiftly changed the subject after that, but when we parted at the end of the night, I to my room in the inn and he to his horse and his home, he clasped my hand and reminded me of the promise we had made.

'Of course,' I said, seeing that he meant it, and we went our ways.

I curse myself now for not seeing something in him that night, for he must have had some inkling of what was happening to him, even if he did not want to say anything to me. But a letter written to me by his brother, just a few short weeks after, confirmed that my Major had been very ill for some time with a cancer of the stomach, which had been steadily eating away at him until it caused his end.

I cannot tell the extent of my grief. It tore through me like a cannon blast, as wide as the sea. The Major had been my truest, dearest friend, the only person I had ever felt had truly seen me – and had liked me in spite of it. My grief distracted me from the strange promise we had made, and I did not think of it as I rode back to Eton for his funeral.

It was not until the sorry deed was done and the Major's body lying in earth, when those who had attended returned to his home to be received by his brother, that I was reminded of it.

It was very strange to think that I had never been to this house where he lived, and I hardly heard the things which were said to me as I wandered through its rooms, looking at books and pictures and trying to imagine things about him which I had never considered. Perhaps seeing

I was unfit for company, the Major's brother took me aside, leading me into a small library stuffed with books and decorated with naval maps.

'He left something for you,' he said, showing me a long, cloth-wrapped parcel. When I unwrapped it, I saw it was the Major's sword in its scabbard. It was the very sword that had saved my life, and I had a sudden image of him that day, rushing to my rescue, wielding the sword so swiftly. It threatened to overwhelm me, and my knees almost buckled when a piece of notepaper fluttered out of the parcel.

My heart leapt as I imagined some final letter to me, perhaps giving voice to something which neither of us had ever spoken of. But I was disappointed when I saw that there was only a single line written on it, with not even his name.

Remember well our promise.

'What does that mean?' the Major's brother asked, but I could not speak. My voice was choked with tears.

I repaired to the Christopher Inn after that, where I determined to remain until I had seen whether my Major would appear or not, as he had said.

I am sorry to say I drank more than I should have, over those long three days, and slept heavily, troubled by dreams. So I was bleary, with an aching head, when it came to the third night after the Major's funeral. I called for candles and, perhaps foolishly, two glasses of the Major's favourite brandy, and then I sat and waited for him in the back parlour where we had always met.

'Two glasses, sir?' said the tapster, raising his eyebrows.

'I am waiting for someone,' I said.

Time proceeded on and the candles burned down. I drained my own brandy, but the other glass remained untouched. Midnight passed and one, and it was almost two when the tapster came to see if there was anything I wanted, as he was about to go to sleep himself.

'Didn't he come, then, the person you was waiting for?' he asked.

Before I knew it I had grabbed his shoulders and was hissing into his face. 'He would have come if he was able, I know it!' I said.

The next morning, I left the Christopher Inn, heartsick and heavy, determined not to see that place again unless it was absolutely necessary.

There had been no sign of immortal life. My Major was gone, lying cold in his grave, and the only thing I had left of him was his sword, which I carried at my side, although I could not bear to remove it from its sheath as the pain of seeing it was too great.

I am sorry to say that I passed the next few weeks in dissipation. My son was at school and I spent much time away from the house. I could hardly bear to look at my wife or at any of the low company I sought out.

I did not want to have to go back to the inn six weeks later, but it was the most convenient stopping point when collecting and returning my son from school, so I found myself there once more. It was nearly Christmastime, and snow had fallen outside, covering the world in a white mantle. But I avoided the cosy back parlour and went to my room early, where I lay in bed staring up at the canopy.

I did not think I would sleep, but I must have slept a little, for I thought I was dreaming when I heard a voice softly calling to me.

'Captain, Captain.'

Thinking it was time to wake and one of the inn's servants was rousing me, I drew back the curtains of the bed. To my surprise, the room was still in darkness, and I could see only by the gleam of the moonlight on the brilliant white snow outside the window.

It was not the chambermaid, but there was somebody there. He looked pale and wasted, but he was as real as my own hand, shaking before me as I reached out to him.

'Captain, Captain,' he said again. It was my Major.

I did not think, in that moment, of how this could be possible. When I looked at him, I was only glad to see his dear face again.

'I could not come at the time appointed,' he said, 'but a promise is a promise.'

'Major, you are here,' I said helplessly. There were so many things I longed to say. How I had missed him. How I had felt the void at my side since he had died. But somehow, I could see by the expression on his face that he knew it all and I need say nothing.

He drew back from me and walked about the room, until he came to the table where I had laid down the sword he had left to me; the sword that had saved my life. Drawing it from its sheath, he held it up to inspect it. I flushed with shame, for I had not kept it as clean as I should have.

'Captain, Captain, this sword was not kept after this manner when I was living,' he said, shaking his head.

I leapt from the bed then, trying to get closer to him, to touch him perhaps, but he backed away from me.

'Do not touch me,' he said. 'I am come to tell you what I always knew but you denied. There is a God, and a very just and terrible one. You have fallen low, Captain, and if you do not turn over a new leaf, you shall find it so.'

There was no more. I would say he vanished, but it was more that he simply and suddenly wasn't there. I stayed rooted to the spot until the chambermaid came to make up the fire. I must have made a terrible sight, trembling and staring, but I had seen my Major. He lived on, despite being dead. It was true.

The first thing I did was to roll up my sleeves and clean his sword so it shone brighter than it ever had, and I determined to follow my Major's orders and mend my life. I broke off my acquaintance with those I should have taken care to avoid and I did my best to be attentive to my wife. I do not know if it will be enough, but I do know that when my own life does end, I shall at least have a chance of being reunited once more with my friend.

4

Hereward the Wake

A Cambridgeshire Tale

England has a fine tradition of rebel kings and lords hiding in marshes. These include one of our most famous and beloved kings, Alfred the Great, who evaded the Vikings as led by Ivar the Boneless in the ninth century by dwelling amidst the Somerset Levels.

As for Hereward specifically, who was also known as 'Hereward the Exile', the invaders he hid from were the Normans following 1066. Hereward's campaign of resistance was recorded in several eleventh- and twelfth-century sources, including the Peterborough Chronicle, *the* Book of Ely, *and the* Gesta Herewardi ('Deeds of Hereward'), *though who he really was is a tantalising mystery – not helped by even the contemporary sources contradicting one another!*

We do know that Hereward existed, at least, but his alleged familial relationships to Lady Godiva and Leofric of Mercia, his initial banishment from England by Edward the Confessor, and his later missions for revenge and various heroic deeds are a bit more ambiguous. Hence his position as a very useful English folk hero: storytellers in Cambridgeshire and beyond have been embellishing his legend ever since, making him another character in the mould of Robin Hood and so many others who oppose tyranny from the wilderness.

As for the narrator here, inspired in part by the Romantic fiction of nineteenth-century writer Charles Kingsley, I made him an ally of Hereward, Morten Lightfoot – a character whose voice was such a hit with Three Ravens listeners that he has since returned for other adventures!

MV

Listen to that rain.

You know, there once was an Englishman who could hide inside the rainfall. I met him in Flanders, fighting in Scaldemariland. A mercenary, he was paid in gold by Robert the Frisian, and that is where we became friends.

Even then, he was a legend. His mother, the naked horse rider, Godiva, was known in all towns, all cities. His father, Leofric of Mercia, Ealderman of the Hwicce, was a Northman – like me. But his son, Hereward, was not like Leofric, Hammer of Harthacnut, obedient to Godwin of Wessex. He was not like Godiva, the holy wife. He was a moon-son, blessed by the Vanir, with blood like boiling rage.

Hereward was a younger son. His brother, Ælfgar, was his father's golden son. Hereward was not a son of gold or silver – he was a son of iron. A child of rage. Always fighting, always hiding, Hereward was banished in his eighteenth winter to the outer kingdoms. It was then, in Fife, fighting for Domnall mac Donnchada, where he duelled with a bear, mighty and fierce, in unarmed combat. Hereward, bear-strong, emerged victor.

It was in Cornwall where he stole the Princess Turfida from the castle of Condor. Later, when he was a tournament fighter in Cambrai, he married Turfida but fathered no sons. His life, bathed in blood, saw Turfida flee from him. She took to a convent, where she gave herself to God instead.

Heartbroken, Hereward went to war for Robert the Frisian. There, I, Morten Lightfoot, became sword-brother to Hereward. By night, we walked long shadows, danced with our blades, and hid in the woods like owls. We were like the goats' eyes, seeing, plotting, fading to the trees like the waves into the sea.

It was then Hereward learned of the death of Ælfgar. William the Bastard had invaded England. His men had murdered Ælfgar, heir to the lands of Leofric, and placed his head on a pike in front of his own castle keep.

With our blood-stained gold, gifted on the death of Baldwin of Flanders, Hereward and I sailed for England. When we found the new lords feasting in the halls of Leofric, feasting in the halls of Ælfgar, we passed through the gates like the night-storm. Fifteen Norman knights were in the banquet hall, laughing, eating, mocking the name of Godiva as a whore. All fell beneath our blades, and from that place of slaughter, riding stolen horses, we went from house to house and raised the allies of the House of Mercia. Our men, our brothers, fled with us to Medeshamstede, and there, above the ancient Hedda Stone laid by King Peada, son of Penda, Hereward was knighted by the Abbot Brand, his uncle, and so he was declared protector of those lands.

In those times, the men of William the Bastard rode throughout Mercia, carving the land into new countries. With such numbers, we could not fight head-to-head. So, we fled back to Flanders – but the reach of the Bastard was long. First, his ally William de Warenne sent his brother, Frederick, to kill Hereward. He came to us with an army, but Hereward outwitted him and sent Frederick's body back to de Warenne as an offering of peace.

So it was that William de Warenne came himself, challenging Hereward to battle. On horseback, William de Warenne rode to Hereward, who, on foot, took down his bow and notched an arrow and slew de Warenne with a single shot.

For strength, Hereward travelled to Søderup and the mead hall of Sweyn Estridsson, King of the Danes. I think you never met him. He had so many sons. But I knew him well. Old enemy of Harald Godwinson and wily grandson of Sweyn Forkbeard, Estridsson was no ally of William the Bastard. From the port of Aabenraa, we sailed north, for the holy Isle of Ely in the Mercian Kingdom of the Gyrwas. Here, the holy treasures of the monks were taken by Estridsson to Denmark for safe keeping, and the campaign of Hereward began.

The Abbot Brand at Medeshamstede, uncle to Hereward, was killed by William's men. In the place of the ancient church, the Norman men built a new abbey, Peterborough, and put in Brand's place a new archbishop. His blood was spilled by Hereward in that place of stone, the cathedral was sacked, and all the treasure gifted to Estridsson for his protection.

These days were days of slaughter and war. But the rising pillars of smoke were as of signal fires, calling allies to our banner. One such ally, Morcar, cousin of Hereward and ousted Earl of Northumbria, escaped from London and joined with us. Then, from the Isle of Ely, deep in the fenlands, we sheltered with the Bishop Aethelwine and planned the battles to come.

In one long winter, William the Bastard sent to us two foes who were much afeared. The first, Belsar, the great siege planner, came with masons, woodcutters, and chests of gold. The second, the witch Sikelgaita, spinner of whispers, came with servants of the dark. Together, Belsar and Sikelgaita surrounded our holy isle, lighting night fires and sending blackest terrors sliding, whistling, through the still waters of the bogs.

We could not hide from these dark powers. And so, Hereward and I slipped from Ely and battled the demons in the dark; creatures without blood or bone. Our blades cut through them as scythes through summer wheat, their forms falling to the fen water as clay. Hundreds of such demons we slew, hunting always for Sikelgaita, whose craft was sharp as ice.

But Hereward, the watcher in the dark, had blood on his teeth. He would never surrender, and like snow melting in winter, he found Sikelgaita, hiding in a tower in the marsh. Here, he burned her, and her demons and her night whispers could not save her then.

Alas for Morcar, who was weak. Belsar, from his fortress, tempted Morcar with gold. First, Belsar bribed the monks of Ely to show him the way to the island. The Normans built a causeway a mile long from timber, but the knights, in their armour and with their horses, sank the ramp into the waters there, and their invasion failed. But Morcar went to Belsar, seeking peace. Instead, Morcar was imprisoned, and so Hereward and I fled from the holy isle, never to return.

For years, we hid amongst the bullrushes there, living in the stinking mire. But Hereward was never one to face a battle head-on. We were raiders; our allies in the towns and villagers knew Hereward in disguise. Dressed as a potter, selling wares, he came to them with word of his resistances. They made gifts to him of food and blades and fresh arrows, knowing he would fight for them until his dying day.

Yet William would never give up. No longer William the Bastard, he was then become William Conqueror, King of England. Outer Mercia was no more, replaced by new shires. Bedford, Huntingdon, Northampton, Cambridge. And to these lands, the Conqueror sent a giant, Ogger the Breton.

For it was known, in these days, that Hereward was once again in love. Alftruda, widow of Gospatric, was beloved of Hereward, and the two made to have a wedding day at the Abbey of Thorney on the fenland's edge. Only, on that day, when Hereward and Alftruda were joined by God, Ogger the Breton arrived with an army from Crowland, to the north.

And so, instead of a bear, Hereward duelled with Ogger beneath the summer sun. And as they fought, the clouds covered the sky, the rain began to fall, and the lightning forked above them, for the Vanir were watching.

Steel clashed on steel, and the earth moved below them, but Hereward was older now, with silver in his beard and the marshland waters in his bones. Ogger the Breton defeated Hereward, and the hero of the marshes was bound in chains. His bones were broken, one eye was lost; Alftruda, the new bride, was imprisoned with her husband, and the march to London began. But Ogger, for all his might, had little wisdom. He took Hereward and Alftruda south, to the edge of the marshes, and that is where we found them.

The battle was one of ugliness. Ogger slew many of our men, and though we struck back with twice the fury, their numbers were too great. Yet, I did not fight that day. Instead, as the rain fell, I stepped through the drops and loosed the chains on Hereward's broken form. So, the hero made one last escape, he and Alftruda vanishing for a final time.

With his forces decimated, the resistance was over. The Conqueror had won.

It is said that Hereward and Alftruda took shelter in the court of Domnall mac Donnchada, his old ally. I will never know, and if I did, I would never tell. For I, Morten Lightfoot, have come home.

As you now know, Harald Whetstone, iron cannot contain me. Stone cannot stop me. Wood is my friend. The knife I have at your throat is an old blade, but it is sharp. And so, I am sorry to disturb your sleep and to come here in the dead of the night, but I seek the treasure your father took into his safe keeping. The relics of Ely and of Medeshamstede are no doubt in your treasure vault even now.

What a shame for such brightness to be gathering dust.

Perhaps, then, you and I can take a walk to see them. If you don't scream, it will be simpler. We both know there are many more brothers to replace you on the throne. And if all goes well, you may yet rule a long time, while those relics and I will vanish from here like owls into the night.

5

The Bells of Rostherne Mere

A Cheshire Tale

The mermaid is one of folklore's most fascinating and often-romanticised figures. They are sometimes beautiful and alluring, but equally they are often associated with perilous events or presaging death.

Rostherne Mere is a tranquil natural lake in Cheshire, which is said to be the home of a mermaid who can sometimes be heard ringing a sunken bell below the surface. Rostherne is also home to a Celtic head, carved into a block of sandstone, which was pulled out of the mere and may depict the horned god Cernunnos.

Still, there are really three separate legends which I've brought together for the telling of this tale. One is the legend of the Rostherne church bell, which dates from 1533 when St Mary's Church was built. This story features an accidental summoning of the Devil by one of the church builders, which caused one of the church bells to roll into the mere and be lost. Church-building folklore like this appears all over England, with the Devil only too happy to frustrate builders' efforts!

Another is the legend of the mermaid in the mere, who rises up to sing and ring her bell on Easter Sunday. The mermaid is associated with the Egerton family of nearby Tatton Park. She supposedly rises from the mere when one of the family is going to die.

There is also a memorial in the church to Charlotte Egerton, a young woman who died near the mere on the morning of her wedding.

In this telling, I connected all three.

EC

It was the night before my wedding, and I felt like a background performer in somebody else's big scene. I was rapidly discovering that everybody else had very firm opinions on what a wedding ought to be, and that the wishes of the actual couple were more or less irrelevant. Hazel and I would probably have preferred a quiet elopement, but with her family that was never going to be an option. Even Hazel's hen party hadn't really been to her taste, although she was far too polite to say so.

If I were being tactful, I would describe Hazel's sister as having a forceful personality. If tact was totally abandoned, I would call Amber a complete nightmare. She had taken it upon herself to organise things Hazel and I hadn't even realised needed organising – and was making herself very unpopular doing it. We had to keep reminding ourselves that we were actually looking forward to our wedding, because Amber really sucked all the fun out of it.

I think Hazel and I were both secretly looking forward to the honeymoon more. We'd booked a cottage and had been deliberately vague about exactly where it was, despite plenty of digs from Amber about not going on an expensive trip abroad.

That evening we were all together in Hazel's family home, a lovely old farmhouse in Cheshire, and the atmosphere had reached fever pitch. Hazel's mum was fussing about making her lasagne for everybody. The lasagne was always perfect, but she worried about it beyond all reasonable level. Amber was alternating between phoning the florist to scream at them every five minutes and frantically tweaking her handmade table centrepieces.

Hazel had escaped upstairs, saying that she wanted to check her dress and shoes, but I suspected she had barricaded the door to her childhood bedroom and was reading a book. I certainly couldn't blame her for that, and when Amber screeched at the florist for the fourth time, I made desperate eyes at Harry, my soon-to-be brother-in-law, wordlessly begging him to get me out of there. He was a much quieter person than Amber, more like Hazel really, and he looked pretty grateful to have an excuse, as Amber had recently been haranguing him about napkin folding styles, a subject I was pretty sure he had never considered in his life.

'Dogs,' Harry said suddenly. 'They need walking. Want to come with me, Robin?'

I leapt up with almost indecent speed and had never been happier to see the mournful expressions of the two floppy-eared basset hounds. We found our wellies and the dog leads and were soon putting distance between ourselves and the pressure-cooker atmosphere of the house.

'All gets a bit much, doesn't it?' Harry said, and I readily agreed. We walked in blessed silence, inhaling the late afternoon air. It was still light, just about, although the weather had been dingy grey all week which made it seem darker earlier. I felt the tension easing from my shoulders as we walked through the beautiful countryside leading down to Rostherne Mere. It was a stunning walk and one I often enjoyed with Hazel when we were visiting her parents. We had to cross a little lane, helping the dogs over the stile, and then we were in the meadow leading down to the mere itself, a gorgeously clear lake surrounded by lush wetlands.

Harry and I walked quietly around the edge of the mere for a while, until the dogs needed a breather and paused to investigate some ducks. Harry picked up a stone and skimmed it perfectly across the water, where it bounced four times before sinking to the bottom.

'That's a knack,' I said, rather impressed. 'I've never managed to skip a stone successfully.'

'Lots of practice,' Harry said dourly. 'Escaping from Amber when we were growing up.'

'Has she always been like that?' I asked.

'Oh yes,' he said. 'Sure you want to be related to her?

'I'm sure about Hazel,' I said, which was probably all the answer to the question he needed. Then I remarked that it was a lovely spot, to change the subject.

'Yes, it is. I like it,' he said. Then he looked at me sideways, with the peculiar sideways smile he has. 'Although if you hear bells, we'd better go home sharpish.'

'Bells?' I asked, unable to imagine what he meant.

'Hasn't Hazel told you the story about the bell?'

'No, she's never mentioned it.'

'Oh, I probably shouldn't have said anything, then,' Harry said. 'Bit inauspicious the night before your wedding, now I come to think of it. Forget I spoke.'

'You can't say that and then not tell me,' I said. As if to back me up, one of the basset hounds promptly sat on his foot to prevent him from leaving before he'd told me his mysterious story.

'Oh, well, in that case,' Harry said amiably. He'd picked up a few stones from the water's edge and had a supply in his hand, and every so often he skimmed one into the water. The rhythmic sound was a comforting accompaniment to his voice as he spoke, and I found myself almost hypnotised by the splashes.

'They say that when Rostherne Church was built in – I don't know – the 1600s or something – it was almost finished, and there were only the bells left to put in the tower. It was the day before Easter Sunday, so they were keen to get it done so the chimes could ring out to celebrate Easter. The builders were lugging the bells up the hill, but one of them kept rolling back down whenever the man pushing it took his hands off it for a moment.

'Well, he got more and more wound up, and after this had happened a few times, he said to the bell, "I would the Devil had thee!"'

'Sounds ominous,' I said.

'Yes, the Devil was obviously listening,' Harry said seriously, as though he really believed any of this might have happened, 'because as soon as he had pushed the bell up the hill and was taking a breather, it rolled down towards him faster than it ought, and squashed him stone dead, then it kept rolling until it fell into the mere here and sank.'

'Serves him right for cursing,' I said, trying to inject some joviality. The afternoon was beginning to feel colder, and Harry's story was not the cheeriest.

'That wasn't the end of it, though,' he said. 'The legend says the bell fell into the mere and landed on the home of the mermaid who lives at the bottom.'

'Mermaid?! Come on, now.'

'Really!' Harry said. 'That's the story! It fell on her home and crushed one of her eggs, just the same as it had crushed the builder. She was so angry, she blamed the people on land for casting the bell, bringing it to Rostherne and being so careless as to drop it in her mere. So, the next morning at dawn, she dragged the sunken bell with her all the way up to the surface and rang it on Easter morning, singing a tragic song the whole time. The noise was so awful that the service was ruined. Apparently, she's done it every Easter morning ever since. If you're ever here for Easter and you're minded to get up early, you might spot her.'

'I imagine she would feel my scepticism coming and stay well underwater,' I said. 'You don't believe it, do you? You haven't actually heard anything, have you?'

'I'm not an early riser,' he said.

'And it's only meant to be at dawn on Easter Day this mermaid appears?'

'Or when someone is going to die,' said Harry.

'But surely she'd be appearing all the time in that case,' I pointed out. After all, somebody dies every few minutes.

'Oh, it's not just anyone,' he said. 'I think they need to be vaguely connected to the family at Tatton Hall, the Egertons. It wouldn't ring for you, even if you were at death's door.'

'Hasn't your family got an Egerton connection?' I vaguely remembered Hazel's dad mentioning the name linked to Tatton Hall, which was the lovely National Trust property near their home.

'Something very far down the line,' Harry said. 'Probably on the wrong side of the bedsheets.'

'But what did you mean about it being bad luck the night before our wedding?' I persisted. The mermaid story was a little macabre, perhaps, but it didn't feel particularly relevant.

'Oh, just that the mermaid was last heard of in – I don't know quite when – Victorian times, I think. She appeared to a young woman called Charlotte Egerton. You can see her memorial in the church if you like, although I expect your mind will be on other things tomorrow… anyway, Charlotte is supposed to have seen the mermaid on the eve of her wedding, and she was dead within an hour.'

'What?' I said, incredulous. 'Was that the official cause of death? Saw a mermaid and keeled over?'

'Oh no, it was apparently a bronchial infection. But you know, people like their superstitions.'

I was a little bit relieved, I have to confess. I'm not superstitious, and I've never believed in ghosts or other monsters. A pre-existing bronchial condition seemed far more plausible than the sighting of a strange woman with a bell. Nevertheless, I was happier when we'd started the walk home from Rostherne Mere, despite not really believing in any of it. Omens of death are not something one really wants to consider before the happiest day of one's life.

Harry skimmed his last stone and we took the dogs back to the cottage, where mercifully everything had calmed down.

I was staying in the spare room that night because it was supposed to be bad luck to sleep in the same bed as Hazel. I didn't really agree with that and would have rather started our married life as we intended to go through it – together – but her family insisted. I found myself unable to sleep after Harry's odd story. Although I didn't believe it and I probably ought to be thinking about the things I needed to do in the morning, like make sure my best man had actually come to the right county, I sat up in the chair by the window, looking out over the fields towards the mere.

I don't think I slept all night, or perhaps I only dozed in the chair, because the sky was getting light with misty wisps of dawn when I opened my eyes. I cracked the window open, hoping the cold air would wake me up a bit in lieu of coffee being made. Then I heard a strange, hollow booming, not like a church bell, really, but something darker. It sounds ridiculous to say, but I could almost hear rust in the sound.

I looked out the window towards the mere, and though it was only just getting light, there was a darker shape in the centre of the water. Hazel's dad is a keen bird watcher, one of those people who keeps a pair of RSPB binoculars on every windowsill in case he catches sight of a lesser-spotted warbler of some sort. With a feeling rather akin to dread I took the binoculars out of their case and raised them to my eyes

I could see what was definitely a head and shoulders above the surface of the water, and a long, thin arm holding a huge, algae-encrusted bell. The arm was emaciated and the skin greenish and indistinct as though it were still underwater. But the eyes of the creature were the worst part – huge green and yellow orbs, curiously slanted and brimming with an expression so sad it sent a wave of emotion through me, as though I too might cry at any moment.

Out of its mouth came a strange, high, wailing sound, which I could hardly call a song. The sound of it made me feel nauseous, so I put the binoculars down and backed away from the window, giving myself a little slap on the cheek to wake myself up. I was still half-convinced I was dreaming at the point, you see, so I staggered down the landing to the bathroom and splashed my face.

When I got back to the spare room there was no sign of the creature in the mere. Still feeling as though I might be sick, I lay down on the bed and must have fallen asleep again, because the next thing I was conscious of was Hazel leaning over me, all rumpled hair and creased pyjamas.

'This is all very nice,' I said, 'but aren't I meant to not see you?'

'Never mind about that,' she said. 'Can you come and help? It's Amber. I don't think she's very well.'

Well, I expect you can guess that we didn't get married that day after all, although we did stay in Rostherne for a bit to help with Amber's funeral. In the end, we had a much smaller wedding ceremony, which suited us much better, and we see a lot more of Hazel's family. I find myself much more inclined to visit them now Amber's not there. But if Harry ever asks me to accompany him to walk the dogs down to the mere, I always have to decline.

6

The Mermaid of Zennor

A Cornish Tale

The church of Zennor in Cornwall is home to an unusual artefact: a fifteenth-century chancel chair carved with images of mermaids. They say that mermaids in church settings reflect the dual aspects of Christ as human and divine.

The church is named after St Senara. There's very little information about her, but she may have been a Breton princess whose husband accused her of adultery and threw her into the sea in a barrel. She was said to have been visited by an angel, then washed up on the coast of Cornwall to found the village and the church. As water is a symbol of the unconscious, Senara's sea crossing is a moment of self-discovery.

The legend of Senara (or 'Asenora') is quite different to the ghastly Mermaid of Rostherne Mere. It's a love story. Often wild, feminine figures like mermaids and selkies are trapped in unwanted domestic situations on land, but Senara brings her man into her world, when she realises that, in order to be truly loved, she needs to be truly seen.

I also expanded the tale to connect it to the Melusine myth, which appears in a lot of medieval romances and later poems, as I felt there was a natural link between the legends.

EC

This tale was made where the sea meets the sky at the edge of the world. It's as old as a barnacled anchor and as new as the sunrise glinting on a sinuous, scaly tail.

On a green and rain-drenched isle there lived a woman named Asenora. She was noble and fair, but she wandered her way through life with no lover to call her own. That was because Asenora had a secret. She was a woman, but she was not only a woman.

Whenever she was completely submerged in water, she underwent a change. Her long, pale legs grew close together, as though they were caught in a fishing net, and a fine covering of scales, glittering like new shillings, crept over them until she had a long, flexible tail, just like a sea snake's.

Asenora did not mind her tail, for it only troubled her when she bathed, but she was quick and observant enough to realise that others might mind it a great deal. In those days, folk condemned faces and limbs which didn't look like their own, and were swift to kindle bonfires when confronted by the strange. It was for this reason that she kept to herself, living quietly in a secluded tower and shunning the company of men.

But one day, as Asenora was walking by the banks of the river and enjoying the sound of the birds in the blossom trees and the sight of the darting minnows in the shallows, everything changed.

A knight came riding towards her, following the bends of the river. At first, all Asenora could see was a tiny dot on the horizon, but soon, far too soon, the dot resolved itself into a coal-black war horse decked in white and gold, with a knight on its back, likewise brilliantly apparelled.

It was too late for Asenora to run back to her tower and out of his sight. The knight rode right up to her and wished her good morning. She hoped that would be the end of it, but he seemed in no hurry at all and was soon sliding from his horse's back and giving it a drink from the river, passing the time of day in a very gentlemanly fashion.

Now this knight, whose name was Revelin, was very much struck by Asenora's charms, not least the expression of slight panic in her eyes and the way she kept glancing over her shoulder as if there was somewhere she would rather be. Ordinarily, he was the sort of knight who would waste no time in urging a pretty woman to lie down in the flower-strewn field with him, but he could see that it would be no use. She seemed so shy and so timid that he knew he would have to find another way.

So Revelin dawdled along with Asenora, telling her all manner of tales of his grand adventures and his great friendship with the young king. As she had never been anywhere or talked to anybody, the pictures he painted in her imagination were wonderful indeed. And while he talked, she stole sidelong glances at him from underneath her eyelashes, and she liked what she saw.

Why prolong my story? By the end of the walk, Asenora and Revelin were promised to each other, and by the end of the week, they were married.

The marriage feast was fine and the guests danced for days. Revelin carried Asenora away to his castle by the sea and showered her with rubies red as roses, pearls as big as plums, and crystal caskets of glittering gold. She promised to love him truly and faithfully, as long as he promised to leave her quite alone every Saturday so she could take a bath. This seemed an easy enough thing to promise, so Revelin happily agreed.

Why is it that the one thing we know we must never do is the thing which seems the most alluring?

I don't mean to say Revelin broke his vow directly. No, far from it. They were delighted with one another and many moons had waxed and waned in their marriage before anything went wrong. But while Revelin enjoyed Asenora's company and had no complaints about her, he became restless and irritable for thinking of the one thing he had promised not to do.

Every Saturday, when his wife sent for buckets of steaming water and pounds of sweet-smelling soap and unbound her hair from its twisted crown of braids, he looked at the closed door to her chamber, and he wondered. Every Saturday, he made himself walk away and ride his warhorse in the forests or fly his hawk to the windy skies.

Until one Saturday, when his own curiosity lit him up with too bright a flame to fight, and he flung back the doors to Asenora's chamber to see her in the bath.

From the waist up, it was his own beloved wife, every inch known to him, with her wet hair all loose and spilling over the rim of the bath. But from the waist down, the bath was filled with a monstrous tail, big as a barrel of herring and tremendously long.

Asenora shrieked and called out after her husband, but it was too late. Revelin rushed from the room, and she could hear him raging through the castle, calling to his men and raising the hue and cry.

Asenora was terrified. He no longer sounded like the man she loved; he had the voice of a stranger. She did not pause to think. In her fear, she slithered from the bath, straight out of the window of the castle turret and into the raging seas below. A fierce current caught her at once, and with a few thrashes of her powerful tail, she was soon borne away from the land.

And she wept, because she knew that Revelin had lost a good and faithful wife, despite the secret she had kept from him.

And she wept because she knew that he would never be able to love her as she was, half-woman and half-fish.

And she wept for the life she had known on the green and rain-drenched island, now lost to her forever, and for the love in her own heart which had been for the whole of her husband, even though his had never been for the whole of her.

She swam for a long while below the waves, longing for the ocean's dark and infinite embrace to soothe the pain she felt.

Now, a long way from those shores, across that tempest-tossed sea, was the Cornish headland, and on that headland near Porthzennor Cove, stood Matty Trewhella, gazing out to sea. Thrift and sea campion grew in tangles round his feet and the wind blew his hair into curly clouds.

He looked out as far as his eyes would allow, but he did not see the ridged back of Morgawr, the serpent, and he did not hear the bells of the lost city of Lyonesse, drowned in a single night – or so they say. Instead, he saw the sunrise, and the haze over the waves.

Some days, the sea shone like a mirror, but that day it was shrouded in mist. Matty was pleased, because he knew the old saying:

Mist from the hill
Brings water for the mill
Mist from the sea
Brings fine weather for me.

He would have stood watching all day, but he wanted to get to the church. It was a Saturday, not a Sunday, but Matty Trewhella had a fine, strong voice, and he sometimes liked to go into the church to practise his singing when nobody else was there.

The church in Zennor was simple and fresh and flooded with light from its high windows. Matty stood in the nave and faced towards the altar, and his voice rose up like a fluttering lark.

As he sang his way through his favourite hymns, the church door slid softly open. Up the aisle came a woman, spattering droplets on to the stone floor as she went. Her hair was long and wild, every shade of gold and brown, and some of it deeper, softer, coloured like the inside of a wave. Her dress was made of plaited seaweed, which had wound itself around her body as she swam. It was Asenora, the lady from the sea.

Matty neither heard her nor paused in his singing, for he was moved by the music and carried somewhere far away from his own self on the wings of a song. And the bright sun which the sea mist had foretold shone through the leaded panes of glass and on to Matty's cheek, making it glow warm.

The softest breath of a sound came from Asenora's lips as she looked at him – no, she did more than look. She beheld him, just exactly as he truly was.

Now Matty finished his hymn, and although he was in the church, it was not Sunday, so he thought nothing of striking up with another song, a merry sailor's ballad in the old language of the land. When he reached the chorus, he heard another voice joining in with him.

Asenora was singing too, and her voice was high and pure at the top and rough and velvety at the bottom, and Matty stopped singing in shock and then he turned, and he saw her, and he beheld her too.

Her arms were wet, and her tangled locks of hair, and at the hem of her seaweed dress he could see a pale white foot with greenish veins, and fish scales vanishing away up her long, smooth leg. For she was only a mermaid in water, but she'd been in the ocean such a long time that it took a while for all the effects to vanish. But she never minded, for this was her true self, half-woman and half-fish, and something about this young man told her that it would be alright to show herself to him.

Well, they sang together, and their voices jumped up and danced together in the space between Asenora's sea green eyes and Matty's bright brown ones, and soon enough they were leaving the church together, arm-in-arm just as though they'd been married, though no words of wedlock had ever passed their lips.

Matty Trewhella's old proverb was right: the sea mist had brought him fine weather, and a fine woman, too.

And that was the last anybody ever saw of Matty in Zennor. His old mother would have gone mad with wondering about him if she hadn't had other grown-up children to care for her. She was sleeping in the graveyard before anybody brought back any news of her missing son.

There was a sea captain sailing his ship back from far-flung shores. His hold was full of barrels of rum and chests of tea, and he was eager to put into port and recover his land legs. But there was some trouble about getting into the harbour, so he anchored the ship a little way out to sea to wait. All at once, he heard a woman's voice calling to him. He looked about for her, and eventually he saw her in the waves, her pale face bobbing against the dark water.

The captain's first thought was that she was in danger, but then he saw the shape of her long tail beneath the surface and realised she was a mermaid.

'Haul up your anchor,' she called to him. 'It's resting on my door, and I can't get home to Matty and the children.'

Well, the captain hauled anchor fast enough, for he was wary of upsetting a mermaid, having some misgivings about their powers over sea and storm. Like quicksilver, the mermaid dived back down to the seabed and vanished from his sight. But when he was drinking in the Tinner's Arms that evening, having finally put into port, he told the company what he had seen, and those of the village folk who had the longest memories all agreed that it must have been the mermaid who had stolen away Matty Trewhella all those years ago.

Neither Matty or the mermaid were ever seen or heard of again. Stories are as changeable as the colour of the sea, so nobody could quite agree if she was really a mermaid, or a saint, or a beautiful woman, but they carved her image on a bench in the church – the very one on which she sat to sing. You can still see it today, if you visit.

And if you stand on the headland at Porthzennor Cove at sunrise on a spring morning, you might just hear the lovers' voices on the edge of the breeze.

And so my tale is told, and now it belongs to you.

7

The Sockburn Worm

A County Durham Tale

It is bonkers to think that, if you visit Durham Cathedral today (which you absolutely should), then among the incredible historic items there (not least St Cuthbert's coffin, which dates all the way back to the seventh century) you can find the Conyers Falchion.

This ancient sword, which was said to have been used to slay the Sockburn Worm, is one of only four surviving examples of its type in the whole world. And it still has a ceremonial use! Traditionally a 'sword of tenure' for the lands the Conyers family held from the Bishops of Durham, it is even now presented to incoming bishops by the Mayor of Darlington each time they enter the diocese for the first time.

As for the legend of the Sockburn Worm, it has been retold time and again in ballads and plays across history, much like the legend of the Lambton Worm and other such slithery, dragon-type beasties who were said to have harassed England in days of yore.

Though the Conyers family died out, and Sockburn itself is now little more than a ruin, Lewis Carroll, whose father was Archdeacon of Richmond, heard the tale while visiting family friends in Sunderland, and was inspired to write his famous poem, The Jabberwocky.

Better yet, you can still find the stone at Sockburn under which it's said the slain dragon was buried, near ancient Viking hogback tombs decorated with carved dragon iconography – all of which lends credence to the tale.

MV

South of Darlington, at the point of the River Tees' northernmost meander, there's a ruined place that was long ago known as the village of Storkburn. Nobody lives there now – only hints remain that it was ever a village at all. A few boulders, a ruined church, an eighteenth-century farmhouse. Then, high above it all, there's a neo-Jacobean country house once owned by the Conyers family.

The wind whips through the vales and down the river there, weathering the old stones – just as the name of Storkburn was weathered away by lazy tongues. First Storkburn became Sockburn, then Sockburn became nothing at all.

Only once, long ago, Sockburn was famous; a holy place and a cultural centre for Anglo-Saxon settlers. It was there, in AD 780, that Higbald was crowned Bishop of Lindisfarne. It's from Higbald's letters that we know of those first Viking raids that changed English history forever. In AD 796, it was the place where Eanbold was crowned Archbishop of York – the same Eanbold who first introduced Roman Catholicism to that ancient city.

To this day, in and around the ruins of Sockburn church, between the long grass, the scrub and the undergrowth, there are hints of this past glory. Nestled in the weeds, you can find elaborately carved hogback tombs etched from granite. They were once intricately engraved, with carved shingles on either side of their peaked, chiselled roofs. These rare houses for the dead are each a Mead Hall, through which their occupants might access Valhalla.

Hogback tombs are found in Scotland, Ireland, Wales, northern England and Cornwall; anywhere Vikings sailed and settled. They have stood for 1,000 years, with many adorned with massive end-beasts, just like the longships that brought their occupants all those years ago. Yet the mythical monsters that ornament these graves weren't always beings of the imagination. Some of the folk at rest in those tombs battled and bested those creatures, earning themselves the glory of being memorialised in stone.

One such warrior rests in a weathered hogback tomb at Sockburn – a hero who founded a long line of soldiers, statesman and rebels.

The last of their line died in a Victorian poorhouse, emaciated and insane. But centuries earlier, one of their number, Sir John Conyers, rebelled against Edward IV during the Wars of the Roses. He became an outlaw king, renaming himself Robin of Redesdale, leading armies in defiance of the crown. And when Sir John was slain, his brother Charles took up the mantle of Robin of Redesdale, creating a new legend: that Robin of Redesdale had the power to rise from the dead.

Long before that, Sockburn had faced a foe wilier than a Yorkist king. For out of the River Tees, for hundreds of years, creatures would hatch and emerge and wreak havoc on that rolling landscape; poison-breathing beasts that crawled on their bellies, slithering through fields and hiding in woodlands.

At night, as these creatures grew, they emerged from the shadows, hiding beneath the cover of darkness, their oily scales twinkling in the moonlight. They savaged and feasted on anything they could find – men, children, sheep – even one another. Then they would retreat to the safety of the forest's maze-like greenery or slide back into the lapping calm of the water's edge.

It was rare for one of these creatures to grow large enough to reproduce. Their hunger was such that often they starved to death. Yet, when a worm became large enough to spawn, it would retreat to the water, seeding offspring like a larval insect. Indeed, the oldest and mightiest of these creatures would grow wings, some strong enough they might even take flight, with worms harrying villages across Bernicia for hundreds of years.

To protect themselves, the ancient peoples of what has since become Durham knew what to do: they fished the rivers, hunting out the young worms and bashing their skulls to pieces with rocks on the riversides. Yet the flesh made for bad eating, and the blood of the creatures was poisonous. If it slipped into waterways then the ground would turn toxic. Crops would fail, forcing families and sometimes whole townships to move on. For this reason, the bodies of the creatures were burned on funeral pyres all through the summer months, black smoke rising high through the clear, warm air.

When raiders came across the whale road from Scandinavia, these new arrivals didn't know about the worms. As the years passed, summer raiding gave way to settling. The Vikings who came to England presumed that those villages that had vanished and the families that had disappeared must have been slain by local people – Northumbrian warbands, wisely hostile to insurgents from afar.

Yet, some of these settlers clung on. Some ventured inland, following the waterways, settling where springs saw holy water bubbling and springing up from the earth.

Sockburn was just such a place; a settlement where black eagles hunted from above and a sacred well drew people together. Clay huts were built, wooden walls and palisades erected, crops planted. Sheep and cattle were raised to graze on the mineral-rich floodplains nearby and the town became rich.

The men who ruled places like Sockburn had to be wise. This earned them names, titles to go by, and so it was that the widowed king, Johannes of Sockburn, who had been chosen to rule and who'd had gold and silver minted in his name, became Johannes the Cunning. It was he who raised a Mead Hall at Sockburn, where the fires burned bright and the drink flowed fast, glinting like gold in the broad hearth's glow.

Wise as he was, though, Johannes failed to see how mischief could grow into disaster, and how disaster could undo all the good work he and his people had accomplished. It started with small things. Shepherds losing a lamb here, farmers losing a foal there. Fish stocks suddenly dropped, then the river started to ripple with strange, stinking eels. Johannes instructed his people to catch the creatures and burn them, but his sole, surviving son, Leif, thought the whole thing was just a game. Not yet ten years old, Leif had never known war or hardship. And one day, he caught one of the wriggling creatures in his net, dropping the stinking beast into the holy well out of jest.

Leif thought the whole thing was a just lark – that one of the women would go to draw water and have a shock – but in doing what he did, the half-orphaned boy spelled disaster for all he knew. For, though the river was dredged of wriggling worms, their bodies burned in crackling pyres that sent up ribbons of black, acrid smoke, deep in the earth of the holy well, Leif's mischief grew and grew, nestling safely in the quiet earth.

Before long, the losses became worse. Livestock, brought inside the village walls by night, started to panic. Pigs squealed and horses kicked at the wood of their stables. Watchmen, keeping guard from the palisades, came to hear the sounds of slaughter coming from inside their own barns. They rushed to see what was happening, their guard dogs barking and straining at their leads. Yet they always arrived too late, unfailingly finding grisly scenes of devastation and slaughter.

They saw blood, torn flesh, broken bones, gouges made by needle-sharp teeth and monstrous claws. Then, all around the clearly mutilated animals, other beasts had perished too, as if struck down by the shock or some invisible plague.

The travelling monks who once came to Sockburn to seek its waters started to avoid it. They prayed, offered totems, icons and spells, but nothing seemed to work. No one could understand what was happening, and panic started to rise.

The people of Sockburn knew of wolves, bears, foxes, wild dogs – knew the marks their teeth made and how to defend against them. But this new menace was something different – an invisible foe that moved like darkness, striking wherever firelight failed to touch.

Johannes the Cunning appealed for calm. He had patrols doubled, told his people to shelter in the Mead Hall. He visited the blacksmith and commissioned the village a new blade. This weapon, he said, should be a sun-bright falchion with which he, the leader of his people, would slay their unkillable foe.

As the blacksmith set to work, folding fresh steel with the skill of a master craftsman, each hammer blow echoed in Leif's mind. The boy's guilt grew like an afternoon shadow, stretching and obscuring, darkening him from head to toe. His joke had grown into something terrible – a jest mutating into a menacing, nameless horror that laughed at the one who'd told it.

Then the villagers started falling ill. They didn't know, could never have guessed, that it was the very water they were drinking that was killing them. That the once holy resource had turned profane, tainted by the shadow growing in its midst.

The animals died first. Then, as men, women and children grew sicker and weaker, most becoming too feeble to rise from their beds, Johannes took a band of his finest warriors and rode out to nearby communities seeking aid. Yet word had travelled. Sockburn was cursed; afflicted with a plague, a wasting disease with teeth and claws, rising like a demon of old.

None of the neighbouring kings would open their doors to Johannes. They feared the illness would spread, decimating their own people. And so it was that Johannes the Cunning came to look inward, considering ways in which he might hope to catch a fiend nobody could even see.

When Johannes and his men returned home, he found Sockburn just a shadow of its former self. His people were either dead or dying, most too sick to dig the graves in which they might bury their friends. He found his son weeping in the Mead Hall, cowering behind the throne, ready to confess to his crime. And when Johannes learned of Leif's folly, he understood what had to be done, binding the boy in a solemn vow.

Johannes had all of his people moved or carried outside of the village walls. Signal fires were lit, his ailing folk sheltering for warmth in a ring of flames surrounding their now-empty village. Then Johannes had the fires of each home extinguished, keeping even the ashes of the Mead Hall cold.

When he went to visit the blacksmith, Johannes found the old craftsman dead at his forge, yet the sword was finished – a gold-bright blade with which a king might fight to save his people.

So it was that Johannes the Cunning took his seat on his throne, his falchion in his hand, all around him bathed in darkness. As his eyes adjusted to the gloom, he thought back through the events of his life – of the good times and the bad. Of his lost love, his wife, who had perished bringing Leif into the world. Smiling, he imagined what it would be like to see her again, to be reunited with all those he had lost at Woden's eternal feast.

Before long though, Johannes was roused from his reverie. He heard the creature moving. It scuttled and slithered through the dark, moving through empty barns and hollow houses, knocking over chairs and surging over tables. He could hear the beast's claws rattling as it moved, listened to it hissing as it neared the edge of the village walls and the fires crackling outside.

In time, of course, the beast moved inwards. It searched like a spiral, out from the darkest edges and in, ever closer, towards the community's heart – to the building in which there had always before been a fire burning, the brightest of blazes. Yet that night there was only darkness in the Mead Hall – darkness obscuring a single heartbeat, and a single point of warmth.

The Sockburn Worm came in through the great wooden doors of the Mead Hall, which Johannes had left open, and as it did, Johannes the Cunning tried his best to keep still. The starlight bounced from the creature's oily scales, and the stink of it was choking, heady, making Johannes' eyes water.

He saw the monster's eyes glinting bright as pearls, and as the worm drew close, rearing up to attack, Johannes leapt to his feet, roaring and dashing backwards, darting behind his throne. Startled, the beast hissed, its stubby wings unfurling, beating the air and sending a smoke-like cloud billowing through the room. The green-black haze, noxious and thick, caused Johannes to stumble, just as the worm darted around behind the throne, gnashing its rows of sharp, needle-like teeth.

The creature caught Johannes in its jaws, biting and holding him fast, but the King of Sockburn raised his gold-bright blade and rained blows on his scaly foe. He stabbed and slashed, pummelled and kicked, and the worm released its quarry, surprised at this barrage of new sensations – the creature's first feelings of pain.

By now, Johannes knew he was slain. His wounds reeked, his mind reeling, his eyes rolling back in his head. Staggering, falling, blood dripping from his chest, he half-crawled, half-ran, rushing to the door of the Mead Hall. As he reached the huge wooden barriers, he tossed his sword through the gap and closed the doors, slamming them shut and locking himself inside.

His last sight, through the gap, was his son, out in the darkness, waiting. Leif held a torch in his hand, the flames flickering, showing his boyish face. The look he bore, Johannes thought, was one of sadness and loss. It made him look so much like his mother.

Then, with the doors closed, Leif did as his father had made him promise he would. Trying to ignore the screams inside, he ran with the torch, lifting it here and there, lighting the thatch of the Mead Hall. Once he'd lit each of the four corners, his face wet with tears, the whole building seemed entirely ablaze. Then, he picked up his father's sword and walked back out to the people of Sockburn, unable to watch as his father and the Sockburn Worm disappeared under fire and ash.

Time passed, as it's wont to do, and Sockburn recovered. The spring again ran pure, and Leif grew into a man. New people came, animals thrived, and each summer eels were caught and burned. Out of the ruins of the Mead Hall, bones were recovered – those of Johannes, which were laid in an intricately carved grave with a dragon's head at one end, and those of the worm, which were sealed under a huge grey stone as a reminder of the dangers that threaten to spring from below. Praise was showered on the people of Sockburn, and king after king honoured the people of that holy place.

As the weathering winds blew, Johannes the Cunning became Johan the Coiner, and Johan the Coiner became John Conyers. Little more than two hundred years later, a son of a son of a son of a king presented a battered falchion to the newly crowned Prince Bishop of Durham.

To this day, when a new bishop takes office in Durham, that same sword is presented to them along with these words:

> My Lord Bishop. I hereby present you with the falchion wherewith the champion Conyers slew the worm, dragon or fiery flying serpent which destroyed man, woman and child; in memory of which the king then reigning gave him the manor of Sockburn, to hold by this tenure, that upon the first entrance of every bishop into the county the falchion should be presented.

The falchion is kept in the Treasury of Durham Cathedral and is on display in a case in a dimly lit chamber. You can go and see it, if you like. It's thirty-five inches long, weighs almost three pounds, and its pommel is engraved with a black eagle. The blade is decorated with dragon motifs and is strangely corroded and bent from use.

The last time a worm hatched in County Durham and lived long enough to terrorise the people was at Lambton, almost 40 miles away, during the times of the Crusades. Others terrorised Fatfield, at Worm Hill, and Penshaw, where a monument stands in memory to those it slew.

As for the graves at Sockburn, they are still there to see, that of Johannes and the Sockburn Worm, all but side-by-side. Although, few go by to visit these days – save the winds, which roll off the river and tease at the ends of the hissing grass.

8

Long Meg and Her Daughters

A Cumberland Tale

One of around 1,300 ancient stone circles in the British Isles and Brittany, Long Meg and Her Daughters, which are located near Penrith, are the third-largest set in England after Avebury in Wiltshire and Stanton Drew in Somerset. The monument is thought to be around 5,000 years old, yet there are many legends associated with it, not least that, a bit like the Rollright Stones on the Oxfordshire/Warwickshire border, if you count the number of the stones there correctly twice, Long Meg and Her Daughters will be freed from their state of stony imprisonment.

Better yet, it's said that if anyone damages Long Meg – the central, red sandstone megalith, marked with neolithic art including a 'cup and ring', spirals and concentric circles – the stone will bleed and storms erupt! Pioneering archaeologists and antiquarians of the sixteenth and seventeenth centuries such as William Camden and John Aubrey fed into this mythology, which also inspired Cumbrian poet William Wordsworth.

As for who Long Meg was in legend, like the Merry Maidens in Cornwall and many others up and down the country, it's said that she and her daughters (or friends, or fellow witches) were up to business they shouldn't have been on a Sunday and so became petrified. Some tales also fold in the occultist and wizard, Michael Scot, as I have done. Born in the eleventh century, he led a fascinating life and is reputed to have died just as I attest in my telling.

MV

Once, there were seventy-seven great stone circles in Cumberland. Some still stand, such as the stones of Souther Fell, where ghostly armies march by night.

There are the Castlerigg Stones, second largest in all of England, and the Mayburgh Henge, left half-buried in the earth since old John Lesh dug one out to build his house and went mad within a week. At Eamont Bridge, there's the Round Table, said to be the site of King Arthur's final battle, and the Swinside Stones, where the folk of Sunkenkirk tried to raise their church, but the Devil kept pulling it down.

But no stone circle in Cumbria has half the fame of Long Meg and Her Daughters. And though others might fall, she never will – not until the curse is broken.

Few dare to so much as touch Long Meg. Some brave soul once set about trying to carve his name in her, but no sooner had his blade touched the stone than it sprang with blood and a storm blew in overhead. Poor fool must not have known the hex laid upon her by the wizard, Michael Scot, he who froze old Meg and all her kin that bright Sabbath day.

She was famous for a time, Meg of Meldon; the flame-haired daughter of William Fenwick, known to all nearby as the Heron Lord. He was master of Harrington Hall and wanted a son. He never got one, and once Meg grew tall she was married off, as was the way in those times. So tall was she that some thought her ugly and some called her a giant, but she mothered seven girls well enough, much to her husband's shame and rage.

Like Meg's father, her husband wanted a male heir, and with no boys forthcoming, he took to drink. It was no matter to Meg who, out of nowhere, found and raised a pup to keep her company. A black mongrel, it grew and grew, and it's said that when the hound barked the rain would start falling, and when it growled the clouds turned grey up above.

One day, so it's said, ripe with drink, Meg's husband fell from his horse and passed on. So, Meg went back to her father seeking money, and by then the old man was on his deathbed. Old William Fenwick wouldn't give her a bean, no matter how loud the dog growled, and when he died at a great flash of lightning, some second cousin became the Heron Lord, and that was that.

So it was that Meg went from village to village, from Penrith to Armathwaite, Whinfell to Kirkoswald, raging until the air turned black with her words on the ways of menfolk. Sure enough, her seven daughters followed, and like the Fenwicks from time immemorial, those girls had magic in their blood. They knew the power of the stones of Cumbria, studied the hedges and the druids' ancient rites, and so many of the women who heard Long Meg's calls dropped their stitching, left their bread half-kneaded, and walked away with the butter unchurned.

It's said over a hundred women followed Meg out into the Pennine Hills. Word was they lived there together in the caves, hunting and fishing, farming and trading with the folk of Winskill, Salkeld and Glassonby. They never went to church and never spoke to menfolk at all. And people came to them for help: cures for the sick, help for the lame, spells for those most in need. All one had to do was walk into the wilderness and there the black dog would find them, leading them to a quiet place where a sister would meet them and do business.

Of course, word spread soon enough – not least of the dances Long Meg led, out in the wilds in all weathers. The women would travel to the stones across Cumbria for their rites. Some said there were sacrifices, fires lit and wailing songs that lasted from dawn until dark. All that noise carried on the wind – well, it drew Michael Scot, and in him, Long Meg met her match.

You see, Scot was a wizard – no bones about it. He'd trained as a priest at Oxford, learning Latin and Greek. Then he went to Paris, learned Hebrew, went to Bologna, learned Italian, and he trained in Arabic at Toledo, unlocking the wisdoms of the East and West. He travelled on, right into Africa, living for a time with the Tuareg people of the Sahara. He solved the secrets of the rainbow, wrote on astrology, alchemy, physiognomy, and the occult, helping Fibonacci with his book on mathematics – which is dedicated to him if you check.

When word reached him of Long Meg, he was in Norway, where he was showing the same trick he'd done in France and Spain, having feasts served by spirits he summoned out of the shadows of the room. And by then, he had learned of the manner in which he himself would die: the spirits told him it would be by a stone striking his skull. So, day and night, Michael Scot wore a steel cap under his hood, never removing it and thinking to live forever.

So it was that Michael Scot sailed to Cumberland, drawn by the rumours of Long Meg. And though he spoke to the Lord Bishop of Carlisle, it seemed none of the priests of the county would dare head out to the wilds to see Meg. All were afraid, having seen the storms above her dances, heard her music on the wind and learned of the many who were willing to follow her, seemingly to hell and back.

He was a brave man, Michael Scot, for as much as he was a wizard, he was also flesh and blood, and though he ventured over the foothills by Thack Moor and through Hartside Pass, everywhere he went a great black dog followed him, watching from not far off. The beast, which some said grew as big as a horse, brought with it gales and lightning and floods, and when Michael Scot battled the weather it only grew worse, the hound mocking his steps.

Yet, Michael Scot was cunning too, and so he laid a trap. For that year, midsummer fell on a Sabbath day, and from studying the stars, the old wizard knew just which stones Meg would choose to dance at. He lay in wait, hiding himself in the Helm Wind blowing off Cross Fell, waiting for Meg to appear.

Appear she did, with her hundred followers. It's said they stripped down to their nakedness, the sisters in a broad ring all about Long

Meg, who was covered in blood as red as her flowing hair. She set about dancing, calling the storms, thanking the spirits for their service. And her black hound was there, and the sisters were singing. But little did they know that in calling the storm, they called Michael Scot, who rode the Helm Wind right to them.

When the old wizard appeared before the women they all gasped in horror, and though they roared and raged, with the witches being of the air, Michael Scot laid down a curse of the earth, turning them all to stone. The daughters in the ring all mingled with the ancient rocks laid down by the druids and the men of the old times, each transmuting to granite, but Meg had a special fate. For her stone was red – red as her hair, red as the blood on her skin. And the hex Michael Scot laid on her was such that only a soul who could count all those stones three times round and come out with the same number would free Long Meg.

But the stones there move, you see. They're never in the same place twice. Which is how Long Meg and Her Daughters were trapped, and still are, sealed in rock forever more.

Of course, everyone in Cumberland knows Long Meg's hound still roams the hills and fells, watching and waiting and bringing the weather. And don't think Michael Scot got off free, either. For, as Dante wrote in his *Inferno*, Michael Scot, the greatest wizard of his day, went to the Devil, just as he always should have.

After laying his hex, you see, Scot went back to Carlisle Cathedral and set himself down to pray. Only, the Lord Bishop bade the wizard remove his skullcap while he knelt to ask for forgiveness.

It just so happened that a loose stone from high above on the cathedral ceiling fell and struck Michael Scot right on the top of his head. He was killed in the blink of an eye, and as an unholy man who died unshriven, his body was laid in an unmarked grave, its location a mystery to this day.

And although Michael Scot is long dead, Long Meg and Her Daughters are far from it. For those old stones live and listen and learn, and one day, some bright spark will count those rocks, and then Long Meg will be free.

9

The Boggarts of Arbor Low

A Derbyshire Tale

One of the very best things about boggarts is that nobody can agree exactly what they are.

Dr Simon Young, one of the world's leading experts in British faery lore, spent years compiling his Boggart Source Book, *which details all the examples of boggarts mentioned in historical accounts from all over the country. From scary, devilish ghosts to giant flaming chickens, expanding monstrous sheep to household spirits like hobs and hobgoblins, boggarts come in all shapes and sizes. They are mostly found in the north of England and are usually thought to be malignant.*

In the case of Arbor Low, the Neolithic henge dated to 2,500 BC *in Derbyshire's Peak District, the site – and the accompanying Gib Hill Barrow – were known locations for ritual execution in the distant past, with gallows still located there through the Middle Ages. Perhaps for this reason, the range of strange, haunting phenomenon reported around Arbor Low and the tiny nearby village of Middleton-by-Youlgreave is really quite remarkable. So much so that, in the year 2000, local residents created the 'Sites of Meaning' walk around the area, which folds in these legends – many of which haunt Mr Strines in this story.*

As for the short story which opens the tale, that of the 'Nameless Horror of 50 Berkeley Square', Maggs Ltd remains one of the longest-established antiquarian booksellers in the world, with the tales of the 'Thing' which haunts its upper storeys first appearing in the nineteenth century and enduring ever since.

MV

It was late January when Mr Strines finally clambered into his motorcar and took the long drive north to Middleton-by-Youlgrave. An antique bookseller of some renown, Strines was resident at Maggs Brothers bookshop in Berkeley Square. Maggs remains a fine London establishment famed both for its trade, since 1853, in rare books and manuscripts and, since the 1840s, the legendary Nameless Horror which once haunted its upstairs apartments.

The hauntings at No. 50 Berkeley Square, with the associated death from terror of Sir Robert Warboys, the creeping madness which corrupted the subsequent resident Thomas Myers (and several maids), and the famed 1872 hunting trip to catch the Nameless Horror by Lord Lyttleton, further embellished the building's reputation. None would live in those apartments, and while book sales continued below, it lurked above, shrouded in mystery.

That was, until 1930, when Strines' grandfather, Ludovico, a German émigré, pianist, and occult historian, solved the riddle.

Whatever he did to cleanse the malevolent spirit, he never spoke of it, though rumours still swirled. The being was rumoured to have manifested as anything from a seething, tentacled demon to a vast and ominous man-shaped shadow. Either way, since Ludovico's great feat of banishment, members of the Strines family had been gifted the use of the attic at 50 Berkeley Square in perpetuity.

By the time of the death of Ludovico Strines, his son, Otto, was already happily ensconced in Golders Green with his wife, Mathilda, and their son, Dieter, along with three other children. In later years, Dieter and his father grew apart, feuding over matters of faith, heritage, and money, but most fractious was Otto's insistence on controlling Dieter's chosen vocation.

While a talented pianist himself, Otto Strines ultimately made his living through owning apartment stores. He was a successful entrepreneur and sought for his son to attend the Royal Academy of Music and become the great pianist of his age.

Alas, while he played beautifully, Dieter truly only cared for his grandfather's other curiosities. He would leaf through the old man's ancient books, his pages of scribbled notes, and collections of orphic apparatus, his shelves of dusty crystals, and homemade, arcane tools. It was perhaps unsurprising that after a particularly heated quarrel, Dieter stormed out of his father's house never to return, taking a steamer trunk filled not with sheet music, but his grandfather's rarest occult treasures. These he moved to the long-empty apartment at 50 Berkeley Square, making it his home, never playing the piano again.

In the years that followed, Dieter, or 'Mr Strines', as he was known to all who made his acquaintance, became someone to whom people turned in times of particular trouble. Stacks of his business cards might still be found beneath the counter at Atlantis Books, Watkins, or Treadwell's, along with other such occult booksellers up and down England.

Throughout his long life and career he encountered all number of spooks and spectres, monstrous beasts, and strange apparitions. This earned him a reputation for the discreet and sensitive handling of arcane phenomenon, although, in his latter years, he focused on his primary means of income: the selling of rare books, which he did with great pleasure and personal sensitivity.

Quite how Mr Strines came to be contacted by Jacob Kendal remained somewhat of a mystery, even as he drove north. Strines' dealings in Derbyshire had been scant over the years, though his grandfather's assistance of John Henry Montagu Manners, the 9th Duke of Rutland, in exorcising the worst manifestation at Haddon Hall had led to a long association between the two families. When Lord Edward, brother to the present duke, had called on Mr Strines to purge the last remaining spirit in the place, that of the wronged mistress Dorothy Vernon, he had, of course, complied – athough that was almost a decade ago. What business Lord Edward might have with a man like Jacob Kendal, Mr Strines could not hope to guess, but his letter had been warm and piqued Strines' curiosity, so of course he replied.

The issue at hand was a set of three ancient cottages at Spaw, a now-abandoned hamlet in a quiet Derbyshire valley. Jacob Kendal was a builder, hired to demolish the cottages and construct a new electricity substation. Only, no sooner had Mr Kendal set about beginning his work than the disturbances began: the noises of people tramping up and down stairs in heavy clogs, the sounds of chairs and other articles of furniture being moved. This was all in spite of the cottages having been abandoned forty years before. Their roofs and ceilings had fallen in, the buildings having no upper or lower floors, no staircases, and absolutely no furniture.

As Mr Kendal explained in his letters, he had persevered undeterred until an apparition made itself known. It was a little girl of apparently three or four years of age, wearing a buff nankeen bonnet, and she had offered him a handful of gold.

Wisely, Mr Kendal had retreated from the place, seeking such advice as led to Mr Strines. This was a sage choice, as the ghost of a child is never what it appears. Indeed, should he have accepted that gold, Strines knew, Mr Kendal's fate would have taken a dark turn, perhaps irrevocably so.

Mr Strines shunned all things electrical on account of their interference with his instruments as well as his mind, so he corresponded with Mr Kendal by letter, as was his way. Missives were exchanged throughout the autumn of 2023, Strines making arrangements to visit Spaw in the new year.

His journey north was initially planned for shortly after Christmas, but was delayed on account of Storms Henk and Isha. This meant it was almost Imbolc by the time he made the trip, ensconced in his trusty Sunbeam Tiger, a classic motorcar he kept running at great expense. He was, at the time, aged 71, and dressed in a warm woollen suit, wrapped in a thick overcoat, scarf, gloves and eight-piece cap of Donegal tweed, all chosen to guard against the cold.

By this time Mr Strines was, of course, semi-retired. His hair was thin, teeth worse for wear, but he was otherwise healthy. He joked that this was because he had never married, although he had loved many men and women across his several decades and knew heartbreak as well as anyone. Still, he considered himself lucky to have avoided the many complications associated with matrimony, including children and home ownership. He was instead content with his work, not least his books, and dined with friends, making weekend visits to those corners of England where he had never encountered a demon, ghoul, or creature of darkness to spare himself from painful memories.

He had thought to take this case because it seemed simple enough, and set out before dawn, travelling up the M1 via Luton, Leicester, and Derby. He knew Mr Kendal would be unable to meet him until the late afternoon, but the builder had kindly arranged for Strines to meet one Mr Winsford, a member of the local historical society, at the Village Stone at the heart of Middleton-by-Youlgrave that morning for a walk around the outlines of the parish.

As Strines drove into Middleton, he wondered whether it might be possible to find a more attractive, less-spoilt village in the whole of the Peak District. Situated on an unclassified loop road, it was out of the way, yet only a short distance from one of Derbyshire's loveliest dales and surrounded by excellent walking country.

This said, Strines was bemused to see, striding out onto the heath beside Rake Lane, a gentleman dressed in not a single stitch. Considering the temperature, which was brisk at best, Strines found himself smiling at the sight. While perhaps invigorating, taking such a bracing, naked ramble at the tail end of winter seemed foolhardy and a sure route to catching exposure.

Strines slid the Sunbeam down Middleton's spacious main street, which was lined with pretty limestone cottages, and came to a stop not far from the village square. He knew little of the traditions of the place, beside that the village held an annual Well Dressing on 25 May, and that once a year, on 10 February, the long-closed pub, The Bateman Arms, was revived in the village hall.

These quaint happenings, which he had learned of via Kendal's letters, seemed suitably esoteric. Yet, as with everywhere in England, there were no doubt all manner of mysteries in the village's past. Having come to know far too much about so many like places, however, had filled Strines' mind with so much history that in his latter days he had become less inclined to read about them in advance. Rather, if commissioned to assist in a case, he would learn as little as possible until there, soaking up salient facts as he went, forgetting as much as he could as quickly as possible. It was, he thought, hard enough to remember friends' birthdays, or where he had left a given umbrella or walking cane. He needed no more reasons to lie awake in his room until dawn.

As such, it was Strines' intention to let Mr Winsford show him the village and its curiosities, but to have the experience wash over him as if he were a rock in a flowing stream. And when he parked up and climbed out of the Sunbeam, he was pleased to see a gentleman, much the same age as himself, sat on a bench beside the Village Stone, and strode over to make his introductions.

'Mr Winsford, I presume?' Strines said. As he did however, he felt the hairs raise on his forearms, which was never a good sign.

The old man on the bench said nothing, though he turned to Strines as if slightly perplexed. This new acquaintance then stood and Strines observed him. He was dressed in a green cardigan and brown trousers, which were tucked into walking boots. His eyes were blue, his cheeks pale, and his silver hair mid-length and tousled by the wind.

In response to his silence, Strines spoke again, rubbing his forearms though he was far from cold. 'Mr Kendal said you would meet me and show me the highlights. He said something of the Sites of Meaning? And, of course, I must see Arbor Low!'

'Arbor Low,' the old stranger replied. 'Aye. And the Sites of Meaning.'

'Is this place… well, no matter.'

'Come on, then. Let's bobby off.'

Strines looked back at his car, considering whether he ought to bring more with him. He already had a tuning fork in his pocket, which was a bare essential, but the rest of his equipment was in the steamer trunk on the Sunbeam's back seat. Likewise, his luggage, yet he knew the bed and breakfast he had booked would not be ready for him until later that day, so shrugged off the unsettling feeling.

He nonetheless implored Mr Winsford to wait for a moment. The old man did just that, standing some way off and watching as Strines changed into his trusty rambler's boots and pulled his long walking stick from its place in the rear footwell.

Carved of hazel, the staff was as tall as Strines, a space in its head socketed for varying purposes. At present, it was embedded with an orb of black obsidian, and no sooner had he touched it than he felt his nerves calm and the uneasy sensation melting away.

'And what have you there?' the old man said on seeing it, peering from a distance.

'Ah,' Strines replied, 'in my line of work, you can never be too careful. Not least when the ground is wet. Don't want to slip! Now, "Lay on, Macduff, and damned be him that first cries, 'Hold, enough!'"'

Mr Winsford was evidently not, Strines thought, a man of letters. Instead of smiling, he turned and began striding away, on towards Roughwood Hollow, speaking roughly over his shoulder. 'Houses here,' he said, pointing to either side of the broad main street, 'built in 1820 by Thomas Bateman. I'm presuming you know of Mr Bateman.'

'Oh yes,' Strines replied. 'A famed barrow delver. Member of the British Archaeological Association and, if I'm not mistaken, author of the *Vestiges of the Antiquities of Derbyshire*. A fine volume, worth a pretty penny if in good condition.'

'Called himself 'The Barrow Knight'. Dug up near three hundred tombs in his day. Buried yonder, with his child, Sarah, in a lonely spot up the hill behind the chapel of St Michael & All Angels. "In quietness and in confidence shall be your strength."'

'Isaiah, 30:15,' Strines replied, bemused.

The old man stopped walking, and Strines noticed he was now pointing to a carved stone seat. Strines looked at it, presuming it was intended for use by weary walkers trudging up from Bradford Dale. Then he spied, engraved in the granite, the quote from the scripture his companion had just muttered.

'Well, well,' Strines said, inclined to take out his spectacles for closer inspection. 'How curious…'

Though, when he turned to look, he saw that the old man had already walked on. Realising there was no time to pause, Strines followed. As he did, he thought Mr Winsford strangely quiet, the old man saying nothing until they were midway across the Bradford Dale bridge.

'"Still glides the stream, and shall forever glide,"' he murmured. '"The form remains, the function never dies."'

Strines nodded, noting that, again, this quote, which came from Wordsworth, was also carved into a stone seat. This one was midway across the stone bridge, its sides worn smooth through use.

Strines inhaled deeply, enjoying the moment, for the air was filled with the sounds of running water and the wind teasing at the trees. He thought it a beautiful spot to sit and rest, so made remarks to that effect, saying, 'Quite the place, Mr Winsford.'

No reply was forthcoming, however, for Mr Winsford was already gone, his shape disappearing off down a nearby lane.

The walk continued in much the same manner for the rest of the morning, including a stop at an ancient sheep dip where, in late May or June, generations of farmers had brought their flocks to wash their fleeces. It was, Strines thought, a hard, cold, murky place, and he was unsettled when the hairs on his forearms again stood on end. This was in spite of the obsidian orb in head of his staff – a sure sign the spot was haunted.

So much so, in fact, that his head began to ache.

Of this sensation Strines said nothing, feeling Mr Winsford was not a man inclined towards superstition. Strines watched him trudging on through damp leaves and past bare trees, and touched the case in his breast pocket. He had no cause to open it, he thought, but was reassured to know it was there.

On they ventured, down the footpath between Rowlow Dale and the road to Smerrill, the view overlooking Rusden Wood. When they came to the old Clapper Bridge, again they stopped, spying another engraved seat, this one from Pope. It read, 'Consult the Genius of the Place in all; That tells the Waters to rise or fall.'

'Men came and said no such inscription was to be made,' Mr Winsford announced. 'But the bridge were broke and down to just one channel. We fixed it, laid the slab. Local folk are the authority here. Besides, there's a boggart, not that outsiders would know to look, and broken things only make them stronger.'

'A boggart?' Strines replied. He acted surprised but had guessed as much from the sweat on the back of his neck, the bristling hairs on his forearms, and the steady ache which had developed behind his left eye.

'Aye, a brownie turned bad. A large something. Long ears, horns, and tail. Glides by and vanishes out of sight. No trouble. Not that one, at least.'

The old man once again walked off, striding quickly away from Mr Strines, who followed on as they passed down Lowfield Lane to Rowlow Brook. Strines thought it strange that Winsford mentioned it, not least as it was common knowledge that to mention a boggart only made it stronger. Still, they continued to walk in a silence which felt frosty and unkind. So, as they made their way, Strines risked a new line of conversation, hoping to warm the mood of his new associate.

'You know, Mr Winsford,' Strines said, 'driving into the village this morning, I saw the strangest thing. There was a gentleman walking up, onto the dale–'

'Naked,' came the reply. 'Aye. Mr Higginson. John. Died 1876. Was a peddler in his day. Likes to show people his backside.'

'Ah,' Strines said, nodding. Winsford was clearly disinclined to say more on the subject, yet this admission, along with the mention of the Clapper Bridge boggart, did at least make clear that the old man was a believer.

This reassured Strines for, though he had only come to Middleton-by-Youlgrave to help Mr Kendal with his issue at Spaw cottages, he knew that any village with this many spectral inhabitants had to hold a deeper set of secrets. A local historian would be a useful resource, though Strines felt it likely that all these phenomena pertained to Arbor Low, a site he had never visited but had read of a great many times.

Located in the midst of the White Peaks, the monument dated from 2,500 BC. It took the same form as nearby Bull Ring at Dove Holes, Cairnpapple Hill and Stenness Stones in Scotland, and Wiltshire's Avebury Ring. Containing forty-three stones, many broken to fragments and all laid flat but one, it was encircled by a ditch seven feet deep and thirty-three feet wide. This was bisected by two causeway entrances, which aligned with sunrise on Midsummer, as did the six stones known as 'the Cove'. These slabs formed what was said to be a central altar of long-forgotten use, and this basic formation was repeated time and again at monuments across the country. Likewise, the earth dug to form ditches at monuments like these had been used to make cremation barrows, the Arbor Low example being known as Gib Hill.

Though the site had not been excavated for over a century, Thomas Bateman, the 'Barrow Knight' himself, had found bone and antler tools, flint scrapers, and arrowheads beneath the earth. It was also reputed, Strines knew, to be crawling with boggarts, something he recalled from his research into St Michael's Ley, back when he had sealed the Wyrdstone at Glastonbury, many years before.

Strines had never been inclined to visit Arbor Low of his own volition, but he had read of its strange significance. Forming an exact Pythagorean triangle, just two degrees north from Stonehenge, one degree east from Glastonbury, a second with the Callanish megaliths in Scotland's Outer Hebrides, and a third with Bryn Celli Ddu on the Isle of Anglesey, it was, he knew, the midpoint or heart of a ley line network. It was a place of ancient power whose language was lost, even to him, but, if past experiences were anything to go by, Arbor Low still wanted to speak, even if its utterances would not be understood.

Strines was shaken from his contemplations by a sudden and almighty roar. It was that of two vast motor engines. They were thundering overhead, yet low – so low as to make Strines' flesh quake and his bones shudder.

Gripping his staff, he spun on his heels, staring into the white-grey sky. And there he saw it, to his amazement: a Vickers Wellington Bomber, a long-range aircraft, belching black smoke and falling slowly but surely out of the sky.

'By the heavens!' Strines exclaimed, watching as the plane sailed, droning, down from above and headlong towards the cold earth of a nearby field. He listened for the sound of the crash, looked to see the rising flames and trail of smoke, but none were forthcoming.

He turned then to look at Mr Winsford, who stood down the lane and stared back, seemingly disinterested.

'It came down 21 January 1944. Killed six. Royal Australian Air Force. But here's what we're here to see.'

Heart thundering, Strines approached, the old man moving off further down the track. And there, nestled in the hedgerow, Strines saw it. A granite hand, carved in the manner of so many guide stoops across Derbyshire. Below it there was another quotation, etched into the stone, which Strines read aloud, '"To see a World in a Grain of Sand, And a Heaven in a Wild Flower, Hold Infinity in the palm of your hand, And Eternity in an hour."' William Blake, he thought, from the *Auguries of Innocence*. Macabre verse, though few ever read it in full.

Again, he touched his breast pocket, quickening his pace as Mr Winsford had long since wandered on.

Their subsequent route took them along the path to Longdale, by the Balderstone and up to Friden Bends. The quote there came from Heraclitus: 'The road up and the road down are one and the same.' Strines knew this particular piece of wisdom to be a lie, but did not remark upon it.

By then, the pair had walked several miles, and though Strines was hungry, he hung back a little, watching Mr Winsford from afar. Indeed, he slowed his pace to a near crawl at the point where Green Lane crossed the path of the old Roman road, after which they finally started journeying north, on toward Arbor Low.

As Strines walked, he kept one eye on Winsford but also stared out onto Middleton Common. It was there that he spied another horror, though he did not mention it. This was, he considered, among the most disturbing examples he had seen in recent years. Having always been slightly unsettled by infants, with their rounded features, wet lips, and shiny eyes, he knew even in his youth that he could never make a good father. Then, when he saw apparitions of children, as he had many times, he assured himself that entities chose such shapes to appear innocent, as if they were vulnerable, intending to fool those mortal souls they were hoping to entrap.

On this occasion, it was the ghost of a baby. Unclothed, yet blood-spattered, it was crawling across the rough scrub of the heath, mewling as if in pain. Strines glanced at it – a tiny, white shape, struggling along the rough ground. Its bandy legs and knees moved awkwardly as it crawled, though the grasses did not shift where it passed.

He tried to look away, to focus on Winsford, but his eye was drawn back to it again and again. That was until an invisible hand seemed to grasp the child's left back leg and lift it into the air, swinging it about before slamming the tiny shape down onto the turf.

Strines shut his eyes at the last moment, unable to watch, listening to the end of his staff clacking on the ground as he walked. Then, when he opened his eyes again, the apparition had vanished.

Strines considered the period when he knew such things happened, the killing of infants, and wondered if there had once been a castle at Middleton. During the Civil War, both the Roundheads and Royalists were wont to kill the children of their enemies by such violent means before leaving the bodies displayed on pikes as warnings to any standing against them.

Though the circular walk around Middleton's Sites of Meaning continued from Arbor Low, Mr Strines never made it along the route south of Lathkill Dale to the Bugle Stone, or up the path on from Cales Farm to Long Rake. If he had, he would have seen the buildings of Castle Farm, built using the ruins of Middleton Castle. That had been the building where Sir Christopher Fulwood mounted a defence against just such a Roundhead invasion.

Sir Christopher had raised an army of lead miners to fight for the king but, when they were surprised, his soldiers fled. During the raid, Cromwell's forces shot Sir Christopher, and he, too, then escaped to the top of the dale. There, he hid in a crevice in a cliff and was discovered days later, having died from his injuries.

After that rout, Middleton Castle was broken down, the stone used in the construction of many buildings around the village, not least Castle Farm, though the earthworks still stand, in the field opposite Chapel House. And Mr Strines would have remarked on them, had he made it that far, considering the final inscription at that spot, which reads, 'Live as if you'll die tomorrow, farm as if you'll live forever'. This was an old Derbyshire saying, the first part of which was an adage Strines had lived by ever since his young manhood.

Instead, however, his journey ended at Arbor Low. For it was there, as he approached the vast circular dyke, that he found his reticent companion waiting, beckoning him inside.

'Quite the walk,' the old man said, offering the first smile of the day. 'But we've made good time. The sun's only now starting to come down.'

Strines stared up at the clouds, feeling the wind whip suddenly so much colder.

'So,' Strines said, 'here we are. The famous Arbor Low.'

'Aye. Come into the ring. I must show you the Cove.'

Strines licked his teeth beneath his lips, almost stumbling. For at that moment, not only did his forearms tickle with prickling hairs, but the back of his neck was hot, his head ached, and he heard his blood rushing in his ears. He made his way forward uneasily, leaning on his staff to stay upright, for he felt dizzy, though he approached the Cove and the figure of the old man standing behind it.

The six stones there were laid out in a rectangle, much like a coffin, yet the grass all about was cut short. This meant that the whole body of a man could lie comfortably within the Cove. This was likely why, Strines thought, the grass of the place looked lush. Much like the turf at Stonehenge, Avebury, Cairnpapple Hill and Stenness Stones, it had been fed for so many years, and not just with sun and rain.

'Come,' said the old man, still smiling. 'Kneel and look into the Cove. What you'll see there is the greatest marvel of this whole place.'

His jaw clenched, Strines smiled grimly, laying down his staff and making his way to one knee. He grunted, spying in the middle of the Cove nothing but grass, neatly trimmed and waiting.

He looked around himself then, out of the corners of his eyes, and saw a dozen or so shapes moving through the half-dark. The naked form of John Higginson. The dark something, with its long ears, horn, and tail. The six airmen stood, their blank eyes staring, while the baby crawled slowly nearer on its hands and knees.

Elsewhere amongst their number, he spied ancients in furs, brandishing clubs. The shape of what must have been Sir Christopher Fulwood, gut-shot, yet smiling. Thomas Bateman, too, dressed in black mourning clothes. His daughter, Sarah, was by his side in a high-collared pinafore dress, looking to have tears in her eyes.

The boggarts formed a circle around the ring of Arbor Low, then advanced as one, stepping down into the ditch, all walking ever nearer, step by patient step.

'And so,' Strines said, looking up at the fiend who had led him there, 'Am I to suppose that, after all this, you are not, in fact, Mr Winsford.'

'I never said I was,' it said, kicking away Strines' staff. The spectre shuddered as it did so, bearing long, jagged teeth and losing its shape for a moment. It grimaced at its nearness to the obsidian, emitting a waft of dark smoke which smelled, ever so lightly, of brimstone.

Strines nodded, then reached into his pocket, and retrieved the case. The boggart watched him, curious and uncomprehending, as Strines unfasted the clip on its side and removed the tuning fork. It was made of quartz, heavy and old, and was tuned to G, the holiest note mankind has ever known.

'Well,' Strines said, peering about as the shapes remerged over the lip of the dyke, 'whoever, or whatever, you are, I bid you and your companions here adieu.'

Strines struck the pitchfork against the stone beneath his knee and the note rang out, clear as fresh spring water. The shapes about the ring paused, halted in their progress, hissing in fury.

Again, Strines struck the quartz against the rock. He saw the boggarts stare at one another, all perplexed, their eerie shapes misting at the edges.

The infant began to cry, and Strines chuckled grimly. 'Now, now,' he said. 'No nearer. And no need for tears.'

As the note echoed away, Strines stood tall, before reaching down and grasping his staff. The being nearest him, the entity he once thought was Mr Winsford, fled, but Strines raised the hazel rod and struck the tuning fork once again, this time on the wood itself.

The forms of the ghouls about him began to loosen and buckle, frozen in place, so Strines strode quickly towards the single upright in the middle of Arbor Low. He clanged the pitchfork against it, then put the base of his staff against the stone and, with a slight bow to the macabre company, touched the fork's quartz tines to the sphere of obsidian in its top.

The sacred sound passed through the gem, down the wood, and into the upright. From there, it spread out through the earth of the ancient ring, its echo humming in each of the fallen stones.

This sacred geometry, Strines thought, was as much as he understood of these places, and he thanked his lucky stars for it. Because, as if at the click of a finger, the boggarts of Arbor Low then vanished as one, like a blazing candelabra extinguished by a single mighty breath.

Strines sighed, knowing this would not hold them for long. In a day or two, perhaps less, depending on their power, the spirits would reform. By then, however, he intended to be long gone, and sooner rather than later.

Turning on his heels, he took the fastest route back to Middleton-by-Youlgrave. On foot, this took him across the common. It was dark, so he took great care not to fall or break an ankle on a rabbit warren. And though he was weary, with no pub open to offer food, a fire, or a stiff drink, he decided to simply head to the car. He would pick up a sandwich from a service station on his route home, letting the electric light bathe him in a pool of frenzied static.

As he walked, he concluded he would have to write to Mr Kendal and make his apologies. Likewise, to the real Mr Winsford, presuming there ever had been a kindly historian who had waited in the village square for much of the morning, expecting his arrival. Nonetheless, Strines would have to send kind words and pass on recommendations that Kendal try another specialist in the field. Spenser & Associates, perhaps, or Henrietta Swann, if she was still in business.

With night truly fallen, Mr Strines reached the Sunbeam, unlocked it, and opened the driver-side door. He tossed his cap onto the old steamer trunk and climbed inside without changing his boots. After slotting the staff into the passenger-side footwell, so it was within easy reach, he opened the glovebox. From within he extracted one of many sticks of sage, and this he lit using the car's cigarette lighter. Placing it into the cupholder behind the gearstick, he watched the smoke rise and sighed. It would have to do, though once home he intended to complete a grander cleansing ritual. Just in case any of them had got close enough to form a bond.

It was unlikely, he knew, but possible.

Though one thing was for sure: he would never again return to Arbor Low.

10

The Hairy Hands of Dartmoor

A Devon Tale

One of those local myths which fascinated me as a child, the Hairy Hands of Dartmoor are an apparition as strange and haunting as the landscape in which they are found.

Stretching over 350 square miles, Dartmoor contains the largest concentration of Bronze Age remains anywhere in the United Kingdom. Threaded through with tors, bogs, and ancient standing stones, there are an estimated 5,000 prehistoric hut circles out there in the wilderness which, alongside more recent ruins, such as the now abandoned Dartmoor Prison, old tin mines, and legends of black dogs and wildcats, makes Dartmoor a landscape teeming with spooky stories.

When it comes to the Hairy Hands, they infamously terrorise drivers passing down the road now known as the B3212. Since 1910, people have reported ghostly, hairy hands appearing and grabbing steering wheels and motorcycle handlebars, forcing vehicles into danger. There have been deaths, too, and close-call survivors, though most people attribute the phenomenon to the route's strange and undulating camber. That said, some people say the hands belong to dead prisoners who perished on Dartmoor after escaping from the nearby jail, while others offer even more macabre origins.

For my telling, I sought to combine real history with something a little more fantastic. And though the Hairy Hands in this account may seem a little outlandish, I would still urge anyone travelling that winding route between Postbridge and Two Bridges to take heed, particularly if they are journeying that way on a misty, moonlit night…

MV

I shouldn't have driven that road, and I knew it before I set out.

The trouble is, the men in my family, we're an inquisitive bunch. Always poking our noses where they don't belong, see? Most families say that's women's business, but not for us. And had I not been born such a nosey sort of fellow myself, I never would have met Gilchrist. And if I'd never met him, then I'd be free to ponder rather than knowing the truth. There are some benefits to letting some questions be.

It all came about because of my Uncle John. Folk from round my way don't move. We're born and live and work and die in the same ground our fathers knew. I had a cousin once who moved to that there London, and he never came back. Some say cities are big enough to eat people up whole, and I think that's cobblers. I've been to Bristol and it's nothing special. But lots of things I once thought was cobblers, I'm now not so sure on.

As for John, he married a lass from Cornwall and moved to Torbay. To my father and brother, that made him as good as dead, fit only for exchanging Christmas cards. But I'd call him up, partly on account that when I was a boy he showed me a trick with a silver penny, making it disappear and run through his knuckles like water, which made me always think of him fondly.

When he died he was already a widower, and his estate, such as it was, was split up, as is the way with these things. And I suppose I was as much a son to John as anyone and was appointed executor. So, I was to Torbay that wet summer to settle John's affairs, meaning I was leaving home for the first time in many years, all on my lonesome.

Now, everybody round our way knows the tales of the Hairy Hands. There's stories going back to my father's father's time of that so-called haunted highway. Of horse and buggies driven off the road, people dying, all sorts. But the big one that all recall was the incident with Dr Ernest. H. Helby.

He was well known, for he was Medical Officer at Dartmoor Prison, looking after all sorts when many folk wouldn't go within ten mile of the place. But one day, he took his wife out on his motorcycle in 1921. She were in the sidecar with the two daughters of the prison governor. It's said that as they were out driving, down the B3212, his hands were grabbed by a pair of strong, callused fists with a grip like iron. He yelled to his wife, and though she survived, as did the two girls, Dr Helby lost control of his bike and crashed, dying of a fractured skull.

That's perhaps the most famous death on that stretch of road, which runs from Postbridge to Two Bridges. But there's been a dozen cases or more in the papers of strange occurrences along that thoroughfare. Army soldiers, journalists, young couples, women driving alone, the incidents stretch out for over a century. Used to make the news, but less so now. People always said the coppers round there hushed it up and made out folk had so many accidents on account of being unfamiliar with the camber of the road. I didn't believe it, but now I do.

Plus, nobody round there calls the bridge Cherrybrook, which is its name on the map. They all call it Hairy Hands Bridge because the stories are the same. People assailed by mighty hairy hands that come out of the dark, stinking of sulphur, trying to drag them off onto the moor.

Now, I can't have been the first to look at a roadmap and think, 'Well, I could go this a-way, but though that way's a bit longer, I wonder if I might take the winding route and make something out of the trip that's more than a journey from A to B.' So, off I went, driving my old Volvo down the B3212, listening to the radio, Dartmoor whizzing by to my left and right. But I made an error y'see, thinking I'd have better luck seeing something by night. You know how it is with spooks and bogeys and the like – nighttime is when they're abroad, or so people say. And after I'd passed through Postbridge, which doesn't have a streetlight, I realised that all I could see outside the car was rough-edged shadows of heath and heather stretching on and on to the horizon.

It was a misty night and cold, and the old Volvo was no good at keeping weather out. I was driving in my old wax jacket, which I pulled close about me, seeing my breath in front of my face. But to encourage whatever horror I imagined there might be out there, I killed the radio and drove on in silence, just the rattle of the engine and the sounds of the tyres for company.

Well, that, and the thundering of my heart.

Must have been some time around midnight, which is just as I'd planned it, only as I sped down that famous road, headed towards that famous bridge, I saw a light up ahead waving me down. I slowed the car and came to a stop by the side of the road – and I could see, in my headlights, an old fella wearing a rough old coat with torn pockets, a waistcoat, flat cap, and walking boots that came up to the ankle. He was holding a torch, one of those with power enough to shine up and light the clouds, and he shone it right in my face, making me squint.

Wasn't until he was at my window that I got a good look at his face. Was ruddy, maybe with weather, maybe with drink, and he had wild, white hair poking out round the flat cap on his head, and he was out of breath, gasping.

He tapped on the driver's side window with his torch, quickly, tap-tap-tap-tap, and I wound it down and inch or two.

'And where are you to then?' he said. He was a good old boy, that was clear as glass, looking something like a lord's gamekeeper down on his luck. He kept looking around him, shining his torch, and when he spoke his breath smelled of whisky and old tobacco smoke.

'Headed to Torbay,' is what I said, and he looked at me with his grey-blue eyes and an upturned lip and a slow nod that said to me that… well, he knew what I was about.

'Down this stretch of road? At this time of night? Pull the other one,' he replied.

I had to grin, 'cause he'd caught me rubbernecking, fair and square. But he didn't rub it in.

'You're not the first,' he said, fiddling with his pocket, 'and you won't be the last, I'd wager. But do me a favour now, if you wouldn't mind. I need to get back up to the Warren House Inn, and sharpish. You passed right by it a minute ago. Sorry to trouble you, but it's a matter of some urgency.'

He strolled round to the passenger side as if I'd agreed to his request and, slightly taken aback, I opened the door for him and he clambered in, pulling out an old mobile phone with the battery pack held on with sticking plasters.

'I'd be quick about it if I were you,' he said, punching numbers into his phone. 'Elsewise, what you came to see may just come and see you. And do yourself a favour – wind that window up.'

I obliged and put the car in gear and set about turning in the road, but just as I did, I caught a smell that made me think maybe my new passenger had had some kind of accident. But he caught it too, and, aged as he was, he was far from decrepit.

'Speed it up now, lad, would you,' he said, looking about the car and over his shoulder. Then he was pressing the mobile phone to his ear. 'Yep,' he said, 'Malcolm, hurry up, you silly goose.' And then he ended the call and locked the door on his side.

It was then that I heard a thump on my windshield.

I was midway through reversing when it happened, swinging the steering wheel left and right, my feet hopping between pedals, one hand on the gearstick. But when I heard that sound, I turned to look at it, and there it was. The wide palm of a hand pressing down on the window glass.

I felt my eyes widen and my mouth fall open, but I had no idea what to say. Only then a second hand thumped down onto the windshield, again, palm-down – bang – fingers spread, long nails scratching at the glass. And I sort of just stopped and stared, but the old fella reached over, whacked on the windscreen wipers, and gave me a mighty nudge.

'Drive!' he said, and I did, watching as the wipers batted those hands on the glass, which tumbled away as I put my foot down and high-tailed it out of there.

We roared back up the misty road and I don't think I said a thing.

Wasn't until we got close to the Warren House Inn that the old fella tapped the dashboard, saying, 'Here we are. Just pull up anyplace.'

I did, stopping the car, and the old bloke hopped out and pulled from his coat something like an old shepherd's club. You know the kind, made of blackthorn with a knobbed head for cracking skulls. And without shutting the passenger door he wandered round the vehicle, the club raised, and then, when he was happy, he tucked it back in his coat and opened my door for me.

'Time for a drink,' he said, standing by as I got out of the car, and he closed the doors, fiddling about with a length of string he wore about his neck. Eventually, he pulled it out of his clothes, revealing an old iron key, which turned out was the key to the pub's front door.

'You know,' he continued, 'the fire in this inn has been burning constantly since 1845. An important date, 1845. What'll you have?'

He walked in, and though the fire was there, burning in the grate, he turned some of the lights on and made his way round the bar, which had me thinking he owned the place. But he didn't. That's when he explained his name was Gilchrist, and that the men of his family had a key as a favour for the duties they performed out on the moors.

He poured me a stiff scotch and one for himself, and he beckoned me to sit on a chair by the bar while he talked.

'Y'see,' he said, '1845 was when the gunpowder factory opened.' He spoke as if I knew this already, but it was news to me.

'It's called the Powder Mills now, but back then, George Frean had teams of folk working, combining saltpetre, sulphur and charcoal. You know much about gunpowder?'

I said I didn't, and he carried on.

'Well, used to be called alchemy, all that. And later came dynamite, but back then, gunpowder was how you blew into mine shafts. As you know, there's tin all through these parts, along with other metals and ores. So much so, if you stand by Cherrybrook with a compass, it's like to go haywire. But old George Frean didn't think too brightly about where he'd put his gunpowder factory, 'cause not a stone's throw to the west is Bellever Tor. Ever seen Bellever Tor?'

I shook my head, and he sipped his whisky, talking to me like I was a child.

'Bellever Tor is an ancient place – 5,000 years old or more. Used to be the start of the Lich Way. Know what one of those is?'

I smiled then, because this old timer knew I didn't have a Scooby-Doo.

'Back before there were a church at Widecombe where people could hold funerals, the Bishops at Exeter made folk from here walk their dead down a-ways from Bellever Tor to Lydford Tor, then from Whitebarrow to Coffin Wood, and on to St Petroc's. And all along that way holy men would wait. This was Saxon times. They called them seers, and they'd guard the Lich Way from spirits and pixies, and keep an eye on the souls what lost their way along the route.

'It's a holy place, Bellever Tor, but George Frean didn't give two monkeys. He used to test his gunpowder on the rocks thereabouts, on the kists and cairn circles, and some who worked for him didn't like it. They thought he was waking the dead, see.'

Gilchrist poured himself another scotch, but I'd barely touched mine, and no sooner had he poured than he'd tipped his second dram down his big pink gullet.

'One of the lads working for him, Jethro Hamlyn, was a bear of a man. Huge. Over six feet tall with hands like… well. With big, hairy, strong hands. And Jethro was born of cunning folk. His hands were craftsman's hands, and his mother had taught him all the wisdom she'd been taught and some, and George Frean took advantage. He had Jethro working on all sorts, using the chemicals and metals and what-have-you, despite Jethro saying how the powder tests were making the spirits upset. Gold will make men do strange things.'

'Ain't that the truth,' I replied, holding my drinking glass.

'Thing is,' Gilchrist went on, 'one day, Jethro Hamlyn's aunt died, leaving Jethro her cottage up by Huccaby Farm. And so Jethro told George Frean he'd be moving on. Frean, well, he didn't like that and lost his temper, so Jethro came here, had a drink, and waited 'til dark. But he forgot something important.'

Then there was sound that made me jump out of my skin. It came from behind me – a clanking of metal and heavy footsteps.

'Alright there, Gilchrist?' came a voice.

'Alright there, Malcolm,' he replied.

I turned, and saw a young man, not thirty I'd wager, dressed in a policeman's uniform. The clanking sound was on account of the thing he was carrying on his back, which looked to me for all the world like an old weed sprayer of some sort. You know, the kind you wear, with piston rods and a tube made of rubber connected to a valve and pressure gauge. It was cast in brass and dented all over, with leather straps and nozzles here and there.

'So,' Gilchrist continued, 'what Jethro Hamlyn had forgot–'

'–was his tools,' Malcolm interrupted, setting down the sprayer, which clonked on the flagstone floor.

'Yeah, thanks Mal,' Gilchrist said. 'You can go now, and thanks for fixing her.'

'Ah, I'll stay,' said Malcolm, 'I like this story.'

'Alright, but you keep quiet 'cause I'm the one telling it.'

He turned back to me, the orange glow from the old fire reflecting in his eyes. 'And so, after dark, Jethro Hamlyn went back to get his tools what he'd left at the gunpowder factory late that night. But he'd had a few by then, and was wearing–'

'–his hobnail boots!' Malcolm said.

'Aye,' Gilchrist said, rolling his eyes. 'And button it, Malcolm. Just cause your mum's my Susan's friend doesn't mean I won't come round there and give you a hiding.'

Malcolm smiled, reaching over the bar and pouring himself a half of dark ale.

'Thing is,' Gilchrist said, 'when on the factory floor, all the workers had to wear boots wrapped in rope, in case of the nails in their soles sparking. Which is just what happened to Jethro Hamlyn.'

'Whole place went up like the fifth of November, didn't it, Gilchrist?'

'Yes Malcolm, it did. The buildings Frean had built were at a safe distance from each other and each had a flimsy roof which carried explosions upwards. But the sparks from Jethro Hamlyn's boots caused a cataclysmic blast which blew him to pieces. People saw from miles around and came running, but wasn't until the next day they found what was left of Jethro Hamlyn.'

Malcolm, who by then had sat down beside me, put his glass down and extended his forearms, wiggling his fingers and crossing his eyes, poking his tongue out of his mouth. 'His hairy hands!' he said. And Gilchrist, right annoyed, bopped the lad's policeman's hat right off his head.

'Nobody knows what happened next,' Gilchrist said, rinsing his glass and setting it out to dry. 'Or understands it. Maybe it was the cairns where his hands landed. Maybe it was the spirits from the Lich Way, woken up by the blast. Or maybe it was on account of all the chemicals that had got into Jethro Hamlyn's skin from all those years of alchemy and potion-craft. Either way, people started to notice taps on the door at night. Scratching on windowpanes. Scuttling shapes, darting about the moorland in the dark.'

I think I must have narrowed my eyes then, taken aback. It all seemed so far-fetched. But Gilchrist was telling the story like it wasn't just true but a chore to tell it.

'What they learned later was, somehow, the hands out there, they breed with another. Most of the time it's not a problem, especially in summer. They keep to Bellever Woods where it's damp. They can catch birds and burrow into the ground, seeking out rabbits and the like. But every once in a while, they scrabble and scratch and dig their way through the earth, making new ways underground, out towards the river or some place else.'

'Did you tell him about the campers?' Malcolm said, smiling. 'That's why we have designated camping zones, you know. And special safe spots for fishing. In 2008, a couple thought they'd pitch a tent on the banks of East Dart and then, middle of the night, a whole swarm came and tore their campsite to pieces. Pretty woman, she was, but she lost an eye.'

Gilchrist nodded to me, indicating I should drink up, but I looked to Malcolm in his police uniform.

'I'm driving,' I said. And Malcolm waved me off like it was nothing.

'Me too,' he replied, clinking his glass against mine. 'Bottoms up. And if you do come back to camp, I'd stay in a caravan!'

We both drank, and Gilchrist carried on, taking out his pipe and filling it with tobacco from a leather pouch, leaves of it spilling across the bar.

'Anyway,' he said, 'you've come on one of those nights they like, when the mists are out. And I was doing my rounds, walking about, just to check they were staying where they're meant to stay, but then– you won't believe it Mal– they're back all over Bellever Tor again.'

'Oh no!' Malcolm said. 'We get tourists there!'

'Yeah, well.'

'Honestly,' Malcolm continued, 'Ever since that newspaper man, Rufus Endell, people never come here to stay. They're scared. Drive on through like bats out of hell.'

Gilchrist struck a match and lit his pipe. Then, with our glasses rinsed, he approached the fire in the grate burning to one side of the room, and pulled the great brass tank nearby. He primed it, yanking the lever, then turned a tap on its top, leaning the head of the sprayer down towards the flames.

'Well done, Mal. You may be thick as mincemeat, but there's not a metalworker in Devon with half the skill.'

The fire leapt up and flickered at the end of the spout of the sprayer, and Gilchrist sucked on his pipe, exhaling smoke from the smiling corners of his mouth.

'Special solution in there,' Malcolm said, under his breath, nodding at the cannister. 'Blessed by the vicar and all.'

'Only one thing they can't abide,' Gilchrist said, taking his pipe from his mouth and pointing it at me. 'That's fire. Holy, cleansing flame. So, this,' he tapped the tank – ding-ding – 'made by my grandfather, is what we use to keep 'em at bay. And, if you like, seeing as you came here to see 'em, you can keep close by if you want, and watch on while we clear 'em off.'

I don't why I agreed. Might have been the whisky. But we went in convoy, Malcolm first and me and Gilchrist following on. And after we parked up a little way off, Malcolm brought out a tin bucket of something he called, 'chum'. Looked like meat and smelled terrible, either way.

Then I watched as the pair walked about through the mist, all about the ruins of the old powder mills and round Bellever Tor, herding those creatures in the dark.

Nobody can quite imagine the sound a hand makes when it screams. Honestly, it's impossible to describe. But the smell of them burning – the smell of the hair, most of all – it's something I'll never forget.

Still, I did see some of them up close, the hairy hands. Must have been hundreds they burned that night, each slightly different from the last. Callused and scabbed, some with long nails curling over, some with stubs where digits must have been lost.

And for all my inquisitive nature, I ended up holding my nose that night, protecting it from the stink.

Anyways, that's how I met Gilchrist, and he's a good bloke really. We still exchange Christmas cards.

11

William Doggett, the Vampire Ghost

A Dorset Tale

Dorset seems an unlikely location for a vampire story, but beyond the county's beautiful hedgerows and picturesque fields lies a dark heart…

The steward William Doggett was a real person, associated with Eastbury House near Tarrant Gunville. There are a number of different legends associated with his life and death, including a dramatic headless horseman picking up his spirit and an indelible stain in the house today that is said to be a permanent record of his suicide.

Suicide in rural communities was incredibly taboo, and there was a stigma around burying those who died in that way in the hallowed ground of the church. Unusually, Doggett was buried in the churchyard at Tarrant Gunville, but his body was exhumed when the church was rebuilt and discovered to be extraordinarily fresh, with its legs tied together with yellow silk ribbons. This played into superstitions about ghosts and vampires, and the unquiet dead walking.

I am hugely inspired by the works of Thomas Hardy, and it seems amazing to me that Hardy didn't tackle William Doggett as a subject for a story, as there are a number of resonances with themes he wrote about too. So, here's my attempt at telling the tale in a 'Hardy-an' kind of way.

Moreover, it is said the sound of the phantom coach and horses, bearing a ghostly passenger, can still be heard by the gates of Eastbury House today, riding by at the stroke of midnight.

EC

The hedgerows were wild with brambles in spiked tangles, their fruit just beginning to darken, as I went towards the little church at Tarrant Gunville where the wedding would be celebrated. I had been out of the area for some time, although I'd grown up there and had an aunt local to the country, but I was still known. People in these parts have long memories for names and lineages and, in truth, I never felt as at home in my adopted town of Bere Regis as I did among the winding lanes and rolling fields of Blandford.

It was high time that I returned, and the design on fate's tapestry had been woven in my favour. A death in the area, an opening for my trade, and my wife's ill health meant that removing back to Tarrant was the best possible choice. The air of the countryside, far from the bustle of Bere Regis, would soon see Amelia restored, and I could continue my calling among my own people.

As I am a doctor by trade, it was half to be expected that, no sooner had I been recognised by somebody as the son of John Symes, I was pressed into service to deal with Carrie Pitfield's toothache. I was able to oblige and the Pitfields invited me to her sister Margery's wedding in thanks. As I knew enough of the players, it was natural for me to accept the invitation without feeling like an outsider, and Mrs Pitfield told me that Margery would consider it a compliment to have a real doctor from Bere in attendance.

The wedding day was soaked in sunshine and brightened by the colourful bonnet ribbons of the village girls, and the feast afterwards warmed with good cheer and good strong cider brewed by Mrs Pitfield. Margery and her groom, Jim, were flush-faced and pleased with one another, and were the centre of the dancing when the pipes and fiddles struck up.

They were ushered off to bed eventually with the customary banging of pots and strewing of fresh flowers, and the few of us who were left sat around the fire enjoying another pot of cider. The light was fading outside, and so we got to lighting pipes and telling stories, as men do on such occasions.

'Who has Eastbury House these days?' I asked, because I had been out of the area so long and was behind with local politics.

There was immediately a shifting around on stools, a clearing of throats and a twinkling of eyes, as though I had said something worthy of note rather than making an innocent enquiry.

'Eastbury House – what's left of it,' said Granfer White, with a wheezing, tobacco-choked chuckle.

'What do you mean?' I asked, somewhat perturbed, as I had always known it to be a grand house and the flower of the country. 'Was it not Earl Temple's?'

'It were always a hard struggle to keep it up,' said Granfer. 'Like a hungry beast it were, always wanting more time, more money, more fine trappings.'

'I heard it were a farm once, before it were a big house,' said Willie Stickland.

'Aye, that it were, and with a fine herd of shorthorns. But the king's own admiral had it built out to suit his ends, though what need he had for such a sprawler of a house, I can't say.'

I nodded, remembering walking over the fields to Eastbury House as a boy. Its five courts and wings were an impressive sight to my young eyes.

'Precious little there is now,' said Stickland.

'What happened?' I asked, wondering how such a great house could have been brought low.

'Well, after George Bubb, the fat devil, had it, it fell into the hands of Earl Temple, and then to his son. Temple the father did his level best with it,' said Granfer White, 'pouring in money like well-water without receiving much reward. But Temple the son soon found it too much for him and had to go off into Italy for his health.'

'A gurt many of our peers do the same, I hear,' said Gaffer Dibben, who thought himself something of a wit.

'And when he went off,' said Granfer, carrying on as though Dibben had not spoken, 'he left it in the hands of the steward to manage the estate.' This was common enough in that time, and it was well-known that the stewards usually lived fine lives, like lords themselves in their masters' absence.

'William Doggett was his name, that steward,' said Granfer. 'Did you ever know the Doggett family, doctor?'

The name was familiar to me, but I knew none of the family personally.

'Ah, I'll tell you of Doggett,' said a voice from the chimney corner. It belonged to a very old man, so heavily lined and wrinkled as to look like he belonged to the grain of the wood surrounding the chimney piece, and who I had not previously noticed because of the thick cloud of pipe smoke obscuring him from view. 'Greedy he was, and sly and canny too, and they say the maids never wanted to work at Eastbury House while he were around, for his hands wandered where they weren't wanted and further besides. He'd been skimming off the top of the estate's profits for years before Lord Temple finally went off to Italy.

'He was deep in with some low-down types too, gambling men, who were no strangers to breaking legs and causing accidents to those who owed them. The dice were his downfall, and he lost all his coin on the regular, so he was always short of money even though his salary from the stewardship would have been a handsome one to a more prudent man.

'Well, when Lord Temple goes off, Doggett sees his chance. All kinds of things start to walk out of the house, things that never had legs before – plates and candlesticks and tea sets, right down to the sticks of furniture – and money changes hands for 'em too. Money that goes right into Doggett's pockets.

'But he loses it fast enough, same way he always does. He's drinking his way through Earl Temple's wine cellar and inviting all sorts to keep company with him in the house, all sorts of folk who wouldn't be welcome in an honest house and never saw the inside of a church neither, I wouldn't be surprised. And all the while, he's writing letters to Lord Temple, telling him that everything's falling apart and he needs more money to keep up the house and the estate and the farm.

'Course, there were no farm left to speak of by then, because Doggett had sold off the cattle and let the men go.'

'My cousin Jack used to work on that farm until Doggett sent him off,' said Charley Rose, and there was a deferential shift around him, as though his familial connection made him more important to the story.

'But then one day Doggett gets a letter back,' said the lined old man, 'or so the tale goes, from his lord, telling him to have two wings of the house demolished to sell off the materials. Well, as you all know, there was more than enough house to get away with smashing down half of it and still leave something which would pass for a palace in these parts. The way the earl saw it, the money that brought in would leave enough to make the repairs and keep the estate going. The stone were fine Purbeck marble, you see, so it were worth a pretty something.

'Course, Doggett was delighted, but he chose to understand his orders a bit different. He had the whole main house knocked down and the parts sold off, all to satisfy his greed. There were only a tiny section of the North Wing and the old stables left, which he kept for his use.

Soon enough, he was going through the same dance as before, drinking and gambling away the money.

'But then Doggett gets another letter and it's one he don't want. Lord Temple's coming home – he's tired of Italy and he's ready to settle down and run the estate and the farm. 'Course, there is no farm, and no house, and not much of anything else either.

'So, William Doggett is a desperate man, a rat cornered by the dogs. He thinks to buy back the stone and wood and rebuild the house, but there's no money to buy and besides the stones is all built into other houses by this time.'

'Parts of it are in the rectory, I believe,' said the parson, who had married the couple, and who presumably lived in the rectory.

'Aye, that's the truth, and there's more in Ashmore Manor too.'

'What did Doggett do?' I asked, eager to learn the conclusion of the story.

'The only thing he could,' said the old man grimly. 'He took Lord Temple's pistol and shot himself, right under the jaw. They say the bullet went right through his head and out of the top of it.'

There was an uncomfortable fidgeting, not least because the parson was among our company.

'Well, Temple gets back to England and finds no house, just a ruin of a stables and his estate piled high in debt. He did rebuild, but it's a much more modest house now, and the farm's never come back.'

'Thing is, though,' said the old man, leaning forward and blowing a puff of pipe smoke out into the room, 'Doggett didn't lie quiet. They say doors in that house are opened by unseen hands, and in the room he shot himself, the floor and ceiling are always stained with blood, no matter how much it's been cleaned and repainted in fine new colours.'

'They've seen his ghost, too,' said Gaffer Dibben, with great relish. 'His face just a mass of blood.'

I looked at the parson, expecting him to disapprove of such superstition, but he was nodding along as eagerly as any of them.

'How do you come to know so much about it?' I asked the old man who had told the story.

'Because Doggett were my brother,' he said, a complicated knot of emotion suddenly twisting his face, 'and I hope he don't sleep quiet, for he don't deserve to.' And he spat upon the floor, a gob of tobacco-stained spittle landing on the rushes.

A general pleasurable shudder passed through the company, and I had the feeling they would settle down to a long night of stories about spooks and spectres. I have never cared for such things, so I excused myself and began my walk back to the lodgings I had taken some three miles off.

The harvest moon was yellow-bright in the sky, lighting a clear path for me to find my footing across the heath. I thought of the moon casting its light on the young newly married couple, but I confess that I thought more of the story of Doggett and his sad and ugly end.

As I approached the crossroads which would lead me to my lodgings or back to Bere and Amelia, I saw a collection of bobbing lights and heard a conference of voices.

'Good evening,' I called, and the owners of the voices started and turned to me, appearing somewhat embarrassed. It was a group of local men, some of whom had been at the festivities earlier in the day and were still wearing their best clothes. Several were armed with forks and shovels and I saw that they were standing round a gaping hole in the ground.

'What are you about here?' I asked, for the look of them in the moonlight was somewhat unearthly.

The men shuffled and muttered. I crossed to the side of the hole they had dug by the handpost and recoiled in horror when I looked down into it and beheld the body of a man, newly dead by his appearance.

'That be the villain Doggett,' said one of the fellows, who I thought might be the husband of Martha Stickland, Willie's eldest daughter.

I started, for it was the very man who had haunted the evening's conversation. But then I made myself walk to the edge of the makeshift grave and look down into it again. After all, I am no stranger to death.

'That cannot be,' I said, and felt that in my heart to be true, for the body of the man I was looking down at was as fresh as though he had died that morning, and as pink and healthy in colour as though he had simply gone to sleep. There was a bandage wound around his head and underneath his chin, but apart from that he looked as alive as I. But it was impossible, for the William Doggett of the story had died many years before. No sign of rot or decay had eaten away at his flesh, and no foul smell arose from the grave.

'It's unnatural,' said one of the men. 'And he walks, everyone knows it. We'm here to make sure he don't.'

I saw then that Martha Stickland's husband was holding in his hand a sharpened wooden stake, and recalled the outdated ideas of my native country, that those who took their own lives were thought to remain on earth for all eternity, emerging from their graves to prey upon the living. The stake was supposed to hold them in position and prevent them from wreaking their mischief.

I had no desire to be part of such a practice, so I bid them a curt goodnight, but I looked down into the grave of William Doggett before I left them. Besides his freshness of appearance, I saw that the legs of the corpse were tied together with a bright yellow ribbon, which appeared ghoulishly similar to the one Martha Stickland had worn in her hat to the wedding.

'To slow 'un down,' said one of the younger men with satisfaction.

I left them in haste and had walked a mile before I realised I was going in the wrong direction, back towards Tarrant Gunville and not to my lodgings. My thoughts were so disordered with visions of phantoms and corpses rising from the dead in a manner I knew I should not countenance as a man of reason, before I knew it I was almost at the edge of the Eastbury estate.

Some unhallowed curiosity in me made me walk on, closer to the house, until I saw its shape loom before me in the moonlight. It certainly was much reduced from the grand edifice I recalled from my childhood.

Suddenly, behind me, I heard coach wheels, thundering along the lane at a breakneck speed. I pressed myself back into the hedge, sure I would be mown down by the horses' hooves. But no coach could I see, and I would swear to this day that none was there, even when the sound was deafeningly close to me and I could smell the sweat of the horses and feel the rush of wind against my face. I would swear, too, that as the sound and the sensation of the invisible coach passed me I heard a hoarse voice, thick with drink, call out to the driver to speed home.

Rooted to the spot with amazement at what I had heard but not seen, I listened to the sound as it drew closer to Eastbury House. It seemed as though a few moments passed before I heard a sudden gunshot, piercing the night like a cry of anguish.

I ran towards the house, certain my services would be required to avert some tragedy, but when I came to its entrance I found it dark and quiet, with no sign that anything had occurred at all. I wondered then if there was more to Doggett's brother's tale than mere fancy, but I feared the work of the men at the crossroads had not been a success, and if anything, had only served to anger the restless spirit.

I did not move Amelia back to the place of my birth after all, and have never been back there myself, even though I am an old man now and have missed many births, marriages and funerals in the parish on account of my most particular aversion to the country around Tarrant Gunville, and its haunting by the vampire William Doggett.

12

Three Knots

An Essex Tale

Weather of all kinds has always influenced agrarian life, and sailors in particular have ever been at the mercy of the wind and its whims.

Versions of the Three Knots story appear all over the British Isles. Across folklore, witches have an affinity for the elements and were believed to be able to control the weather. From Mother Shipton to the three crones of Shakespeare's Macbeth, *this strange power has helped and hindered witches and those who consult them.*

This incarnation of the tale is peculiar to Leigh-on-Sea. The Sarah Moore pub can still be visited today. It's named after Sarah Moore, a witch who was known to have the power to control the winds through knot magic. Not a great deal is known about Sarah, or when she lived, so I chose to set the story in the seventeenth century – a time both of tall ships and witch-hunting fever.

The practice of selling sailors a good wind was a common one along the coast. A length of string or ribbon would be tied in intricate knots to catch the wind within it. When out at sea, a sailor could then unleash a single knot to summon a breeze, a second for a strong wind, and a third to let loose a storm.

Sometimes they might untie more than they had bargained for…

EC

The wind is a wild soul and hard to tame. It cannot be pinned for long, and it laughs away every attempt. Even those who think they can contain it have their spirits broken, for the wind will always dance away. People who can control its rough magic are few, and you may never meet one.

One such soul was Sarah Moore. She knew the secrets of the wind, and some of the secrets of the sea as well, although it has too many to ever know fully. Gulls perched on her shoulders and told her tales of their flights to distant shores and shimmering fish jumped from the water to giggle at her jokes. Sarah Moore was strong and tall, and the four winds liked to play in her storm-grey hair. She had quick, clever fingers and she wove charms from colourful wool and twisted net fibres.

Sarah's speciality was harnessing the wind into her knotted charms, which she gave to sailors to afford them a little extra help. The knots she wove were intricate and beautiful, and each charm was like a tiny picture of something nobody could fully see – the dance of the wind. She created many different sorts, but the one she most often gave to others was a charm of three knots.

Three knots Sarah tied into her charms, and each knot had a different purpose. A sailor could carry her charm aboard and, as needed, untie a knot. The release of the first knot would produce a light breeze, just enough to catch the sails of a ship. The second knot let out a strong wind, which could carry a ship to its intended point much faster. But Sarah always tied a third knot into her charms – a balance of sorts, which she told sailors never to use. Within that third knot, a storm was contained, and if it was released it might rage unchecked until it had claimed something from the seas.

Most people listened to Sarah when she warned them not to use the third knot, but there are always exceptions.

For instance, I heard of a man over from Sheerness who used one of Sarah Moore's charms. I don't know why he'd come to Leigh-on-Sea to do his wife's shopping, but he had a list and he'd made the trip. The shopping was done quickly and cheaply, and this man decided he'd spend the rest of his day in the quayside inns.

Still, when the sun started to get low, he thought he'd better start for home to avoid angering his good lady. Worry beset him when the waters were calm, with no wind to catch a sail. Luckily for him, Sarah Moore was walking along the quay, feeding the seabirds, and she offered to sell him a charm.

Just like she always did, she told him never to use the third knot, and he nodded and paid her.

Well, this chap was just delighted. He released a knot and a light breeze fluttered through his sails and set him on course to sail back to Sheerness. He was enjoying the sunset, looking over the bows, when he thought it was still quite a distance home, and he might just have a little more wind just to help him get along a little faster. So, he took out Sarah's charm and untied the second knot. Oh, didn't he get along beautifully then!

The ship cut through the water like a cormorant skimming along the surface, and this man thought there was nothing better. He decided he'd never do the shopping anywhere but Leigh-on-Sea. But the sun had dipped well and truly below the horizon by then, and he thought of his wife waiting back at home in Sheerness, wanting the things he had bought, and he thought perhaps he'd have a little more speed, just to get home faster. Sarah's charm had worked so beautifully up until now that he could just imagine how it would be with a little more wind.

So he let out the final knot, and held on to the mast, ready to fly into Sheerness port like a shooting star.

Well, just as he had been warned, a fearsome storm blew up. It battered and buffeted his ship and he had a job to cling on to the mast. He was lucky not to be sunk or dashed to pieces, but on that occasion, the wind fiercely blew the ship off-course, away from Sheerness and all the way back to Leigh-on-Sea.

And who should be waiting for him on the quayside but Sarah Moore, with her hands on her hips and a smile on her face, and what did she say but 'I told you so'?

But most of the time, the people who used Sarah's charms listened to her words and were well satisfied with the service. Of course, it wasn't free. Magic had a price, and Sarah Moore charged it happily. Selling her spells kept her cottage by the sea well supplied with salty fish and red-heeled shoes, and it was a happy place, filled with pretty shells and gull's feathers and dangling charms made of sea glass.

Most days, she sat outside on the Leigh-on-Sea harbourside, talking to the winds and watching the ships and selling her charms to anyone who wanted them. The people in Leigh-on-Sea accepted Sarah Moore as part of the scenery, as much a feature of their landscape as the sea or sky.

But one day, a foreign ship sailed into Leigh – a mercenary crew who had come to patrol the seas and keep them safe from the threat of invasion. The captain was a solemn, cold man who had read the words of Matthew Hopkins, and when he looked at Sarah Moore, with her twists of thread and her chattering birds, he saw only a witch. When he passed her on the quay, he spat at her feet, and he told his men not to buy her charms at any cost.

About the town of Leigh, he spread vicious rumours about Sarah, telling people she'd sold her soul to the Devil and the seabirds she fed were her hellish familiars. At first, nobody listened, but the insidious talk gradually spread, and the sailors and fishermen who'd bought charms from Sarah for years started to avoid her too. Sarah soon found that people stopped saying good morning to her, and she wasn't welcome in the pubs she always went to. Even the landlady of the Bent Bowsprit Inn, who had been her friend, was rude to her, and Sarah started to feel as though Leigh-on-Sea wasn't the happy home it had always been.

It didn't take very long for her to trace the problem back to the foreign captain. His rude remarks and the way he crossed himself whenever he passed her or clutched at his silver crucifix, and the way he pointed at her and muttered things to his crew – oh, he was the source of it, alright.

Now, Sarah Moore was no wallflower, so she lost no time in marching up to the captain's ship the next time it was in dock and confronting him. But he didn't have the grace or the face to speak to her. He turned away and shut himself in his cabin and wouldn't meet her eyes.

'You'll see,' said Sarah Moore, 'you'll see.'

For she was full of a tearing fury, spiralling through her like a whirlwind, and she vowed to have her revenge on the foreign captain and his shipmates

The captain opened his sea chest and looked into his book of maleficium, and after long hours of pondering he had an idea of what to do about Sarah Moore, but he kept it to himself for a little while, in case nothing happened at all. After all, the coldness of old friends is sometimes enough to send someone away from the home they have loved.

But Sarah wasn't to be seen off so easily. Her anger was growing, as rain swells a dark cloud. The next overcast day, when the captain sailed his ship out to patrol the estuary, Sarah Moore stood on the quay with a bundle of threads in her hands. As she stared at the ship, she twisted the threads into a new, dark shape, not her usual three knots, but a tangled, bramble-spiky knot of malice.

And she tossed that oily dark thing into the air, until a whispering wind caught it and carried it right to the top of the mast of the captain's ship. There it tangled itself around and around, and when Sarah Moore spoke some words to it, it stuck fast as though it had been carved into the grain of the wood. The knot began to glow, drawing the storm clouds around itself in a web of wind and rain, until it was the eye of a fearsome storm which raged only about that ship, for Sarah Moore had no anger in her heart towards the other sailors and fishermen of Leigh.

But around the bows of that ship, the estuary churned and roared. The crew clung to the masts and the bows, their stomachs rolling as they went for the barrels of rum, vowing not to die sober if they had to go that day. The captain stood at the wheel, and as he looked back towards Leigh he saw Sarah on the shore, and he knew that the time had come to put into practice the things his book of maleficium had told him. He knew that a witch needs a connection, a magical link to the spell she's cast. So, he looked around for the source of the raging wind and rain, and he saw the glowing knot at the top of the mast.

All in a trice, he ran to fetch the great axe he kept in his cabin, a relic from another life, and he swung it back and chopped into the ship's mast as though he were cutting down a great tree in a forest. Righteous fire fuelled his strokes, and in three chops the mast was toppling from its great height and crashing into the waves below.

As soon as the mast hit the surface of the water, the storm stilled. The sailors cheered the bravery of their captain, and they didn't mind that they had to row all the way back to the harbour, for they all knew how close they had come to dying that day. They knew that the burn in their muscles from pulling at the oars would soon be relieved by strong liquor and prayers of thanks that their captain's foresight and knowledge had saved their lives.

But when they arrived back at the quay in Leigh, there were no bright smiles or words of welcome for their safe return. Instead, they found a group of people gathered around a fallen shape, lying near the harbour wall. It was the dead body of Sarah Moore, lying in a pool of her own blood, with three great axe wounds sliced across her chest.

Nobody in Leigh knew exactly what the captain had done, but they knew he was to blame. It didn't take long before they forgot that they had listened to him and colluded in Sarah's misfortune. Leigh-on-Sea made it quite clear that the captain wasn't welcome there anymore, not in any of the pubs, and nor were any of his crew. Soon enough, they set sail for other waters, and they weren't seen again in those parts.

The landlady of the Bent Bowsprit Inn changed its name to the Sarah Moore, in honour of the witch of the winds, and it remains named for her to this very day, though it's a long time now since she sold her charms by the sea there. Many a sailor has wished he held three knots in his hand to unleash a wind, and many more has longed for the spells Sarah wove to keep them safe at sea.

But as for Sarah, she lives on in the winds which lift the waves into carrying ripples, and in the fluffy clouds which darken with rain. If her spirit takes a fancy to a handsome seafarer, she might help a ship along by blowing a breeze through its sails. But too much zealotry and cold looks aboard, and Sarah Moore might just knot her spirit around the mast and whip up a fatal storm.

13

The Torbarrow Guardian

A Gloucestershire Tale

This strange tale comes from a broadsheet published in 1685 entitled, A Strange and Wonderful Discovery Newly made of Houses Under Ground at Colton's Field in Gloucester-Shire.

In the past, it was commonly accepted that barrows were haunted places believed to offer entryways to the Otherworld, elf or faery halls, or the world of the dead. For this reason, they were seen as suitable spots to position gallows or stocks, which was exactly what happened in communities up and down England. In this case though, the intrepid explorers who went down into the Colton's Field barrow found something else entirely.

As such, my retelling here is a very straight one. The original account plays out just as I've written it, including the gravel diggers, the antiquarian, and the crypt's mysterious contents. The men involved even sold the treasure they found, and for a rather good price. Yet the precise location of Colton's Field has proved an enigma; these days, the best guess is that it happened at Torbarrow Hill, just outside of Cirencester, where there are two prehistoric burial mounds. This seems unlikely, though, as they have not collapsed.

Bearing all of this in mind, my addition of details including alchemical explanations for the ever-burning lamp and the pool of mercury as found in Ancient Egyptian and Mayan tombs, and those of occult icons like Ferdinand II of Aragon, Tycho Brahe, and Anastasia Romanov, might seem fanciful. Yet, those particulars are the least weird thing about it.

MV

Ah, my lovely, I am an old man now, and shan't be digging no more holes.

Aye, I do still have the letter and, since you ask, I'll speak on it one last time, for the venturing of me and Groves and Dr Parsons into Torbarrow was the strangest event of my life. Besides, soon I shall be dead, and if you don't speak it on thereafter, then the tale will die with me, sure enough.

Oh now, chin up. Your pestering to hear it once more gives me no pain. You were like to hear it ever since you came no taller than my knee. Besides, save sitting here in this chair, and going abed each night after saying my prayers, and gumming on what gipping scraps your dear mother gives me, I have little else useful to do.

So, may this telling make you smile and quake in terror as it did when you was young, and as it has all manner of person for many a year.

Put another log on the fire, then, and lean in close.

There now, I shall begin.

It was the year sixteen-hundred and eighty-five, which I remember on account of Monmouth's Rebellion. I wasn't the sort to be caught up in such nonsense, never being a fighting man. Rather, I was a good worker, and put my hand to labour, as God would have it, through all my days until then.

So it was that I and my good friend Groves – who were a layman such as myself, though older, may he rest in peace – were hired to dig at Colton's Field. There were good gravel there, see, all about that great mound folk knew as Torbarrow. Though they speak less of it these days.

Was a famous spot betimes, for atop that knoll, itself standing sixteen feet above ground, were gallows made in the Civil War. Many traitors and scoundrels danced the hempen jig at Torbarrow, and it was said, though planted up with beech trees since, that the mangy place was haunted by all manner of wandering souls and spirits of the damned.

Those were cold days when we were set to dig there, the ground going harder each passing moment by the workings of Jack Frost and his sprites. The labour was slow, but Groves and I set to it, digging at the ground with shovel and pick, making a pit almost a furlong in size all about that eerie mound.

We never went there alone, of course. For though it's common to see a mist rising in the early morn or as the gloaming makes way for night, about Torbarrow a mist did hang all the live-long day. It would rise up your ankles, tickling your leg-hairs, spinning in shapes that looked, in some ways, like men.

Old Groves would scratch his silver whiskers and say he heard whispers in the mist, voices speaking words he couldn't ken, but I never knew nothing like that. Though I did hear, like Groves, the knocking. It came from deep under the earth, slow and strong. Knock, knock, knock.

I said to Groves it must be on account of the cold – water below ground freezing or some such. But Groves were a good old country lad and said it were fairy folk in the hill, telling us, 'Leave off'. I laughed, but Groves told Dr Parsons, who were then Vicar of Driffield, and Parsons came to the gravel pit and blessed it to silence the spirits, for all the good that did.

Day after day, we dug that pit, loading gravel into a hand barrow, emptying that barrow into a cart and driving the cart loaded with shingle on to Hidcote Manor. What they used it for, I don't know. Day after day it was the same, and Groves would shake in his boots, not least when the knocks came, always keeping a lantern near him in case of sudden darknesses.

And be not mistook, for sudden darknesses sometimes did come there, and when they did, the mists rose thicker than blood, tickling us here and there, making us jump.

On one such day, dark as mid-December's like to be, our spades were set close to the Torbarrow itself. As we dug down to about four yards deep, the gravel hissing as we struck it, my spade clattered on something not gravel. Neither were it mud, nor an ordinary stone.

Right curious, Groves and I dug out about this rock and came to find it were an arch made of ancient stones. We thought it must be a door of sorts, packed with mud and roots and shingle. But Old Groves and I were interested, hoping for treasure, though Groves was quaking, clutching his lantern, looking here and there for fear of evil spirits.

I'm shamed to say it, but dark thoughts weren't on my mind. Rather, my thoughts was golden, for it's known all through England that men find treasures in barrow tombs.

I'm no grave robber, but at Belas Knap, Uley, Nympsfield, and Windmill Tump, men dug down and found fine wonders. Crowns of dead kings, silver coins, and cups glittering with emeralds and rubies. But none of them found what we did, as Dr Parsons would admit, if he spoke to our like since he became Chancellor of the Diocese.

No matter. The work was hard at first, clearing the stone from the mouth of that place, us two labouring with cold fingers and our wooden spades. But as we worked, we wondered, heaving and digging, if other men had been there afore we. Seemed likely, for, as a gallows place, crowds had come to Torbarrow in their droves, ringing that mound like druids in the ancient times, watching men pass to the hereafter.

Yet, the deeper we went, the more our hearts thundered, beating with hope. We felt we may find fortunes, meaning no longer would Groves and I spend our days digging at gravel or anything else. No more would our clothes be filthy, knuckles red and singing on dark frosty mornings. We were to be rich.

Once we'd cleared the entrance, which appeared very strange to us and more of art than nature, we ventured a little way in. I went first, Groves following behind with his lantern. The way in was tight as a bailiff, so when I first went down it was into total darkness.

Good as blind, I felt my way, touching the stone walls made of rough-hewn blocks laid together like bricks. And I found, in time, a second such arch in the earth, this one blocked with rubble.

Clearing that rock took hours, and no sooner had we opened even the smallest gap in the stones than a wind blew through that moaned. It were a horrid sound, like a gasp of a poor man dying. Groves whimpered at that, of course, but by the glow of his lamp we saw shapes within – shadows, which made us work quicker than we had before.

In time, we moved all the stones and passed through the inner arch and down into a hall of sorts. It was large, with two long tables, benches each side, laden with what once must have been a feast. By then it was thick with dust and fine dirt, wooden plates and mugs all of nothing.

I went to touch one table, to run my finger across it and clear the scurf, but no sooner did I touch the table than it crumbled to dust, collapsing at my feet. This ruined what must have lain there for many centuries, filling the air with a cloud of powdered sand and earth, obscuring our sight in a moment.

Coughing and blinking through the haze, we pushed on to the room's far side, finding a passage to another room. In there we found what had been a kitchen, containing furniture and utensils proper to it, with pots and kettles of brass and iron which in places continued firm, though eaten through in others with rust and canker.

Beyond was a parlour of sorts, furnished according to the fashions of bygone days, with carpets worn and eaten away and other such thrones and chests. All were so aged we feared they might fall to pieces if disturbed. And in one corner, we observed what appeared as stairs leading downwards, but the earth had fallen in and stopped all hope of our descent.

We did, though, find another passage, leading to a room curiously beautified with carved icons and several works of art. We supposed it was some place of worship and devotion, filled with graven images of gods long forgot, with a stone altar at the end of it. This altar, carved with faces of, to us, grotesque aspect, was surrounded by several urns. Greedy, these we searched, finding in most only ashes. Though in a few we found coins and medals of gold, silver, and brass, some with inscriptions we could not read, bearing heads of emperors, gods, and kings.

With these we filled our pockets. As we did so, behind the altar where once had hung some great work of tapestry long decayed, to our astonishment we spied a door. It had been latched strongly with iron, but the wood, being rotten, proved no barrier. I put my shoulder to it and heaved, and with little force it fell to pieces, revealing behind an earthen stair leading down. Though I tell you now, it was not to darkness it led, but light. Golden-blue and shining, glinting at the foot of the steps.

This, we thought, was surely impossible – a light deep in a darkness that had stood since afore the Conqueror came to England. At the sight of it, Groves was terrified, shocked pale as death. His white hair and whiskers all but stood on end with fear. He started saying his prayers as a murmur, telling me we had found the lights of a fairy hall and were set to be cursed, for we had travelled to their kingdom uninvited.

Well, I chuckled at him, which mayhap I should have not. But he would go no further, and neither would he part with his lantern. Thusly, alone I descended, slow and quiet, step after step, down and down, toward that mysterious light.

I thought it wise not to rush, and so it proved. Holding my breath as I neared the bottom, I sought to peek only into the room. And when I did, to my great astonishment, I saw a wide pit had been dug, filled with what most folk call quicksilver, others mercury, though much of what had once been in that pool had long since drained away.

I held my breath, seeing the pit was square, though in the middle was a raised island bearing a tomb of stone, sealed and still. And over this tomb stood the image of a man in full proportion, gripping a great truncheon in his hand, and a light above him burned, held in a ball of glass, turning and turning, bathing that place in that eternal glow of golden-blue.

I was affrighted, of course, for the figure looked perhaps to be devilish, with horns upon its helmeted head. And I wondered if it were a statue of a guardian spirit set there to defend some hidden treasure, which made me step forward.

I took but one pace into that chamber, then froze. For, though it may sound like madness, or foolishness, or even mayhap deceit, believe me when I say it: at the sound of my footfall, the statue there, the shape of that horned man, moved.

The sound it made was like a grindstone milling flour, setting my teeth on edge. And the image cast shadows all about the space on account of the strange light which swirled there within the orb of glass. The gold-blue glow made echoes in the shades it cast, repeating the sight of the shape – no statue, no icon, but something else – as it raised its truncheon like to smite me for entering that heathen place.

I'm no fool, and so I fled back up the steps to Groves, grasping at him, wordless, my voice lost in the tightness of my throat.

Speechless, we passed back through the passages and rooms. Through the strange parlour, kitchen, and feasting hall, and back into fresh air. And each step we took, our pockets jingled, heavy with plunder.

No sooner than we were outside once more, the mists there turned, pouring down into the tomb we had since uncovered, and we realised night had fallen. I remarked on it, then Groves set about emptying his pockets of the coins and medals he had taken. I asked him why, and he said such things were cursed, all without my even mentioning the strange guardian I had laid eyes upon.

I don't recall exactly what I said to Groves, but I did shake him by the shoulders of his jacket and used speech rougher than I ought've, not least to one older than I. But I gave him instruction to calm his nerves and gather his wits, though he wouldn't listen.

'God will forsake us,' he said, looking not like a man of four score years and more like a frightened child.

So it was that I decided to stay and guard our discovery, and sent Groves to go by the horse and cart to Cirencester to fetch Dr Parsons. I did so, in part, for Parsons was a vicar and might save Groves from his panic with holy words, but also because Dr Parsons was an antiquarian of some renown, learned in Latin and other ancient tongues.

This, of course, left me alone there, stood by Torbarrow, the sun down and mist turning all about. It was a clear night, bitter cold with a light breeze. From on high, the stars shone down and the moon began to glow, and weren't I where I was, I might have called it pretty. But pretty it was not, and I recall standing, breathing slow, hearing the wind in the beech trees, rattling like wheezing lungs. Moreover, as I looked about me at the shifting vapours, I saw what I thought was eyes looking up at me, glinting and hungry for my soul.

Was nothing of the sort, of course, but rather the coins Groves had dropped, reflecting the light of the heavens back at me. So, I gathered up that treasure, taking time about it to distract myself from gloomy thoughts. For it felt as if phantasms moved in that mist or the shadows of the trees might stop in their gentle, wind-driven dance to birth a revenant, one to come to me and recall its own hanging, seeking absolution for past crimes.

As I waited, listening for the sound of the horse and cart's return, I heard a sound most unnatural, echoing up from deep within the earth. It was that familiar sound, that old sound – ancient – but with new meaning to me now.

It boomed out. Knock! Knock! Knock!

I thought again of that devilish shape below, the stone guardian of the tomb, wielding his fearsome club. But relief then came in the click of Groves' tongue as he drove the horse and cart. Alongside him was Dr Parsons, carrying his own lantern, full of excitement at our discovery.

'Come along then,' he said as he approached. 'Show me what you've found.'

And so we did, leading the vicar down out of the night's darkness and into the heavy shadows below. Yet, Groves came no further than the first chamber, the feasting hall, leaving Dr Parsons and I to push on toward that strange and final chamber.

Being alone again with the vicar gave me time, in whispered tones, to explain to him what I had seen below. I spoke first of the ever-burning lantern, saying it seemed a miracle, for no fire should burn for hundreds of years untended.

I'll never forget his reply, not least for I had him repeat it in parts. He said, for one, that there was once a wise alchemist, Christian Rosenkreuz, who died. Only then, about his crypt, was built a temple, special to his own design. And this Temple of Rosicrucias, Parsons said, was later opened by monks in the year of our Lord 1604, 120 years after his decease. Parsons said that within were found, beside other mysterious articles, lamps of special and peculiar construction; sepulchral lamps, he said, ever-burning with brilliance.

Yet, he said, this was no rarity in the middle ages, though the destroying hands of the Goth and the Vandal had left few ancient tombs for modern folk then to explore. Though in 1540, in a catacomb in the Appian Way at Rome, supposed to be that of Tulliola, the daughter of Cicero, was just such another ever-burning lantern found. She had died forty-four years before the birth of Jesus Christ, Parsons said, yet the lamp within her tomb had burned over 1,500 years.

As we walked on, the vicar spoke of theories of such ever-burning flames. Of a 'divine afflatus' he called it, a portion of the spirit of God. Of electrical methods exhibited by Zoroastrian Magi. He spoke of the immolation of Salamander's Wool, the holy fire of Nehemiah, the ever-burning flame of Trivandrum, as written of by some abbott. On and on he went, and I could see his ardour at the notion he may himself study the truth behind an arcane mystery such as the flame behind that ball of glass.

'A miracle imitated is not a second miracle,' he said.

And I'll always remember it. A miracle imitated is not a second miracle. Those words gave me courage, for if a country vicar could hope to explain the secrets of that tomb then the things within could not be devilish or worthy to fear, but things out of nature. Things to know and tame and master, and not miracles at all.

When we then reached the room with the altar and the urns and other such religious items, Dr Parsons stopped still. For he spied, in an ancient tongue, an inscription upon the altar top. It read something like, 'Get ye hence, most wicked thieves, What do you desire with your rolling eyes? Get ye hence with your broad hatted Mercury, Carrying a wand with twisted snakes.'

I thought this but a riddle or a message of foreboding, but Dr Parsons thought it of great import. Yet, as I told him, don't you wonder over an engraving, for down these stairs are things of greater mystery. An ever-burning flame and the guardian of the tomb below.

So, we descended once more into that crypt, observing that square pool half-filled with quicksilver, shining with the light of that gold-blue flame. With wonder and delight, Dr Parsons viewed the room, holding a kerchief to his nose. Then I pointed to where the image stood: the man of stone with his horned head and his mighty truncheon raised.

Dr Parsons supposed the figure to be made by some great artist of past days, and when it set to move, he thought mayhap it was as a water clock or similar, built to strike at certain times. Therefore, without any apprehension of danger he went forward, and again the man of stone made as if to strike.

I heard that same grinding, like a mill at work, and Parsons sought to inspect the glass there, so filled with flickering light. Yet, the disharmonious sounds of the guardian's limbs moving grew and grew, for then, not just the arm of the figure moved, but its whole form. Legs, waist, head, all turned, twisting. Then, with great, thudding footsteps, the thing began to walk, advancing to Dr Parsons at a quick and steady pace.

As it moved, wading through the shimmering, liquid silver, I saw the thing's face. Carved, though dirtied by the grime of centuries, I saw its beard, its aspect, which was of a Roman general or ancient king, though its eyes were fixed, unmoving. About its chest I spied what looked like engraved icons and ensigns of martial honour, pinned, though carved, to fixed, stone robes.

'Remarkable,' said Dr Parsons, as if there were no danger. But then I saw, in the figure's other hand, the one not grasping the great stone truncheon, two heads dangling upon twisted cords of ancient bronze, long decayed.

The heads there looked as if embalmed, for the flesh was shrivelled up and looked like scorched parchment. They had long hair on their chins, one once being red of beard, the other black, though there was little time to make inspection.

I dashed to Dr Parsons, dragging him aside as the guardian processed, bearing down and striking with its truncheon the spot on which the vicar had stood. The stone of the floor there was cracked then, splintered, while the figure's club appeared untouched. I saw this as the demon again raised its weapon, up and behind it, as if preparing to strike again. And as it did, it struck the orb of glass, casting all the room in blackness dark as pitch.

I screamed then, I know, as did the vicar. I grasped my companion, backing away toward the nearby wall. Still, on the grinding went, stone on stone, sliding. Then crashing footsteps sounded, all amidst the noise of quicksilver splashing, washing about in great, unseen waves.

Hastily, I pulled Parsons along the walls and to the door, seeing atop the stairs a light there bobbing and glowing bright. It was Groves, come near after hearing our screams, though our anguish was far from over.

We ran up the earthen steps, but the danger followed us. The guardian was intent on pursuing us, though it appeared unable to leave that chamber. Still, it struck at the stone and earth thereabouts with mighty blows, once, twice, thrice. Knock! Knock! Knock! And so it was that the roof of that ancient place began at once to give way.

As all about collapsed, earth showering us like rain, we adventurers quitted those apartments, fearful to stop or gather more of the treasures as we passed. Good thing, too, for no sooner had we squeezed through the entrance than the hollow did give out the noise of a deep sigh or groan. Then, the hill sunk down before us, no longer a mound but flat and broken earth.

All the treasures therein, the mysteries, coins, and medals, were buried. All save those rarities in my pockets. Those, as you know, were given mostly to the Church, for the doing of good. Elsewise, they paid for Groves' last years and bought this house in which your father's lived since a boy, which you shall one day inherit.

After, Dr Parsons wrote me the letter you know so well, which I have here, see, kept in my breast pocket? And here it says, 'Nature herself lay witness, for her laws are overridden, replaced by a power to which she, the mighty mother, has herself to bow. The darkness of death and the darkness of the tomb are no match for the light of such wisdom.

'The great tendency of our times has been to reduce all men to a level, a dead level, of mediocrity. Yet this is an effort fatal to the authority of each man, which has tended to discourage research into ancient, hidden mysteries as opposed to the study of what we know as modern science. Yet, there are such things to learn of and to know revealed in antiquity, since hidden in that same darkness underground. I know it, you know it, and we must never be afeared.'

All grandly expressed, that's for certain. But what he wants is for poor folk to go burrowing about for treasure, while rich folk stay nice and warm.

And, like I said before, I learned my lesson that night and shan't be digging no more holes.

14

The Netley Abbey Phantoms

A Hampshire Tale

Ghostly monks are so common in English folklore that they are almost a cliché.

Often they are said to have been walled up alive, interred with the nuns with whom they had affairs, a little like Abelard and Heloise. Sometimes, they move down ancient progress routes, appearing half-buried in the soil as the ground level was so much lower in their day. Usually, though, there is no particular reason for their haunting, their appearances acting as a ghostly reminder of the shock and trauma of the Dissolution of the Monasteries, or the nation's collective guilt (or historic suspicions) related to Catholics.

In the case of the Netley Abbey phantoms, they are said to be Cistercians, guarding treasure. Indeed, there are legends at the site of the ghost of an old abbot, nighttime chanting, the sounds of ringing bells, and a group of three grey ladies who appear each Halloween. Even more curious, from 1863 until it was ruined by a mysterious fire in 1963, there was a military hospital and mental asylum on grounds once owned by Netley Abbey, which saw plenty of famous inmates and visitors, including Siegfried Sassoon, Wilfred Owen, Queen Victoria, and Florence Nightingale.

In my telling, I have done my best to blend historical fact with an M.R. James-style ghost story, where ancient treasure is disturbed, such as Oh, Whistle, and I'll Come to You, My Lad, A Warning to the Curious, *or* The Treasure of Abbot Thomas. *Fingers crossed it does not give you nightmares…*

MV

From the Private Papers of Dr Isaac Watts, Physic of Netley, nr Southampton, dated 10 April 1704

I feel a fool, committing these grisly thoughts to paper. Yet, in the days since Mr Taylor's demise I have been unable to shift the thoughts of it from my mind. A fallen lintel feels an apt icon for my distress, for it is as if the idea has collapsed upon me, too heavy to shift. Yet, while apt, the analogy is in poor taste.

No matter. It is my intention that no living soul should ever read these pages. I only seek to write my account and, in doing so, free my mind of the whole affair so that I might know peace.

It started with a man named Slown. Whether Slown was his last name or first I never learned, but he was where it began. I believe he was a midshipman once, though that's but tittle-tattle and speculation. I inspected his body, which was riddled with scars and new small wounds, but I learned little of his history or character and no relations have since been traced. Besides, who Slown was is of little import – rather what he did is what matters. For though my friend Mr Taylor had always been a man of ambition, the obsession which latterly overtook him would not have entered the course of his thoughts had he not encountered that shameful bandit.

This is to say that anyone living in Netley, Southampton, or our nearby districts cannot help but know of the abbey. Its shape protrudes from the landscape like a row of broken teeth, biting through God's green earth and standing rot-grey against the clear southern sky. Its story is as twisted as the place, for though constructed in the thirteenth century by Peter des Roches, who was then Bishop of Winchester, the abbey has not been used for a holy purpose since 1536. Since that time, it has been a private residence, a manor owned variously by Marquesses of Winchester, Dukes of Somerset and Earls of Hertford, Ailesbury and Huntingdon.

As just this brief history would imply, the buildings in the abbey grounds have never been loved since the days of Henry Tudor. Rather, the place has been feared, hated, and sometimes speculated upon. Indeed, it may be thought of as a bad penny – a tarnished coin, rotten in its very metal – traded back and forth by any gentlemen fool enough to think a bad penny spends the same as a good one.

These conjectures were gross folly, as the people of Netley know too well. For legends of the abbey's haunting abound, godless as such tales may at first appear.

Still, around any Eastleigh landlord's fire, you might hear the same God-fearing people tell the same irreligious accounts: that the abbey's grounds are haunted by the spectres of two Franciscan friars of the strict Observant part of that order.

It is said that when the abbey was dissolved, those monks were placed into the custody of the abbot, Thomas Stevens, though the bodies of the friars were never found and no further records made of their movements or transfers between authorities. Duly, it has long been surmised that the king's commissioners, Sir James Worsley, William Berners, and the brothers John and George Paulet, had the monks slain and their bodies buried somewhere in those deconsecrated grounds.

Word of this slaughter first emerged when the Paulet family were gifted the abbey estate by Tudor himself. The father, William, never lived there, but he and his sons oversaw the demolition of much of the edifice. They turned the church nave into a great hall, the transepts to luxurious apartments, the monks' dormitory to a long gallery.

Servants there began to report unsettling nocturnal appearances. It was said the spectres of the two Franciscan friars appeared by moonlight, robed and bathed in blackish blood, carrying reliquaries in their gory hands. These rumours spread like moss, slow and steady – not least of them being that the two Franciscans had before death hidden a cache of papist ornaments in an undiscovered crypt deep in the abbey's grounds.

Whether the Paulets knew the gossip or simply ignored it was of little consequence, for they soon sold the estate. And though it passed through many hands, and new owners came and went, the rumours lingered.

Indeed, it was those arcane whispers which drew Slown to Netley and which, in due course, prompted his undoing. This is to say that latterly, with the manor house having fallen into rack and ruin, it was sold to the enterprising Sir Bartlet Lucy of Charlcote Park. Lucy, hailing from Warwickshire, cared not a jot for the abbey itself, but saw value in its stone. So, he sought resourceful entrepreneurs to dismantle the edifice and sell the best of what remained for the highest profit.

The contract was advertised hereabouts for some time, though none in the borough would take it. All knew of the legends and feared such curses or dark fates which might befall them at the phantom hands of the blood-drenched friars.

So it was that Slown, knowing the abbey to be desolate and unguarded, sought to pursue the opportunity for graverobbing. Evidence he left shows that he had taken a spade and quarried at several points, digging down into the earth in search of the hidden crypt.

None would have guessed at his endeavours, or even known he had been there, camping alone in a lowly copse, had he not burst into Mrs Pyke's one night, covered head-to-toe in cold earth and pale as Death himself.

Though Slown was known to none at Mrs Pyke's that evening, all listened close enough to recount his ravings. I was told by none other than Barbara Findlay, one of the most God-fearing women in the village, that the stranger pleaded with all who would listen to shrive him of his crimes.

He had been digging, he said, seeking the lost treasures of the abbey, when he found a tunnel, part collapsed, lined with rough-hewn stone. Gingerly, Slown had clambered down into this underpass, lighting his way with a candle. And lo, he said, though it was tight and dank down in the causeway, he wriggled on through, struggling for a long while, all before finding a buried chamber filled with glinting silver and gold.

As Mrs Findlay told it, it was then that Slown realised a grim truth. In crawling into the tomb, he had clambered over some fragments of human remains. Though the habit was decayed and the skin on the cadaver darkened as if to leather, he could see the face of the fallen fellow, and believed he had, therefore, moved into such a position that there was then a long-dead monk laid below him.

Panicked though this made Slown, he was intent and the trove of relics was within reach. So, Slown said, he reached out with his free hand, his candle held tightly in his other. Yet, no sooner had he grasped one of the dusty icons than did the corpse beneath him shudder, twist, and stare at Slown with smoke-white eyes.

Frightened out of his wits and feeling the cadaver moving about beneath him, Slown made to escape – and as he did, the very cavern and tunnel in which he was crawling started to collapse about him. So afeared was he that, muttering prayers, he laboured and struggled back through the cold ground as if gifted an angel's strength. Somehow, he made a miraculous escape, intent that all around should know that the tunnel should be sealed and never trespassed upon again.

Of course, the fine people of Netley aren't known as fools, and none would have given credence to Slown's ramblings, save for a single, dire fact: in Slown's fist he gripped nothing less than a pectoral cross of pure gold, inlaid with garnet and slivers of silvery shell. Alas for Slown, he would not release his grip on the cross. Perhaps if he had, it might have saved him. For, though the priest was called, and so was I, by the time either of us reached him Slown had fallen down stone dead. Most horrid, his fist was still wrapped about the golden icon. So strong was his grip, even in death, that I could only prise the relic from him with the use of tools borrowed from Mr Sellwood, the ironmonger.

Curious as this incident was, the matter may well have been settled then and there, and the cross buried back in the abbey's grounds, had Mr Taylor not been present. For Mr Taylor, as everyone knew, was a very fine builder indeed. Hailing from Southampton, known as William to his friends, he listened to Slown's story with great interest and, within the hour, accepted Sir Bartlet Lucy's contract. He returned the agreement by a rider, dispatched not long after midnight and at great expense, rousing stonemasons from their beds by dawn.

Not two days later, the agreement was returned, signed and sealed, and William Taylor set to work. He hired men, more in number than his usual team of capables, and set to work shifting the abbey's stones. At the same time, though, he had men work at digging, for William's drive was less for Bartlet Lucy's money than the treasure he might find buried deep in the abbey's earth.

It had been agreed, in the meanwhile, that I should maintain possession of the pectoral cross, and for the longest time, or so it seemed, I kept the infernal object in my chambers. I did not want it, but William swore me to silence on the matter and paid all who'd been in Mrs Pyke's that night to also hold their tongues. Even the priest stayed mute, though I suppose he's begging forgiveness now.

'After all,' William said to me, 'you prised the cross from a dead man's hand. Surely you've earned the right to keep it in payment?'

He said this in jest, but the matter became more and more serious, for something about the relic got as deep under my skin as it had once been buried in the abbey's grounds.

Perhaps it was a matter of conscience, but when I closed my eyes I would see the cross there, glinting and sparkling as if lit by the sun of a pure summer sky. Yet, despite its fire, a shadow soon fell across my mind's eye, and I would shiver like a babe left out in the dead of winter.

As days passed, I came to feel I was no longer alone in my lodgings. No matter where I placed it, the cross would move from room to room, cupboard to worktop, and I would hear steady footsteps walking in the dead of night. More than once, sat in my chair of an evening, I thought I heard whispered voices outside my door, hushed in Latinate prayer.

Then, or thereabouts, the dreams began.

It feels ghoulish to recount them but recount them I must. They came not at once, but rather they built, like a terrible edifice or words on a scroll unfurling nightly.

First I saw them alone, the two pale Franciscans, walking the streets of Netley. From there, in my dim awareness, I saw them wander through Abbots Wood and over the Itchen and the Hamble. The pair moved in a ghastly procession, always progressing towards the abbey, yet each night they would journey a little nearer. Moreover, each night, as dawn approached, their march would break and they would turn back towards me, as if I were following on behind, and would reveal to me their ghastly wounds.

One was slain by sword, I saw, stabbed at first then, with his throat cut, rendered unable to speak or scream. Instead, he would gabble, his gory tongue lapping at his blackened lips. Then there was the other, the friar who had been blind in his life. I knew, somehow, that while his brother's name was John, the blind friar was named Peter. And Peter, unseeing, had been beaten and clubbed, knifed, and speared with a dagger, and it was his mangled form which Slown had found crushed and crippled in that tunnel beneath the ground.

I told William of my dreams and he laughed at me, much in his manner, assuring me that the visions were nothing more than the prickings of a guilty conscience. 'If you're so worried,' he said, 'throw the cross into the sea and let it sink to a spot where it will trouble you no more.'

Perhaps this would have been the wisest course, but it was not the one I charted. Instead, night by night, I followed the phantom friars, John and blind Peter, trailing their way to what I knew must be their eventual destination.

Such was it proved to be. For not much more than three nights after I spoke to William, my dreams were filled with the sounds of hammers and masons' chisels. The sounds came before the sights, but the visions followed soon after. Those of William Taylor and his teams, digging and working on the abbey, knocking away at the ruin stone-by-stone.

After this, the terrors came to their climax. For I saw then, in the dream, William Taylor smiling, overseeing the destruction of an arch. Stood below, surrounded by his men, he pointed and spoke in wordless silence, instructing his fellow craftsmen.

Only, beyond his sight, flanking him, one on each side, I saw in my dream the two friars standing, pointing up at that same arch until the lintel crumbled and spiralled downwards in a storm of rock which buried my friend beneath.

The night I woke from this final vision, my heart was thundering in my chest, dread making every nerve tingle. I felt there was nothing to do but immediately dress and walk to Mr Taylor's residence before the sun had time to rise. This I did, knocking at his door until, in due course, he might be fetched to speak to me.

'Watts,' he said, 'you look as if you've seen a ghost.'

I explained to him, as best I might, begging and pleading him to stop the works on the abbey. Only William, being a jester, refused to hear the subject of my dreams as anything more than fantasy, laughing them off.

I know I tried as much as I could. More than many men might. Yet, all my imploring served only to anger William, who slammed his door in my face and instructed me never to darken it again.

With great regret, I travelled home, hearing the cock crow like Judas after Jesus' betrayal.

I returned to my bed, heartsick, and was only roused from it when a desperate rapping sounded on own door later that day. It was a workman attending to report that during the works at the abbey, a high arch had collapsed, crushing Mr Taylor under tonnes of ancient stone.

The men worked hard at digging him out and, in the meantime, I rode out to the scene on horseback. Few could believe him still alive after that ordeal, yet he was, clinging to life by a thread.

Alas, he had taken a part of a great timber beam to the head. The plank itself had splintered in such a manner that his skull was run clean through. His heart still beat in his chest, but he would not survive. So, I pulled the shaft away, in doing so sending the soul of my friend soaring to the hereafter. It was a grim sight, truly, for the wound affected his eyes in particular, leaving him gored in much the same manner as Peter, the blind friar.

So it has come to pass that William Taylor is scheduled to be buried.

Though the dreams have stopped, as have the works on the abbey, I can't but fear the visions will return. Thus, I have decided to have the pectoral cross buried with Mr Taylor, so he might have a fraction of the riches in the next life that he craved in this. Moreover, perhaps through that act, if not through this testimony, I might be freed from the Netley Abbey phantoms forever.

15

The Dragon of Mordiford

A Herefordshire Tale

There is an element of mystery to eggs, which is perhaps why they have always been powerful symbols of potential. The fearsome Dragon of Mordiford, hatched from an egg hidden among ordinary chicken eggs, had the potential to become many things.

Whenever I discover a story about a murderous beast, I always try and look at it from the beast's point of view. In the case of the Dragon of Mordiford, we have a dragon befriended by a lonely little girl. The pair are really the only ones who understand each other and, at the end of the story, nobody is exactly happy.

The legend dates from at least the sixteenth century. There was a picture of the dragon, green and with a very long tail, on the wall of the village church until it was removed in 1811 by a rector who thought it was heathenish. In the church there are also some 1670 verses which tell us the dragon was slain by 'Garston', which corresponds to the name of a local family who are mentioned in the parish records.

The dragon's legacy continued well into the nineteenth century. If Mordiford people saw newts near the River Lugg, they identified them as 'the seed of the dragon' and killed them, as they believed that if the newts were allowed to live, the dragon would appear again and devastate Mordiford.

And who knows? Perhaps they were right…

EC

The chickens pecked and fussed around Maud's ankles as she scattered grain for them, picking up the eggs as she went and putting them into her basket. Each morning, she gathered the eggs for her mother to take to market, along with the cheeses she made and the wool she spun. Everything they owned was for the same purpose – to be turned into money. Even so, the money Maud's mother brought home was only just enough to keep them, and if they hadn't been able to grow their own vegetables and eat their own eggs, they might have starved.

They lived on the outskirts of Mordiford village, in a little ramshackle cottage surrounded by a yard full of animals. Maud didn't go into the village much, and she had never managed to make friends with anybody. She and her mother had to work so hard that they didn't have much time for anything else. Maud's father had died in the war, so it was just the two of them, and the other village children didn't like Maud because she was small and quiet and strange.

She did love the animals, but she had learned the hard way not to get too attached to them. Most of them were destined for the same end - except the chickens, of course – but Maud's mother wouldn't allow her to take one into the house. Still, she talked to them and couldn't stop herself naming them all, even though she never knew which of their necks might be wrung to make a pot of stew.

As she bent to pick up an egg, something strange nestled half under the straw caught her eye. Maud pulled the straw away from it. It was an egg, undoubtedly, but it was the strangest egg she had ever seen. It was much larger than a hen's egg and rough to the touch, as though it were covered in tiny little chips of stone. But the strangest thing of all was that it was a bright, vivid green, like meadow grass in summer.

Maud put the egg into her apron pocket and waited until her mother was outside milking the goat before she went back into the cottage. She left the basket of hens' eggs on the table, ran into her little bedroom and put the strange green egg on the window sill, where the sun could shine on it. She didn't want her mother to see it, in case she tried to sell it at the market.

For a long while, the egg did nothing at all. Maud collected more eggs and cleaned the cottage and made dinner each day as she usually did, but each night when she went to bed she sat with the egg in her lap, stroking it and talking to it, telling it everything she had done that day and how the world around her looked. More than anything, she wished and wished for the egg to hatch.

One morning, when spring was in the air and the world was fresh and bright with blossom and birdsong, Maud woke to find that her dearest wish was coming true. There was a tiny crack in the shell of the egg, which spread and widened as she watched. Maud could hardly contain her excitement as the shell finally split apart and a tiny head poked out.

The creature hatching from the egg was no hen. It was not even a bird. Although it was as small and delicate as a sparrow chick, it had a long, scaly snout, and four tiny feet with glittering, dark claws, no bigger than poppy seeds. It had a tail which flicked and lashed like a newt's, and shimmering, translucent wings sprouted on its back. It was as green as the egg it had climbed out of and, oh, it was pretty.

'Hello,' said Maud, holding out her hand to the baby dragon. It nuzzled its snout into her palm. It was the most adorable thing she had ever seen. The dragon flicked out a tiny bright green tongue and started to lick Maud's fingers. She thought that it must be hungry, so she ran to the kitchen and brought back a small bowl of milk. She watched with delight as the little dragon licked up every last drop.

Maud had never known such happiness. She finally had a pet of her very own, to love and care for and bring up, and to tell all her thoughts and secrets. The dragon was happy too. After it had finished its meal, it climbed on to Maud's lap and would have sat there for hours if she hadn't had to leave it in her room to do her daily household tasks.

But as soon as her mother left for market, Maud went to see the dragon and talked to it and played with it and had a wonderful time. One night, she took the dragon into bed with her. It curled in the hollow between her shoulder and her neck and she stroked the tip of its nose until they both fell asleep.

Maud's happiness was short-lived. She was woken the next morning by a scream. 'Maud, get up! There's a terrible wyrm in your bed!'

Maud opened her sleepy eyes and saw her mother standing at the foot of her bed, pointing at the dragon and wearing a look of terror.

'It's not a terrible wyrm,' she said. 'It's just a baby, and it's very friendly. Look.' She lifted up the dragon and petted it, scratching it gently under its wings. The dragon made a sound like a cat purring.

'Monster!' Maud's mother screeched. 'Maud, people will think we're witches! You'd better drown it in the duckpond!'

'No!' Maud said, cradling the dragon tight against her chest. 'It just hatched from its egg. It's harmless, I promise. See, it's only small.' The dragon opened its glittering eyes wide and wrapped its tail around Maud's fingers. 'It needs me,' Maud said. 'Please can I keep it?'

'I'm not having it in this house,' her mother said. 'But if you won't take my advice and drown it, you'd better take it into the forest. I mean it, Maud! That beast means trouble, for sure, and I want no part of it.'

Maud was very unhappy about having to take the dragon into the forest when it was so young and couldn't look after itself. She felt responsible, as she had hatched it from its egg. She was all the mother the poor creature had, wasn't she? But her mother said that if Maud wouldn't put the dragon out to fend for itself, she would take it and drown it in the duckpond, so Maud finally agreed.

But she hunted in the forest until she found a cave which she thought would be perfect to hide the dragon in and protect it from wolves and foxes. The cave was dark, but it was warm, and Maud left a brimming bowl of fresh water from the river and a clutch of berries she had picked on the way. She wove the dragon a cosy nest from twigs and wool she had secretly taken from the spinning basket and promised to come back the next day.

Maud hurried through her chores as fast as she could, and by midday she was running through the forest towards the cave with some milk and cheese she had sneaked from the store cupboard.

The dragon was thrilled to see her. It frolicked and tumbled for her and ate crumbs of cheese from the palm of her hand. She stayed talking to the dragon for as long as she dared, and then she reluctantly turned her steps towards home. She felt sad at having to leave the dragon alone in the cave, but in her heart there was a warm kernel of happiness, because she knew that she had finally found a friend.

Things went on in this way for some time, with Maud creeping out to visit the dragon every day, bringing it fresh milk and any little treat she could manage. But strange things were starting to happen.

For a start, the dragon was growing. It was growing much faster than Maud herself, in fact. It was now the length of a dog, and its small, fluttering wings had become thick and powerful. If such things were possible, its green scales seemed to be becoming even brighter and more vivid.

One day, when the dragon was the size of a calf and Maud was very nearly a young woman, the dragon no longer wanted the milk and little bits of food Maud brought it. It paced the cave angrily, lashing its tail, which had developed vicious spikes.

'I know it's not much, but I don't know what more I can bring,' Maud said. 'My mother's frail now, you know that, and she's fussy with it, and she'll notice if I try to take any more food than I should.'

The dragon made a sound like the screech of a dying owl. It was very unpleasant.

'I don't know what to tell you,' said Maud. 'When I'm a woman grown and can make my own way, we'll live together and share everything, but we're not there yet.'

But the dragon roared, and Maud was almost frightened. Although it spoke no human language, she could understand its meaning well enough, after all this time, and the look in its eyes seemed to say that the time Maud spoke of was not coming soon enough and perhaps it would have to take matters into its own hands – or rather, claws. The dragon's claws, incidentally, were now very long, black as pitch and curved like the blade of a sickle. Maud left with her mind in a whirl and her heart in a muddle, wondering what on earth she ought to do.

She hadn't come up with an answer by the time she went back to the cave the next day, but the dragon who was waiting for her was a different dragon. Instead of the dull tinge which had spread over his glittering scales, it was glossy and green as a canopy of leaves. If possible, it seemed to have grown even bigger. It ate a few of the berries Maud had brought along, but it certainly didn't seem to be starving any more.

When Maud sat down with her mother that night over a pot of stew, her mother's eyes were wide and her tongue rich with news. 'The talk's all over the village,' she said. 'There's been a terrible attack. So many of Farmer Beech's sheep, all killed! Their bellies ripped out as though by some great beast, all the good meat scooped out like something was eating from a bowl. They're saying it must have been wolves, but it sounds to me like the work of the Devil.'

Maud turned pale and looked down, her spoon clattering into her untouched chicken stew. She clenched her fists in her lap, desperately hoping that her mother wouldn't remember all those years ago when she had hatched and helped the green dragon.

When she next went to visit the dragon, she asked it outright if it had killed Farmer Beech's sheep. The dragon, sitting on a pile of leaves and flowers it seemed to have gathered, looked extremely pleased with itself.

'You must be careful!' Maud said. 'If the people in the village were to see you, I don't know what might happen. Please don't go there again. Can't you fish in the river for salmon?'

The dragon snorted and spat a gobbet of acid-yellow saliva on to the floor of the cave, which sizzled where it landed, making it very clear what it thought of the idea of eating fish. All Maud could do was repeat her pleas to be careful and throw her arms around the dragon and hug it as she usually did, but she had a horrible feeling her wishes had fallen on deaf ears.

Her mother was waiting at the door to greet her when she got back to the cottage. 'Where have you been, Maud?' she said, looking around fearfully. 'Come inside! It's dangerous to be out. You might be killed where you stand and scooped out like a sheep!'

Maud's worst fear had come true. Her friend the dragon had been seen and things had gone from bad to worse in a very short space of time. Farmer Beech had caught it tearing into his prize bullock with its three rows of razor-sharp teeth, and when he had run towards it, shouting and waving his arms, the dragon had eaten him as well. There was no middle left to him at all, Maud's mother said, only legs and a head. Farmer Beech's son had seen it from the turnip field and heard the dragon let out a great satisfied belch as it flew away.

'So, you must stay indoors, Maud,' her mother said, 'and we'll bring the chickens and the goat inside, just for now.' She darted a quick glance out of the window, as though she feared that the dragon would swoop down at any moment.

Her mother didn't go to market the next day, so Maud had to wait until night fell to sneak out of the house to see the dragon. She wasn't frightened, because she knew the dragon would never harm her, but she knew that trying to convince her childhood friend not to kill people would not be an easy task.

It was worse than she feared. The dragon didn't listen, and it even turned its scaly back, now as wide as a river boat, and wouldn't let Maud give it the usual cuddle.

The situation in Mordiford grew worse and worse. Maud was distraught, for she had no idea how to stop the dragon going on murderous rampages, and while the dragon was happy to eat livestock, it was just as happy to gobble up any people who tried to get in its way. It was brazen, flying about in broad daylight and snacking on anything or anyone it fancied. Every time Maud saw the dragon she begged it to stop, but the dragon just snorted and tossed its head as if to say that a person has to eat.

The villagers of Mordiford were sick at heart, too. Every time they tried to trap or attack the dragon or chase it away from their animals, someone was killed. No human person seemed to be a match for the ever-growing green dragon, especially with only simple pitchforks and farm tools as weapons.

Eventually, some of the men travelled to the great house of the Garstone family, a few miles outside Mordiford, to tell the squire about the goings-on with the dragon. Unfortunately for them, the squire was a deeply practical person who didn't believe in dragons. He suggested that the villagers must have been standing too near mouldy crops, so they were imagining local wolves to have scales and wings and fly in the air, and told them to be on their way, build better fences, and perhaps take more water with their ale next time.

The squire was dismissive, but his son, Bartholomew Garstone, stood at the back of the great hall and listened to every last word. He had read romances in French and grown his hair long and curling, and the dearest wish of his heart was to perform a brave and courtly feat, perhaps to attract the notice of a benevolent king or the attention of a beautiful maiden, or both.

Although the villagers left Garstone Hall in deep disappointment, ideas flew round Bartholomew's head like bats in a church tower. It seemed to him as though the villagers were struggling to best the dragon due to their lack of weapons and equipment, although he thought it might also have something to do with their lack of intelligence, chivalry and curling hair. So he made his preparations, strapping on the best armour from his father's war chest and arming himself with a shield and lance. He saddled the finest destrier in the stables and decked it with heroic plumes, and then he rode forth from Garstone without telling his father where he was going.

Along the road to Mordiford, whose house should he reach first but that of Maud and her mother? As he rode up, Maud was in the yard, distractedly feeding the chickens and worrying about the dragon.

'Excuse me, fair maid,' said Bartholomew Garstone, flipping up the visor of his splendid helmet and bowing low over his horse's neck, 'I'm looking for a terrible beast that has desecrated the farmland hereabouts. Might you have seen such a foul creature?'

Maud went white and trembled all over, because she knew why he had come, and his lance was sharp and his armour tightly plated and she feared terribly what might come. Bartholomew mistook her fear for shyness and came closer, thinking that here would be an excellent chance to prove his bravery. For Maud, despite her loneliness and strangeness, and conversations with a bloodthirsty dragon, had grown up to be very pretty. She could only stammer a reply to him, but Bartholomew was in no way discouraged, and vowed to come back for Maud later, once he had slain the dragon and made his name as a hero.

As soon as his fine horse with its fancy nodding plume had vanished down the lane, Maud ran as fast as she could to the forest and picked her way through briar and bramble to the dragon's cave. As soon as she ducked into its dark entrance, she could see that it was empty, and there was a curious finality about the way it appeared, as though her friend had left forever.

Despite the burning in her lungs, she turned and ran back to the village of Mordiford as fast as she could. She could see her friend flying overhead before she got there, its powerful wings beating and carrying it towards the outlying farms. But galloping below the dragon, his destrier's hooves thundering on the hard earth, was Bartholomew Garstone, lance pointed and shield raised.

Maud called for the dragon to fly higher, to get back. The dragon heard Maud and swerved, then it opened its mouth and belched out a plume of flame intended to roast the young knight like a pig upon a spit.

The flames never hit the knight, for his huge shield protected him from the blast and his armoured glove prevented his hand from being burned as he held the shield. It seemed that the dragon had no more fire to breathe, and it swooped low over Bartholomew instead and opened its jaws wide, ready to bite through his middle. But his armour scraped and clicked against the dragon's teeth and the dragon made a moaning sound as it felt the pain of its very first toothache.

There was a worse pain to come, though, for while the dragon was howling at its damaged teeth, Bartholomew Garstone raised his lance and drove it hard into the dragon's soft underbelly.

Maud let out an agonised scream and ran to the body of her fallen friend.

'Never fear, dear lady!' Bartholomew said grandly. 'I have slain the terrible beast!'

'You've killed my only friend!' Maud said, and she pushed the young man so angrily that he stumbled into a cowpat and sat down hard on his behind.

Maud threw herself down next to the dragon and wrapped her arms around it. Her tears fell on to its scales, which were rapidly losing their bright green hue and dulling into a misty grey. Its great dark eyes blinked up at her and Maud saw that the dragon was weeping too.

Before the sun had closed its eye to dream, the dragon was dead. Maud was inconsolable. She soon left Mordiford behind, for there was nothing for her there any more.

As for Bartholomew Garstone, while the villagers were grateful to him for ridding them of the ravenous dragon, he had nothing but terrible luck for the rest of his days. He never met a king, and even the long, curling hair that he was so proud of fell out before his twenty-fifth birthday, leaving him as bald as his father, the squire.

The people of Mordiford painted the dragon in their church as a reminder of what had happened, and when the women went to the river to wash clothes, they killed every newt they saw, for fear one might grow into another dragon.

Maud found another home, where she lived alone for the rest of her days. She kept all sorts of animals – goats and geese and dogs and cats and, of course, plenty of chickens. Every day when she fed them, she kept her eyes open for another special egg that might hatch into a dragon, but she never did find one.

And there you have it.

16

The Blind Fiddler of Anstey

A Hertfordshire Tale

When a tale can be traced back to the beginning and the first version found, people call this the 'ur-narrative', meaning the original. And from what we can tell, 'The Blind Fiddler of Anstey' is one of those.

Acknowledging that the violin has long had associations with the Devil, as cultivated by Faustian virtuosos like Niccolò Paganini, this story is special. It is different to most Devil tales. Not least because Old Nick seems to win – and not against a foe who deserves it either, such as in the Devon legend, 'The Parson and the Clerk'.

Anstey is also a very old village, mentioned in the Domesday Book. The tunnel in the now-derelict castle was real and the Blind Fiddler Pub in the village truly was a coaching house called the Chequers at least as far back as the eighteenth century.

The story requires a blind person to be the one playing the fiddle, as the tunnel in which he meets the Devil is pitch dark. Versions of the story now recur in plenty of places, and urban explorers love to seek out 'Devil's Tunnels'. This is testament to the power of Blind George's intrepid journey, even if, with no gravestone, details of exactly who he was have been lost. All we know for sure is that he was a very brave fellow, if rather unwise. And the echoes of his subterranean journey, like the music he played as he went, have resounded across the world ever since.

MV

Come on over, old friend. Take a seat. Yeah, bring your pint, come on. Blimey, you look like you've seen a ghost.

Not seen one so much as heard one, eh? Oh yeah. Yeah, yeah. Well, that'll be Blind George, won't it?

What do you mean, you've never heard of Blind George? Mate, listen, you've been living here for what, ten years? And this is the first time – I mean really, learn the culture, mate. I've seen you banging nuggets in the fruit machine, you've been wasting your time! And if you'd asked, I'd've said, 'Mate, never, ever, ever walk through Northey Woods at night.' You should know, don't do it. Yeah, I know it's a short-cut from your place, I get it, but it's a bad idea, and I'll tell you why.

See, it's an old story, this one, but a good one, so kick back.

Now, this starts in the days of Bad King John, when there was a full-on castle here in Anstey. You know where it was, right next to the church – there's that huge mound of earth, ringed by that pond. Yeah, mate, that's a moat. Wasn't always full of ducks.

Still, there's nothing left of what it once was, save that mound, that duck pond and bits of the church. If you look in St George's, and I know you don't go to church, blah, blah, but if you go in, there's a coat of arms above the doorway. Big shield. And then there's the old-old parts, like the font with the four mermaids – nobody knows how old that is – but the shield, the nave, all that – the stone, you can see it's all different, and that's because it came from the castle.

Now, the bloke who owned it was Nicholas de Anstey. The whole village, all this, was de Anstey lands – maybe not a surprise the place is called Anstey.

What do you mean, '*How'd I know all this?*' Mate, I've lived here all my life. Plus, I like to read. You know, books. Remember them? From before you got into Candy Crush and became another *Love Island*, *Strictly Come Dancing*, *Britain's Got Talent*, *Gogglebox*-solo act? Yeah, yeah. Look mate, don't get argy – I've been in your house. There's no books anywhere. What do you mean, Jamie Oliver? Jamie Oliver isn't a book. That's a cookbook, mate, it's not the same. You're hilarious. Now, what was I saying? Oh yeah, Nicholas de Anstey's castle!

Right, so, Nicholas de Anstey. He was a rich lord and a knight – a Norman. No, not like Norman, the window cleaner. Like a French knight from Normandy. You're hopeless, mate. Just try and follow me.

Nicholas de Anstey was a knight in the 1200s. And like a lot of knights, he wanted a son to carry on his family line – only de Anstey didn't have a son. He had a daughter called Dionysia. Yeah, I know it's a weird name. It's old, named after the ancient god of wine and fertility and insanity. And the insanity part is important because the de Ansteys, mate, they went mental. All of them, to a man – fine as kids, fine as they grew up, but the older they got the stranger they became. And de Anstey had a sister, nobody knows her name, but he kept her locked up in that castle because of family shame and all that.

Anyway, Nicholas' father dug a tunnel out from the castle all the way over the fields, under Northey Woods, right the way to a spot called Cave Gate. You got it, Cave Gate Lodge, that massive mansion up on Biggin Hill. Yeah, well that's where it came out, this tunnel. It went all the way from Anstey Castle, right under the woods, under the fields, right by the new houses they built, then out at Cave Gate. And everybody knew that back in the day, Nicholas' father, Herbert de Anstey, he dug the tunnel to sneak stuff in and out, and also to take his daughter out secretly, so she could run about the woods and do whatever and nobody would see.

So, Nicholas, when his dad dies, all of a sudden it's his job to take his sister out. And down they go, walking through that tunnel – and it's a long tunnel, that walk isn't short. Still, he does it, year after year, and people in the village, they start to know about it because this sister, everyone says she's a witch – that she gathers mushrooms and herbs and whatever, and does black magic in Anstey Castle.

Of course, it's no secret Nicholas has his daughter, Dionysia. And Dionysia, sure enough, learns about witchcraft from her auntie. She uses that tunnel to go out in the woods, and soon enough she's meeting a boy in the woods – a local boy, a common boy – and when Nicholas finds out about it he hits the flippin' roof. And he's a knight, so he does a trick, he kidnaps that boy, drags him back through the tunnel, and that boy just disappears. Poof! Gone, like a puff of smoke.

Now, that only makes the rumours worse, and people from the village find the entrance to the tunnel, smash their way in and sneak into the castle. Yeah mate, I did say, it's a good story. It's the good ones that last, isn't it? Anyway, so the villagers break in, flaming torches, pitchforks – they're a mob, mate. And Nicholas de Anstey has guards, there's a scrap, people die – check the graveyard, there's stones there from people who died in this fight. But not everybody dies, and what the people find in that castle is all sorts of freaky stuff. Altars to the Dark Lord, sacrifices, magic cauldrons – it's all in there, and some of them manage to get away and tell everyone about it.

Afterwards, Nicholas de Anstey is known by everyone to have done a deal with the Devil. His sister, his daughter, his wife – they're all witches, and everyone knows it. Sure, de Anstey marries Dionysia off to some lord in Kent, but things are never the same. People in the village, they're all planning what to do – burn the castle, maybe. Do something when His Lordship is out riding. Either way, de Anstey disappears one day, off to fight the Barons' Wars, and next thing you know, the king himself, Henry III, has ordered Anstey Castle taken down. Brick by brick, they do it, and those cursed stones from that castle are used to build the new end on old St George's Church.

Well yeah, mate, that is exactly the question. What about the tunnel? Well, ever after, the people in Anstey village know that tunnel as the Devil's Hole. And they called it that because the old de Ansteys had their deal with Old Scratch, see, and people believed for years and years that anyone who went through the Devil's Hole would meet the Devil himself down there, or one of the old witches, or one of their ghosts, or whatever. Point was, it was cursed, and for years and years nobody would ever go down into the Cave Gate and walk the Devil's Hole.

Only – yeah, of course someone did. Yeah, that's the point of the story. Yeah, mate, do you want me to tell it, or? All right then, well let me tell it then. Oh – all right Sandra… how's the kids? Yeah, all good, all good. Nah, I'm all right, still drinking this one.

So, where was I? Oh yeah, so hundreds of years go by – literally hundreds. And then, some time in the 1800s, this pub that we're sat in, back then it's called the Chequers, right. And it's called the Chequers 'cause it's also the old bank. This is where people came to keep their money and travellers stabled horses, it was the full deal. And like a lot of places, Anstey had an old church band. Local people, some singers, someone scraping the cello, someone tooting the hautboy, so on – with the best of the bunch in Anstey at the time being Blind George, the fiddle player.

Now, Blind George was blind from birth, right. Lived all his life that way, never married, but had a big old dog called Trumpeter. And people said the Devil had done a deal with old George back in a past life, where he'd sold his sight to be born with a gift for music. This isn't the first time people did things like that. Italian bloke, Paganini, he done it: sold his soul for skill with the violin. Another one, Tartini, he was the same. And people said, back in the day, the fiddle was the Devil's instrument – Old Nick's favourite, see. They also said that if a fiddler was really good, he could make any woman fall in love with him, capturing her soul through music.

Blind George, he wasn't like that. He was a good old boy, went to church, said his prayers, went everywhere with old Trumpeter, who was his best friend. But even George, from time to time, came close. He'd play here, at the Chequers, in this room, and he'd work those strings with his fingers and tap his toes, and the people would go crazy. Literally, they would lose their minds. And 'cause he couldn't see, he didn't know. He'd just play and play and, sooner or later, hours would have gone by.

It was said he'd come to, always because Trumpeter would bark and bark to make him stop. But when Blind George stopped playing, and everyone who'd been dancing and jigging stopped wheeling about, they'd wake up as if from a daze with no memory of the hours from when Blind George started playing 'til when he stopped.

No, yeah, I realise, that isn't what happens when you listen to Bananarama. Or Culture Club. Still, mate, ask about. People never forgot about Blind George. That's why this pub is called the Blind Fiddler – it's named after him. But not because he was so good at music. Nah. Blind George is remembered because he's the very last person who ventured down into the Devil's Hole.

This all came about because people said to him, 'George, you're devilish good with your fiddle. Maybe Old Scratch himself would like to hear your music.' And it was a joke. But, like a lot of jokes, it went on and on and on and on. Year after year, people said, 'George, go down into the Devil's Hole, walk the tunnel. If anyone'll be safe down there, it'll be you. And the Devil won't take ya, he'll just dance to your music, and before you know it you'll come out the other end.'

Eventually, they did a deal with him. Made an agreement. Said, 'If you walk that tunnel, we'll all chip in and keep you in pie and ale for the rest of your days.'

Now, Blind George liked the sound of that, as did Trumpeter, who was partial to a bit of steak and ale, as any dog is known to be. And people knew the route to walk, as every winter, when it snowed, you could see the outline of the tunnel through the woods and across the fields. That's because when the snow fell, it always melted along the line of the Devil's Hole, on account, people said, of the patches of hellfire burning down below.

No mate, you don't have to believe me, you can literally look with your own eyes. Next time it snows, go and have a look. You can walk all the way along it across the surface. But Blind George, he didn't just walk along on top. He went under.

The whole village thought it was all fun and games. They all went out to the Cave Gate like a mob, dancing to Blind George's fiddle. They walked and they hopped, and everyone was merry. And when they got to the Cave Gate they cleared the opening, which years back had been blocked with stones, and Trumpeter barked and barked.

People brought shovels, see, with the plan being George would play his fiddle all the way down the tunnel, and above ground people would follow the music, knowing where he was. Trouble would come at the other end, as the way up into the castle mound was lost years back. But as soon as they heard Blind George's fiddle down in the earth there, they'd dig the entrance out again, pull him up, and that would be that – pie and ale guaranteed for life.

Everybody laughed when Blind George went into the Devil's Hole. And they laughed as he played his violin, jigging and reeling about on the earth above ground. The rest of the church band came too, and they sang and played to the tune he fiddled. And the first verse they sang, it went:

The Devil swapped my eyes for song in 1756
To free me from the chains of life, though I'm doomed into his pits
I'm bound to feel his tongs one day, but 'til I meet my doom
I am a blind old fiddler, who's never far from home.

And on they danced and jigged, the ladies dancing, lifting their skirts, swirling them about. And the gentlemen hopped and skipped, and those who'd brought shovels clanged them in time, along with the second verse:

I've been to the cunning woman who lives along the lane
She looked to raise my curse from me, but nothing could I gain
She told me that I'd never see, and it's no use to mourn
I am a blind old fiddler, who's never far from home.

They crossed the fields, the banks of the River Quin twinkling as the sun went down. And Blind George played and played, and they heard Trumpeter down in the earth, barking and barking, joining in with the third verse of the song:

I have no wife or little ones to fuss and bother me
I'm spared from all those troubles, whatever they may be
My footstep's ever careful, while I'm compelled to roam
I am a blind old fiddler, who's never far from home.

Next, they moved into Northey Woods, and that's where it happened. Of course, above ground all was merry and on they sang, but as they did, only a couple of them heard it – the wild screech of Blind George as his bow scraped across his violin. Nah, they kept singing:

So while my fingers dance along these narrow cat gut strings
Let's pour a drink and never think of dark or evil things
Come jig and dance unto my song, you'll never hear me moan
I am a blind old fiddler, who's never far from home.

But when that verse was finished, the rest of them realised Blind George had stopped playing. And they heard Trumpeter's bark, not below their feet, but racing back along the tunnel down the way they'd come.

And the villagers, well, they didn't dig down, oh no. They ran, sprinted, back through the trees, back across the fields, back to the Cave Gate.

Once there, they found Trumpeter all right. Poor animal. His tail was gone and his fur all burned away, skin all singed. Some said the dog's eyes were burned away. Whatever the case, the sad old creature ran off into the dark of the night, howling, almost like the Lords of Hell were behind him.

They found the dog dead the next day, drowned in the river. And the villagers waited for Blind George to come out, but he never did. So, the priest came and blessed the tunnel, and they put the stones back, then went so far as to brick it up to stop others going down or whatever was down there coming up.

But as you felt, walking here – if you go out to Northey Woods around nightfall and you wander about over that tunnel, it's said you'll know if his ghost is down there. You'll feel it, on your skin. In your heart. In your guts.

And from time to time, just like you did, you'll hear Blind George down there, playing his fiddle, scratching out the Devil's tune.

And that's that. Now, I've told you a lovely story, and I must say my throat is feeling mighty dry.

Pffft. Pfft.

Yep, see, I desperately need something to wet my whistle.

How about it then, chum? Go on, up to the bar. I reckon it's your round.

17

The Lantern Men

A Huntingdonshire Tale

Being out alone at night does something to the imagination. In darkness, every breath of wind and rustle of leaves is heightened. Perhaps it isn't the darkness we should fear, but the tantalising promise of a light.

The folklore of the Fens of historic Huntingdonshire describes the lantern men. They are believed to be evil spirits who tempt their victims to their deaths in the reed beds with the light of their lamps. I wanted to bring ideas from the folk tale 'The Buried Moon' together with local beliefs about the lantern men. I have also woven in the true story of a horrendous murder which took place in the Fens in the nineteenth century. This happened, more or less, exactly as it appears in the story, except on the road to Royston and not in the marshes.

Thomas Weems really was executed, and his dead body experimented upon. Doctors attempted to reanimate him using electricity, likely inspired by Mary Shelley's Frankenstein, *which was published the year before. An anthropodermic book bound in a square of Weems' skin can even be found in the Christopher Wren Library today! Meanwhile, the grave of Mary Ann Weems can be visited in Godmanchester, although its rather forbidding epitaph blames her for her fate.*

EC

Have you ever walked across the Fens at night?

If it weren't so dark, you'd see for miles and miles, for the land is as flat as a disappointed lover. It was made flat, you see, so you could never hide. Someone will always see what you are doing.

You are never alone in the Fens. For we are here. You might have seen our dancing lights, hovering above the black, stagnant water. Their reflections make them seem near, then far away. The darkness and the stench of the marsh gas will so disorientate you that you won't know whether the lights are before or behind you, until it's too late.

Some call us boggart, some Will o' the Wisp, some simply the lantern men. There are other things here too – the nightshades, the slithering, dark eels, the dead hands which thrust from the water and grab, grab, grab – but we are the oldest.

We've been here since this twisted mess of a world was made and then discarded, and we've had a powerful hunger ever since. We all have different methods, but I like the old way, the simple way – use my lantern to guide the lonely traveller into a treacherous patch until they stick fast in the mud, and it pulls them down, down, down, drowning them slowly, the black foulness of swamp mud forcing its way into their nose and throat.

And then I consume them, savouring every last delicious moment of horror and regret.

We do not haunt the Fens – we *are* the Fens. We are the damp, rich scent of the place, the mists escaping the meres. Night after night, I seek flesh and bone through the reeds and sedge. We are the darkest of the darkness, except for the warm, almost comforting glow of our bright lanterns. You would never see one of us, even if you came close enough.

We caught the moon once, and we would have kept her too, if we hadn't been tricked. How we laughed when we trapped her in a mere and plunged her down under the water, slapping wet mud over her bright, shiny hair. I danced myself on the heavy stone we used to weigh her down. But she got away from us, and now she shines as bright as she can over these Fens to take her revenge on us and keep wanderers safe.

Our prey are always trying to trick us. They know no other defence, so they seek to outwit us with cunning. They have their little ways, things they do, thinking to protect themselves from us.

Whistling is one. If two are travelling together, they split apart a little way, leaving a wide enough gap between them that it seems as though they aren't together at all. Then one will whistle, drawing the lantern men in his direction, but just as our bobbing lights get close, the other whistles, drawing us away and back to him, and so on, until they've reached safe ground.

Of course, we're wise to this now. Our lanterns have shutters – and we can split up, too.

Even more pathetic is the way they clutch their little safe-keep bags, which are supposed to scare us away. Packed with sad relics – eel slime and bits of dismembered wood creature – what is that supposed to do, other than add a little sauce to the dish?

And they think that lying face down on the ground, mouth in the mud to stifle any noise, will see us off too. If I come across someone lying in the mud, I don't go in the opposite direction. I close in and enjoy the splendid meal laid out before me.

Oh yes, we know all the tricks.

Aside from the moon, there's only one man who ever got away from me. The lying down trick did work for him, for he kept so silent that I passed by without either seeing or hearing him. I didn't have an inkling there was anyone there but me until I'd gone some distance past him.

Well, he scampered back to his farm, and I wasn't quick enough to catch him. His farm was at the edge of the marshes, and I saw there was a horn tied to a pole outside. Was that supposed to scare away me or the birds? Either way, it was ridiculous, and I burned it to scorched black scraps with my light so he would see it and know to stay off the marsh. I won't be deprived of my dinner twice.

Usually, it's very easy. Like the one I've just eaten. He thought to bring a dog to protect him, as if a dog would do anything against a phantom of the marshes. Stupid creatures. Tasty, though, if you don't mind the hair sticking in your teeth. Of course, it raced away from him, and of course, he whistled for it to come back.

He whistled; I answered. Man and dog I took pleasure in drowning, and man and dog I ate in wet gobbets and sucked the marrow of their bones. Another missing person, lost to the marshes – lost to the misty delirium of this place.

I please myself, you see, toying with life as I like. Humanity doesn't like to play with its food, but we lantern men are bound by no such rules. Food tastes all the sweeter once it's muddled and mixed up and turned all around.

Sometimes, once in a while, when that cursed moon is sleeping and the sky is as dark as our ground mists, I'll choose to let one go. But only sometimes, if my hunger is already sated.

And sometimes, what happens next is sweeter.

I'll tell you a tale of one, if you'll follow my light just a little way…

It was a night much like this one. The moon was playing coy, just a sliver of her peeping out from behind a cloud. Show yourself again, I urged her, come down here and show yourself in all your shininess, and I'll have you this time, and I'll bury you where nobody will ever find you.

I heard them before I saw them, footsteps sloshing thick in the marsh mud. A young couple, exchanging words. His voice was brusque and rough, and he answered her questions abruptly as if he would cut off her speech. Hers was hopeful, piping, chattering to him about all manner of things. When they hove into my view, she was clinging to his arm, worried about the dark. He was a huge brute of a man and she a tiny little fairy with an ugly face.

She was twittering to him about starting a new life together somewhere, and he told her that they would. I could hear the lie in his voice – smell it in his sweat. It's something I like about humans. They trick each other the way they like to trick the lantern men, and so his lying words caught my interest.

I like my food to have a little spice, after all.

So I delayed flicking open the dark panel of my lantern, though my long, shrivelled fingers were itching for it. My hand doesn't look like yours, because I live in the dank marsh water. We're always wet, and our skin wrinkles and bloats like the flesh of the drowned.

She told him she was scared of the dark and he told her he would look after her, and something in the way he said it let me know he did not mean it. And so I waited, for I wanted to see how it would play out.

He suggested they sit down and rest, and he gave her some bread from his pack – good, soft, white bread which shone palely against the dark night. She took it gratefully and seated herself carefully on the verge despite the darkness, as though they were having a lovely picnic.

He stayed standing, and when her mouth was stuffed full of that fluffy white bread and she wasn't twittering any more, he grunted out, 'Now I will be the death of you!'

Oh, it was sweet to watch, as he choked her with his fingers and thumbs. And when he was finished and she lay still, he untied her garter from her leg and tied it tight around her neck just to be sure. The half-chewed bread spilled from her blue-tinged lips and her eyes started out as though somebody had pinched her.

Now, I was enjoying this so very much and thinking how good they both would taste, so full and rich in fear and sin and murder, when I heard a little sound in the reeds, not far from me: a tiny noise like a gasp. And I had almost missed it.

A girl – yellow hair, bright and sweet – must have been making her way across the marshes, too. She had a little light of her own, which was as foolish as anything. As soon as one of my kin saw that, she'd be doomed. She was just the sort I like to eat – but I paused for a moment.

She was crouching down, hiding, and looking at the man dragging the body of his girl into the reed beds. And I thought – there's more trouble to be had here than I can cause.

You see, we like trouble, we lantern men. We like chaos. We like the swirling of thunderclouds and the ringing of alarm bells and the screams and swoons and the fearful pointing fingers of accusation and the slammed windows, and we'll cause it any way we can, even at our own expense.

I could see that she would go and inform on him. I could smell the goodness in her, shining brighter than the weak light of her little lantern. Sure enough, when the murderer had dumped his girl's body and made his way off through the marsh, she gave herself a shake and said a prayer.

I stuck my fingers into the sticky grey wax in my ears when she did that, for I hate the words of prayers and the sounds of hymns more than I hate the moon.

And then she said to herself, out loud, right there in the marshes with no regard for who might be listening, 'Susannah Bird, you do the right thing now by that poor girl.'

And I knew she meant to get that man caught.

It was with great regret I let her go, for a girl like that with yellow hair, great handfuls of it like that damned moon, is just the kind I like to drag into my pool and devour. But sometimes there's more fun to be had when you leave things be, and I haven't got to the age I have without learning that a long existence craves variety.

I was not disappointed, when I made my way along the waterways that night, following the scent of the yellow-haired girl, to find out the result of my selfless act.

All the way to the waters of Granta I went, through the roaming ground of the night shuck and to Cambridge, where his trial was being heard. I wasn't in the court, of course, but I heard enough of the gossip from lurking under the town's many bridges, and from my kin who cluster there, flocking like carrion birds to death and tragedy.

His name was Thomas Weems, my murderer, and the girl he'd strangled was his wife, Mary Ann. The naughty boy had a second wife he liked better, who didn't have an ugly face, and he wanted to get rid of the first.

And she'd tricked him, too – she was no angel, make no mistake – making a play for him when she'd been just a girl, then telling him her womb was swollen with a baby when it wasn't.

Humans are so delicious.

Susannah Bird, all glowing with the light of righteousness, testified about what she'd seen in the marshes that night. I could have done, too, of course. But nobody asked me.

It all came out in the trial and the questioning, and Thomas Weems was sentenced to death.

And oh, the things they did to him. It was beyond even my imagining. Acid and electricity and steel plates, a thousand jolts and volts. What a flavour his corpse would have, if I could get my hands on it now! What's left of it, of course, for it was dismembered in a public gallery for anyone who cared to watch.

I heard from listening under a bridge that a piece of his skin was kept and stretched out to cover a book, which was tucked into one of their grand libraries. Someone in that university must have a lantern man's sense of humour.

My only regret in the whole affair was that I let Susannah Bird go. But if I had not, nothing would have played out quite so wonderfully and I would have soon forgotten her. As it is, I can't get her out of my wrinkled, curious mind.

Perhaps she'll come back across the marshes, one day. After all, with Weems dead, she'll think the danger past and that only human men are lurking in the darkness to squeeze their hands around her throat.

But I can wait.

When the time comes, I'll beam my light out so bright, so enticing, she'll be drawn towards it like a summer bug to a flame. And then, in her last moments, she will fear the Lantern Man.

18

The Queen of Bones

A Kent Tale

Leeds Castle in Kent was the prison of two women who were accused of witchcraft and necromancy – Joanna of Navarre and Eleanor of Gloucester. Although I have chosen to explore the superstitions about Joanna of Navarre, it was Eleanor with whom black dog sightings at the castle have become associated.

It's difficult to disentangle Henry V from his folk hero status in England, helped along by Shakespeare's rousing lines, so I found it interesting to explore his more vindictive streak. Accusing Joanna seems a clear case of political manoeuvring to get a troublesome woman out of the way, manipulating widespread fears of dark magic and the Devil.

Almost anything can be a sign of witchcraft – being too old, being too young; having no children or having too many; having lots of moles, having none; laughing too much or not at all. In Joanna's case, there were some very inconvenient things which worked against her. The legacy of Charles the Bad, her supposedly monstrous father, is close to an ogre fairy tale, and his daughter was tarred with the same brush. And it was also very easy for Henry to play on xenophobic superstitions to convince others of Joanna's treachery and witchcraft.

As for Leeds Castle, it was listed in the Domesday Survey as Esledes and is often called 'the Castle of Queens, and the Queen of Castles'. Set on two islands in a lake, it has been the home, or prison, of seven English queens.

EC

Many moons ago, when Blessed Julian of Norwich was old and I was young, a queen came to Leeds Castle – a queen who could talk to spirits and raise the dead. She was French, of course, which Roger the steward said went just to show, and what more did you need really, and it was only a surprise she hadn't been found out before now.

It was a lot of horse manure, said the cobbler who came to the castle to mend our shoes. It was money, that was all. Money is the only magic of our age. King Henry wants money for his wars and the Dowager Queen has got it.

There were those who agreed with him and those who did not, but I was green as grass back then, and my ears pricked up like a spaniel's at the slightest hint of a juicy tale or a slice of gossip. I won't say I've changed my coat too much where the gossip is concerned, so if you can stand me a cup of ale one winter's night I'll tell you a thing or two. But the tall tales, I've learned to take with a sprinkling of salt.

The rumours travelled between us like spreading fire as we went about our daily work in the castle, and everybody was stopping to chatter much more than usual, leaning on brooms and letting pots boil over. His Majesty King Henry had arrested the Dowager Queen for treasonous necromancy. She'd plotted and schemed for his death and destruction. Objects had been found in her private chambers, said Mary, idling over the cheese curds. Bottles of potions from the Witch of Eye and strange charts reading messages in the stars.

She could raise up corpses from their graves, Alys told me as we were washing the floor, and charm both fiends and fairies to do her bidding.

When I went out to collect herbs, John the gardener told me that she was as crooked as they came, and that she accepted bribes and was greedy and stingy, hoarding all the money for herself. Even her late husband King Henry IV had been kept on an allowance.

And when we gathered around the kitchen hearth in the evenings, Roger the steward told us about her wicked father, Charles the Bad.

When you're young and impressionable, you don't need much more than a name to form your opinions, and 'Charles the Bad' was fairly conclusive. He'd been a murderer many times over, preferring to hang his victims upside down in chains and slowly behead them. He'd been in league with the Devil, so whenever the people of France caught him and tried to lock him away, he changed himself into air and slipped away undetected.

But the wager he'd made with the Devil for power and influence took its toll on Charles the Bad. In return, the Devil was slowly eating away at his limbs, decaying them one at a time. The ends of his fingers were black and rotten and every time he spoke a stink came forth from his foul and broken teeth.

Terrified of death, Charles the Bad sought the help of all the doctors in the land, but none had an answer for him, until one day the Devil came to him in disguise as a doctor and advised him to have himself sewn up into a bedsheet soaked with the finest brandy, to preserve his flesh. Well, Charles lay down and they wrapped him up in yards of the best linen and doused him with gallons of expensive liquor.

But then the Devil changed himself into a seamstress and appeared to help stitch him into the sheet, and when nobody was watching, the Devil tipped a candle over and there was Charles the Bad, gone to Hell in a blaze of fire with no chance to pray. We can only assume, said Roger the steward, that the Devil had a fine old time feasting on his soul drowned in all that delicious brandy.

Somebody else piped up that they'd heard Charles the Bad had been a necromancer, too, and a poisoner, and all sorts of other things. The Dowager Queen was just the same. Like father, like daughter.

Well, by the time she actually arrived, we were all good and terrified and nobody wanted to be the one to serve her alone in her chambers, so we drew straws for it. Margery got the short straw, and I thanked all the blessed saints it wasn't me.

The Queen was tiny and pretty with a round face and a high forehead. In hindsight, she probably didn't look quite as we'd imagined a necromancer might look, but at the time we saw all sorts of foreboding in the thundering hooves of her tall black horse, the noiseless sweep of her gown and the glow of her eyes. I remember how white her hands were, slipping out of her jewelled gloves.

It was a strange sort of imprisonment for treasonable necromancy, we had to admit to ourselves. Queen Joan had plenty of luxury and an allowance. She came with her own clerk, Thomas Lilburne, who we tried in vain to get to gossip with us, but he was as tight-lipped as a priest. She had her own household of nineteen grooms and seven pages – which was great news for all of us maids, I can tell you, and so can the man who's now my husband, who arrived with her that day.

The extravagances kept arriving while she was settling into the castle. Chests of fine clothes of silk and linen, and more bolts of cloth and metres of grey squirrel fur to trim capes. Three dozen pairs of shoes. Golden girdles and silver buckles, medicines and a personal physician from Portugal to prescribe them.

Our eyes widened as we saw the parade of things carried in. Books, more than we had ever seen. A gilded harp and a popinjay in a birdcage, which shrieked loud enough to wake the dead. Rosewater, cinnamon and aqua vitae. A pot of green ginger, lying on its own bed of straw like a wealthy invalid.

All this bustle meant that we almost forgot the dark rumours about her, but that was when strange things started to happen around the castle – or so it seemed. I doubt my memory now, but it was real enough to me then.

There were noises in silent rooms, you see, and sudden blasts of cold air when you walked down a passage alone. Once I thought somebody pushed me hard in the small of my back, but when I turned around there was nobody there. We heard footsteps, heavy and determined, crossing the gallery above our heads, but when John and Roger ran up there with the fire irons and shouted to whoever it was to stop in the name of the king, the room was empty.

People started to hear the scrabbling claws of a dog skittering on the flagstones after dark, and soon after, we started to see it. It was a monstrous black hound, long in the back, with a collar of gold and rubies the same red as its flashing eyes. I never saw it myself but plenty of people did.

Sightings of the beast were terrible luck, because Nell from the still room saw it and she got an awful toothache right after it, so we knew it must be something sent from the realms of the Devil. After that, we all looked away or closed our eyes tight whenever we heard the dog's paws or its hungry, panting breaths.

The worst of all was when I woke up in a cold sweat after a dream of buried skeletons forcing their way up through the orchard soil, one earth-encrusted finger bone at a time, and limping and rattling slowly but surely towards the castle. When I looked down from the window, I could see the Queen in their midst, her white hands raised and the dead bones ready to do her bidding.

Now, I was lucky for a good long while and never had to go into her chamber alone, but one evening I certainly drew the short straw and there was no going back from it. I had to go in there, and as the others said, my turn was long past due.

I was shaking and my back was clammy with sweat as I knocked softly on the door and went in. Night had just fallen, one of those autumn nights which comes down all of a sudden. The chamber was dark, lit only by a few candles.

The first I saw of the Queen was the reflection of her face, white in the glass of the window and floating like a haunted moon. The waves in the glass made her eyes look black and bottomless. She was sitting, staring out, and she was surrounded by silver and gold and things in bottles. Though they might have been cosmetics, they looked unearthly to me, like the concoctions of a witch.

I fumbled my way to the fireplace and started to build up the fire, not liking to turn my back on her but not having any other choice. She was behind me in a trice, and I swear to this day I never heard her move. Her skirt had made no sound, for there were thick rugs on the floor, and her stillness and poise stays with me now, because it was so unnatural. I was used to people with constantly busy hands, fidgeting, working, scratching themselves. The Queen was like a statue over a tomb.

I am not ashamed to say that I dropped one of the logs loudly on the hearth.

'I know what they're saying about me,' she said. Her voice was low, with a slight French accent. 'But it's all nonsense, you know. There's no need to be afraid.'

I thought there was every need to be afraid, what with the demonic hound giving people toothache and the invisible people walking about the castle and the dreams of clanking bones.

'If I could raise spirits,' the Queen continued, 'the only one I'd raise up would be my husband, for I miss him sorely, and my heart yearns to see him again.'

Well, I finished making up the fire and I got out of there swiftly, but I thought about what she'd said and I started to feel a bit sorry for her after that. I certainly wasn't so quick to listen when the others prattled about the black dog having given them a pimple or a swollen stomach.

In fact, I started thinking that the Queen was probably alright, and I never minded going in to serve her after that – until one night.

I was bringing her a jug of Rhenish wine, which was her favourite. As I approached her chamber door I could hear voices within, and as I got closer, I could especially hear her voice. But the door was so thick that I couldn't actually make out what she was saying.

Now, the door didn't fit very well in its frame and there was a gap underneath it, and I was as little able to control my curiosity back then as I am now. So, I bent down and had a look under the door. I couldn't see much, only that there were two shadows on the floor, which was a bit disappointing, so I straightened up and squinted through the keyhole instead.

I could see the Queen, and by the heavy curtain there was the very dark, shadowy shape of a tall, gaunt man with strange, old-fashioned hair. Then I heard a scratching and a skittering, like a dog's claws, but no dog did I see – only a dark massy shape near the man's feet.

Well, she never got her wine that night. I had it myself, sitting on the stairs, to calm my shaking hands and shattered nerves.

Eventually, the King pardoned her and released her from Leeds Castle, and things went back to normal. I wasn't at the castle much longer myself, and one of Queen Joan's nineteen grooms certainly didn't follow her to her next residence, for he's even now sitting by the fire with his feet up, snoring. But my niece who works at the castle now says that they still hear the dog around sometimes, so it must have lingered.

The years have passed and Queen Joan's spirit lies quiet now. They built her a fine tomb in Canterbury Cathedral. I had a shock when I went to see it, for there, lying next to her, was the late King Henry

– King Henry IV that was – but it was the man from her chamber that night, with the funny hair and everything. And there at their feet, sleeping with them, was a dog.

I felt a bit dizzy, so I stepped away for a moment, but when I looked back, there was an expression on the face of the effigy of Queen Joan which I was sure hadn't been there before. She was smiling.

19

The Cockerham Devil

A Lancashire Tale

Fondly remembered through a truly toe-tapping folk song, this iconic Lancashire tale has it all: a clever and kind-hearted schoolmaster, three tricky riddles, and the Devil acting like an absolute swine before being outwitted.

The solution the schoolmaster eventually comes to, deceiving the Dark One through asking him to make a rope out of sand, has a long heritage. In Scotland, it occurs in the 'Legend of Donald Duival'. In Ireland, it features in the story of 'The Devil's Mill'. In Cornwall, it is a torture exacted by the Devil upon local villain Jan Tregeagle. Across the sea in Scandinavia, it occurs in Black Book stories, and English playwright Ben Jonson even featured it in his 1616 play, The Devil is an Ass.

The earliest version we could find linking the story to Cockerham was published in the nineteenth century and, as Lancashire legends go, it has a huge amount to recommend it. Not least Cockerham itself, which, despite being a small village today, has a fascinating history.

Once a Roman settlement with shrines to local gods, it later boasted the rather grand Cockersand Abbey, now almost entirely ruined. Medieval records show it was once a wealthy manor which traded in peat fuel, sheep, cattle, shoreline mussels, and salt – a resource which used to be big business back in the day. Plus, it is a place so beautiful that, like much of the county, it is quite understandable why the Devil would want to claim it as his own.

MV

As many know all too well, the Devil is fond of Lancashire. Quite why is a mystery, for as long as stories have been told the people of the county have been playing the Devil at his own games – and the Devil, angered by their wit and cunning, has earned a reputation for kicking huge hunks of stone in frustration.

We know this because the Devil's footprint leaves its mark, and you can see these shapes on stones and boulders all across Lancashire today. For example, up on Pendle Hill, near the haunted house at Stainscomb, up on the moors where the Devil used to meet his witches, there are piles of stones bearing the shape of Old Nick's cloven hooves – people say they came about when he danced jigs at having claimed the witches' souls.

Then there's the case of the builders on Scribner Hill, who found a stone nobody could shift. No matter how hard they strained and heaved, there was no moving it. That was, until one of the men said he'd sell his soul to the Devil if he'd only move that rock. Lo and behold, the Devil appeared, lay on his back, cackled once, and kicked the stone, which went flying off into a nearby field.

No one knows what happened to the builder or his soul, but if you look at the wall of North Manchester Meeting House, you can see that very stone used in part of what was once the old cemetery wall.

My favourite Devil's mark, though, is on Broadfleet Bridge in Pilling. And that one came about because the Devil was hopping mad, all from the doings of a wily old schoolmaster called Hallowes.

See, on the coastal plains of west Lancashire, a little way south of where the River Lune meets the sea, there's a pretty old village where, so it's said, no one ever wanted for much. The lake in Moss Wood seemed blessed somehow and was always rich with fish. The forest was likewise filled with game and was a fine place for mushroom picking. Best of all, for a time, the village was famous for salt. To this day, you can follow the winding river out to the sea, but where the land ends and the waves begin is not as it once was. The salt strands that were there are all inland now, though once, by wetting the rocks on the strands with sea water, the people of Cockerham would pike out the saltness, the water sliding off into a pit of sod while only the flavour remained.

This sweet, briny taste brought gold to Cockerham. Not much, mind you, but enough. Few merchants ever stayed there for long, hurrying to do their trading and moving on, keeping their coin purses closely guarded. Not that the people of Cockerham were dishonest – far from it. Rather, the word was that the fairies liked Cockerham, and in summertime they would buzz round the salt strands like clouds of shimmering flies, eager for a lick of the salt.

Perhaps this is why, when you meet folk from Cockerham, you can note a sort of twinkle in their eyes and a different kind of spring in their step. People say that this is because maybe, just maybe, somewhere back along the line, a great-great-grandmother or a great-great-grandfather did a trade with the fey to bring their kin such good luck. Or maybe, as unlikely as it seems, on one Midsummer Eve, one of them fell in love with a fairy and the babe born afterwards was blessed with a share of their magic.

Nowadays, it's still said that fairies will swing by Cockerham from time to time, just to see how the folk there are doing. And part of why they do, even now, what with the salt being gone, is that the fairies know the story of the place – the echo of the legend lingering like a pinch of salt on the tongue.

You see, what with Cockerham being such a fine village, with all a person could want or need on any given day, the people there were happy. Not haughtily so, mind you, but they were a jolly lot, living lives without much care. And perhaps it was because of this, or perhaps it was down to the monks at nearby Cockersand Abbey, whose bells and prayers chafed in his ears, but either way, one day, long ago, the Devil came to Cockerham and looked to make it his permanent home.

The people of the village didn't realise at first, because the changes were subtle. The children all spied peculiar things, like birds flying backwards and flowers hiding their petals, growing down into the earth. Children being children, they reported this on, telling their mothers and fathers about it, but parents being parents, they took no heed, busy as they were with splitting wood for fires, planting crops in the rich earth, or piking salt to give their lives more flavour.

At the schoolhouse, though, Ambrose Hallowes the schoolmaster, well – he listened to the children prattling. Hallowes was just one of those fellows with a spring in his step and a twinkle in his eye. He never knew love, save a love of books, and liked to play pranks on Mr Schofield, the rector at St Michael's Church. Hallowes took a healthy penny from each household for every child he taught, and he'd heard plenty of gossip from children over the years but knew firstly not to take it too seriously, and secondly, not to pass the chatter on, for that was a sure way of losing pupils.

After school each day, Ambrose Hallowes would walk around the village, saying hello to this person and that, checking the place was as it should be. For, as we all know, village life relies on people like Mr Hallowes – the first ones to start a snowball fight, the voice at the back of the pub who calls out for a wager, or the person who suggests that a fair might be nice to mark this occasion or that from time to time.

And one evening, just a few days after the prattle of children had reached his ears, Mr Hallowes came across Mary Briarcliffe on one of his walks, with Mary all in a mess and a muddle.

'What's occurring now Mary?' Ambrose asked.

And through the blubbing of tears and the catching of breath, Mary told Mr Hallowes of a very strange thing indeed. 'It's my Bessie,' she said. 'I was milking her, see, not thinking of much while I did, and there I was, with my bucket and my cow, sat on my milking stool, squeezing her duds, when you'll never guess what happened, Mr Hallowes, not in a month of Sundays.'

'What was it then, Mary?' Ambrose said. 'Don't leave me on tenterhooks.'

'Well,' said Mary, 'I'd never believe it if I didn't see it with my own eyes, but the milk, you see. Instead of yellow-white and creamy as it ought to be, Bessie's milk… it came out black.'

'Black, Mary?'

'Oh yes. Black as pitch, and sticky too, like tar that's stuck to my fingers.'

Then Mary held up her hand, which she'd been clutching and hiding in her pinafore. And would you believe, no word of a lie, her skin was stained black as night.

Just then, the wind blew, but instead of a sweet-smelling summer breeze, Hallowes caught something else on the edge of his nose. Unmistakable, he thought, even though it was just a slight whiff. That, he said to himself, is the smell of brimstone.

Making his apologies to Mary, off Hallowes strode, making a beeline for St Michael's Rectory. Once there, he knocked three times on Mr Schofield's door.

Young Mr Schofield, who hadn't long been out of short trousers, opened his door and grimaced. 'What is it this time, Mr Hallowes?' he asked, with an edge of hard-earned scepticism.

This is because, out of a healthy liking for mischief, Hallowes had made a fool of Schofield once or twice. This came about because once Schofield had been one of Mr Hallowes' pupils, only being such a bright lad Schofield had gone off to university, becoming a man of letters. Yet, instead of going off to do great and good things, Mr Schofield had come back to his old parish, which Mr Hallowes thought was a waste.

One April First, for one reason or another, Mr Schofield had made a fuss over people eating no meat. He called it 'April Fish Day'. And so, Mr Hallowes had ensured there'd be fish everywhere Schofield looked. In his larder, his writing desk, even the nave of the church.

Another time, not long after Schofield had come to the village, Hallowes had all the schoolchildren pretend that Cockerham was being harassed by a magical goat, visible only to young eyes. The children would point at empty space and holler whenever Schofield was near, making play of watching the creature bound off over a gate or boundary wall. When something was lost, broken, or one too many sweet buns went missing, the children would blame it on the magical goat. So, before long Schofield was walking about the village with his wooden cross, uttering holy rites in an attempt to rid Cockerham of the mischiefs of the invisible goat. Trouble was, none of the adults in the village had ever heard of such a thing, making Schofield look daft as a brush.

That night, though, Hallowes was serious when he made his report of Mary and her cow's black milk and of the children's stories of the birds flying backwards, flowers hiding their colours, and the smell of brimstone on the breeze.

'I'm afraid it's the Devil,' Hallowes said. 'And I think this is more your area of expertise than mine.'

'Pah!' Schofield replied. 'The Devil in Cockerham? Pull the other one, Mr Hallowes. And good evening to you.'

With that, Schofield slammed the door in Hallowes' face.

Though he wasn't quite so brash and confident in a few days' time, when all across the village things were going wrong. The River Cocker, for example, started to flow upstream. The chickens at the Townley farm laid only eggs that were already rotten and, worst of all, when the girls of Cockerham played the Lovers' Game, their apples were bitter and had no pips inside.

To explain, the Lovers' Game was famous in those parts. The idea was that a maid would eat an apple and then, when they got to the core, they would sing a song and tip out the pips as a way of telling their fortunes. The rhyme, which remains famous, is as follows:

Pippin, pippin, paradise,
Tell me where my true love lies;
East, west, north, or south,
Pilling Moss or Cockermouth.

What with Pilling Moss being just a short walk away, it was said the Lovers' Game was as good a means as any for finding a handsome swain with whom to whisper sweet nothings. But, what with the apples gone vicious and with no pips inside, people started to fear there would be no new love in Cockerham from then on.

With all these strange goings-on and the air becoming increasingly unbreathable on account of the brimstone smoke and smells, Mr Schofield was minded to take Mr Hallowes a little more seriously. But no matter the prayers he said or the songs he had the congregation sing, in Cockerham, things only went from bad to worse.

The skies grew cold, dark clouds gathered, and people started to spot the Devil peering round fenceposts and street corners. They'd give chase, following the thickening stink of sulphur, but all they'd find was a trail of salt – for the Devil had taken to gobbling up all the crystals out on the salt strands in the greedy sort of way Devils are famous for.

Yet, by night, they would hear the Devil walking the streets, whistling a happy tune, his cloven hooves clattering and sparking on the ground. They'd see evidence of his passing – grassy verges singed by the whippings of his forked tail and nasty messages detailing changes he would like to see, scrawled on pieces of parchment and left pinned to things. No more smiling, for example, and absolutely no laughing. No attending church, no reading or telling stories, and only sweet foods and strong, boozy drinks to be consumed by anyone.

Some people quite liked all this, but not Mr Hallowes. And that's when the old schoolmaster struck upon a novel idea. He asked Mr Schofield for his help, but Mr Schofield was cowering in fear, hiding in the church and muttering scriptures over and over. So, late one night, after quite a lot of thinking, just like with the Yuletide Feast, the Mayday Dance and the Spring Festival, Ambrose Hallowes rolled up his sleeves and took matters into his own hands.

He started, in as sure a way as any, summoning the creature up by saying the Lord's Prayer backwards.

No sooner had he uttered the words than poof! In a cloud of black and stinking smoke, the Devil appeared – right there in Mr Hallowes' kitchen.

'Well, well,' said the Devil. 'Mr Hallowes. It's nice to finally make your acquaintance. Although, as I look around, I see vegetables on your kitchen counters. There are well-thumbed books everywhere. And, what's this? A calendar to remember peoples' birthdays. I feel, Mr Hallowes, that you are a good person. Yet, all good hearts have scope for corruption. And here you are, summoning me. Your soul smells deliciously pure. I wonder, what might I offer you in exchange for it?'

'I've called you here for a wager,' said Mr Hallowes, 'as I understand you like that sort of thing.'

'Oh yes,' the Devil purred. 'I do love to gamble. So, tell me, what did you have in mind?'

And this is when Mr Hallowes laid out his terms.

'You like Cockerham,' he said, 'as do I. It's near enough heaven on earth to me, yet we both want to make it our home. So, I challenge you to three tasks. If you best me in all three, you can have my soul and Cockerham too, but if I win just once, you'll leave our village and promise to never return.'

'Done,' said the Devil, without really thinking, confident in all that he was.

'Right then, first challenge,' Mr Hallowes said nervously, looking out of his window at the sun starting to rise. 'The long hedgerow at the bottom of Milner's Hollow. By morning, I want you to tell me how many dewdrops are on it.'

The Devil cackled, clicking his fingers again and transporting himself and Mr Hallowes to the very spot. And although the hedgerow had been covered with dew, the very act of them appearing and the Devil beating his wings saw all of them fall save thirteen.

The Devil counted them up rather sarcastically, then announced the result to Mr Hallowes. 'There are thirteen dewdrops on this hedgerow, Mr Hallowes. It's almost as if you want me to have your soul.'

Annoyed, Mr Hallowes huffed for a moment, then thought of the largest field he knew. 'The corn field off Crimbles Lane – take us there,' he said.

And with a click of his claws, the Devil vanished himself and Mr Hallowes, depositing them on the ground not far from the Cocker's banks.

'Since you're so good at counting, manage this. Tell me, how many heads of corn are there in this field.'

'Are you sure?' asked the Devil.

'Aye, I am,' Hallowes replied.

The Devil snorted with laughter, sparks shooting from his nostrils, and he raised his hand, closed his eyes, and in but a few seconds announced the result. 'Six million, six hundred and sixty-six thousand, six-hundred and sixty-six.'

Mr Hallowes, angered, squinted at the Devil out of one flashing eye. 'You're a cheat,' he said. 'There's not. You've made that number up.'

'Oh really,' said the Devil. 'In which case, why don't you count them? I'll wait.'

Mr Hallowes, by now feeling rightly outsmarted, thought of one last gambit. 'Fine then. To the salt strands. Let's go.'

With a click, woosh, and smouldery puff, the pair arrived on the salt flats, looking out at the churning waves. Confident in himself this time, and swearing he saw fairy faces hiding in the undergrowth nearby and watching on, Ambrose Hallowes made his stand.

'Weave me a rope,' he said, the Devil sniggering, 'using nothing more than the sand on this beach.'

'Oh, very well,' said the Devil, sighing in a manner which made it clear he was bored. And so, without much effort, the creature tucked his wings in neatly, sat down cross-legged on the beach, and set to work.

It didn't take long, and just at the moment you might have said the sun was really up, which made the Devil squint, the creature raised his creation aloft. A length of rope woven from the sand of the beach.

'All done,' said the Devil, handing Hallowes the rope and standing up and brushing himself down. 'Now both your soul and Cockerham Village are mine.'

'Not so fast,' said Mr Hallowes, weighing the rope in his hands. And then, feeling more than a little proud of himself, the old schoolmaster walked down to the water's edge. Once there, he knelt, washing the rope in the salty brine. As he did, it fell to pieces and washed away through his fingers.

'You're a cheat,' said the Devil, angrily.

'Oh really?' replied Ambrose Hallowes. 'In which case, why don't you tie me up with the rope you just made me. I'll wait.'

And with that, the Devil screamed and stamped and flapped his leathery wings, spitting at Mr Hallowes and leaping angrily into the sky. Where he landed at Pilling Moss, before taking flight again, is where you'll find the mark on Broadfleet Bridge. But suffice to say, the Devil never came back to Cockerham.

As for what happened to Mr Hallowes, nobody knows for sure. In all likelihood, he died as humbly as he lived, albeit with a salty vein of mischief and a little fairy sparkle lighting him up round the edges.

20

Black Annis

A Leicestershire Tale

An infamous English bogeyman-type creature, Black Annis has been studied at length by very clever people like Dr Ronald Hutton and the good people of the Folklore Society, with her heritage seeming to date back to the eighteenth century.

Said to live in a grotto called Black Annis' Bower Close in the Dane Hills, she was believed to appear, or at least to have appeared, as a blue-faced hag with iron claws and a taste for human flesh. Local people used to try and bait her out of her cave and hunt her with hounds (hunting with dogs being a famous Leicestershire pastime) each Easter Monday, and she has variously been associated with monstrous prowling cats, the consumption of naughty children, numerous ancient pagan goddesses, and a real-life historical figure, the late medieval anchoress, Agnes Scott.

Conflations between Black Annis, Leicestershire's local cave-dwelling monster, and the crone-form of the Celtic goddess Anu have only served to further enhance and muddle her mythology, which has also appeared in poetry, such as in the popular ballad of 1797 by John Heyrick, as well as in plays and other media. Either way, painting Black Annis as a villain is nothing new and follows in a long tradition of vilifying solitary women as baby-eating witches.

With all of this in mind, my ambition in this tale was to weave what we know of her together with what we know of human nature, and in doing so, offer Black Annis a little bit of redemption.

MV

Long ago, between the banks of the River Soar and Rothley Brook, Leicester Forest stood tall and dark and wild. The Earls of Leicester hunted there, staining the earth with the blood of beasts caught on their spears, and out of that unholy ground grew men of an unholy order.

For centuries, the monks of Leicester Abbey were known as Black Canons. They dressed as shadows, rearing barking hounds which fouled the flagstones of the house of God. If you wander the ruins of Leicester Abbey now, you will find, amongst the grass and rubble, the ghost of Cardinal Wolsey, who died there on route to his trial for treason.

That place was ever a den of corruption, and few wept when it was razed to the ground in the Dissolution. And fire liked that place, whether the fires of Hell or some other primal force. The blackened stones were used to build Cavendish House, but by 1645 that too had burned, licked by the lapping tongues of flame. This left little but a mess of jagged ruins, haunted by the spectres who freely wander the remains of Abbey Park.

Centuries before, however, Leicester Abbey had held a tortured soul whose soul was destined for a darker fate. A hostage of Richard of Gloucester, the hunchbacked, cripple king, who sallied forth in 1485 and left his own blood in the earth of Bosworth Field – although he perished there, hacked to death amid the clashing chaos of the fray, his corpse was ridden back to Leicester naked and slung into the choir of Greyfriars Church to be forgot.

Yet, Richard had known he was riding to his doom, having sought wisdom from the very soul whose name echoes in infamy: Black Annis, a seer he kept in his bitter retinue.

Though her legend now is monstrous, she was once a holy maid. Her name was Agnes Scott, and she was one of many hostages Richard kept to dampen the fury of his foes. A bastard daughter of Edward IV and his mistress-witch, Jane Shore, Agnes carried her mother's gifts within her blood. Unlike Jane, who had honed her talents out of books found in her lovers' libraries, Agnes had no such advantage.

While her mother had been known as 'The Rose of London', charming Thomas More, William Hastings, and Thomas Lynom, the King's Solicitor General, Agnes was more like her uncle – born with a twisted spine, the only hints of her royal lineage shone through her moon-white skin, pale and spiderwebbed with dark blue veins. Her eyes were red and wet with ever-flowing tears. From girlhood Richard coveted the wisdom she offered, hating her all the while for being so ugly, so malformed, and so much his own crooked shadow.

It was Agnes who told him, 'Where your spur should strike on the ride into battle, your head shall be broken on the return.' Her prophecy came true, even though no sooner had it slipped through her youthful lips than Richard struck her for it. He had her sent from there to the care of the abbot. But on the ride to Bosworth Field the king's spur struck the bridge stone of Leicester's Bow Bridge. The dark omen's second part was realised when his corpse was carried back from his great defeat, the dead king's mangled skull striking the same stone and breaking open, just as his niece had warned.

While Richard had died in infamy, Agnes was kept locked in a cell by the Black Canons. When Henry Tudor ascended to the throne, she was spirited away, and for years she lived as an anchoress, locked within a simple cell beneath St Martin's Church.

To keep off the rats, cats became her companions, with the poor of Leicester coming to hear her holy wisdom. They were screened from sight of her by a leather curtain, which was stretched and pinned across the hagioscope which bordered the street. Through this squint-slight window, she told passers-by of her dreams, offered help in times of trouble and advice in all matters. Through another slot she was fed, though only the simplest food, and through a third, she heard mass and could view St Martin's altar. In all weathers, all seasons, that place was her home; through sickness, health, hot summers and long winters.

From her cell, Agnes heard the construction of Wygston's House, listened to the talk of rolling sicknesses, and of changes in the nation's fate. But while bishops and abbots grew old and died, Agnes lived on and on, her feline friends keeping her warm, bringing her news of the outside, slipping through the holes in the walls through which she could only peer. Generations of cats throughout the city knew her name, and some said she learned to change shape, to become a cat herself, visiting the fishmongers at High Cross and stalking the Saturday Shambles in Market Square, hunting for bargains.

As the new century unfurled, the Guild of Corpus Christi was dissolved and St Martin's Church, which had stood since the times of Penda of Mercia, fell into disrepair. The bricks of her cell were removed to be sold and Agnes moved on, seeking ways to use her wisdom elsewhere.

For a time, she took up residence at the leper colony at Burton Lazars, hiding her own ageless, deformed shape in much the same manner as the ailing souls she served. Though wrapped in lengths of cloth and surrounded by the dying and the damned, she was feared and pitied, even in spite of her good works. And, alas, even the Order of St Lazarus was not exempt from the fires of the Dissolution, so Agnes journeyed back into Leicester Forest, finding there, in the blood-rich earth, a hollow in a cave at the top of Dane Hill to finally call her home.

By then, the woods about that place were thinned, felled to fuel the growth of Leicester and the villages nearby. In the places where lords had ridden in thundering bloodsport, calm had settled, with men rearing Longwool sheep and minding them in the meadows thereabouts. But as years rolled by, rumours grew of the woman who lived in the cave at the hill's top. She had taken to pinning sheets of leather over the hollows in the rocks, hiding herself from view. Some brave souls went to her grotto seeking wisdom and cures, but all about, perched in the trees, cats watched and stalked and hissed, guarding her from unwanted visitation.

In payment, so it was said, she accepted lambs, which she reared and slaughtered in strange rites. Others left her gifts of gold, though she never made to spend it. Some said she had a hoard of treasure, and greedy men from time to time would try to lure her out to steal it. To do so, they would catch a cat and kill it, dousing the beast's remains in aniseed, tying it with rope, and riding by her cave, dragging the creature's tiny corpse behind. Yet it never worked, though on moonlit nights many spoke of the blue-skinned hag who roamed Dane Hill, the sky filled with yowling, the trees marked by claw-like slashes from the creature none saw but all knew as Black Annis.

But one man did see her, and lived to tell of it. His name was Bailey Drover, and he hailed from Thorpe Astley, born of humble stock. His son, Fulke, was his helper, and together they led their flock from Enderby to Peckerton, on to Ratby and back down, ever fearful to avoid Dane Hill as all folks did. Alas, one day, while Bailey and his boy were leading their sheep from Glenfield down to Braunstowne, one fled, running deeper into the forest, and Fulke gave chase, headed off towards Black Annis' hollow.

Bailey well knew that his son had heard the tales and would never risk meddling with the witch woman of Dane Hill. Yet, as afternoon moved towards night, Fulke did not return, and Bailey determined he had little choice but to go off in search of his son.

He took his shepherd's crook with him, a dagger tucked in his belt and a flaming torch to light his way. And as he wandered Leicester Forest, he heard them in the trees: the cats spitting, mewling, skittering through the dark. They warned him off, telling him to stalk no further into that domain with such dark thoughts in his heart.

His jaw grimly set, Bailey pulled wool from his coat, twirling it to stuff into his ears. This blocked out the wailing of the beasts, whose eyes glinted in the dark, yet they watched him still, their tails twitching, considering whether to pounce. His breath rattled out as jets of steam floating aimless through the night air.

Where he walked twigs snapped, which to him seemed like the cracking of children's bones. And the wind roved through the trees, the branches shaking, blocking the stars above, though he heard nothing save his own pulse thundering in his ears.

In time, he saw through the trees the orange glow of a fire burning. He extinguished his torch and moved towards it, the shapes of cats moving to keep pace with his passing. In time he came to see by the fire a shape dressed in rags which trailed about the campfire. It was the witch, he knew, and atop the blaze was a cauldron bubbling. He watched as she tipped herbs from wooden bowls into the kettle, stirring them with a black iron ladle. The cave behind her was said to have been dug with the witch's own monstrous claws.

Crouching low, Bailey hid behind some briars, peering about for signs of his son. As he did, he smelled the stench of tanning, and noticed all through the trees, hung up in frames, leather drying – the skin, he feared, of Black Annis' victims. And though he could not hear her, he saw the shrouded figure's lips moving. It was an incantation, he knew, which sounded like a haunting lullaby; a song she was singing over a small, shadowy form.

His heart ran cold as Bailey saw that shape. It was Fulke, his boy, laid out on a pallet of sheep's wool and dry leaves. And beside Fulke was the lost sheep, tethered to a pole as if ready, like his son, to be slaughtered.

Gathering his nerves, Bailey drew his blade, standing and dashing out of his hiding place. As he ran, cats skittered and yowled, some tripping him, others darting across his path, all seeming as demons, black in the shadows cast by the fire. And Bailey raised his blade, dashing towards

Black Annis, seeking to bring the dagger down into the witch's black heart and end her nights of terror up in that savage place.

The shrouded woman turned as he ran towards her, raising her hands, screaming in broken-toothed terror. Bailey, roaring, saw her long, dirty, talon-like fingernails and the crone fell away, muttering, begging. Yet Bailey's ears were blocked, and he could not hear a word she said. Instead, he closed in on her, backing her against the wall by the entrance to her cave, seeing her look desperately from Fulke's pallet towards Bailey and back again.

Bailey saw her lips moving, and twisted his own, horrified by the red-eyed face he saw. And what he failed to hear was Agnes Scott's entreaties that he stop, be careful, for Fulke was awake.

This was because she had found the boy injured, fallen in a gully, and had brought him to her grotto for food and rest. She had helped the boy to find the lost sheep and secured it until morning, when it would be safer to make the return journey. And in those brief hours, looking with his innocent eyes, Fulke had seen Agnes as anything but a monster. A kind soul, patient, fearful, yet mild, he had laughed with her, prayed with her, and come to think of Black Annis as his friend.

It was the boy's instincts which impelled him to leap to his feet and dash forward; his good heart which saw him run between Black Annis and his father's blade. But all was doubly in vain, for as Bailey's dagger slashed through the dark, he did not hear his son's last words, nor did he slay his intended target. Instead, he plunged the blade deep into his own son's heart, killing him stone dead.

Appalled by his crimes, the shepherd staggered back, falling and knocking Agnes' cauldron. The boiling contents spilled over him, the bubbling stew scorching his eyes, blinding him forever more.

The rest of Agnes' night was spent in tending to Bailey Drover. She saved his life, though his face was scarred. The clods of wool within his ears were extracted and she sang to him, whispering calming words as he drifted in and out of consciousness. And all about them, the cats sang to the stars, mewling over the death of Fulke, who was buried not far off in earth all too accustomed to slaughter.

The following day, Agnes led the blind shepherd back down from Dane Hill, guiding his steps, but without his sight Bailey Drover could never again find his way back up to Black Annis' hollow. And though he told all who would listen that their rumours were not true, that the blue-faced hag they all called Black Annis was no monster or beast with a taste for human flesh, her dark legend only grew.

The hunts continued, the dead cats dragged past her bower. Songs were written in fear of her, windows were built smaller to stop her fitting through and hung with charms and bundles of herbs. Yet, all the cats of Leicestershire know her, and if you ask them, they will say so, attesting that to this day, Black Annis will run with them at midnight and feed them milk from wooden bowls and stroke them with her long-nailed fingers.

Alas, this is the way with ugly things. People make up stories far darker than the truth, for if they are not maligned then they are forgotten, no matter how good they may be of heart or how kind they are, in spite of all the cruelties of the world.

21

The Tiddy Mun of Ancholme Vale

A Lincolnshire Tale

First appearing in the Legends of the Cars, *a series of articles by writer, translator, and folklorist Marie Clothilde Balfour, a 'Tiddy Mun' was a kind of Fenland bog spirit particular to Lincolnshire. Known for making characteristically bird-like calls and standing no taller than a toddler, interest in the tiddy mun seems closely linked to campaigns to drain the marshy flats of Lincolnshire, Cambridgeshire, and East Anglia in general, as were undertaken by Dutch engineers from the seventeenth century onwards. The lore Balfour collected from local people detailed what the tiddy mun looked like, their magical powers, the dances they performed around marshland fires (likely, those phenomena known variously as* ignes fatui, *hinkypunks and Will o' the Wisp), the sacrifices local people made to placate them, and their anger at their habitat being destroyed.*

Diseases linked to stagnant and polluted water are many and varied – malaria, cholera, and typhoid, to name just a few. Before the advent of modern medicine, it is quite reasonable to associate so many English folk tales about evils emerging from wells and bogs with concerns about disease, including those of dragons, cockatrices, basilisks, and drowned-or-drowning revenants. That said, it feels too simple to justify the tiddy mun away as pure superstition, not least as the people of Ancholme Vale knew so much about them.

So, even if the Fenland drainage did perhaps make them extinct, it seems only right to remember them and that Fenland way of life that has all but vanished from Britain today.

MV

At the town of Glanford Brigg, where the mud is green and stinks of the sea, men have crossed the River Ancholme for as long as there were souls in England. It's said the first boats made there were stitched; oak tree boards darned together with needle and thread. For oak is a holy tree. When one grows a catkin beard like a wise old king, its flesh is supple enough to be sewn, boards tacked with Goat Willow thread, yet strong enough to keep out the wet. Not to mention the darker things that dwell below the waves, if ever they come a-knocking on the hull.

For the longest time at Glanford, and those droves around it, Kettleby as was, Scawby Brooks, Wrawby and Wressle, all were at the mercy of the waters. Floods came in upon doorsills, the marshes breathing in at winter, belly swoled like a maid with child, then out they flowed come Midsummer's Day, revealing earth richer than Croesus.

Until the Dutchmen came, through all those dark months, the bogs spilled over. The stink of the Fens rolled in on the wind and the cold salt kisses of the water wives were wet on the lips of all at Glanford and for miles about. So to get around, most went by on boats – oak boats and elder. Seeing kin and making trades, they stayed inland – though away from the ruins of Thornton Abbey, where the restless shade of Thomas de Grentham, fourteenth Abbot and wizard as he was, speaks silent words of his lost black arts to this day, though he's been dead many a hundred year.

Such folk as dwelt in Ancholme Vale were in times past known as Carrfolk, and to please the waters they kept to strange ways. For in the Fens, come winter, where mists rose up by night thick enough to clutch your tongue and lapwings peeped, the mud was yare enough to stand and reach to grasp a man and pull him under. Many knew it, and saw pale and creepy fingers in the mire, which were called 'dead hands', for that is what they were. To keep safe, all gave tithes to the boggarts who held the Fen waters at their command. Gifts to the dead hands of chickens' eggs and fish; bone things to the water wives; and to their husbands, those that some called Greencoaties and some called Yarthkins, all manner of delights.

Though the Carrfolk called them 'Strangers,' to most beyond Ancholme Vale those men of the marsh were known as tiddy mun, for they grew no taller than a three-year child, no higher than your knee. All had beards and great big hands and feet, and ugly heads rolling about on their shoulders. They walked limpelty-lobelty, mayhap as they was lame, looking like dearie-wee grandfathers with long, white hair and whiskers all cotted together and tangled.

Most times, the folk of Glanford kept well-in with the tiddy mun. For, if left alone, those Strangers harmed no one, and if people were good to them, they never forgot it and helped them back. Come summer, it was said they wore grass-green jackets and breeches, and yellow bonnets like toadstools atop their queer little faces, with long noses and wide mouths, their tongues hanging out and flapping about. They were mischievous and playful, folk said, and in the harvest fields they pulled the corn-ears about and tumbled in the stubble. They wrestled with poppy-heads, tweaked the flower buds, and chased butterflies, tugging worms out of the earth in jest.

In the spring, they fell to shaking and pinching the tree buds to make then come open, and if happy they helped the corn to ripen. The crickets played for them with a right good will, and they painted the pretty colours of the flowers, and made the reds and browns of the fruit come autumn. It was well known that if you'd only stand quite still out of doors then you'd see the tiddy things running and playing all around you. They were never heard to speak, but if made angry they grinned and yelped like dogs. But when gay, they'd come croodlesome, and twitter and cheep as soft as birds, laughing like pyewits, making the sound of 'Oie! Oie! Oie!'

Though that were only in the bright months, when they gave. In the cold times, they'd take, and they'd take and take and take away, for that was when their bills came due.

When the cold rains fell and Ancholme River ran quick out onwards to the sea, and the Fens grew fat and black and wet, by night the Strangers danced on the glebe underneath the moon. Gowned in grey for wintertime, they could scarce be seen through the thick mists, but came out from their water holes with the sound of running water and a sough of wind. And there were large, flat stones found here and there in the valley, where the waters never touched. The Stranger Stones, they were called. By day, people smeared those stones with blood and lit fires on them for the tiddy mun to dance about, for if they didn't, there were hell to pay.

People did all they could to keep in with them. Laid on those stones the first flowers of the garden, the first orchard fruit, first ears of harvest corn, a bit of bread and salt, a drop of milk or beer. And the givers went home quick once they'd set down their gifts, paddles racing through the gloom, for none would want to see the tiddy folk eating their victuals.

And when deepest dark came on, people walked about with lights in their hands and smeared the sills of windows and doors with blood to keep the horrors off. At Yule, priests would call such actions 'sin' and 'heathen', but the Carrfolk did their part – made cakes of grain to roast beside the hearth, then left them on the Stranger Stones, bobbing out upon their boats to keep the tiddy mun sweet.

When they was happy, you knew it, for they'd screech out like pyewits, 'Oie! Oie! Oie!' but when angered, oh, you knew that, too. Things withered, harvests failed, folk went missing or hungry. And the waters rose and rose, right up to doors, sometimes pouring in. The mists turned green, and from out of them came the tiddy mun to take what should have been gave.

Folk that did give had nowt to fear. But those who shirked, who kept food back in hoards – the Strangers knew and took their share with their tiny little hands.

One year, just such a thing occurred to Balfour, preacher of Kettleby, back in the reign of Charles I. A proud man, Balfour thought that to go without was good, so he deprived himself and his daughter Kate, who were larch-thin from when she were a girl. Balfour saw this all as sacrifice, but the tiddy mun thought him a miser. More's the shame, for a good sort was Kate. Pretty, and fond of Gilbert Tyrwhitt, son of Sir Ralph, lord of the manor there.

In the summer, young Gilbert came from Glanford upon his pony, and Kate would walk with him amongst the fields and orchards full of life. Balfour, who were priest, was in no place to offer up her hand to folk such as him. But still, she'd come home with flowers in her hair and a glow on her rose-apple cheeks.

Some said the money didn't matter, that Kate would wed Gilbert and become a fine lady, even though she were Carrfolk. But in those sunny times, the tiddy mun must have seen her out a-walking and taken a liking to Kate greater than Gilbert Tyrwhitt.

Back then, see, the Dutchies came. Sir Ralph had monies from the Crown to drain the Fens and make all Ancholme Vale good farming land. So, the Dutchmen dug out dykes and drained the Fens, and the Greencoaties – well, they hated that. They spat and raved and wanted more and more from people laid upon their stones. And though

Dutchmen disappeared, pulled beneath the mire, more were sent and the work carried on, with Balfour blessing the Dutchies and their work.

More though, Balfour... well, he never gave. He thought the Strangers outside God, not knowing the Bible and born of Cain. So, one winter, with the waters up, the bog spilled into Balfour's home, and the Strangers came and snatched young Kate, taking her away beneath the mud.

Once Kate were took, Balfour aged right quick. His hair turned white and eyes pale blue, outstaring like he saw a ghost. And Gilbert, course, without his Kate to walk with and canoodle by the fire, he came no more to Kettleby from Glanford on his pony, and the girl was never spoke of, save for when folk whispered she was taken by the Yarthkins and eaten in the mist.

In winter, no work was done by the Dutchies. They kept to their camps and spoke their foreign tongue, and if we speak in truth, the Carrfolk all despised them. Like oil and water, the Fen folk and the Dutch stayed well apart, and through the dark months, when the tiddy mun went hungry, all who knew their ways feared spring, while the Dutchies gave not a fig.

Years passed this way, and things got worse and worse. Cattle died, no crops would grow, and the green mists came, claiming old and young. But the king's gold was good, so the networks of dykes were dug, summer after summer. Though little did folk know that Kate, though took, was far from dead. Instead, she were beneath the earth, down deep below the still, green water, within the Strangers' caves.

To them, you see, Kate Balfour was much as like a jewel. Bright and shimmering, her white skin was as moonbeams, and she were a treasure to them. Not wicked and tantrummy like their water-wives – she was a giant to them, too. Tiddy as they were, they clambered up all on her, round her legs and in her hair, tying in it elflocks full of curses far too dangerous to lift.

They knew not their strength and hurt her with their graspings, their twistings and their pokes, but her voice was pleasing to them, so she would sing them lullabies to make them calm. And she washed their tiddy clothes ready for spring and cooked the things the Carrfolk left upon the rocks, lighting little fires in their caves and living with the Yarthkins down below.

Within the dark and wet, away Kate's clothes did rot. She was never seen by men, so felt no shame, dressed up in muck and slime such as it clung upon her. Moss grew on throughout her hair and tree roots curled about her here and there. In summer, she wished to go and walk about beneath the sun, to see Gilbert, and her father, too, before he died. Yet, the tiddy mun kept her hid, so her eyes came all but blind in the dark, and where the tiddy hands and fingers touched her and moved her this way or that as pleased them, she lost her ways to care. And she never laughed, even when the Strangers did, cheeping and twittering, 'Oie! Oie! Oie!'

As time went by, of course, Sir Ralph saw to it that Gilbert wed, marrying a maid from Goole. And the Dutchies dug and dug, so the land grew dry and hard, but the Dutchmen watched amazed as the Carrfolk went about the fields and offered water to the four corners, singing to the Yarthkins. 'Tiddy mun, without a name,' they sang, 'Here's water for thee, take the spell undone!' But it was of no matter. The tiddy mun were bold as brass.

Children withered and died, and food was scarce. Seeking help from God, the people stoned the wall-eyed witch from Gorby out of the market place and ducked Sally of Wadham in a pond until she nearly died. They said 'Our Father' backwards and spat to the east to keep the tod-lowries' pranks off, but it was no use.

This was as, you see, the Strangers would no longer give to them but only take. Their water-wives had drained away and their dead hands turned to bitter sod from which no life would spring. Beside this, the tiddy muns' powers were for nought good, or so it seemed. Until one day, a Dutchy captain called Egbert Baas did a cunning, cunning thing.

See, through all the years, Egbert saw to Balfour's wants. The priest came, ragged and half-starved, and blessed the men at work. So, the Dutchies fed him, meat and potatoes and fine, fine things, hot and rich and holy in their way. And the priest prayed on over the Dutchmen's work, so Egbert learned the old man's language. Enough, at least, to understand the sadness in his heart. So, he wished to help him, and when winter came once more, shivery like, with skirls of bitter wind and water, Egbert waited out one night, hidden by a Stranger Stone, a long, dark musket on his back, a fire burning beside a high pile of gist.

Afore long, out came a tiddy mun, gowned in grey. He was, the Dutchman saw, no bigger than a child of three, just like old Balfour said. He'd come up, darkling with the mist, creeping limpelty-lobelty, his long, white beard and hair glinting in the firelight. And Egbert watched as he gathered up the sausage meats and hams, dancing a leaping jig, laughing like a pyewit, 'Oie! Oie! Oie!'

Though right amazed, Egbert did not take his musket up and shoot the Stranger dead. Rather, he watched it moving off, back down into a water hole. And then he blew a whistle, called his men, and that's where his team of Dutchies started to dig.

It took them time, of course, for the Yarthkin caves ran deep. But on and on they worked, through sun up and across the day until, all of a sudden, there broke out the awfullest wailing and whimpering all about them. It was a sound like a lot of crying babies, sobbing as if their hearts would break. Like lost children, the tiddy mun reached up with little hands, cheeping with their cold lips, for the Dutchies had broken through into their deepest grotto.

And there they saw, covered in the tiddy beasts, a thing most of the Dutchmen thought was their mother. A strange fiend, they spied, not so unlike a pretty maid, clad in nought but mud and moss and roots. And as the winter sun fell on her, she wept, for the brightness caused her pain and she shrank from it in a terror.

Though the Dutchies sought to shoot her dead, Egbert Baas bade them not. Rather, he took out his sabre, shaking it and prodding 'til the tiddy mun left off. Then up he scooped the Yarthkin mother, who was no more than Kate Balfour, and he dressed her in his jacket and carried her to Kettleby, to the house wherein her father lived.

The commotion all about was great, for the Dutchmen lit fires then, burning down into the water holes and blasting out the Yarthkins with black powder. The Stranger Stones, too, they broke down, striking them with hammer and pick 'til nowt was left but gravel.

Wild as this day was, wilder still were the faces of the people who saw Kate Balfour as she was that day, come back from the dead or so it seemed, tangled up in mud and roots, brought home by Egbert to Balfour's cottage.

Alas for Kate, when her father saw her, his pale heart gave out. Old as he was, he fell flat upon his back and died, so she never did see him alive again. But Egbert watched as she made her way about the place where she had grown, crawling on hands and knees. She touched her father's form, then held and sniffed at all the items in the place, creeping into the corners of the cottage and weeping, for she had returned, ever-changed, to a half-forgotten land.

For days Egbert Baas stayed with her, sat near or just outside the door. And Kate washed herself clean in hot water he fetched her. But none of her old clothes fit, in spite of her father having kept them in a heavy trunk. So Egbert sent his men to Lincoln and bought her back linen and lace, thread and wool, and the folk of Kettleby gathered about in clumps, waiting and waiting until she reappeared.

This she did, dressed in a new gown of her own making. Her sight was never good again, but she told the Carrfolk of her time beneath the ground, living with the tiddy mun. And Egbert listened too, in spite of all the Fen-dwellers making it clear they sought him gone. Few gave her tale much credence, but word reached Gilbert Tyrwhitt, and he rode by from Kettleby Hall, bearing witness to Kate Balfour as she was then, years older and stranger than ever she had been.

It's said Gilbert wept on seeing her, for she was so beautiful, but not for him. As for Kate, whose heart was broken long ago, the sight of Gilbert was not of great import. He was a fatter man than the boy she'd loved as a girl, and balding, with bad teeth. Far more handsome was Egbert Baas, and when Gilbert rode away it was the Dutchman who stayed behind, keeping at a distance, asking her what more there was that he could do to please her.

With her father buried, and the people of Glanford Brigg, Kettleby, Scawby Brooks, and all about observing her with suspicion, like some strange being not of the earth, Kate thought at last of what she sought from Egbert Baas. This was, in time, to be his wife, and to travel with him far away to Holland, where life might begin for the pair of them anew.

Egbert had loved on first sight the fae maiden hatched from out the Fenland ground. So, he of course agreed, and come spring, with the dykes finished, the pair set sail, never to be heard of in Lincolnshire again.

As for Ancholme Vale, once the Siege of Hull was won, the Tyrwhitt line ended and Kettleby Hall was torn down. Time ran by just like the river there. The earth grew lush and fruitful, the people less inclined to go about in boats. Still, for many years, on each new moon, the Carrfolk went out to the nearest dyke-edge and teemed water in the foss, singing, 'Tiddy mun, without a name, here's water for thee.'

Who knows if this old prayer was answered. The land there's good to this day, so who's to know?

But on a misty night, it's still said you'll hear the tiddy muns' cries, and sometimes see a fire for them burning in the dark. Whether they dance about them as they once did though, well, you'll have to ask a braver soul than I.

22

Brutus of Troy and the Giant Gogmagog

A Middlesex Tale

When the Romans left Britain, some of the remnants of the buildings left behind were so sophisticated that civilisations who followed believed they must have been built by giants. Perhaps some of them were.

The legend of Brutus of Troy, founder of London, came about when a ninth-century monk called Nennius made a spelling mistake. Geoffrey of Monmouth, chronicler of the history of English rulers, expanded wonderfully on his error and the idea of the 'New Trojans' was established.

The Brutus story was taken up and regarded as fact well into the seventeenth century. It appears in Spenser's Faerie Queene, *Holinshed's* Chronicles, *William Blake's poetry, and that of Chaucer and Shakespeare. John Milton even almost wrote a* Brutiad *instead of* Paradise Lost, *with many British monarchs having claimed descent from this entirely fictional person.*

Sources for the tale of Albina, the founder of Albion, and her sisters are equally wide. She is also called 'The White Goddess', which is another story.

These days, Gogmagog the giant has been split into two brothers, Gog and Magog, whose effigies are still carried on floats in London's Lord Mayor's show. As for Leonard, he is a real demon, the grand master of nocturnal orgies, listed in the Dictionnaire Infernal.

I couldn't resist.

EC

These days, Britain is the best of islands, as everybody knows. Its rivers are abundant with fish, its forest glades grow flowers of every colour, its meadows are green with grass and its skies alive with birdsong.

But Britain was once wild and empty, lashed by rain from every side and bogged down with thick, muddy slurry. Nobody at all lived here, and even the birds gave its frowning black clouds a wide berth. It was not until Albina and her sisters came and dug their blood-stained hands into its claggy soil that Britain started to become the pleasant land we know today.

Let me tell you about Albina. She was the eldest of fifty sisters, and while that may seem like a lot to you now, let me tell you that it was far more common before the days of libraries and other such excellent distractions.

Now, these sisters were the daughters of the King of Syria, and they all had fine qualities and skills in all sorts of areas. Kings were very headstrong back then and were often in the habit of making decisions for other people without consulting their feelings. Nowadays, kings are much calmer sorts of beings and can usually be placated with a nice quiche.

But the King of Syria wasn't interested in quiche. He was interested in power and in making the right alliances. So, he determined to marry all fifty of his daughters off to influential people of his choosing, all on the same day, for he was strong-willed, determined, and also extremely good at planning.

While the palace was all in a bustle sewing seed pearls to fifty silk veils and trying to work out how to support the weight of a fifty-tier wedding cake, Albina and her sisters gathered in secret for a council.

'I don't think we can cancel the wedding,' said Justina reasonably. 'The invitations have been sent out and it would be a shame after all the hard work everybody has put into it.'

'But we've never even met these men,' said Tristina, bursting into tears. 'They might be horrible!'

The sisters discussed it for hours, and I'm not quite sure how they reached this conclusion, but they decided that the best course of action would be to go through with the wedding, marry the men, and then murder them all in bed on the wedding night. That way, everybody in the kingdom could still enjoy the party and they would all still be free.

Even their father couldn't complain, said Georgina, because they would inherit all the husbands' worldly goods anyway. It would be doing everybody a favour.

The wedding day came, and the bells were rung and the sisters curled their eyelashes and tied their garters and stuffed their faces with wedding cake and danced the night away, and then, in the early hours of the next morning, when their new husbands were snoring beside them, they each took out a jewelled hairpin and stabbed their hapless man through the heart.

Perhaps unsurprisingly, the move was less popular in Syria than the sisters had anticipated. The king wrung his hands and the courtiers protested and the people rioted in the streets. It was hard to save face after what had happened, so the poor king thought that the best thing to do was send Albina and the rest of his daughters off in a boat and forbid them to ever return to Syria. But he did keep all the dead husbands' worldly goods, after all, so in time, he recovered from the whole unfortunate episode.

You may be thinking that the sisters didn't stand much of a chance, having very little sea-faring experience, but they took to it well and were soon enough plotting their course by the stars and reading the winds and fishing for great swordfish and salting them in barrels. In some little while, they arrived on the shores of Britain, which they named Albion after their eldest sister, and travelled about until they found a nice place to settle. It was somewhere near the area we called Surrey today, for the sisters called it Little Syria, in honour of their home, and it's been abbreviated and mispronounced ever since.

Well, they really did wonders for getting everything going in Albion. They cut trees and built halls and homesteads. They captured the wild cattle and ponies and farmed them. They made their own laws and lived the way they chose. Some of the sisters went off to found their own settlements, but each traded with the other using money made from stones with holes in them. If you look into streams and shallows today, you may still see them, those coins of Albina and the first women.

But there started to be a slight feeling of loneliness and worry for the future, since all the women were sisters and nobody was getting any younger, and backs and knees were starting to go, and they were running out of options. So, Albina and the others gathered together for another council.

'We should take the boats and sail to another land,' said Sabrina, who was the chief boatbuilder and responsible for all Albion's bridges and dams.

'We could conquer France!' said Martina, hopefully. She was in charge of Albion's armies, training the sisters for battle, and she was always talking about conquering France. It may be that her spirit lived on in many later English kings.

Florentina thought that they should train the beasts of Albion to talk and work for them, and Valentina thought they should send out letters summoning men to the island. There were many more ideas too, and again, I'm not quite sure how they reached this conclusion, but they decided that the best course of action would be to gather in one of their great stone circles and summon up a demon.

This demon's name was Leonard, and he was very interested to hear about the sisters' little problem. You see, Leonard and his various friends and cousins had been rather lonely too.

The demons were not altogether the picture of chivalry. Some had wings and some had tails and some were mostly composed of knees, apart from the bits which mattered, but they were good for a laugh and eager to please, and that was all that was important really. They made many visits, popping into Albion through the stone circle, and to all reports, it was an arrangement which satisfied everybody.

Sooner rather than later, Albina and her sisters welcomed the pitter patter of small feet, which became larger and larger feet as the years went on. Sometimes, that's what happens when demons and people have fun together – they create descendants who are larger than life. That's right – the sisters' offspring were all giants!

But let's spin forward through time a little while, years after Albina first peered into the extra-long cradle of her enormous baby, and peer into the destiny of another baby – one who was born to be a hero.

The soothsayer frowned at the child's mother's belly, dangling a strange talisman over it.

'Well?' said the proud father-to-be anxiously. 'What'll it be?'

'A boy, certainly,' said the soothsayer, as the talisman span and danced on its chain. Well, everybody was very happy, and the soothsayer really should have left it there, but for some reason he carried on talking and went on to prophesy that the baby boy would be the death of both his parents, would wander through many lands and eventually become the father of a nation.

There is such a thing as too much information and it's fair to say that the soothsayer was not seen around any more.

The baby was born and they named him Brutus, but his mother did not live to see his first sunset, so that was one part of the prophecy fulfilled. His father kept a close eye on him for fifteen years, but one day, when he and Brutus were out hunting, Brutus mistakenly shot his father, believing him to be a stag.

After that, his relations thought it was high time Brutus started fulfilling the next part of the prophecy and wandering to many lands, preferably those as far as possible away from theirs, and they exiled him without further delay.

Brutus wandered for many moons, and he grew great in strength and nobility. He freed his Trojan ancestors from slavery under the unscrupulous Greeks and built himself an army. He solved land disputes, he enchanted princesses with his skilful swordsmanship, he rescued stranded kittens from trees.

One of the Trojans he had emancipated was named Corineus, and this man became Brutus' greatest friend. They had many escapades together, and their bond strengthened because neither truly had anywhere to call home.

One day, Brutus and Corineus were engaged in manly pursuits – shooting, hunting, braiding each other's hair – when they came upon a deserted city. The buildings were in ruins, all except for a temple to Diana. The friends had the inspiration to pray to the goddess, so they poured libations and called to her as the hope of all who ride in the wild woodlands to guide them to a safe haven they might call home.

The goddess appeared before them with her silver hunting bow bent bright like the moon's crescent, and she told them of an island surrounded by sea, now the home of bloodthirsty giants, where Brutus could make a second Troy and rule it as its king.

Well, Brutus and Corineus called to their forces and they set sail right away in search of the island Diana had promised. There were no compasses in Brutus' youth, so they managed to visit Africa, Aquitaine and Andorra before eventually sighting the green and misty shores of Albion, where they sailed straight up the River Dart and landed at Totnes. If you go to Totnes today, you can still see the stone touched by Brutus' toe as he jumped ashore.

All was going very well as Brutus, Corineus and their forces made their way north-east from Totnes, exploring the apparently empty land Diana had directed them towards. But Albion was not available to anybody who cared to claim it. It was inhabited by the giants, the descendants of Albina and her sisters and their demon lovers, and Brutus found this out one night when he had made camp and a monstrous giant came crashing through the tents, crushing soldiers under his size-nineteen boots and roaring with rage. Brutus and Corineus realised that they had a rather large problem on their hands.

The giants weren't too keen on the arrival of the Trojans, either. When the news of their landing was brought to the Council of Giants, there was a great uproar amongst them.

'They'll get into our stores and nibble all our cheeses!' said the giant Brackenbog, who imagined the Trojans to be something like mice.

'They'll knee-cap us with their nasty little clubs!' said the giant Froggenhog.

'Calm down,' said the King of the Giants, whose name was Gogmagog. He was the grandson of Albina herself, and he was particularly repulsive in appearance, being covered from head to foot in thick, grey-green hair.

These giants, rather like their grandmothers, were not known for the quality of their decision making, and they hadn't reached any kind of positive agreement before a challenge arrived in handwriting which seemed to the giants to be excessively and awkwardly small.

'Pass me my glasses,' said Gogmagog, and he proceeded to read out the challenge. Brutus of Troy called the giants to a wrestling match between their champion and his, with the winner declared king of the land, once and for all. Some of the giants were worried, thinking that it must be a trap, but Gogmagog scoffed at the thought of wrestling Brutus or one of his tiny friends. After all, how could he possibly lose?

The day set for the wrestling match arrived. The giants gathered, drumming tree branches on the ground and howling, and the Trojans gathered too. Brutus' old friend Corineus was their champion, for he was the best wrestler among them all. He was on the pitch early, limbering up, doing his stretches.

Gogmagog showed up fifteen minutes late with a horn of mead. 'What did I miss?' he said, scoffing at Corineus. This, he thought, would be an easy win.

Fifteen seconds later, the giant was lying in a puddle of spilt mead, as Corineus had easily toppled him with a blow to the back of his ankle.

Realising that this might not be as simple as he'd hoped, he roared in fury and surged into action. The contest began in earnest. The two champions rushed towards each other, grabbing each other in a tight hold.

Gogmagog used all his strength and broke three of Corineus' ribs and gave him a fair few bruises too. Brutus, watching the fight and fearing for his best friend's life, closed his eyes and said a prayer to Diana, asking her for her aid. In a voice like the silken whisper of an arrow flying past your ear, the goddess spoke to him, telling him not to be afraid.

She was as good as her word. There seemed suddenly to be a silver light about Corineus, which flashed in his eyes and outlined his muscular limbs. He heaved the giant Gogmagog up on to his shoulders and ran as fast as he could to the edge of the cliff nearby. There, he hurled the giant down on to the sharp reef of rocks below.

The seas below the cliff ran greenish grey with the giant king's blood as his body was dashed into a thousand pieces. That place is still called Gogmagog's Leap to this very day.

The giants were defeated, and that is how Brutus of Troy became king of the land once and for all. The land which had been Albion was renamed after him, and it is still called Britain to this day. Those Trojans who had travelled and fought alongside Brutus began calling themselves Britons, and even their language, which was a sort of crooked combination of Trojan and Greek, was now the British tongue.

As for his dear friend Corineus, Brutus rewarded him by giving him the southernmost tip of Britain to rule as his own, and from then on that place has been named Cornwall, after the hero who defeated the giant Gogmagog.

Brutus travelled the length and breadth of his new land searching for a suitable spot to make his capital. At last, he came to the banks of the River Thames, in the heart of Middlesex, and there the goddess Diana appeared to him and he knew that he had found the right place. He built his great city there, and called it New Troy, which name it was known by until the days of Lud – but that is another story.

And in time, the remaining giants, who were the descendants of Albina, and the friends of Brutus, who had been Trojans, all settled down with each other. Over time, the tallness has mostly been bred out of them, although every so often one comes along who grows over six foot five.

There's the music of my story; long may it last in peaceful harmony.

23

Black Shuck

A Norfolk Tale

Black Shuck. Old Shock. Snarleyow. The ghostly black dog of East Anglia has many names, and there are a huge number of accounts of the creature's appearance echoing through centuries of folklore.

Shuck's nature varies considerably. Sometimes an omen of death or an active bringer of destruction, the dog might also act as a protector to lone women walking home at night.

The starting point for my telling of the Black Shuck legend is the 1577 text, A Straunge and Terrible Wunder, *written by the Reverend Abraham Fleming. It's an account of Black Shuck's attack on St Mary's Church in Bungay and its murder of some of the congregants. There are great tempests of rain and lightning, and it's very dramatic and well worth a read.*

I was also interested in the black dog as an allegory for depression, and for the suspicion and fear which can destroy communities. My characters are archetypes who might be anyone at any time, but they reflect the ways we can behave if we're maligned, left outside of things or seen as 'other' or evil.

Signs of Shuck's presence can still be seen at Holy Trinity Church in Blythburgh, Suffolk, where he was also said to have rampaged, with Shuck's claw marks still scarring the church door.

And devils can be without or within. Sometimes we have to go through the dark forest to confront them.

EC

Times like these, the waiting's heavy.

Each breath crackles with the expectation of a storm. Fraught and spawning times, like a mother dog puffed up with puppies. Something seeks someone. Someone seeks something. Something must be given, and something must be taken away.

I'll tell you of a strange and terrible wonder, and I need you to believe me, although not for long. Follow me. Close your eyes and let yourself be led astray. Wander from the path. Breathe in deep. Go on. Inhale the candles.

Let the scent carry you back, across the centuries. Beeswax and tallow twining round the pillars. A church, a place of sanctuary in the saltmarshes, the heath and pasture. Follow me to sweating, sultry August, where darkness hovers like clouds of blood-drunk flies. Darkness, so close at hand.

It might be now. Some things are not so different. Famine, taxes, arguments about religion. A war going on, somewhere, though it isn't here just yet. People. People you've met before, probably. You might even have been some of them. A soldier. A dancer. An orphan.

And a big black dog, of course, but we'll get to that.

Everywhere like this, each comfortable community, needs whatever telling of a witch conforms to fashion at the time. The poor, the old, the different – somebody to take the blame. A vessel for the demons the righteous are too scared to claim. There are those who can fit in, and there are those who never have.

On the outskirts of acceptable, an orphan lived uneasily, a true-blue orphan of indeterminate age. Nobody had known her parents, but everybody had their views. Child of the foul-mouthed gravedigger, long since dead, or that woman who'd been hanged for theft. But all they knew for certain was that she'd been left, abandoned at the almshouse, growing up grieving without knowing what for.

Living untethered to parents or place is an unquiet thing, but she did survive, though the village children mocked her and the cats all spat. Narrow streets make narrow minds and hearts, which offer scraps like roses. She never asked for charity, but charity's what she got. She was taken in, but it was sharp, that charity, a charity of hard hands and bitter words. They told her she was like the dog, the storm that threatened the village. For all they knew, she was the Devil's puppy too.

There was a legend in the village, you see. It started when the priory fell. The monks' wolfhounds, all left behind in shards of smashed stained glass and broken effigies, began to kill and eat each other. They killed and ate until just one was left alive, a vast hound-bitch, the size of a donkey – accustomed to the taste of blood.

In kindness, a farmer took her in. Fed and tamed her, or so he thought. But soon she ran and was lost for days. The farmer gave her up for dead. When she returned at last she was exhausted, tongue lolling, paw-pads torn, and belly swollen huge with pups. All right-thinking folk could see it, plain as a nail in a bronze horseshoe. It was the Devil's work.

Just one puppy came from the hound-bitch's brood. A beast. An abnormality. A red-eyed hellion.

Black Shuck, we call him. Skeff. Snarleyow. He gallops in the mist along the marshes, grinning carnage with his filthy teeth. One look will kill you or someone you love. He's the hand of night, spreading its fingers over our heads.

They told her she was like Black Shuck. Appeared from nowhere to cast a shadow. But still the shadow was just a shadow. The storm had not yet broken, and all things were imbalanced. There was neither enough of one nor too much of the other.

To this fragile peace returned a soldier, home and yet not home.

Some run towards war and others run away. For the soldier, it was both. The cause was not the reason for his going, though he believed that something would be changed. Good deeds notched gradually on his soul's shield, fighting fire with fire.

He met the orphan as she carried water in the red poppy sunset of the ruined priory, as hellhound voices sounded through the forests. He asked her what it meant, the village dogs all howling in one voice. What's eating all the dogs tonight?

Better to ask what the dogs are eating. Those aren't the village dogs, she told him. Black Shuck and his terrible spawn. Ghosts and demons. Evil portents, omens.

That's what's said, anyway. That's what they believe.

The soldier gave no weight to these prattling yarns. The worst stories always come from the firesides. People will say anything until they've really lived it. Then, they keep quiet.

If he saw something in her eyes, he could not name it. And she herself was nameless, nobody. If he saw the traces of another life there, he could not touch them. He had believed the war so far behind him, salt water acres rolling out between them. But standing in the ruined priory, where ghosts stretch out as long as shadows, he heard the hungry hatred of the howling and wondered if he had stepped into a new one.

You've almost met them all, our players, though one at least still stalks the forests between midnight and dawn.

In the village there was a dancer. She ran light-footed from sorrow and swayed her hips to nudge aside all woes. The rains of melancholy sizzled when they touched her skin, and grief and regret poured from her twisting hands, libations on the earth. Her smile was a fortress against memory, her hair a net to catch bad dreams. The past she did not speak of, when something small was taken and something greater given.

In the inn she met the soldier, but they could not say the words which rolled around in the silences of the past. He could not speak of the war to her, of the new scars on his body and in his eyes. He could not tell her of the things he saw. The little girl whose hair was falling out from fear and the old man who did not understand how his hair has become white and his betters still could not agree. For the clouds of musket dust, there were no words, and for the stench, still fewer. Instead, he told her that he thought of her, sometimes, when the mud wasn't so deep and the cloud of hungry flies buzzing around the dead men could be mistaken for a handful of hawthorn blossom.

And she couldn't hear him, seeing no good in mere thoughts. What were thoughts but smoke, easily wafted aside? Thoughts don't cook geese. Instead, she told him of the Devil's hound, who all were afraid of but her, and how it came to her when she walked the marshes on a moonless night. How she'd seen Black Shuck, sitting in her way as bold as steel, with marsh light and murder in its monstrous eyes. Each tooth the memory of a scream. Fur matted with a dank whiff of despair.

He asked if she was frightened. The dog is death to those who see it. Why not you?

Maybe it wanted to do some good, she said. The strange part – it ran from her a little way, then turned and bounded back again – again – again, as though it wanted her to follow it. So, she did, and she'd swear on any book you like that Old Shuck took her safe back through the marsh, the dog running beside the woman until the crossroads, when it vanished.

Talk lessened after that, and things unspoken were lost in hazel eyes and grazing thighs, in touches as soft as the dust from ruined abbeys.

Are you still with me? Follow me into the church. It's just a short step away. Creaking door gives way to evensong. The air hanging humid with the smell of sweat and hay fresh from the field. Candles make the place a smoky beehive. Like an itch between the shoulder blades, the congregation shifts, awkward, unable to reach to scratch. A lazy rivulet of perspiration on the rector's forehead, and the angels on the roof obscured by haze.

Blessed are they that do his commandments.
Their right may be in the tree of life.
They may enter in through the gates into the city.
For without shall be dogs, and enchanters, and murderers, and whosoever loveth or maketh lies.

The faces of the figures carved on bench ends seemed to twist, their oaken features smirking, while the sky frowned black displeasure, and with a sudden hammering, the rain escaped the clouds.

Blessed are they that do his commandments.

A clap of thunder split apart the blackness.

Their right may be in the tree of life.

All at once, a pounding on the church door. Once, twice, thrice, it struck the wood.

They may enter in through the gates into the city. For without shall be dogs–

The door burst open. Black Shuck was everywhere, his eyes as bright as braziers, his tongue a flaming ribbon, his growl a thundercrack. Each barrage splintered the floor tiles. Where he leapt he devastated. Those he touched, he killed. His howl pierced the heavens, calling the lightning to lash down. Calling hell to open and unleash its very worst.

A whip-fast bolt of lightning hissed from sky to earth, cleaving the tower and rending the steeple. It sent the bells into furious chiming

pieces and smashed the spire down. As fast as worry, Shuck had gone. The wrecked church tower his calling card and the smoking claw marks in the door, and all the people he had touched stark dead.

After, though the storm had broken, the darkness had not melted away. Instead, the sky was bruised, like sleepless shadows behind the lashes of the trees. Every tear was like a stone, and the stones dropped on the village, shoring it up, blocking the windows, damming the streams.

It's easy to become a stone, you see. Hard to be a fox, slipping slyly from a snare. Hard to be a starling, fluttering fast for freedom. But easy to be a stone. Heavy. Stubborn. Cruel.

The soldier and the dancer's silences burst like swelling warts in an eruption of anger and accusation. Why did they do it? They could full well see the cuts they made, yet still persisted.

Where they could have been together, they pushed at each other, until they were as alone as they had ever been. And scenes of a similar nature played all through the village, in a non-stop run without an interval. Kindness was left out in the cold and given a few kicks just for good measure.

Black Shuck had claimed the village, captured, chewed and slurped it, making it his own. Nobody saw what the dog had done or noticed what they'd become. Frowns were knitted into every shawl and spite baked into puddings.

But somebody had seen. Somebody knew. It takes a homeless dog, sometimes, to recognise another. To see the anger, fear and pain which makes us cast our longest shadow.

As the raven who carefully gathers twigs to build a nest and shrouds her fragile eggs in lambswool safety, the orphan went from door to door to ask for help against Black Shuck. As the raven who can find nothing for her fledglings to eat battles helplessly with the winter blizzard and gets no reply to her crying, she too knew there was no answer. Everywhere she found closed doors, closed faces, unfeeling words.

We must do something, she said. If we don't do something, together, all of us together, Black Shuck will destroy our village. Like a serpent, he'll tighten his coils around us, panting, salivating, until we've coffined ourselves in darkness and served ourselves up steaming. We must do something.

But her words were met with cruelty. None of us ever wanted you, stray dog child. Go back to the gutter and sing your mad songs there. You were in the church that day – why didn't Black Shuck murder you?

As the raven who can fly no further, whose wings are wet and heavy with the snow, she could scarcely drag herself along. She could not feel her heart.

But the raven did not die and the orphan did not die. She did not know how to do it, but she knew what must be done. Something seeks someone, so someone must seek something. Something had to be given, and something taken away. Determination gave her the strength to straighten her shoulders, to lift her face and let the light stroke it for the first time. To hear above the beat of wings, as though someone passing in flight had stopped to listen.

She went beyond the village gates. She crossed over the river. She went through the salt marshes and deep into the forest. She walked into the dark.

Every sound was a claw being sharpened to rip and tear. Every movement was a beast, limbering up to pounce. Every rustle was a promise – you'll be dead meat.

Her hopelessness was greater than her fear. She knew that people like her don't fight great battles. People like her don't ever win. And in the dark, he sniffed at her defeated loneliness as though it was the sweetest perfume.

With savage puffs of stinking breath and eyes like clots of blood, Black Shuck stalked through the forest. Each footfall thundered. His swiping tail scorched the tree bark where it brushed, his fur writhing like black maggots. His teeth as long as grudges. Each step he took towards her swelled his power. The Shuck was one huge, gaping maw, ready to devour, to suck all joy down to the marrow and leave only emptiness behind.

She flung a hand out and in her open palm was all her isolation, all her yearning and her dreams. This orphan girl, her history so unknown that even the lines in her palms were blank, had quite by accident shone a light that a passing angel could take a shine to, a celestial light in an unwashed hand, which shuddered through the village.

It made its way to the inn and its air of desperate merriment, where people put themselves through the motions, forcing themselves to boisterous mirth. In this furious whirlwind of biting words, of spilt ale and broken friendships, the soldier and the dancer refused to see each other. His hands shook as he spiced his draught with self-pity. He could not look at her, and yet he could not leave the inn. Her hands were fists, her nails dug in as she turned and turned. She could not look at him, yet every second she knew he was there.

The thunder rumbled once, then the clouds parted. The light was without and within, pouring through the cracks in the floor and ceiling and through the cracks in hearts. The most curious thing, which nobody ever understood afterwards, was where the feathers came from. A soft, white snowfall in the August heat. Was it a flock of fleeing herons, startled, shedding as they soared away? Most people, when they tell the tale now, agree that an angel must have passed.

Something had been given. Now something could be taken away.

While the inn was in the sudden clutches of joy and a few stray feathers still drifted from the ceiling, a rumour chanced to join the crowd, of an orphan girl and how she'd left the village, crossed the marshes and gone to meet Black Shuck. Slowly, it dawned on the villagers what had been given and what might have been taken away, and that if there was a chance to save her, they had to take it now.

A dancer who had held in all her woe let it go, as she laughed and sobbed at once, and a soldier who had never known his father allowed himself to imagine what it was to be a father, and what it was to lose a daughter in the moment he had found her, as he raced towards the forest of Black Shuck.

Stories can change, you know. We're afraid of dying, but death is so small. It happens once. It's a tiny mouse-squeak when the hawk dives down – and gone. Life is long and huge and sprawling, beginning after beginning, and a great big middle.

The orphan touched the black dog's snout. I was a mouse, she said. A mouse, scared of all the hawks which might be waiting. Now I can be brave, uncurl my shoulders, look the whole world in the eyes. You don't have to run on fury either. Once you walked a woman safely home. Even the biggest dogs can stop to chase the butterflies.

And when the soldier found her, the dog was calm and the sky was clear. She didn't know yet why she felt like a memory to him, but she would know. The nameless can be named.

Stories can change.

In the village, great plans were made. The church was rebuilt, the bells gilded anew, and sea-heather and dog roses brought inside to garland the angel roof. Other, smaller things were patched as well, carefully polished and mended so they were better than before they broke. Old rivalries, bitter words and jealousies. All were put aside.

And on the road with rowan trees, out of the forest and by the marshes, a soldier and an orphan went on foot. The night was past and the dawn had nicked her finger, seeping blood into the edges of the horizon.

Among the rowan trees, a small bird was pouring her heart out, singing of a life both cruel and beautiful. As she sang, the storm clouds sighed and slunk away and the rain softly spun the sky into dreamy silk. With it fell kindness, drop by drop. A heartfelt word, bread shared, a goose bought with a soldier's last penny.

Night by night, the shadow of Black Shuck was shrinking. The stories changed.

As the rain fell, a soldier and an orphan went back to where a dancer was waiting to forget – and to remember what it was to kiss with a mouthful of blackberries, and how to find the blue feather of love in the magpie's black and white.

As the rain fell, a dog was playing, bounding and stalking in the priory ruins, hunting a butterfly, then letting it fly free.

All fears can be overwhelmed with words. All flowers grow in dirty, fertile mud. And all homeless dogs have hope.

24

Dionysia, the Female Knight

A Northamptonshire Tale

From the ancient Briton Queen Boudicca to Joan of Arc, the mythological figure of the woman warrior is a part of our cultural heritage.

There are plenty of records of women in the Middle Ages fighting alongside or in place of men. For example, in Catalonia, the members of the Order of the Hatchet were a group of women who fought valiantly to defend their town, Tortosa, from siege.

The actual history of Dionysia of Clopton has become muddled with that of Agnes de Hotot. They may well have been related through the same Northamptonshire family. Agnes and Dionysia were certainly both real people, perhaps numbered among the many, many children of Sir Walter de Clopton.

Both Dionysia and Agnes were said to have dressed in armour and duelled with men in place of their fathers, either because their fathers were too old and incapable or too cowardly. In either case, it seems to have been that the woman was the best person for the job!

I have also always wondered how lady knights in films take off their helmets to reveal their identity with a cascade of perfectly coiffed hair. Poor Dionysia doesn't quite manage it…

EC

In the reign of King Stephen there lived a man called Walter de Clopton. His family name was originally Grauntcourt, but the local people in Clopton, where he lived, found it difficult to pronounce, and so Walter had absorbed the name of his home. He was, technically speaking, a knight, but Walter had never been much interested in the kinds of things knights usually get up to. He hated the sight of blood, disliked travelling far from home on quests, and perhaps most crucially, he had poor depth perception, which made jousting a kind of personal hell.

No, what Walter de Clopton really liked to do was to have children. His children were the passion of his life, and after his wife produced their first, he swiftly fell into the role which suited him most – that of the insufferably proud father who wants to tell anybody within a fifty-mile radius about the brilliance and beauty of his offspring and show them miniature portraits of his rosy-cheeked baby.

Walter's dedication to having children was such that he managed to father eight of them, until his exhausted wife eventually tired of the whole affair and died. According to those close to the family, her final words on expiring had been, 'At last – five minutes peace!'

She left Walter in a mess of children – and it was a real mess, given that there were eight of them and their father was very good at telling them bedtime stories and bouncing them on his knee in endless games of horsey-horsey and playing Norman invaders with their bath toys and wearing pointy hats and giving his best impression of snooty Saxon princesses – but he was very bad at tidying up after them.

There was William, who had taken the games of horsey-horsey to heart and developed a fascination with breeding and racing horses, and little Walter, who read voraciously and was soon writing his own poems, to which his delighted father subjected any guests to Clopton Manor. There was Robert, who had from birth an almost pathological aversion to wearing clothes and would leave any garments his father and siblings attempted to apply to him in scattered piles over the house. There was Richard, who had a variety of hobbies and skills, although it was probably fair to say he enjoyed picking them up and trying them more than he enjoyed seeing them through for any length of time. Then there was Reginald, who had been born with his tufty baby hair growing in a natural tonsure. Reginald, who showed a propensity towards the priesthood even as a stocky toddler, was often to be found conducting High Mass with his teddy bears and occasionally dropped a large and heavy Bible on his loving father's toe when he was playing horses with William.

In addition to the five excellent Clopton sons, Walter had three daughters, Alicia, Rohesia and Dionysia. Alicia was devoted to music and in no way allowed the similarity of her singing voice to the cry of a hunting falcon to stand in her way. It appeared to a casual observer as though she was attached to her harp, which went everywhere with her, and the air of Clopton Manor was almost always filled with its gentle plucking and the scratchy yowl of Alicia's voice raised in joyful song. Rohesia, the middle daughter, had been blessed with the kind of startling good looks which cause horse-riding accidents. Numerous poets had immortalised her grass-green eyes, mesmerisingly long eyelashes and ripples of auburn hair in their works, most of which are tragically lost to posterity.

And the youngest daughter was Dionysia.

Walter loved all of his children equally, but it was fair to say that Dionysia was the only member of the Clopton family with a sensible head on her shoulders. Having so many children, Sir Walter had no money to keep any servants, and so it was quite a challenge to keep the eight of them in clothes, food, and the toys their indulgent father was constantly having made for them. So Dionysia, who seemed to be the only one who noticed things like tankards with little dribbles of ale left inside them being left everywhere, had her work cut out even from a very young age. Between trying to make sure they all got to bed on time and occasionally ate vegetables, and persuading Reginald to stop preaching to the goats, which they disliked, and getting Robert to put his tunic and hose back on, she barely had a moment to herself.

Dionysia did not have a talent for music or the magic touch with a horse. She did not have long auburn hair or a vocation to serve God. She quite liked her clothes to stay on her body, especially when it was cold, and she didn't have much time for hobbies. She did, however, have a barrowload of determination to make sure her family thrived and ensure its various members didn't embarrass themselves in front of their peers.

When Sir Walter had once generously invited a large hunting party back to Clopton Manor, forgetting there was no food in the larder, it was Dionysia who uncomplainingly whipped up a giant batch of chocolate mousse. As they didn't have a cooking pot large enough for the hunting party, she made it in the bath tub. Nobody minded as it had been so chocolatey and delicious, even if little Richard did get chocolate on his rubber duck and between his toes and in a few other places it ought not to have been possible to get chocolate.

Sir Walter was a wonderful father and doted on his children utterly, but as he grew older he became more forgetful. Although his chest still swelled with immense pride when he regarded his offspring, who had all grown into fine young people, he often forgot basic things, like closing the front door of Clopton Manor when he went out or the gate to the goat pen, meaning the manor was quite often completely overrun with goats. Whenever this happened, Sir Walter would scratch his fuzzy, grey head and look at the goats with faint puzzlement, as if they were yet more children of his whose names he had temporarily misplaced, and who mysteriously had managed to develop extra legs, horns and tails.

And as is so often the way when people become older and more forgetful, they start to offend people quite by accident. It started out as quite small things, like getting the messenger's name wrong, even though he'd been carrying post to the Clopton family for well over a decade, or not paying the butcher's bill. These things were easily taken care of by Dionysia, who always knew how to discreetly smooth ruffled feathers. But then he started doing rather more serious things, like promising Rohesia's hand in marriage to three different eligible young bachelors at once because he'd forgotten that he'd done it, or loudly commenting that he thought Empress Matilda's fashion sense was really fabulous in the hearing of King Stephen.

These incidents started out as few and far between, but they were soon happening with increasing frequency. It was all Dionysia could do to run around tidying up the messes her alarmingly doddery father kept getting himself into.

Now it came to pass that a new young lord, Sir Robert de Hofford, moved into the neighbouring estate to Clopton Manor. Robert was one of these newfangled lords who believed in things like landscaped gardens and dinners with vegetables in them. He had never allowed a goat into his home nor made chocolate mousse in the bath. In fact, he had never done anything outrageous in his entire life.

When he encountered Sir Walter at the boundary of their two estates, the old man did not make a great impression on the young lord. Sir Walter's hose were worn at the knees from having played too many games of dolls and dragons on the floor and his hair increasingly resembled a windswept dandelion head. It may be that this negative first impression was the cause of a slight frostiness in tone when Sir Robert brought up a piece of land between the two estates, which each gentleman considered to be his property.

It wasn't much to look at, this land. It was really just a scrubby piece of nothingness. But Robert de Hofford thought that it would be nice to turn it into a kitchen garden and grow all sorts of modern things, like heritage carrots and three different types of sage.

He may well have been right, and if he'd smiled and complimented Sir Walter on his eight children then the whole thing might have gone differently, and I wouldn't be sitting here telling you this at all. But Sir Robert wasn't especially friendly in this first conversation, and then he started confusing Sir Walter by waving land deeds at him. Sir Walter, who by this point had got rather fussy, told him that he was a very rude young man and also remarked that he disliked Robert's haircut – a floppy, layered confection which Sir Walter thought made Sir Robert look like a minstrel.

So, the two men found themselves at odds, and one thing led to another, and as we all know, no true knight will stand to have his hair insulted. And that was how Sir Walter came to find himself challenged to a duel.

Well, the silly old man went home fretting about it, and he was so worried and bothered by it that he even remembered to close the front door of Clopton Manor, leaving the goats gathered around the porch desperately disappointed. However, he didn't mention it to any of his children, hoping that if he kept it himself, Sir Robert might forget all about it.

Nothing happened for a few days, and Sir Walter did actually manage to forget about the duel himself, until a challenge arrived by post.

'Thank you, Horace,' Sir Walter said to the messenger.

'You're welcome, Sir Walter,' said the messenger, whose name was not, and never had been, Horace.

The family clustered around the scroll with its fancy green wax seals and ribbons, thinking it might be an invitation to a banquet or perhaps another proposal of marriage for Rohesia, who had rather lost track of how many she had received. But when Sir Walter opened it and found it was a challenge, he started shaking all over.

'I can't. I can't. I'm too old! I can't even lift my sword and spear, and my knees have gone all funny,' he said, dropping the scroll. This was only too true. Many years of getting down on the floor to play knights and princesses and dragons with his children had left Sir Walter's knees in a poor state of repair indeed.

There was a great deal of consternation amongst his children. They were excellent young people, but they were absolutely blind to the faults of their parent and could not imagine a set of circumstances in which somebody could be so cruel and unfeeling as to challenge him to a duel.

The problem was none of them were fighters. They all had their skills, to be sure, and to the credit of the Clopton children, they did all offer to try and solve the problem in their own inimitable style.

'Fighting's a sin,' Reginald said primly. 'I shall visit Sir Robert and preach peace, at the peril of his immortal soul!'

'Horsedung!' scoffed William. 'I shall challenge the bounder to a race, and to the victor the spoils!'

'What about a bout of naked wrestling?' said Robert, who had never developed the habit of clothes and preferred to have his skin to the wind as much as he could. Even now, he was wearing only a small pair of breeches and a smile, and all I can say is that it was lucky the messenger was used to the family or he would have been very shocked by Robert.

'I could challenge him to a poetry writing contest,' said young Walter hopefully. 'I've been refining my haiku and if I say so myself, they slay.'

'How about a rap battle?' said Alicia, with a discordant twang of her harp.

'I could marry him, I suppose,' said Rohesia, tossing her waves of auburn hair. 'But I don't really want to, as he's been so rude to Dad.'

This was immediately shouted down by her siblings, who refused to allow their divinely beautiful sister to waste her charms on a vulgar ingrate who thought root vegetables were more important than people's feelings. The family went round and round in circles about it, arguing about who would use their unique talents to represent their father in the duel.

While this was going on, Dionysia stayed very quiet, and when they were all distracted trying to develop a very silly yet involved plan which featured dressing up in potato sacks with skeletons painted on them to scare Sir Robert away from Northamptonshire entirely, she picked up the challenge scroll with all the details of the engagement on it and carried it off to read in the kitchen. Dionysia privately admired the neat handwriting of Sir Robert and the forthright lines of his signature, but she had to admit that the challenge was unequivocal in its wording. It gave a time, a place and laid down in no uncertain terms that failure to turn up would mean that Sir Walter would ever after be known as the worst kind of coward throughout the whole county, and also that if he didn't show, Sir Robert would win by default, meaning he could claim the contested land for his vegetable garden.

Meanwhile, poor Sir Walter had got himself so worked up that he had been forced to retire to bed with a hot drink and a cuddly toy dragon, and all the other children had descended into plotting elaborate revenges against Sir Robert, totally having forgotten the more pressing matter of actually fighting the duel.

So the next morning, before anybody else was awake, Dionysia got up. This was quite normal, as the rest of the Clopton family liked lengthy lie ins, reading the latest chivalric romances in bed, taking long baths and spending at least an hour and a half over breakfast. Dionysia preferred to be up early so that she could feed the goats and get a head start on the day's chores. It was also the only time of day she could keep the manor looking tidy, before her siblings inevitably messed it up with their various hobbies and interests.

She crept downstairs and into the great hall, and she looked at her father's suit of armour, which was in extremely good condition as Sir Walter had always been more of a lover than a fighter – hence the eight children. With some difficulty, Dionysia got herself strapped into Sir Walter's breastplate and greaves and pinned a flowing cloak to her shoulders. She slammed down the visor of his helmet.

When she caught sight of her reflection in one of their silver goblets, she thought her head looked like it belonged to a particularly shiny pig, complete with snout, but she couldn't deny it made her completely unrecognisable. The armour fit quite well, because Dionysia was broad and strong in a way Sir Walter had never really been, due to all the lifting and shifting she had taken upon herself. It fit her much better than it would have done her father, in truth, because he was skinny in the calves and round in the middle, which was quite the perfect physique for the lifestyle he had chosen, but not so great for fighting.

When she was satisfied that nobody would know she wasn't Sir Walter, apart from a certain bandy-leggedness to his walk, she clanked her way out to the stables and borrowed William's most fearsome-looking horse.

The horse actually had an extremely gentle personality, but it had been blessed with a coal-black mane and tail, large, flared nostrils and immense hooves. William had rather hopefully called it Killer, in the hope it might live up to its name, but this had not noticeably helped.

Dionysia mounted Killer and galloped out in the morning mists to meet Sir Robert de Hofford. Sir Robert rode a white horse, and Dionysia had to admit that he made a fine and exceptionally shiny figure in his cool, modern armour. He had a forest-green cloak pinned to his shoulders and his horse was positively prancing in that smug, self-satisfied way some horses have.

Killer immediately stopped moving and dug his heels in.

'Come on, Killer,' Dionysia said under her breath. 'Don't let me down. We can't make Dad look silly in front of this pompous ass.'

Maybe Killer heard her, or maybe he had just spotted some nice yellow flowers he wanted to smell on the other side of the meadow, but he managed to trot towards Sir Robert.

Sir Robert immediately issued a challenge, which might have sounded very impressive if his helmet hadn't made it sound all tinny. 'I challenge you, Sir Walter, to determine who has the rights to this parcel of land and to satisfy the insult you have given to me regarding my hair, which is very stylish, thank you very much!'

Obviously, Dionysia could not reply or her voice would have instantly given her away. So, she shouldered her lance and pointed it at her opponent in what she hoped was a suitably deadly fashion. Killer snorted menacingly, but this was because he was thinking about what he was going to have for lunch.

Sir Robert's prancing white steed was soon thundering towards her and Dionysia felt suddenly extremely out of her depth. She held firm to her lance, but before she knew it, Sir Robert's lance was slamming into her chest, shoving her breastplate into her and winding her. Dionysia lost her grip on Killer's reins and felt herself begin to slip from the saddle, but as she fell, she was able to plant her lance firmly into Sir Robert's soldier and unhorse him too.

They fell in an ungainly, clanking heap of armour. Killer, the treacherous beast, immediately galloped off to investigate the yellow flowers he had been much more interested in to start with, and Sir Robert's horse returned to admiring his own reflection in the lake.

Dionysia scrambled for her sword, but Sir Robert, who had much more practice at standing up quickly while wearing a suit of armour, reached his first. He raised it high above his head, preparing to whack it down hard on Dionysia's helmet, but she had decided that enough was quite enough of these shenanigans.

'Stop that at once!' she exclaimed, holding up her armoured fists. 'I've humoured you this far, as you were so insistent, but really, there are far better ways to resolve a dispute.'

Sir Robert was so surprised to hear a feminine voice issuing forth from the pig-faced helmet that he allowed his sword to hang stupidly at his side.

'Sir Walter?' he said uncertainly.

'Of course not, you silly man!' said Dionysia impatiently, and pulled off her helmet. This did not go off quite as she had imagined, with the helmet coming off smoothly and unleashing her somehow perfectly coiffed chestnut curls. In fact, it involved the hinge of the helmet's jaw piece getting stuck in her braid and Sir Robert having to help her untangle it.

By the time he had unwound the hair from the metal, however, he had got a good look at Dionysia's bright eyes and determined jaw, not to mention the way the helmet had left imprints around the edges of her eyes and her slightly sweaty forehead, and he was thoroughly charmed.

'Who are you?' he said wonderingly.

'I'm Sir Walter's daughter, of course,' said Dionysia. 'And I've come out to tell you that I think it's very unfair of you to upset him over something so minor, when he's got so much to worry about as it is, with eight of us at home and the animals.'

'S-sorry,' stammered Sir Robert. 'I didn't – realise.'

'Do you think you could take your helmet off, please?' Dionysia said. 'I can see my own reflection in your face and it's a bit disconcerting, honestly.'

Sir Robert immediately obliged, and his helmet removal was much smoother and more glamorous than Dionysia's had been. She looked at his chiselled jaw and green eyes, and she had to confess that she did not share her father's opinion about the qualities of his haircut.

If I tell you that Killer was distracted from the yellow flowers by the sight of Sir Robert's horse, whose name was Percy, and he cantered over to Percy and started nuzzling at his shiny mane, then that perhaps gives you a fair idea of what was going on across the meadow between Dionysia and Sir Robert. The early morning mists cleared and the sun came up on a warm and beautiful day.

The wedding was held in the Clopton estate chapel, and it was the happiest occasion imaginable. There was no father prouder than Sir Walter as he escorted Dionysia down the aisle, with tears of joy in his eyes and to the sound of Alicia's harp playing, made all the sweeter by her frown of concentration. They were married by Reginald, who felt the event to be the culmination of all his religious learning.

Dionysia arrived on Killer, carefully groomed by William, and she wore a crown Richard had crafted from flowers and beads and all sorts of fabulous twiddly bits. Walter Junior read a celebratory poem of his own composition and Robert even wore a pair of hose for the wedding, although he regarded a flower in his hair as a perfectly appropriate replacement for a tunic, or indeed for anything else. As for Rohesia, no sooner had she locked eyes with Sir Robert de Hofford's best friend and best man, also rather confusingly called Robert, she knew that she was finally about to receive the only proposal she would ever accept.

Dionysia and Sir Robert were ideal for each other. He was the calm she needed after any time spent in the loving chaos of her family, and with her help, he was able to loosen up just a little bit. In time, I've heard, he even came to do one or two outrageous things. They stayed living on the neighbouring estate in Clopton, and no family Christmas was ever so happy as those when the two families were united, and the array of fresh, homegrown vegetables at the feast table was quite astounding.

Dionysia never had call to wear her father's armour again, but she kept it well polished and displayed in her own Great Hall – just in case she ever needed to defend any of her family's honour again – and when the time came for her to have her own daughters, she made sure they not only knew how to get into the armour, but how to gracefully remove the pig-faced helmet without getting their hair caught in it.

25

The Fish and the Ring

A Northumberland Tale

As some of the wealthiest, most powerful landowners in all of English history, it's perhaps understandable that the Earls of Northumberland had rather fractious relationships with other noble houses over time, not to mention several monarchs.

The Percy family did not always play nicely with others. Their feud with the Nevilles prompted the Wars of the Roses. They led the Rising of the North and were involved in the Gunpowder Plot, all the while holding lands containing some of the most beautiful castles and holy sites in England – not least Bamburgh, Alnwick, and Lindisfarne.

In this story, I picked at a thread from a fascinating moment in time when Henry Percy, known in his day as 'The Wizard Earl', became embroiled in a set of conspiracies involving occult magic, spies, and famous historical figures like Christopher Marlowe, John Donne, and Sir Walter Raleigh.

With the 9th Earl of Northumberland's relationship with his son, Algernon, having been so strained, and Algernon's love life so peculiar, I connected their real-world narratives to the truly ancient tale of 'The Fish and the Ring', which, considering Percy's links to the arcane, felt only right. A story which appears in legends dating to before the Common Era, such as those of Herodotus and the Talmudic tales of King Solomon, reappearing throughout European Medieval and Renaissance literature to today, it's an old one but a good one. Moreover, in my view, it fits over this bizarre era in the Percy family's saga surprisingly well.

MV

It is no secret that the reign of Queen Elizabeth I was a time of magic. And though the list of spellcasters, mavens, and alchemists of that age is long, none of them were as wealthy or powerful as Henry Percy. The 9th Earl of Northumberland, Percy had gold enough without changing it from base metals. He was the head of the School of Night, which met at Syon House in London – a group which had amongst its members over time Dr John Dee, Christopher Marlowe, George Chapman, Sir Walter Raleigh, and John Donne. Indeed, when John Donne married Anne More, resigning himself to a life of penury, it was Percy who carried the letter announcing the news to her father.

Many know of Percy's imprisonment in the Tower of London, after he was tried in Star Chamber for his involvement in the Gunpowder Plot. Though today we know, just as they did then, that there was no evidence of his involvement. Still, the Tower was a familiar setting for the Percys, for Henry's father had been imprisoned there three times for aiding Mary, Queen of Scots, and died there, shot in the heart at the orders of the Vice Chamberlain – a murder announced to the public as a suicide.

This was in contrast to his grandfather, Thomas, who was hung, drawn and quartered at Tyburn for his rebellion during the Pilgrimage of Grace, and to his uncle, who had loved Anne Boleyn and had been the one who, as a juror at her trial, collapsed when the verdict was passed and died of a broken heart.

Still, from their seat at Alnwick Castle, a little inland from the North Sea, the Earls of Northumberland were always some of the richest men in England. As such, the Wizard Earl Henry Percy took his sixteen years of imprisonment in his stride.

Attended by twenty servants in the Martin Tower, which he had lavishly decorated and furnished with one of the finest libraries of the age, he continued to meet Thomas Harriot, Walter Warner, and Robert Hues, men known as Northumberland's Three Magi, right up until they died and he was freed.

It was his magi who did his bidding beyond the prison walls, for Percy was a furious man, vindictive and preoccupied with matters of blood. A descendent of the brave knight Henry Hotspur, he came from a long line of rebels resistant to the Crown.

In his mind, his children should only marry amongst the most powerful and noble families in the land – for this reason, he kept his daughter, Lucy, imprisoned with him at the Tower to prevent her marriage to James Hay, the Earl of Carlisle. Percy said he would not have Lucy 'dance to a Scottish jig', but for all Percy's power and cunning, she escaped, aided by the Earl and Countess of Somerset, and married Hay, who, in turn, fought for Percy's release.

When he was finally freed, due to his son-in-law's endeavours, the Wizard Earl was deaf and almost blind and he never recovered his strength. He died at Petworth House in 1632, too weak to journey back to Alnwick Castle, recently restored to his only son and heir. And on his deathbed, the Wizard Earl muttered wildly of his greatest regret – of his battle with fate which drove a wedge between himself and his only son, Algernon.

The matter of their great feud began when Algernon was but a newborn. In those dark days, at the end of the Nine Years War, months before the queen died and his ally, Raleigh, was imprisoned for treason, Henry Percy drew a thimble of Algernon's infant blood; he sat before his obsidian mirror, burned the blood and summoned angels to the 'shew-stone'.

They told him news he did not want to hear. His line would soon end. It would be Algernon's fate to marry a girl named Ann – a woman of inferior blood, who would bear him only daughters.

For Henry Percy, such a fate for his son was unthinkable, and so, with iron determination, Percy set about controlling Algernon's life from daybreak to sunset, his every hour prescribed, his every movement monitored. Simultaneously, Percy set to seeking Ann, sending his men to scour Northumberland.

And though it took him some weeks, he found her: the girl unto whom his son was betrothed by destiny. She was the daughter of a lowly fisherman, living on the banks of Devil's Water.

He knew her on sight, having seen her in the obsidian mirror, though she was then still but a wordless babe, dabbling at the edge of that fast-flowing brook. She was a dark-haired creature with snow-pale skin and fey-like eyes of greyish green.

He approached the lowly fisherman and reached for his coin purse, retrieving three gold pieces and offering them as payment. The fisherman, though flushed with shame, accepted this sudden fortune and sold Ann to Henry Percy. The fisherman presumed she would now live in Alnwick Castle and be raised as a lady. Yet the Wizard Earl had other plans.

Percy placed the child before him on his horse and rode to Corbridge. There, he took the smiling babe in his arms, stood high on the bridge above the River Tyne and dropped her into the black-green water.

His quest accomplished and fate defied, Percy rode back to Alnwick and continued Algernon's instruction. Since the boy's mother had been executed in 1601, after allegations of treason, Henry was free to ignore the will of her side of the family, the meddling Devereuxs.

With other business to attend to in London, Henry therefore appointed the accomplished tutor, alchemist, and natural philosopher Edward Dowse to raise his son, proceeding south at his earliest convenience. His parting gift to his son was of a ring made of pure gold, inlaid with the symbol of the House of Percy: a lion rampant carved from the bluest lapis lazuli, the band inscribed with the family motto, *Esperance en Dieu* – Hope in God.

Only, Ann had not drowned in the river where the Wizard Earl dropped her. Instead, as if rescued by forces beyond sight or knowing, her frail body tumbled downstream and was discovered by chance, by Henry Nevill, the Baron of Bergavenney.

Nevill, out hunting with his men in the Forest of Kielder, was astounded to find a child emerging from the river's foam, not least one he thought so beautiful, so intriguing and so strange. He considered it an omen and so took her with him to meet with his friend and the wisest man he knew, Sir Robert Cecil.

Cecil, a hunchback known for years as the Queen's Pygmy, had long been spymaster to the Crown. Once protégé to Francis Walsingham, Cecil had inherited his father's interest in the occult, including his rafts of letters from Edward Kelley, and he remained a patron of the secretive alchemical alliance known as the Society of the New Art. Though Cecil held little stock in the transmutational experiments of William Medley, he was a great friend of Robert Fludd, whom he had inspect the girl to learn more of her mysterious lineage.

It was many years until Ann appeared again in public, though when she did, it was as Lady Ann Cecil, daughter of King James' most trusted advisor. By then Cecil was known as the King's Little Beagle, having long since revelled in the success of the Treaty of London, for which he had hired the playwright William Shakespeare and his actors to serve as diplomats to the Spanish delegation. A member of the Order of the Garter and discoverer of the Gunpowder Plot, Cecil had since swept the board clean of his old enemies, one amongst them being Henry Percy, Earl of Northumberland.

Since the Wizard Earl's arrest, he had, for long spells, ensured that Algernon was imprisoned alongside him. They were not lacking in amusement, for Percy's prison included a bowling alley and tennis courts, and he would watch Algernon fencing or have the boy taught from ancient books, with the same seemingly ageless tutor, Edward Dowse, never far off. Yet Percy knew that Algernon should have a fine marriage match, and so, under Dowse's watchful eye, with Percy's Three Magi – Harriot, Warner, and Hues – observing from the shadows, Algernon attended social occasions with members of King James' court.

A student at Cambridge attending St John's, where his father had gone before him, Algernon was known as man of great fortune. Which is why, when Sir Robert Cecil presented to him his daughter during a masque at the recently completed Hatfield House, none present thought it in any way untoward.

Cecil said to Algernon, 'I am told, your Lordship, that like your father, you are adept at reading horoscopes. Please, permit an old man's folly and be so kind as to read my daughter's.'

This Algernon did, and no sooner had he begun that arcane process than a strange set of coincidences emerged. He read in the stars, in her blood, in the great many almanacks and books he had studied so well, copies of which stood in Cecil's own library, that the fate of this girl and his own were inextricably entwined.

'It is as I thought,' Cecil declared with a wry smile. 'This child, the apple of my eye, is to be yours, as decreed by the heavens themselves.'

Dowse, who knew no better, thought Ann a fine match for his ward – not least as the dark-haired beauty was the daughter of the Lord Protector. No sooner had Algernon given his golden ring to Ann, bearing his family's crest and motto, than Dowse had written to his master, appealing for the stars to be studied and the date set for the pair to be wed.

The intended union was a cause for celebration and all the great families present bore witness to the ring on Ann's finger. Somerset, Hertford, Arundel, Pembroke, and Shrewsbury all saw it, and all thought Algernon well matched.

Rather than pleased, of course, from his position in the Tower of London, Henry Percy was furious. He knew nothing of Ann's true identity, but it was Cecil who had seen him tried and imprisoned – Cecil who had routed the School of Night, replacing them in the Crown's esteem with the Society of the New Art. And so, Percy dispatched Harriot, Warner, and Hues, setting them on a secret quest: to prevent the marriage, whatever the cost.

While simple murder was considered and favoured by Harriot, Northumberland's magi were far from fools. Each a learned academic, they discussed the merits of curses, poisons, and spells, but Warner knew that Cecil was a man whose homes were all defended against the dark arts.

Cecil's allies included skilled natural philosophers like Nicholas Culpepper and Peter Coles, as well as great minds and thinkers such as William Byrd and Orlando Gibbons, who wove spells into music which echoed through Cecil's halls, banishing shadows and any dark forces within them. Sat amid all this protection, like a faerie at the centre of a hoard of gold, was Ann, the dark-haired daughter, so unlike Francis and Catherine Cecil, both of whom were years older with hair like golden wheat.

The magi turned to simpler means. During a madrigal at Arundel Castle, Hues approached Ann Cecil and, with a deft touch, slipped from her finger the Percy family ring, for the magi knew that without that ring Ann would never again appear before Algernon. Its loss would be so shaming and such a dishonour that the marriage would be cancelled by default.

Thinking themselves wise to dispose of the evidence in the most thorough manner possible, the magi rode all the way up to Northumberland, where the ring began its life. At Bamburgh Castle, they conducted an unholy rite, commanding the ring to only return to the rightful heir of the House of Percy.

Then they tossed the ring into the sea, rode south once more, and considered the matter settled.

Algernon was, of course, heartbroken. His father continued to attempt to control him, but Algernon was wilder now, a child of passion, just like his forefathers of old. He studied law at Middle Temple, but so close to the court, with Ann always kept from him, and away from all eyes at the time, he felt he had no other choice than to go abroad.

So it was that for six years Algernon toured Europe, always in the company of Edward Dowse. He travelled first to Italy, then back through France and the Dutch Republic, ever-seeking a beauty to rival the woman whose face he saw in his dreams. His star wife, his bride of fate – Ann – the only one for him.

In the meantime, Cecil died and Ann became the ward of his son, William. Much older than she, William assumed the role of her father, yet he was unnerved. Though he grew older, his hair threaded with grey, Ann did not, her pale skin, raven hair and twinkling eyes appearing alike to him as when his father first introduced them so many years ago.

The Wizard Earl, Henry Percy, was then freed from prison in 1621, by which time he was but a shadow of his former self. Abandoned by his magi and banned by the Crown from returning to Alnwick, he took shelter at the Bath Inn, recently renovated by Inigo Jones. Sickly and bitter, even though living in luxury, he tried to restore relations with Algernon, who returned to England three years later – but the rift between them was wider than it had ever been.

Edward Dowse died and, now despondent and alone, Algernon was elected to Parliament. He represented first Sussex, then Chichester, but he had become a bitter man. Still handsome, with flowing auburn hair, by the time he entered the House of Lords he had grown frenzied with his fury towards the new king and his allies.

Attempts were made to placate him and he was appointed Lord Lieutenant of Cumberland, Westmorland, and Northumberland, but at every opportunity Algernon chose to pick at the scab on England's heart. The target of his ire was George Villiers, Duke of Buckingham, favourite to the new king Charles I, whom he embarrassed and belittled and enraged.

Word then came to Algernon in the autumn of 1628 that his father was finally dying. Out of pity, and at the behest of the Duke of Somerset, Algernon met once again with the Wizard Earl – the man whose tyrannical treatment had made his childhood so bitter. A date was set for the pair to dine together, and at the Bath Inn, with the Duke of Somerset also present, they ate. The talk was light and airy, of matters of no consequence, all parties fearing a slip of the tongue which could explode into violence.

The Wizard Earl, almost blind and wracked with fits of coughing, tried to pour honeyed words into his son's ears, but Algernon was resistant. Indeed, it was not words that did for their relationship, but a dish, served on a silver platter. It was one of many served to those present, but on that salver lay a fish cooked in lemon, garlic, and butter, into which the Duke of Somerset cut, making a remarkable discovery.

'By the Fates!' he declared, holding his knife aloft and stepping backwards, dumbfounded and fit to collapse. 'I never thought I would see it again…'

Algernon rushed about the table, bringing a chair near for his friend, and then saw it, glinting in the belly of the fish. He pushed his fingers inside then raised it aloft – the ring he had given Ann, bearing the lion rampant, inlaid with lapis lazuli and inscribed with that motto: *Esperance en Dieu* – Hope in God.

The Wizard Earl, though sickly, saw the glinting gold and stood, recognising the ring in an instant. 'Impossible!' he roared. 'My magi stole it from that stupid girl and threw into the sea! You must never marry her – never! No child of that cripple Cecil may wed a child of mine!'

Algernon, furious, replied, 'She is not a child of Cecil's, father. She is a child of heaven. With hair as black as a raven's wing and skin as pale snow, and eyes as green as the seas from whence this ring has returned to me!'

The meal did not continue, and Algernon never spoke to his father again.

Less than a year later, he married Ann Cecil, who had not aged a day until that point. And the pair bore only daughters – four in fact – but it was as if the years that had passed while they were apart came rushing in on Ann all at once.

Of course, Henry Percy died alone, sheltered by the Duke of Somerset at Petworth House. The old man never saw his granddaughters nor came to realise that the same child he had tried to drown had grown into the woman his son had married. Neither did he live to see Algernon welcomed into the Order of the Garter, appointed Lord Admiral of the British Fleet and serving as one of the great leaders on Parliament's side in the Civil War.

But that was his just desserts, for Henry Percy had tried to defy fate, who is a cruel mistress indeed.

And although Algernon Percy loved Ann with all his heart, the time rushed in on her, and her beauty and health faded quickly. She died in 1637, never seeing her children wed.

In the wake of her death, Algernon was once again heartbroken. He rebelled against Cromwell, retired to Alnwick and never returned to the heart of politics. He did marry once more, to Elizabeth Howard, daughter of the Earl of Suffolk, but their son, Josceline, died without issue and the line of the House of Percy was ended forever.

Still, Algernon and Ann are at least united in death. They are buried side-by-side at Petworth, in a crypt in the South Chancel of St Mary's Church, as perhaps they were always destined to be.

26

Buttermilk Jack and the Blidworth Witch

A Nottinghamshire Tale

In folk tales, witches are often victim to the same pitfalls which trap the Devil. They can be easily tricked, and their greed is often their downfall.

Still, the maxim that you should give a witch something she asks for does have some basis in fact. There are numerous accounts of cunning folk and healers refusing to accept traditional forms of payment for their spells and charms, instead being offered gifts of food or useful household items.

The 'Buttermilk Jack' story follows a classic 'power of three' folk tale structure, but I thought it would be fun to tell it from the witch's perspective rather than the hero's. Sack tricks are also rife in fairy tales, along with the general trope of the magic bag.

Although it might fit into any collection of European folk tales, this one is firmly placed in Nottinghamshire. The idea of a 'familiar spirit' in the shape of a cat is also a classic trope. It stands to reason the cat would be the brains of the operation, especially in a case where the witch is a bit forgetful.

I borrowed my witch's name from an eighteenth-century text, The Tale of the Lancashire Witches, *and was rather taken with the idea of Cecily Cuthbert being bribed to part with her immortal soul with the promise of a really fabulous dinner.*

EC

Always give a witch what she asks. Unless you can think of a way to trick her instead.

There was once a witch in Blidworth who was as houseproud as a new bride. Her cottage was always kept spotlessly clean and tidy, with the magic books stacked neatly, bundles of fresh herbs scenting the air, and the copper cauldrons shining like the morning sun. Her pride and joy was her collection of fine china, which was displayed complacently on a broad dresser.

This witch's name was Cecily Cuthbert, and she liked everything around her to be pleasant. That was how she'd become a witch in the first place, in fact. She'd grown up in poverty until the Devil, in the form of a hare, had appeared to her and her mother and sister and persuaded them to join his cause in exchange for a seven-course dinner with wine pairings.

That first dinner had awakened a hungry fiend in Cecily Cuthbert, and from that moment on, she just couldn't get enough of cinnamon sweetmeats, juicy chicken legs and lashings of butter and cheese. Her cheeks were round as apples and her skin was smooth and pink from all the eating and fine living.

Despite her love of the most luxurious food, Cecily Cuthbert didn't like to pay for it. After all, she'd already paid the Devil with her soul, so she thought she shouldn't have to pay for anything at all after that. Everything she owned, from her soft leather boots to her geranium-scented hair oil, she'd acquired by other means. In fact, the saying in those parts that you should always give a witch what she asks originated with Cecily. She had only ever had to do one piece of real magic in Blidworth, but it was enough for word to get around.

One day, she'd been about to board the cart bound for Nottingham and she fancied some of the carrier's pipe tobacco to smoke herself, so she asked him for a pinch. But the carrier refused and told Cecily Cuthbert that she should buy her own tobacco as he had done. So, she never rode the cart that day, but she fixed the horses with a fierce stare and then they wouldn't move. They stood stock still, rooted to the spot, and after nightfall the carrier knocked at Cecily Cuthbert's door with a great pouch of tobacco.

From that day on, people always gave her what she asked for.

I should tell you that Cecily Cuthbert had a familiar spirit to help her in her enchantments – a hobgoblin from the Devil's own breeding grounds. It looked like a cat to the eyes of others, and it fed from a mole on Cecily's left arm and was known as Rutterkin. It was just as well that Cecily had a familiar to remind her of things, for she was very forgetful.

Now, one day Cecily put on her new heeled boots and tallest sugar-loaf hat, hung her willow basket over her arm and rode the cart into Nottingham to do some shopping. She didn't shop as you or I do, for she never paid for anything, and more often than not, she didn't remember the things she had really needed but came back with lavender soap instead of eggs or gingerbread instead of ribbons. Rutterkin twined about her ankles trying to remind her that she needed oil, bread and potatoes, but she hardly listened.

Nottingham was a fine place to spend a morning wandering around the shops and stalls in those days, and Cecily's basket was filling up nicely with pieces of lace, sticky currant buns and other good things. But by midday she had a powerful thirst and a craving for something sweet. She could almost taste the sugar in her watering mouth as she imagined biting into a delicious pudding. She was thinking about calling into an inn for some lunch, when she heard a thin cry from a deserted alley.

'Who'll buy my buttermilk?'

Something you may not know is that witches are excessively fond of buttermilk, and no witch was ever fonder than Cecily Cuthbert. So she followed the sound of the voice, down the dark little alleyway, until she saw a small, skinny boy holding a pail of delicious frothy buttermilk.

This boy's name was Little Jack, and he was the only son of a poor widow. They only had one cow to their name, and it was their whole fortune, that cow. Every day, the widow milked the cow and made fresh cheese and butter to store ready for sale at the great Nottingham Goose Fair, while Jack took to the streets of Nottingham to sell the buttermilk.

His prices were reasonable and he would pour a generous helping of buttermilk into your jug for just a few pennies, but that meant nothing to Cecily Cuthbert. She went up to Little Jack as bold as brass and asked him for the milk.

Little Jack didn't like the look of the crow's feather stuck jauntily into Cecily Cuthbert's hat or the way mud didn't seem to stick to her grass-green petticoat, so he clutched his pail tight in his trembling hands and told her that he and his mother were poor and couldn't afford to give the milk away for free.

Cecily Cuthbert was astonished, for nobody had ever refused her since the trick she had pulled with the carrier's horses. She was hot and thirsty, and the sweet, creamy milk in the pail was calling to her. 'You'd better hand it over,' she said crossly to Little Jack, 'or I'll put you in my sack and take you home with me, and then I'll eat you for supper instead.' Cecily always carried a sack when she went shopping, in case any of the kind townsfolk wanted to make her a particularly large present.

But Little Jack put up his chin and refused to give her the milk.

So, Cecily Cuthbert took out her sack, grabbed hold of Jack and stuffed him inside it, along with his churn and pail. How delicious he would be baked in a pie, she thought, with a flagon of lovely buttermilk to wash him down!

It was a fine day, so Cecily thought that she would walk back to Blidworth. Besides, she could work up an appetite for eating Little Jack. But a little way out of town, she started thinking about Rutterkin's reminders to bring back certain things. What could they have been? One had been potatoes, she was sure of it. Could she manage without them? Perhaps, but wouldn't a pie filled with little boy taste better with some nice mashed potatoes on the side?

Cecily determined that she must have those potatoes. Ahead, she saw a pair of fellows cutting a thorn bush, so she asked them if they would mind the sack for her while she just popped back into Nottingham. The men agreed, and off Cecily went.

But as soon as she had gone, Jack started wriggling and kicking and making a noise in the sack, so much that the hedge cutters opened the top of the sack to see what all the fuss was about. They were all for leaving well alone, for they had recognised Cecily and knew that it would be a bad idea to get on the wrong side of her, but Little Jack gave them all a free drink of buttermilk and they agreed to let him go.

The sack was a bit flat without Jack in it, so he picked up some of the thorny hedge cuttings and stuffed them in instead. The hedge cutters watched doubtfully, but Little Jack gave them more buttermilk and they promised not to say a word.

When Cecily returned with the potatoes, she thanked the hedge cutters and went on her way with the sack slung over her shoulder. But the thorns from the hedge cuttings poked through the sack and stuck into her back, so that she thought Jack was pinching her. It was a long way home, with the thorns pricking her, and Cecily angrily calling out to the supposed Little Jack to keep his fingers to himself.

When she got back, Rutterkin rubbed up against her ankles and asked her if she had remembered the potatoes, oil and bread.

'Oil and bread went out of my head,' said Cecily, 'but potatoes I have, and something better!'

She shook out the sack with a flourish, expecting to be able to show off the basis of a scrumptious dinner. But all that scattered on to her clean floor was a bundle of thorny clippings. Rutterkin yowled and hissed, and Cecily said some words which were never found in Mr Johnson's *Dictionary*. There was no pie and mashed potatoes for dinner, but instead the witch and the cat sat sadly eating currant buns and planning revenge on Little Jack.

The next day, Cecily put on her sugarloaf hat again and trotted back off to Nottingham. Rutterkin cautioned her to remember the oil and bread this time, but most importantly to capture that slippery Little Jack.

Jack believed he had got clean away from her, so thought nothing about selling his buttermilk in the same streets as usual. Imagine his surprise when Cecily Cuthbert's shadow in its pointed hat fell across the end of the alleyway. She didn't wait to ask him for his buttermilk, but stuffed him straight inside the sack, churn and pail and all!

Cecily marched straight out of the town gates and past the thorny bushes, giving the hedge cutters a fearsome look which made one turn pale and the other have to sit down suddenly. But she hadn't got a little bit of the way back to Blidworth when she started thinking about Rutterkin's reminders. What could they have been? One had been bread, she was certain. Could she manage without it? Perhaps, but wouldn't the gravy she'd make from Little Jack's bones taste better with some fresh, springy bread to mop it up?

Just up ahead she saw a couple of stonecutters mending the potholes in the road, so she asked them if they would mind the sack for her while she just popped back into Nottingham. The stonecutters agreed, and off Cecily went.

I hardly need tell you that just the same thing happened. The stonecutters had their buttermilk, Jack got clean away, and Cecily Cuthbert walked back to Blidworth with the heavy stones in the sack banging against her back, thinking Little Jack was kicking her.

Rutterkin jumped down from the dresser and asked her if she had remembered the bread and oil.

'Oil we'll not have for the boil,' said Cecily, 'but bread I have, and something better!'

Well, she shook out the sack, but all that thundered on to the floor was a pile of clattering stones. Rutterkin spat and screeched, and Cecily kicked a chair leg in an unusual show of pique. There was no roast boy and fluffy bread for dinner, and the witch and the cat went to bed with a wheel of Colton Basset Stilton and plotted their revenge on Little Jack.

The next day, Cecily laced up her boots with renewed determination and set off for Nottingham town. Rutterkin reminded her thrice times nine about the oil, but most especially to let nothing distract her in bringing back Jack.

Little Jack had wisely gone to sell his buttermilk in a different street, so it took Cecily half the morning to find him, and when she did she was good and hungry and ready to take a slice out of him then and there. But she was as good as her word to her familiar and went straight back home, passing the hedge cutters and the stonecutters with her nose in the air.

When she got back, she put the sack down on the floor in front of Rutterkin and shook it hard to check that Jack was still inside it.

'What about the oil?' said Rutterkin.

Cecily was all for managing without the oil, now she'd actually got Jack home, but wouldn't his flesh taste better if she lightly sealed the meat in a pan first?

This time, Cecily put Rutterkin in her basket to make quite sure that she wouldn't forget, and she shut up the cottage windows and locked the doors, and tied the neck of the sack as tightly as she could so that Jack wouldn't escape. As soon as he was alone, Jack started to wriggle and jiggle inside the sack. He fairly well danced a Nine Men's Morris in there, until the rope around the sack loosened enough for him to worm his way out.

He was surprised to see how clean and tastefully decorated the witch's cottage was, but it gave him an idea to teach her a lesson she wouldn't forget. He took all of her fine china plates and delicate tea cups from the dresser where they were displayed and put them into the sack. Then he retied the rope around the sack's neck. Although the doors and windows were locked, it was lucky for Jack that forgetful Cecily Cuthbert hadn't remembered to light her fire, so he could climb up the chimney with his buttermilk churn and pail and run back home to his mother.

Some little while later, Cecily and Rutterkin returned in triumph with a large flagon of oil and lots of other nice things too, which the kind folk of Nottingham had been practically begging them to take. They were ready to cook a wonderful dinner and drink up every last drop of Little Jack's buttermilk.

Quick as a flash, Cecily upended the sack and shook it out, but all that fell out was her beautiful collection of china – and every last bit of it smashed to smithereens on the polished flagstone floor. Cecily Cuthbert howled in rage and vowed that this time she would put a curse on Little Jack which would last for seven generations.

But Jack wisely moved his buttermilk operations to Mansfield, and after a few days of prowling the streets of Nottingham in search of her foe, Cecily forgot all about him too.

27

Lord Lovell's Bride

An Oxfordshire Tale

A perennial Yuletide favourite, also known as 'The Mistletoe Bride' and 'The Legend of the Mistletoe Bough', this is a story whose origins are claimed by dozens of stately homes and country houses across England. These include, though are not limited to, Basildon Grotto in Berkshire, Castle Horneck in Cornwall, both Bramshill House and Marwell Hall in Hampshire, Brockdish Hall in Norfolk, Exton Hall in Rutland and Bawdrip Rectory in Somerset.

The tale is older; it first appeared in a printed form in 1822 in a poem by Lord Byron's friend Samuel Rogers entitled 'Ginevra'. It was then turned into a ballad by T.H. Bayly and Sir Henry Bishop. This version became one of the most popular songs ever written, sung in households all over the England each Christmas.

It lives on in stories like Henry James' The Romance of Certain Old Clothes *and Thomas Hardy's novel,* A Laodicean*; features in Hitchcock's classic thriller,* Rope*; and my setting of it, in the haunted Romantic fifteenth-century ruins of Minster Lovell Hall, is further enhanced by the discovery of a skeleton in a hidden vault there in 1708. As recounted in my telling, those bones were thought to belong to Francis Lovell, ally of Richard III, who was believed to have fled back to the Cotswolds and hid there after the Battle of Stoke, subsequently dying of starvation.*

As for the Lord Lovell the tale is said to pertain to – William – he was born a generation before, in 1397, and is buried in Greyfriars Church, Oxford.

MV

In the quiet parish of Minster Lovell, on the bristling banks of the Windrush River, you'll find the empty ruins of a barren hall. Built of grey rubble and once faced with fine ashlar, the roof fell in over a century ago. The stairs have long since crumbled away and the vaults beneath the house are filled in now, but in 1708, those very vaults were excavated, and a secret chamber found inside.

Within that secret chamber, there was a body. It was male, entirely wasted away, and within minutes of being exposed to fresh air the corpse crumbled away and turned to dust. Some say this was the body of Francis Lovell, heir to the house and the last in a long line of Lovells dating back to the Norman invasion.

Francis had been the ninth, but he made a mistake – supporting Richard III during the Wars of the Roses.

The Lovell family held estates all over England, including at Middleham Castle in Yorkshire, Acton Burnell in Shropshire, and Old Wardour in Salisbury, but after the Yorkist defeat at the Battle of Stoke in 1487, Francis Lovell disappeared. His estates were searched over, but Lovell was nowhere to be found. The theory goes, he escaped to Minster Lovell Hall, which by then had been gifted by the Crown to Jasper Tudor, Duke of Bedford, and there he hid, secreted in a little-known chamber deep underground.

Whether Bedford locked him in or a servant abandoned him there, or if he was already ill and just wasted away, whatever the case, the ninth Lord Lovell starved to death in that secret iron cage and was forgotten about for almost three centuries.

Yet that discovery was hardly the first macabre story associated with the Lovells. For it was William, the seventh Lord Lovell, who built the hall in Oxfordshire. And William was known as a kind man, unlike his father, John, the Mad Lord Lovell, who spent a fortune on an elaborate four-storey octagonal tower there. The Mad Lord built the tower for his own defence, so he said, against evil forces that had cursed his family's blood.

It was defensible, and the Mad Lord lived in that tower almost entirely alone. After the death of his wife, it was just John and William. At the top of it, in the room above his bedchamber, the Mad Lord kept his greatest treasures, heirlooms of past Lovell victories, safely locked in a grand chest with a stiff iron lock, sumptuously carved of the finest English oak.

As a boy, William Lovell was scared of the tower, suspecting he knew the things his father and his father's father, and men before that, had done to acquire that gold and silver. Bright as they were to others, for William those treasures were stained blood red.

Unlike the Mad Lord, William was a man of peace. As soon as he could, he moved away from his father. He went to Oxford University, training to become a priest, but when the time came to take Holy Orders, the Mad Lord died. William inherited the family's wealth, so he declined a life in the Church, but dedicated himself to good works nonetheless.

He set about having the oak chest emptied, using part of his father's treasure to renovate St Kenelm's Church – the place where many of his ancestors were buried. You can see them there still, and the marble busts William had commissioned, hoping to buy their way into Heaven years after their lives of brutal war and slaughter.

Alas, the renovations at St Kenelm's did not clear out the chest with its thick oak sides and banded iron loops. Besides, new money kept flowing into William's household with such rapidity that it threatened to fill it once more. So William crept up to the top of that tower, opening the chest, embellished as it was with the grotesque faces of goblins and dragons, monsters and trolls, and he filled a sack with those goods, those heirlooms, that treasure, carrying his legacy off to sell, giving half to the poor and using half to build Minster Lovell Hall.

Gentle, softly spoken, charitable – after William built the hall, it became a warm and happy place. A grand house, the old tower was the coldest part, situated in its corner up a flight of twisting stairs that William knew to avoid. And though William entertained and paid his servants well, and was loved by the people of the parish, the grand home he had built felt shockingly empty. At night William struggled to sleep, wandering its halls and rooms achingly alone.

As the years went by and silver grew into William Lovell's beard and speckled his temples, he became more and more lonesome. Friends tried to interest him in hunting and sport, revelry and drink, but Lord Lovell – he pined for something he feared he would never know.

And that thing? Well, it was love. Not a roll in the hay or a sowing of wild oats. William sought true, meaningful love, the kind of which he had once felt for God but, since his father's death, he worried he might never know again.

Happily, while out riding on one bright autumn day, William saw a woman who he knew was the one. Her name was Elizabeth. She was playing with children in the road, laughing and running, dirt on her skirts. And though she was only the daughter of a tenant farmer, humbler in background than he, from the moment William laid eyes on her his heart skipped for joy.

For weeks he was too nervous to speak to her, and though she was some years his junior, Elizabeth knew of William Lovell's good works. And he was a handsome man as well as generous. She never might have imagined a person as grand as he might choose her for a wife, but he did, and her playful smile, her laughter, and her sense of irrepressible mischief brought joy to William Lovell of a kind he had never known.

So a wedding day was set. Christmas. A day of charity and goodwill. And at the very church William had helped to rebuild, St Kenelm's, the pair were joined in holy matrimony. All and sundry were invited to the wedding feast, from neighbouring lords to washerwomen, gentry to chimneysweeps, and to cope with them all, Lord Lovell opened the hall's windows and doors wide, the feast stretching from inside to out, tables laid end on end in the garden. Fires and torches were lit, people dressing in their thickest clothes, and with the brisk air pinching their cheeks, the tables decorated with ivy, mistletoe, and holly. All ate their fill and made merry, feasting and drinking long into the night.

It's said Lord Lovell was dressed as the Lord of Misrule, his new bride as his Lady, wearing a mistletoe crown. Games were played, laughter echoing down the river, bouncing off the fast-moving water. The party was wild, food abounding, and the wine poured freely.

As darkness fell, however, Lord Lovell, keen to take his bride to his bedchamber, turned to her and smiled a wide smile. Knowing his meaning, and with warmth in her heart, Elizabeth grinned.

'One last game, please, My Lord, and a good one to boot,' she said.

'As you wish, My Lady,' William replied. 'What sport would be your pleasure?'

'Hide and seek,' she replied, standing and planting a kiss on his red cheek. 'Count to a hundred and then come to find me.'

So it was that Elizabeth Lovell walked away from the feast, disappearing into the grand hall she could now rightly call her home. And William, the Lord of Misrule, wearing his crown of holly, closed his eyes and counted just as he had been bade.

His first port of call, as you might imagine, was his bedroom, but he searched all his cupboards, under his bed, in his wardrobe, and Elizabeth was nowhere to be found. Perplexed, he moved on, searching the other rooms on the second floor, rifling through each with growing desperation. He sought on – the upper floors, the third and the attic, then proceeded to the kitchens, beginning to worry.

As the hours wore on, those guests who remained formed a search party. The torches were pulled from the ground and the house and grounds scoured. The nearby woods were walked through, Lady Lovell's name called out into the night, the riverbanks combed until dawn broke.

Some felt it the worst of all fates. That William had been taken for a fool right and true, and his new wife, faced with the thought of marriage, had simply fled and would never be found. Others feared she had fallen into the Windrush and drowned, her body carried downstream or claimed by the creatures within.

Yet, as the days wore into weeks and the weeks into months, the chill of winter giving way to spring and spring giving way to summer, the cold never left William Lovell. The lord grew older so quickly that friends who had not seen him since the fateful wedding day would see him again and mistake him for his father, the Mad Lord, withering away.

By night, Lord Lovell once again wandered the rooms of his hall, which now felt all the more empty. As he walked, he wept, crying out in the night, fearful of heading to bed. For when he slept, he was haunted by dreams; the voice of his mistletoe bride calling out to him from deep in the dark.

'William, it's dark, why don't you come find me? I'm so aching for you. I can barely breathe.'

He would wake bathed in sweat, his heart thundering. And sometimes he would search, looking over the same places again and again, hoping perhaps somehow he had missed something – some clue that would reveal where his true love had gone. Yet, it was no use, and each night, as he lay down to rest, her voice would sound in his mind.

'William, it's dark, why don't you come find me? I'm so aching for you. I can barely breathe.'

The months turned to years, and as the memory of Elizabeth waned in the minds of so many, Lord Lovell was left alone in his grief and pain. His servants found him no longer so kind, no longer willing to smile, and as the money came in from his lands and estates, questions arose as to what to do with it.

So it was that one day, a maid opened the old turret door, recalling that once, people said, the Mad Lord had kept his treasure in a trunk. Thinking to dust it down and return it to its old purpose, she was sent by the steward up to the fourth floor. And there, in the middle of that dusty, unused room, she saw the old chest, carved with grotesque faces, banded with iron, its stiff lock firmly closed. She went for help, and eventually, after great labour and the application of whale oil and a length of iron, the lid was prised open.

And concealed inside, in a tattered silk gown, wearing a mistletoe crown, was Lord Lovell's bride.

They told William, who rushed to the chamber and saw her there, his own greatest treasure, lain in that forsaken box. And though he raised her up out of it, her body was so frail it fell to pieces in his arms, the words of his dreams echoing in his mind.

'William, it's dark, why don't you come find me? I'm so aching for you. I can barely breathe.'

A sad tale for sure, not least because William Lovell never recovered. His hair was white for the rest of his days, and though he married again and fathered a son he called John, after his own father, he only grew more and more mad. So, his wife and son moved away, repairing to Titchmarsh Castle, where they lived in great comfort.

William, meanwhile, stayed in Minster Lovell Hall, moving into the tower, making a bedroom in the room below the garret where the chest remained. People say they used to see him walking through the rooms at night, long after his bride was found. Some said he danced as if on his wedding night, though with a partner invisible to all but him. Others even swore he kept searching, rifling through wardrobes and cupboards and chests as if she'd never been found at all.

It's even believed that Lord Lovell kept on with his nighttime wanderings after death, long beyond the time the house was bought by Sir Edward Coke in 1603. Which is why, over the years, Minster Lovell Hall fell into disrepair – abandoned in 1747 and desolate ever since.

So, while it might seem like a fun sort of place to play hide and seek, the locals of Minster Lovell village recommend against it. Though it's also said that if you're very quiet, in the still of the night, you might yet hear them laughing together, at play forever more – William, Lord Lovell, and Elizabeth, Lord Lovell's bride.

28

Four Eggs a Penny

A Rutland Tale

Considering its relative size, it is perhaps understandable that Rutland has a fairly small bank of local folk tales, yet it still punches above its weight. Standing out against the tales of mythical knights and monstrous huntsmen who are perhaps the hallmark characters of Rutland's legends, this rather quiet, good-natured ghost story speaks to a different side of the county's character.

It came to me via the good people at the Leicestershire Guild of Storytelling, and tracing it further back, it is a variant of an older kind of tale known as 'The Grateful Dead', as kept alive by the likes of the iconic twentieth-century storyteller Ruth Tongue (she who taught Taffy Thomas his trade, long before he became England's first-ever Storytelling Laureate).

A version appears in the Medieval Romance Sir Amadace, *it was recounted in Gaelic by Highland storyteller Alexander MacNeill as 'The Barra Widow's Son' for John Campbell's nineteenth-century collection,* Popular Tales of the West Highlands, *and it seems that all of these variants link back to the apocryphal story of 'Tobias and the Angel'.*

Considering Rutland's rich history – Oakham Castle, with its vast collection of ancient horseshoes, is the best-preserved Norman building in the country – there have no doubt been many Toms and many Blind Joes who have lived and died there over the centuries. As such, it behoves us to remember them and seek to avoid their fate repeating and therefore haunting us in the centuries to come.

MV

Back in the days of Bad King John, there lived a man called Tom Thistledown. A poor man and an orphan since childhood, Tom made his living by foraging in the county's hedgerows and all through Rutland Forest. He lived on mushrooms and berries and roots, and camped under the moon, free as bird. That said, what Tom sought and prized most of all was eggs as laid by the wildfowl that lived thereabouts.

Of course, Tom sought pigeons and doves, for both made good eating, but most of all he prized duck eggs, whose silky yolks were worth more than any other. In fact, duck eggs were a precious commodity at the time, and Tom knew that if he could find them and bring them to Oakham Market he could sell each for a farthing, or four eggs for a penny.

With enough pennies, Tom could afford to sleep in a comfortable bed and buy himself a hot meal, a bath, and maybe even the odd mug of ale. And this he deserved as hunting for eggs could be tough work, especially when it rained or the weather was cold.

Now, Tom was, it's worth saying, a fairly lonely sort of fellow, as many poor men are wont to be. Folks don't take kindly to people who know what it's like to wake with frost in their hair, and somehow they can always tell. Thankfully, though, in time Tom did make one friend – a man even poorer than himself, whom everybody knew as Blind Joe the beggar.

Joe, who lived in Oakham, had lost his sight and two fingers fighting for King Richard's army in France. Yet as he was old and poor and disfigured, he was not much loved by the people of the town. They resented his sleeping in doorways and other such spots that were sheltered from the worst of the weather and they chided him for begging by the wall near the town gates, even though he had little choice.

Thankfully for Blind Joe, when Tom came by on market days the pair would enjoy each other's company. After selling his eggs, Tom would lead Joe out of the town to the hollow halfway to Barleythorpe. There, beneath the trees, they would share such food as Tom could afford and some drink, if there was some. And Joe would sing with Tom, ballads from when Joe was a boy, and tell him stories round fires that Tom lit and kindled, the pair laughing long into the night.

As the years went by, of course, Blind Joe became thinner and thinner, all on account of a lack of charity in Oakham. So, it became Tom's habit, on his way into Oakham to market, to leave one of the eggs he'd found in a hole in the bricks by the town gate, right at the spot where Blind Joe would sit and beg for money. And sure enough, when Tom would see Joe later that day, Joe would thank him for the egg, saying, 'Without that egg Tom, I don't think I would have made it through until evening.'

Well, on one such market day at dawn, Tom went to the hollow halfway to Barleythorpe, and he laid kindling and stacked wood ready for the evening's fire. He knew he was coming to town with a huge haul, for spring had come. He'd managed to find several nests, so was headed to market with two dozen eggs. This meant he was going to earn a whole silver sixpence and he'd be able to afford an entire loaf of bread to share, and butter, and beer, and much more besides.

Still, as he walked into Oakham, Tom thought to himself, 'You know, I'd best leave an egg for old Joe.' So he did, picking one that looked particularly beautiful, with a sky-blue shell and speckles all down one side in a shape that looked like Orion's Belt. This, of course, only left Tom with twenty-three eggs, which would earn him just five pence and three farthings, but he knew such a sum could still afford him two slices of bread and some butter, and some beer to share with Joe, so although it was less than he might have earned otherwise, he left the egg in the hole in the wall and wandered off to the market.

Amongst the hubbub of the stalls, Tom got down to business. Sure enough, he sold his eggs for five pence and three farthings. Only then he spied, laid in the road at the edge of the market square, a shape that was face down in the mud. It was none other than Blind Joe, who was dead as a doornail, and when Tom saw him there, he dashed over and fell to his knees and wept.

'I don't know why you're crying,' said one woman passing by. 'He can lie in the dirt for all I care. I leant him a penny once and he never paid me back. I suppose that's just the way it is with some people.'

Appalled at this, Tom paid the woman back the penny she had given to Joe out of the coins in his pocket. Then he spared two more, one to rest on each of Joe's dead eyelids. These would mean Joe could pay St Peter to enter the gates of heaven, although before that could happen, Tom realised, his friend's corpse would need to have a Christian burial.

Quick as he could, off Tom went to the coffin maker, and there he bought a coffin for Joe which cost him a whole penny and a half – the price of six eggs. Desperate now, for almost all of his money was spent,

Tom sat outside the coffin-maker's shop with Joe's body in its box. He was weeping again, in a state of despair, as he could not for the life of him think of how to get the coffin to the churchyard without spending the last of his earnings.

Then, thankfully, a farmer was passing by with his horse and cart, and he spied Tom weeping beside the coffin. 'Who's died then, son?' the farmer asked.

'Only Blind Joe the beggar,' Tom replied. 'I'm trying to get him to the churchyard, but I can't afford to pay anyone to carry him.'

'Oh, I knew Blind Joe!' said the farmer. 'He told me any number of wonderful stories over the years. He made me laugh and made me cry. Tales of King Richard and France, of love and ghosts and adventure. You know, he was a hero, too, once. So then, come on and help me lift him into my cart and I'll take you both to the alderman.'

So, off Tom and the farmer went, chuckling away about Joe and his stories. Unfortunately, once the farmer had dropped Tom off at All Saint's Church, helping him with the coffin before driving his horse and cart away, Tom learned that the alderman was not quite so jolly.

'Well, we can bury him,' said the alderman, sucking his teeth. 'Only, won't be cheap.' The priest told Tom that to bury Blind Joe he would need to donate two pennies, plus pay his last farthing to the gravedigger.

So it was that, with a heavy heart, Tom parted with his last few coins. Then he watched on as evening turned to night and the gravedigger made a space for Joe – six feet under, yes, but way off in the darkest, loneliest corner of the churchyard.

The priest said his holy words, and as Blind Joe's coffin disappeared underneath the earth Tom thought to himself that although the view wasn't as nice as he'd have liked, Joe couldn't see to know. Besides, it was at least holy ground, and he couldn't afford to pay for better anyway.

All this did mean that when Tom Thistledown left Oakham that night, he did so with less than he'd come with. Less his eggs, of course, but less, too, a friend, and Blind Joe's company was worth more to Tom than all the pennies he might ever hope to earn.

Not thinking too much about it, Tom let his feet lead the way, and soon enough, he found himself approaching the hollow halfway to Barleythorpe. As he did, anger bloomed up inside him, because he saw that someone had lit the fire he'd laid and the logs he'd stacked were crackling away, throwing orange light and dancing shadows all about the hollow.

Tom dashed forward, wanting to see the scoundrel who had lit his fire and stolen his spot. But when he did, he saw, laid about the fire, two mugs of ale, a full loaf of bread, butter, and twenty-four eggs. Tom fell to his knees and inspected the eggs one by one, eventually noticing that one of them was particularly beautiful, with a sky-blue shell and speckles all down one side in a shape that looked like Orion's Belt.

Well, nobody lives forever, and sure as eggs is eggs, you won't find a gravestone in All Saint's Church marked with the name Tom Thistledown. Yet, for many years, down in that hollow, it was known that Tom would sit around a fire on nights after market days and feast and dance and laugh. People thought him mad, for as they passed it seemed he was talking to no one.

But Tom knew, as you do now, that he was hardly alone – just like he knew that the songs he sang, though from a time long ago, were ballads, and always duets.

29

The Legend of a Cat, and by your allowance, his Earnest Friend Richard, Latterly of Whittington

A Shropshire Tale

While Dick Whittington is most famous today as a pantomime stock character, it is worth remembering that he was a real person, who was three times Mayor of London.

Being born the third-eldest son – and so denied the familial wealth of his Gloucestershire siblings – Richard Whittington came to London in the fourteenth century with nothing, then set about learning his trade as a merchant. He quickly rose to such a position of power that monarchs relied on him for money, which always struck me as a little uncanny. Indeed, we all agree he had a magic cat, so why do we presume that this cat's magic was good?

The association between cats and the Devil goes back a long way. They enjoyed sacred status in Ancient Egypt, were linked with the witch goddess Hecate in Ancient Greece, and then a papal decree of 1233 sealed the deal. According to Pope Gregory IX, in the Vox in Rama, *cats were the creatures of Satan, responsible for spreading the plague. So across Europe cats were rounded up and killed in huge numbers. Which, ironically, led to a boom in the rat population and an escalation of the Black Death.*

Putting these ideas together, I rather like the idea that Dick Whittington was a hapless fool and his cat was actually a demon, if not the Devil himself, pulling the levers of power from behind the scenes. Indeed, if you are a cat owner, do ask yourself who is really calling the shots…

MV

You would think people would care for saints. But they don't. Not really.

Some people wear icons about their necks and call on them in times of strife, rubbing them optimistically between their fingers and their thumbs, but in idler moments saints are forgotten. Dead things, waiting for things to do.

Take Oswald. Murdered by the brute-king Penda, Oswald's arms and legs were cut away, and he later became a saint. What people forget is the why of it, for a raven flew down, collected one of Oswald's severed arms and brought it to a sacred tree. There, Oswald's blood fell from the tree and a spring bloomed forth – a miraculous, healing well later called Oswestry. At this holy place, a castle was built by the Fitzwarines.

Some remember the first Fulk Fitzwarine, the bandit king, but none remember me. This is perhaps by my own design, and I am, no doubt, like a saint in that regard. And though my old bones ache and my fur is thinner in places than perhaps it ought to be, the magic waters of Oswestry have helped me live a thousand years, and through dozens of adventures. Battling alongside Fulk Fitzwarine was a fine thing, hiding in the woods and drawing battle plans, raiding the rich and giving to the poor in a dozen dashes of derring-do, but if you're anything like me, you'll know that a price in blood buys half the pleasure of a price in gold.

Which is where that idiot boy came in useful.

He came at first from Ellesmere, the boy – Richard. And I liked him straightaway as, in addition to being incredibly stupid, a product of the fine tradition of inbreeding within Gloucestershire families, he was also exceedingly greedy. So it was that he came to the Fitzwarines seeking work. Sir Ivo Fitzwarine took him on as a prentice. It was then, while in Ivo's service, that young Richard, still a scrawny boy, came to the wellspring to draw water. I, of course, was slinking through the shadows minding my own business, terrorising a community of mice who had taken up residence in a nearby castle wall and, as Richard dropped his bucket into the well, I couldn't help overhearing him prattling on to himself about a girl.

'Oh, Alice,' he said, 'I do so wish you would notice me. Your beauty shines bright as the light of the moon. Your hair is gold like a sheaf of wheat, your voice as joyful as a songbird's music.'

'Oh, give it a rest,' I purred. And the boy near soiled his britches.

'Who goes there?' he said, drawing a dagger and swishing it about cackhandedly.

'Come off it,' I replied, padding forward and swishing my tail in what I considered a most elegant manner. 'You evidently don't have a clue how to fight, and that's not a problem, dear boy, as if it's love you want then steel is a worthless commodity.'

I could see he was terrified, which was most pleasing, and as he stuttered and mumbled and staggered slowly backwards, I saw he was a ready fruit, ripe for the plucking.

'You… you… you're a talking cat!' he said.

'Bravo,' I replied. 'Now, put your little bodkin away and let's talk business.'

I explained to the boy that base metals are no way to seduce a maiden. I'd learned, long ago, from a very wise alchemist that while pearls and rubies, silk and silver all have their place in this world, truly, the safest and quickest route to beauty is through gold. And certainly, poets are alchemists in their way, spinning air into gold with nothing but their tongues. This foolish lad, well, he was no poet.

'My fine fellow,' I said, 'there's no particular reason for you to trust me, but here you are, talking to an enchanted feline beneath a magic tree. Give me the benefit of the doubt and perhaps try taking some advice. For example, why not suggest to dear old Lord Ivo that you would like join the Mercers' Guild? If you do, he'll say yes, because Ivo likes money as much as the next fellow – and most importantly, your beloved Alice will see you are a man of substance. No mere water-fetching squire – you will become, in her eyes, a golden proposition. One to match her golden hair.'

Well, thankfully, young Richard accepted my guidance, and before long, he was back at the well, a feather in his cap and a ghastly moustache sprouting all along his top lip.

'Cat,' he said, creeping through the shadows in search of me. 'I've done as you told me and Alice's father has granted me the honour of accepting my plea. I'm to marry Alice and all my dreams are set to come true.'

Well, I didn't think much of that, and I jumped down from the branches of the Oswestry in a sequence of graceful, dramatic bounds, landing at the young boy's feet. 'Oh, Richard,' I said, 'your dreams are so small. You're still but a lad.'

I looked him up and down, very much in favour of the brass buckles on his boots, less so the gormless expression on his face, and I licked a paw absentmindedly. 'Dick,' I said to him. 'You don't mind if I call you Dick, do you? Only, Dick, I think we could achieve great things together, you and I. And you trusted me once, so trust me again. How would you like the idea of becoming the richest man in England?'

Well, the boy paused for a moment, and I could see the cogs turning, and eventually an answer rattled forth, falling from his lips like ingots of lead. 'I think,' he replied, 'that I would like that very much.'

'Of course you would,' I said, scampering up his skinny left leg, around his belly and into his doublet. 'In which case, why don't you and I go on a little adventure?'

And that was the beginning of a very exciting time. Our first port of call was the Stiperstones, which we clambered up on Midsummer's Eve. I say 'we' clambered, but Dick did the climbing while I stayed safely stowed in his jacket. We popped by the election, and naturally all were familiar with me. I'd been part of the community for generations and when I explained that Dick and I were throwing our hats into the ring of local politics once more, well, there was a resounding upswell of support.

Our only real competition was a witch called Bianca, who I had Dick poison, and a half-giant named William Ball. And all William, who people called Billy, was interested in was iron, and I made the case that iron was hardly the thing for witches. All it does is get in the way. So it was that the votes were counted, and from his great stone chair, the Devil declared Dick his King for the year – after which we had everything we needed to really get to work.

Dick married Alice and inherited the title. Richard Whittington, Dick to his friends. Alas, back in Gloucestershire, Dick was the youngest son so stood to inherit nothing. And so, though we gradually worked away at diminishing the number of heirs, we also started a rather profitable imports business.

We started in velvet, which is a splendid material, I think we can all agree, and from 1388 we were the go-to people for monarchs and nobles alike. On our first trip to London, Dick was terrified, quaking in his boots, so I more or less had to wear them for him. He turned back, fearing the place, but after the sage administration of a simple tonic, the poor fellow fell under the illusion that the bells of the city were calling to him.

'Turn again, Whittington,' he heard them say.

'Once Lord Mayor of London!

'Turn again, Whittington.

'Twice Lord Mayor of London!

'Turn again, Whittington.

'Thrice Lord Mayor of London!'

I didn't want to push much more than thrice as the boy was never much for counting, but suffice to say that turn again he did.

To start with, I had to get my paws a little dirty. I caught rats, hundreds of the things, and through this Dick made a great many friends – friends who were very much in need of hosiery. And our successes in velvet opened up new markets in silk and broadcloth. The king, also named Richard, spent over £3,500 with us – in today's money that's almost four million. And from there, we started lending money, which was always the real aim of the game. Good old Richard II. Poor fellow had a terrible head for figures, and before the year 1399 he was in debt to us up to his eyeballs.

We also started a very jolly sideline in selling cats. You see, mogs were everywhere in those days, much the same as they are now, in all honesty, most of them dumb as a box of old hammers. But with a judicious enchantment, we could pass them off as magic, and so it was that Dick sold his magic cat a dozen times over. Of course, the enchantments wore off, but a deal's a deal.

In the meanwhile, we had further election successes. In 1384 Dick was elected Councilman to the City of London, then in 1394 the Sherriff of London, before the king very wisely appointed us mayor after poor old Adam Bamme had a terrible accident involving a brick dropped from above an alleyway – well done to Dick on that one, he timed it perfectly.

Well, poor old King Richard II. Bolingbroke led a coup against him. The same Bolingbroke who was incredibly fond of our merchandise. I claim no particular credit in the plot, only suffice to say both sides were admirably clad. Still, Bolingbroke, who became Henry IV in short order, also couldn't count for figs.

So it was that we rode a wave of success, re-elected Mayor of London in 1406, becoming a Member of Parliament in 1416, and all the while we became best of chums with Henry's son, also called Henry, because if ain't broke, don't fix it. Henry the Younger, who would become Henry V, also borrowed huge sums, all the while thinking we were the best of friends.

When they extended Westminster Abbey, who better to oversee the finances than us? And after we were re-elected mayor for the third time in 1419, and people started piping up about usury – a dirty word, no mistake – who better to sit as judge over the whole sordid affair than trusty old Dick Whittington?

People overlooked his habit of referring to his doublet for advice. Not least because we engaged in a great many charitable works, and who wants to criticise a rich man who does so much good with his money?

We rebuilt the Guildhall, in part because the previous iteration was an absolute abomination, and a jolly good chunk of Greyfriars Library, which was very useful to me as some of the books I needed were tricky to find elsewhere. We opened a ward for unmarried mothers at St Thomas' Hospital, one of my favourite places to visit for guaranteed stroking and cosseting in warm bosoms. We dug drainage systems all through Billingsgate and Cripplegate as – well, I have a sensitive nose and the smell beforehand was positively dizzying. Indeed, we opened Whittington's Longhouse, a veritable palace of lavatories – 128 seats, if you can imagine, all positioned so that at high tide every last turd was washed out to sea by Old Father Thames himself.

I felt a little sorry for Alice, who always wanted a baby, but through careful management of her meals, with little additions of fennel, parsley, pennyroyal, and a pinch of arsenic, I managed to keep her womb reliably empty. Nothing would have been worse than the pitter-patter of tiny feet. People barely think of the cat when there's a baby around, and even I draw the line at infanticide.

When it came time and Richard had out-served his usefulness, I did a few very clever things about which I remain incredibly proud. I had his will drafted, leaving millions to good works. His bequests rebuilt

Newgate Prison – after all, one never knows if they might end up in hokey, so it's best to ensure the brig is in tip-top condition. Likewise, we built the brand-new Sheriffs and Recorder, which later became the Old Bailey. For it's always good to keep judges happy. You can have that advice for free.

We also created some super alms-houses, including at St Michael's, and a number of very useful drinking fountains, through which, should one ever have the need, all sorts of tonics might be administered to the local populace en masse, whether that be for their betterment or their ill.

I also, rather nattily, had one of those enchanted cats done in, mummified, and entombed with Dick's corpse at St Michael Paternoster Royal. They found it in 1949, which people found very exciting.

Knowing what's good for me, of course, I never took up permanent residence in the capital. The well at Oswestry is my true home. And there is nowhere in the world quite like Shropshire, I'm sure you'll agree. Speaking of which, there are fresh elections coming up on the Stiperstones. I still have a rich vein of savings – it's prudent to ensure one squirrels at least part of one's fortune away for rainy days – but it's been a while since I had an adventure. The term only lasts a year, and with the judicious application of bribes and a little underhand dealing, a face like yours would make you an outstanding candidate for kingship.

So, how about it? I think you and I could achieve great things together.

30

The Restless Witch of Sandhill

A Somerset Tale

My family has a centuries-long history in Somerset which, along with much of the West Country, is famously a land of rebels and non-conformists.

From King Alfred hiding in the county's marshy levels before repelling the Vikings to the Western Rebellion of 1549, or the county's pivotal role in the Civil Wars to the Monmouth Rebellion of 1685, there has always been something a bit different brewing in Somerset. And not just the cider, I hasten to add…

It is perhaps for this reason that there is quite such a legacy of witchcraft and witch stories in the county, along with buckets of faery lore, tales of King Arthur, and other magical characters linked to Glastonbury. So, rather than picking one of the 'big stories' from the county, I therefore chose to be a rebel myself and tell one of Somerset's smaller, much stranger tales. One linked to Withycombe, Dunster, and Sandhill Manor, near the county's north coast on the edge of Exmoor.

The legend of Joan Carne, as recounted here, is a rare thing, factoring in real historical figures, the Welsh, mysterious deaths, ghosts, and breakfast foods. Moreover, with Joan's defiant progress back towards her home presumably continuing at a rate of one cock-stride a year, I have my fingers crossed that she will soon return and give us all yet more stories to tell.

MV

Somerset is a county rich with witch stories. There are dozens – so many it can be hard to choose whose story to tell.

For example, there's Mary Ann Bull, who people knew as Nan, a healer and wisewoman who roamed West Somerset in a wagon during the nineteenth century. It's said Nan Bull sold goods from her cart, which was also her home, venturing as far as Wool in Dorset to hawk her cures and curses. That was until the townsfolk of Crewkerne turned against her. Like so many witches, she was buried at a crossroads in a spot now known as Bull's Grave.

Then there's Mother Shipton. Born in 1472 in Knaresborough, she lived and died in Porlock and was famous for knowing when storms were coming – essential in a fishing community. It's said Mother Shipton could forecast the tides and predict squalls with such regularity that she didn't so much read the weather as control it.

Of all the witches of Somerset though, perhaps the most interesting is the story of Joan Carne, the Restless Witch of Sandhill. She died in 1612 and is famous for having murdered her three husbands. The truth of her story is a little more complex though, as is so often the way.

Born in Dunster, just a short walk from Minehead, Joan seemed to spring from nowhere. A great beauty, the first record of her existence was her marriage to John Newton. The Newton family had owned Sandhill Farm since 1427 and Sandhill Manor Farm stands on the same spot to this day.

Today, Sandhill Manor sits in 250 acres of wood and farmland. It has its own freshwater spring, manicured gardens with an ornamental lake, stables, and over a hundred horses. You can rent part of it as a holiday home. But back in the time of Queen Elizabeth I, the house and its grounds were more modest, even if their owner, John Newton, was in the prime of his life.

The day John met Joan, the unmarried lord was out riding. A perennial bachelor, he prided himself on his work. He had grown his father's estate, turning it from a run-down, if beloved, semi-wilderness into a profitable, tidy, happy farm. That afternoon though, as John ventured through his thriving empire, he caught sight of a figure scrumping apples from his orchard. He only caught a glimpse of her; a face through the trees and a swish of skirts. Then, the next thing he knew she was gone – vanished from sight.

John rode up to the walls of the orchard, dismounted, and searched desperately between the trees with his heart in his throat. The only trace of life he could see, besides the trees and the insects, his horse and himself, was a pale brown hare running off into a nearby copse.

As the days wore on, John could not put the vision of the woman from his mind. He couldn't eat, couldn't sleep, and would talk of little else. Her face, her shape, that flash of skirt, haunted him. So it was that John Newton pursued Joan, not the other way around.

As days turned into weeks, John made more and more enquiries. He rode west to Old Cleeve, north to Cleeve Bay, and east to Carhampton, the nearest village, which sits beneath the shadow of Bat's Castle. Everywhere he went, he described the woman he'd seen. Though some faces flashed with recognition, nobody wanted to tell the young landowner anything about the person he was seeking. The best he got was a nod in the direction of Rodhuish Common, a wilderness surrounding the ruins of an Iron Age hillfort. So, that was the way John Newton rode, scouring the hills of the common, combing through them day after day.

The people of Sandhill started fearing for the health of their patron. Little did they expect John to one day ride home with Joan on the back of his horse, lured by a promise to make her his wife.

All this time, you see, Joan had been living in a hovel out in the wilds, nestled in a space between two scrubby hills. When John Newton rode down into Joan's glade, she had fear in her eyes and thought once again to flee. Yet Joan recognised the man and, being a decent sort, offered him a little payment for the apples she had stolen from his orchard. When he refused her paltry collection of coins, she thought that would be that. But instead, John asked her for a different form of payment. His price? No more than a conversation.

It was during this chat that John learned of Joan's sad history. How once, when she was barely more than a girl, she had met a man from Blackdown who told her he had stolen a golden mug from the Fairy Fair, after which the fairies had caught up with him and exacted their revenge.

The man had been tricked, bewitched, and became pixy-led – unable to think for himself. The traveller told Joan that he'd been led from town to town by the malevolent elfin folk. They'd spat in his eyes, giving him pixy sight, helping him see the world as they saw it. Then for years they kept him with them, using him to carry their goods from forest to vale to beach and back again.

The only way he'd escaped, the man told Joan, was that one day he had put his coat on backwards, sleeves the wrong way out. It had only been an accident, he said, but the moment it happened he felt himself freed, so he ran off and escaped to live the rest of his life in leisure.

The way Joan told it, ever since that day, the man she met had enjoyed great luck. He could win at dice, dance the finest of jigs to any old tune and, with just a look, any girl would fall in love with him. Which was just what had happened to Joan, who the man led off on a merry jaunt that lasted through spring, summer, and until the leaves started to turn.

As the seasons passed, Joan said, and her love blossomed and bloomed, she convinced the man to show her the world as he could see it. So it was that he spat in Joan's right eye, and from that day forth, Joan could half-see the world of the fairies and all their pixy mischief. Their footsteps in the dew, their language in the spiderwebs, the future written in an apple cut clean through.

Joan and her swain lived a life of mirth in those days, but as the West Wind turned and winter came knocking, Joan came forth with news. She was pregnant, she told her lover, no doubt about it, and wasn't that a wonderful thing?

Alas, in response to Joan's admission, the swain did what swains are wont to do, albeit with a twist. For, not content with just running away, the man turned himself into a hare, shooting off into the undergrowth, and Joan didn't know how to follow him.

Times were hard then for Joan, for although she could see part of the hidden world, had hedge wisdom, and might earn herself coppers for telling fortunes, she didn't have the luck her lover had boasted. Before long, she found herself all but penniless. Moreover, when the baby came, she found her son proved not to be a normal sort of child. He was a half-fey baby, or part-fey at the very least. Everything Joan tried to feed him only made him sick, and the harder she worked to heal him, the sicker the boy became.

It was then that, one night, there was a rap at Joan's door. She opened it, her heart swelling with hope that her errant lover had returned. Instead, it was the fairies, come to take her son to live a secret life as their kind always ought.

Joan refused, of course, but the fairies wouldn't take no for an answer. They spat in her face and forced their way inside, gathering the boy up in his swaddling clothes. Joan had known what to do; quick as a flash, she'd turned her skirts inside out, freeing herself from being pixy-led. But it was still too late, for out of the windows and up the chimney the fairies vanished, spiriting her son away. And their curse was twofold – although, like her lover before her, Joan had now accrued new knowledge and could turn herself into a hare when panicked, had luck at dice, and could dance the finest of jigs to any old tune, it seemed that from then on, whatever good thing she touched she tainted, marking it with fairy charms.

John Newton listened to this story and felt for Joan, loved and stolen from and left alone. Moreover, like most important people, he did not believe in curses so, despite Joan's warnings and after much begging and pleading, he convinced her to make him the happiest man in the world by marrying him and becoming his wife.

Trouble was, and just as sure as eggs is eggs, it didn't take long before John Newton fell ill. Like a true lady of her time, it was only after the wedding bells rang that Joan agreed to offer John a first embrace, but even that first kiss, sweet as it was, was laced with poison.

Joan begged John not to, but he wouldn't hear otherwise, and morning, noon and night he kissed his wife. He had her cook his meals and prepare him medicines, yet everything she made for him only made him sicker. She pleaded with him to call on others for help, a doctor from Taunton perhaps, and beseeched him to visit the priests at Exeter or Glastonbury, but John wouldn't hear of it. He only wanted to stay at home at Sandhill with Joan, his one true love. For there he might die happy.

Which is what he did, of course. And people were sad, not least John's workers, who were suddenly afraid, for John had died without issue, meaning their futures had all become abruptly uncertain. Most afraid was Joan, who in a short time had grown to love Sandhill, just as she had loved the man who'd made it a success. Indeed, with Joan's fairy sight, she could sometimes still see John Newton wandering the house by night. Though she went to the funeral and put his body in the ground, she knew, in her heart, that while John might be dead, he wasn't really gone.

It was at that very funeral, though, that Joan was seen by all the great and good of Somerset. Many of them had heard of John Newton's sudden wedding and were curious to meet his widow. Sure enough, all the major families were there – the Hickses, the Hastings, the Clarkes, the Pophams, and notably, the Wyndhams.

Indeed, though all the men who caught sight of Joan seemed to covet her, most of those men at John Newton's funeral were already husbands. One who was not, and who fell in love no sooner than he had seen the hem of Joan's mourning clothes, was Charles Wyndham, heir to Orchard Manor in Watchet.

The kindly John Popham, who inherited Sandhill, was sufficiently enamoured with Joan that he agreed to give the conveyance fee to the estate to whomever the pretty widow married next. And though Joan begged and pleaded with Charles, warning him off as she had warned off John, telling him of her past and imploring him to leave her be, Charles wouldn't hear of it. He married her, though in jealousy towards John Newton's ghost, he knocked down the old farmhouse and commissioned a new, grander building be erected in its place.

Joan was bereft at the destruction of the old Sandhill farmhouse, mourning John Newton's loss all over again. And although Charles Wyndham was a jealous man who took her away from the home she had only just come to feel she belonged in, he loved and craved and showered her with kindnesses, just as her first husband had. Just like him too, in spite of Joan's begging and pleading, Charles sought her kisses morning, noon and night, and made her cook his meals, pour his wine, and when Charles fell ill, he had Joan prepare his medicines. Duly, she sat by his bedside at Orchard Manor, and watched him as he wasted away, powerless to convince him to seek succour from anyone but her.

None of this was lost on the great and good of Somerset, of course. The Hickses, the Hastings, the Clarkes, and even the Pophams spoke whisperingly of Joan – of her great beauty, her bewitching powers, and her strangely intoxicating influence. The rumours spread through court – a little tittle-tattle to most, but for Sir Edward Carne of Ewenny in south Wales, the talk of Joan made him prick up his ears.

For Sir Edward, you see, was a widower. Not only was he a widower, in fact, but his first wife, mother of his son and heir John Carne, had once been Catherine Wyndham, Charles' sister. And Sir Edward was a tricky character; his father had been Queen Mary's Ambassador in Rome. His entire family had refused to convert to Protestantism. In 1574, Edward even allied himself with Mary, Queen of Scots, and he and his men led several frays into neighbouring Welsh lands, rebelling and seeking to enforce feudal rights.

In short, Edward Carne was not the sort of man who believed in curses – but he did believe in money. He knew that if Charles Wyndham died, as all who knew him supposed he would, then by marrying Joan he could secure increased wealth, power, and a grander title even than Sheriff of Glamorgan.

Alas for Charles Wyndham, of course, who never got to see Sandhill Manor completed. He died happily though, shortly before the final bricks were laid in 1588, with his will of 1585 specifying that Joan should be able to live in the house until her death, after which the estate should pass to his godson.

Joan, meanwhile, was heartbroken all over again. Alone again, grief stricken, given an unfamiliar house in a familiar place where the ghosts of her past husbands seemed to shimmer and shake in and out of existence. She wondered if, somehow, she might untangle the mystery of their afterlives and thought to perhaps appeal to the fairy folk for aid. Before she had much time to follow up on such plans, though, Edward came calling and refused to take Joan's 'no' for an answer.

So it was that, before long, Joan Newton, who had become Joan Wyndham, became Joan Carne – though Sir Edward considered himself cannier than his precedents. He listened to Joan's words, took them to heart, and after moving Joan to Ewenny, he at first managed to keep his life and hers almost completely separate.

Yet, like Charles before him, and John before that, try as he might, Edward could not keep Joan from his thoughts. He dreamed of her, and glimpsed her reflection in every puddle, mirror, and windowpane. As weeks turned into months and months turned into years, he at first craved the sight of her, then to brush her lips against his, and suddenly Sir Edward Carne was just as infatuated with his Joan as her two prior husbands had been. He could not bear to be parted from her, hung on her every word, and soon demanded that only Joan prepare his meals, only Joan pour his wine and, as he became more and more ill, that only Joan tend to his sickness.

Edward Carne's will, dated 20 October 1602, was proved on 27 May 1603, and Joan returned to Sandhill Manor, where she lived until her death in 1612. It's said that in the final years of her life Joan became a recluse. She covered herself from head to toe in black cloth, fearful of letting anyone see her – though many still came seeking prophecies and advice. Often the auguries Joan gave her visitors were not what they wanted to hear, and by the time she died, the people of Withycombe were most pleased to learn she'd passed on. Indeed, by then they had come to fear her, creating a special iron coffin in which to bury her, barring it to the ground deep in Watchet Churchyard.

One of the things the people of Withycombe wanted to know, though, was how much money Joan was leaving behind and to whom. The great and the good were just as curious as the folk who'd worked Sandhill Farm during John Newton's heyday so, one and all, a crowd of inquisitive mourners travelled back to Sandhill Manor House to hear the will being read.

It was of great surprise to all in attendance when they opened the doors to the grand Elizabethan house to find within it none other than Joan Carne. She was in the kitchen, dressed in black, cooking eggs and bacon – presumably enough to share with her three dead husbands. The priest was sent for, exorcising Joan's ghost, which, true to form, turned into a hare and made an escape. What followed was a scramble – a hunt across hill and vale, with Joan's spirit eventually driven to a body of water known to this day as the Witch's Pool.

It's said that the priest, whose name is lost to antiquity, sealed Joan there by blessing the pool, turning it to holy water. It's also said that Joan Carne's ghost can only return to Sandhill by one cockerel's stride a year.

Measurements of the precise distance between Withycombe's Witch's Pool and Sandhill Manor House vary somewhat, but by most estimates it's imagined that Joan Carne, the Restless Witch of Sandhill, ought to be home by now. Judging by the additional exorcisms that took place at the manor during the last century, in fact, there's every chance she's already there.

31

The Children of Cannock Chase

A Staffordshire Tale

Reports of sightings of black-eyed children around Cannock Chase Forest in Staffordshire first cropped up in the 1980s, making this a relatively modern folk tale by Three Ravens standards. Although a more recent story, it plays on archetypal things we find frightening, such as unsettling children and white figures on lonely roads glimpsed in a rearview mirror. The things the character experiences on encountering the children – headaches, nausea, dizziness, and fear – are all based on true accounts of sightings.

One of the theories about the ghostly children is that they are the spirits of the victims of a real series of murders which took place in the area in the 1960s. Although multiple children disappeared and were later discovered dead, a killer was only convicted for one of the murders, leaving a feeling of unfinished business about the whole affair.

For that reason, I wanted to see things from the perspective of a police officer who might be trying to get to the bottom of a case, and to offer a possible explanation for why these children might appear.

In situations of awful tragedy, it is very human to want to try and solve such a mystery. Plus, Cannock Chase is evidently a place of intense supernatural activity. Other entities reported in the area include the Cannock Chase Werewolf, spectral soldiers, a screaming woman, and the notorious Pig Man.

EC

Rain rattled against the windscreen, too heavy and fast for the wipers to clear. They left wide smears in their wake, making it almost impossible to see.

Lily crawled the patrol car down the deserted lane, unable to go any faster. If she had to give chase, she'd be putting herself at risk, especially as the road was littered with broken-edged potholes which would bounce the car and make the suspension shudder.

She shouldn't be out on her own – they weren't ever supposed to be, but they were always understaffed, and the Chief Superintendent had called them all in to explain that the budget cuts meant there might be occasions when the second officer would be at the other end of the radio and not in the car. Budget cuts were all very well, but they didn't account for officers' shift patterns, which meant that, more often than not, Lily was left alone.

This was the graveyard shift in more ways than one, slowly zigzagging her way around the narrow lanes crisscrossing Cannock Chase Forest, headlights dipped, watching for – well, anything, really. Cars exhibiting any unusual behaviour – don't stop everyone, the Chief Inspector had stressed – or any sign of strange activity at the edges of the forest – don't go into the forest alone at night.

So far, Lily hadn't seen a single car, and the trees were so thickly clustered at the edges of the dark forest that she would have been hard pressed to spot any kind of activity, strange or otherwise. It was dangerous, being alone, and if there was any trouble, Lily was under strict instructions to call for back-up immediately. Patrick's patrol was in Milford, so he could screech down to Cannock Chase quickly enough if Lily needed him, or she could go to him.

Actually, Lily had volunteered for the Cannock Chase patrol. It was Friday night, and she didn't much fancy being verbally abused or vomited on outside the Walkabout in Lichfield. Besides, she'd made sergeant last year and the drunks' rescue service was for junior constables. She would much rather be here, despite the dreary, dark night and the lashing rain.

And yet, she didn't think she was doing much good. She felt, in that instinctual, lower gut way which had got her into hot water in the past, that Cannock Chase Forest was the place. They hadn't had the resources to comb through it without a single solid piece of evidence, but Lily was sure that if they'd had a couple of dog units and an uninterrupted week, they would find something. After all, both bodies had been found in ditches surrounding the forest, although on different sides.

The first, Caroline Blackwater, was discovered at the side of the A51 and the second, Alba Johnson, near the golf club on the Rugeley Road. DCI Harris said there was no evidence, but as far as Lily was concerned, the forest had to be the key. Where else would the killer have been able to do the things he'd done without somebody seeing or hearing?

She rolled down the window, peering into the dark forest. There had to be something. She had to find something. For those poor little girls. To stop there ever being any others.

But she knew, in the deep part of herself which throbbed with self-loathing in the middle of the night when she couldn't sleep for thinking about it, that there would be another one, because they hadn't caught him yet. When they'd found Caroline, everyone hoped it would be a one-off, but Alba's body, with the exact same injuries, proved them wrong.

Lily slammed on the brakes, jarring her lower back and making the car's underside grind along the road, because she could see a child reflected in the wing mirror, standing at the edge of the forest. How had she driven past her? The girl must have only just emerged. Lily couldn't quite make her out through the rain, but she could see that she was wearing something white, like a nightdress. The brake lights shining on her made it appear doused in red.

Lily leapt from the car, leaving the engine running, and made her way back down the lane towards the girl. 'Hello?' she called. 'Police. It's alright, I'm here to help.'

The rain buffeted Lily, soaking her face and hands and getting under her hat. She squinted, but she couldn't see the child any more. Had she gone back into the forest? Surely she wouldn't have done. She'd looked small – only about six or seven years old, Lily thought, although she'd only seen her for a moment.

'Police!' she called again. 'Please step forward if you can. I'm here to help.'

Don't go into the forest alone at night. The Chief Inspector's words came back to her just as she was about to step off the road and into the oozing black mud of Cannock Chase. He had spoken to Lily particularly, giving her a look which said he knew that she would if she thought it necessary. She had been on the receiving end of his rage, and almost had a caution, for going haring off doing her own thing contrary to orders.

She'd caught the woman running a drug ring out of the back of her chain of nail salons, though, so the telling off hadn't been too heated.

Lily shone her torch into the woods, but she could see nothing except trees and vegetation. Then she put her foot on something and swore softly when it gave way with a soft wet crunch. Shining the torch down, she saw that she had trodden on the rain-soaked, half rotten carcass of a deer. There was a spot of blood on its cream front and the back legs were broken.

She wiped her shoe on the verge and went back to the car, shutting the doors and flipping the central locking. Her hands were shaking. '10-45,' she said into the radio. 'Deer carcass on the Slitting Mill Road, over.'

How many too-late nights had she had, to think a dead deer was a little girl needing help? Too many, and far too many on this case alone. When was her next day off? This time, Lily told herself, she would actually use her day off to rest instead of trying to clean the flat, do the shopping, get a haircut and catch up with four old friends.

Her radio buzzed, making her jump. '10-99 – wanted, a beer and a smoke and an umbrella please, over.' Patrick's cheery voice came out of the radio in Lily's lap. She smiled, because they weren't meant to use the radios for unofficial chat and reached for her phone to call him instead. There was no signal in Cannock Chase Forest, but she could call him over Wi-Fi.

'How's it going?' she asked, when he picked up.

'Dull as my cousin's stag do,' Patrick said. 'You know, the one where we all had to stand around and watch him practise his golf swings. You?'

'Nothing much,' Lily said. 'Thought I saw something, but it turned out to be roadkill. I should be so lucky.'

'Are you going crazy in the forest by yourself, Lil?'

'Maybe,' Lily said.

She liked Patrick a lot. She definitely didn't approve of workplace romances – they were cops, for goodness' sake, they had to be realistic – but his voice over the phone was comforting and his face across a briefing room always made Lily slightly less interested in what was being said and slightly more inclined to think about asking him out for a drink. They chatted for a while longer, Patrick telling her about the thrilling sights and sounds of the Milford Industrial Estate he'd stopped to eat his sandwich at. There was nothing really to share, but having the moment of human contact was something. When they hung up, Lily pulled away and began the slow circular route again, driving at a snail's pace through the rain, trying to keep her eyes peeled for any sign of life.

The second child was in the centre of Post Office lane, right in Lily's rearview mirror. She must have stepped into the road just as Lily drove past. There were two of them, Lily saw, as she jerked on the handbrake and brought the car to a stop. One of them was very small and she was half-hidden behind the other.

Lily reached for the radio, but a sudden blinding stab of pain flashed through her head and sinuses. White spots swam in front of her eyes. She tried to focus, looking at the steering wheel, her hands, anything, but her vision was blurring. In the mirror, she could see the two children coming towards the car.

Something about the slow, purposeful way they were walking made Lily hesitate before unlocking the doors. Her head hurt, and her breath was coming in shallow pants, as it did before she was going to sick. What was wrong with her? Had she forgotten to eat something before she'd come out on patrol? It was a feeling like fear, she realised.

A loud noise echoed through the car. One of the children, the taller one, had slammed her hands against the back window. With shaking hands, Lily picked up her radio. '10-78, need assistance, Cannock Chase patrol, over,' she said. She felt jittery, out of control, even though she was a trained officer and these were only two children.

Where were they? She couldn't see them in the mirror any more. Lily craned around in her seat to look out of the back window, but the children weren't there.

When she turned back around, her head feeling as though a pickaxe had been driven into it between her eyes, one of the children was right outside the driver's window.

Afterwards, it would be difficult for Lily to put into words the feeling of intense, all-consuming fear which gripped her. The little girl's eyes were black, treacherous black ice on a frozen road, in a chalk-white face. She was only small. She barely came up over the edge of the car door, so Lily couldn't see if she was smiling or in distress. All she could see were those black eyes, drilling into her.

Lily squeezed her eyes shut, then almost screamed when her radio buzzed.

'Lil, come in. Are you okay? Over.' It was Patrick's voice.

Slowly, Lily opened her eyes. She couldn't see the little girl next to her window any more and there was no sign of the other one. She picked up the radio. 'Yeah, I started feeling ill,' she said, 'migraine or something, I think. I might need to come off shift, over.'

'Give me a minute to clear it and I'll come down there, over,' he said.

'Okay.' Lily made herself drink some water. What was wrong with her? Why was her heart pounding and her palms sweaty? Where had this sudden, piercing headache come from? And why was she seeing children when she was fairly sure there were no children there to see?

There was something happening here tonight, but Lily had no idea what it was. The pain in her head made her less inclined to find out than usual. She pulled away, torturously slowly, the rhythmic sway of the windscreen wipers sounding loud as a pneumatic drill in her throbbing head.

The last child was standing by the junction of Penkridge Bank and Birches Valley. She was the smallest, and she waved at Lily. Like the others, her face was white as chalk, and she was wearing a pale dress which looked as though it was made of the same flimsy nylon as Lily's grandmother's dressing gowns; the kind that was used a long time ago. Her eyes were almost completely black, from edge to edge.

Lily rolled the car right up to the child and wound the window down. The headache was almost blinding.

'Will you take me home?' the little girl said. 'I need a lift.'

'Of course, sweetheart,' Lily said, even though the child was barely dressed despite the freezing night. There was some quality in her black eyes which made Lily unable to look away from them. It was as though she was falling into those eyes and drowning in tar. 'Get in the back and I'll take you. Where's home?'

She unlocked the back doors so the girl could climb into the car.

Her radio buzzed again.

'Lil, I'm on my way,' Patrick said. 'Are you ok? What's your position? Don't drive any more, ok?'

'Wait, I'll talk to you in a minute,' Lily said, and cut the channel.

The little girl had climbed into the patrol car. With her came a damp smell, like soil and leaf mulch, and something older and darker – the sharp scent of something which never should have been there. Her black eyes met Lily's in the rearview mirror.

'It's not far,' the little girl said, pointing down the Birches Valley road. 'That way.'

Despite the stabbing pain behind her eyes, Lily put her headlights up and turned the car down Birches Valley.

'I'm Sergeant Shaw. What's your name? Where have you been tonight, sweetheart?' she asked the girl. 'Why aren't you at home now?'

'I got lost,' the girl said, almost dreamily, not really answering Lily's questions. 'I got lost, but it's time to go home now.'

Lily drove along the lane until the black-eyed girl suddenly said, 'Here!'

The entrance to the track was almost invisible, but closer inspection showed Lily the broken pieces of a rusty five-bar gate, half-hidden behind overgrown brambles. It might have been the entrance to a farm. It was thickly lined with trees, creating a kind of black, leafy tunnel.

'This is your home?' Lily asked doubtfully.

The child answered by opening the car door and scrambling out. She stood next to the car, a little way from it, as though she was waiting for Lily. Lily killed the engine and got out.

'You were looking,' the little girl said, and the expression on her face suddenly made her look much older. 'You were looking, and now you'll find.'

Lily took a step towards her, meeting her impossibly black eyes, but just like that, the child simply and suddenly was not there. Lily would never be able to explain the sensation adequately. There was no lurch of the world on its axis, no ripple of change, no rush of tiny feet or rustle of the bushes. The little black-eyed girl simply ceased to exist.

Lily looked down the narrow track, and she knew what she had to do.

Her headache had lifted, curiously, as though it had never been there. Lily grabbed the radio from the car, called in her position and asked for back-up again.

'Lily, what's going on?' Patrick's distorted voice crackled across the channel.

'Just get here,' she said, clipping the radio to her jacket.

Then she made her way down the narrow track, not daring to use her torch in case it gave her away. Now the painful haze behind her eyes had lifted she felt no fear, not even a little. There was just an extraordinary sense of clarity, that she had been brought here by those children, whoever they might be, to do a job.

You were looking, and now you'll find.

The track was long and Lily almost missed the point where it veered off sharply, because the turning was covered with thick brambles. Not caring that she scratched her hands, she pulled them aside. Just beyond, in a little clearing, there was a corrugated-iron shed.

It looked shabby, abandoned, like a farm outbuilding which had been long forgotten. There were no lights inside, and there was a shining new padlock on its door. Lily ignored the door and picked up a piece of wet wood to smash the window. It was a single pane of glass and broke easily.

Then she heard a voice.

'Help me, please help me. I want to go home.'

Her hand now steadier than it had ever been, Lily clicked on her torch and shone it through the window.

She saw the little girl on the floor first, dressed in a dirty blue tracksuit. She was terrified and shivering violently, but she looked as though she was in one piece. The smell hit Lily next, that old smell of fear and suffering. There were dark patches on the floor which might have been urine or might have been blood. And on the walls–

Lily did not linger long on those photographs, pictures which belonged locked away in an evidence room or in the heart of a bonfire. She had seen enough to make the call.

The girl's mother had only just reported her missing. It had only been a few short hours. When the armed response unit arrived and cut the padlock, the girl rushed into Lily's waiting arms. Patrick arrived soon after, and the three sat in his car together, drinking lukewarm tea while forensics moved in.

They caught the man not long after, coming on foot to that little shed in the forest where he'd murdered Caroline Blackwater and Alba Johnson. He'd looked like anyone, DCI Harris said. Just another dog walker. But Lily caught sight of him as they brought him in to the station and she thought she would have known what he was and what he'd done. It was his eyes, she thought. They were strangely blank, as though he'd been thinking of nothing at all when he'd killed those children, and they were far more horrible than the black eyes of the children of Cannock Chase.

Lily never drove the forest beat again, but she never heard of anybody seeing the little girls with their dark eyes either. She didn't know entirely what she had seen that night, but she knew it had stopped at least one other child being hurt. Afterwards, all she would ever say was that she had been in the right place at the right time, and that was all anybody could get out of her.

32

The Wild Man of Orford

A Suffolk Tale

The sea has captured the imaginations of storytellers since the beginning of time. From merfolk to monsters, ships to storms, there are so many tales and possibilities for tales floating in the ocean's ever-changing colours.

'The Wild Man of Orford' story first appeared in the Chronicum Anglicanum *of Ralph of Coggeshall, written in the thirteenth century. Ralph gives the story in a very blunt and matter-of-fact style, without speculating as to whether or not it actually happened.*

I think it's quite a universal story about a small community's suspicious reaction to otherness and difference, with an ultimate message of defying social and religious norms in pursuit of freedom. We know that Christianity of the period could be oppressive, as portrayed in the figure of Bartholomew de Granville. De Granville was a real person, and it's possible to visit his castle, the church, and the quay in Orford today, although the coastline has altered somewhat.

In St Bartholomew's Church, there is a woodwose figure on the medieval font, though he is more a 'wild man of the woods' type than a merman. I gave my wild man a fish tail, as he does have one in some accounts. He appears that way in the logo of the Butley and Orford Oysterage restaurant, too, serving dishes of seafood!

I like to think he went on to have a long and happy existence, after slipping from de Granville's clutches…

EC

When the sea's dreaming before a storm, and the sound of it rolling over the shingle rises and falls like the gentle beating of a heart, and the cormorants skim under the surface of the water and burst free shaking shining drops from their oil-dark feathers, and it's so bright and clear out there that you can almost hear the waves whispering their secrets to the sky, then I remember that strange time.

Our stories here are fashioned by the sea, just as our coast is beaten and battered into new shapes, its juts and hollows the bony elbows on the arms of England. This is a tale from the deepest depths of the sea, written between the lines of its strange, wild song. Monks and men tried to capture it, the scratch and stab of their goose-feather pens determining history. But they weren't there, that stormy spring when the marvellous catch was made.

I was. I saw it all.

I was young then – young and new with the shine still on me – but I remember it, clear as the bells ringing under the sea to warn of a storm. I saw it all.

This is how it started. With a sea salt taste on the tip of the tongue and a boat bumping and bouncing down the beach. The day was full of possibility, with dreams of nets groaning full of snappers and sturgeon and sticklebacks and salmon. It wasn't my story then. Then it belonged to a clout-headed pair of fishermen, Rafe and Hugh.

Every single day, Rafe and Hugh sat in their boat and waited for bounty to swim into their nets. Every. Single. Day. But that day, something was different.

A dark shadow wriggled and rippled under the boat, bigger than an eel, bigger than an elephant fish. Rafe and Hugh saw what looked like a tail, but then they saw arms, hands, and fingers.

'It's a man down there!' cried Rafe. 'We best save him, or he'll be fair to drown!'

Sweating and straining, they heaved and hauled, hand over hand, muscles moaning and backs berating. The net protested and clung to the water but at last it came free and over the bows, thumping and slithering into the boat.

Rafe and Hugh pulled at the net, trying to see if the drowning man lived, but they saw no man inside. No man, but a huge, glossy mass, flopping and quivering and taking a great, gulping breath.

'That's no man!' said Hugh. 'It's a monster!'

It was market day in Orford town when they brought their monster up to show us. A stiff sea breeze urged the sharp smell of fresh catch into my nostrils as gossip and news flew about like seagulls. Money slipped from purses quick as salmon from nervous hands as the rows of stalls heaved and seethed like the sea herself.

Fish was our life and our living. The sea was always our friend, but we worked it hard back then. There was nothing so sweet to see as a full net of wriggling, slithering beauties. Silver and bronze and green, better than any hoard of treasure.

And there was no fishing without me, for I made the nets. Twisted hemp and pine tar as I netted and looped back and forth. From my corner of the market, I could see everything when they brought him up.

There was a huge crowd around the net, gawping and poking at something huddled in one of my nets. I heard mutters of monster or demon, fish or fowl, but when I pushed through to look for myself, I saw none of those things. Oh, he was scaly and glistening slick as a snipe eel and tailed like a fish, but when I looked into the great dark pools of his eyes, I knew he was a man.

Some said we ought to put him back in the sea where he came from, and I was with them, but Rafe and Hugh were for taking him up to the castle to show him to Lord Bartholomew. They were prinking and proud of themselves, you see, wanting to show off what they hauled up. So, they lifted the net on their shoulders and up we all went after them to see what our betters made of it.

In those days, Bartholomew de Granville was Orford's protector. High in his smart new castle, he looked down on us all with his knife-grey stare and his too-clean hands. He was a devil-digger, a churchgoer, and mean and cold. Being such close friends with God, he didn't need to be friends with anyone else.

When we brought the wild man into the castle, Lord Bartholomew's sharp gaze sliced into all of us before it came to rest on the man in the net. The jewelled clasp of his prayer book clicked shut as he stood and commanded Rafe and Hugh to untangle the net.

Twisted fibres of the net came loose from the wild man's body and for the first time I saw him – I really saw him. Not a fish, no, something other, something all its own. I saw green skin, glittering scales all barnacled over like the treasure of a long-forgotten wreck. His hair was coarse, strong tendrils waving weed-like round the rock pools and shallows of his face. And that long, sinuous tail, flicking up and over. The sound it made, beating against the floor. A pumping heart. A quivering tattoo of fear.

We asked Lord Bartholomew if he was a man or a fish, but the lord said that he was a devil. I said no, because the wild man was frightened, but Lord Bartholomew said it was a trick.

'Devils play tricks,' he said, in his cold, distant voice. 'Lies are the only language their tongues know. This creature's unnatural tail and hideous skin proclaim it for what it is – a flawed and jagged fragment of God's image.'

He threw us all out then, and I only found out what happened when I sneaked back to the castle after dark and spoke to my friend Jack, who washed the pots there. Jack said Lord Bartholomew and his guards had taken the wild man down to the dungeons beneath the castle. They'd questioned him for hours, Jack told me, asking him if he was spying for the French, if he was a fish pretending to be a man, if he was an evil spirit possessing the body of a drowned sailor, and all manner of nonsense.

When he couldn't answer or understand them, they thought he must be a fish. But Lord Bartholomew reached out and pinched the wild man until he called out in pain, and then he said that fish couldn't feel pain, so the creature from the deep must be a man.

Jack said it had gone on all day, after that, with the Lord Bartholomew insisting that the man must acknowledge and recognise Christ, our saviour. Of course, the wild man hadn't responded, so the lord had called to his guards to strike his limbs and sprinkle hot oil.

They carried on and on, pain from every point of the compass, changing from burning to pinching to hitting to tearing. The wild man made sounds at last – hollow cavernous notes of pain – but he spoke no words, and he didn't understand the cross, the bread and the wine, the holy book.

Long after night had fallen, they left him, but he wasn't what he had been any more. They had tried to make him different, like them. Their blades had ripped and his scales had fallen like snowflakes on the stone floor. They hadn't killed him, but they'd taken his life from him just the same, breaking where they thought they mended.

The last thing Lord Bartholomew did, Jack told me, was to bring the cross towards the wild man. And when he hung his head, Bartholomew believed that he had won.

‘Why does he hate him so much?’ Jack asked me.

I didn’t know then, but I know now. Lord Bartholomew hated the wild man because he didn’t understand him and he couldn’t control him, and he hid his fear in a cloak sewn from prayer and authority.

It was late then, and most in the castle were in their beds, so we sneaked down into the underbelly of the castle where the dungeons were. There were no guards on duty, and it was a lonely, desperate place, thick with the smell of pain, a foul fog you could almost taste in the air.

The wild man was huddled in a corner, his webbed fingers scrabbling for purchase on the walls. Blood thickened on the floor in the cracks between the stones. His tail was a ruin.

Jack had a bucket of fish he’d brought and we offered it to the wild man. He was suspicious at first, but hunger soon won. To this day, I’ve never seen anyone eat like that. He took hold of the fish and brought it to his mouth, squeezing it hard. Blood and juices poured down his chin, and he drank it like it was the best thing he’d ever tasted. Then he guzzled down the rest, cracking and crunching the bones until there was nothing left.

He let us help him then, unfolding himself and showing his tail to us. I had my tools with me, and it was easier than weaving a net after all. With each stitch, I drew the ripped flesh together and brought him back to himself. And as I stitched, we talked to him, Jack and I, telling him that he was whole, that he was before and he would be after, that Lord Bartholomew couldn’t make him something he wasn’t.

We were about to leave, Jack and I, but the wild man caught hold of my arm. He held out his hand to me and his green palm uncurled. Nestled in its hollow we saw a marvellous shell, iridescent and dazzling. It seemed to draw all the light to it and drag it into itself, so it was the only bright thing.

I took it in my hand and Jack put his hand on it too, and we suddenly heard a swirling rush of water as though we were plummeting into the deepest depths of the sea. The water grew blue and still, until it was like being inside a jewel. We could hear music, but it sounded as if it were coming from a long way away, through water. The light from the shell expanded and stretched until it was everywhere.

It played across the flickering, twinkling skin of the fish – yes, fish! They were with us, or so it seemed, nudging at our hands and feet, playing in our hair and tickling our noses with bubbles. The murmur and swell of the ocean seemed louder and louder, drowning out voices and gossip and rules, until the sea was everything.

Well, after that, Jack and I were determined to get the wild man back to his home, though we didn't know how we would do it, and we didn't get a chance until much later.

The summer had come right in and we were readying ourselves in Orford to celebrate the Feast of the Star of the Sea. We'd scrubbed behind our ears, soaked the scent of sea and scallop from our hands, and we were ready for a party.

Lord Bartholomew was pious and everything, but he couldn't resist the chance to show off. So, he ordered that the wild man be brought out of the castle dungeons and down to the harbour, so that people could look at him. But he didn't want him just swimming away, so he called for some nets to stretch across the harbour mouth to make a pen for him so he couldn't get away.

My nets were the ones that were brought.

Everyone hastened and hurried down to the harbour, hustling for a good place. They all wanted to see the wild man in the water. He was carried down in a net, and he looked different to the way he had when he'd been caught. He was thinner and paler, somehow, as though being away from the sea for so long had leeched the colour out of him.

Lord Bartholomew gave a speech about the Star of the Sea being our guide on the way to Christ, lest we capsize amid the storm-tossed waves, and then he commanded that the wild man should be released to swim in the water, just for one day.

The guards shook him out of the net, dropping him into the harbour like a coin in a well. He stretched and flexed, feeling the sea water on his skin, then he was sinking into it, rolling over and over in it, wrapping himself in its arms.

But then he was swimming, pulling himself through the waves with arms that suddenly looked stronger towards the line of nets, faster and faster.

Mine were the best nets in Orford, you know. No fish could escape them, for they were woven to do the job – or they would have been, if I hadn't cut a hole, right there in the middle.

And like an eel, the wild man was through, he was out, he was free! Lord Bartholomew was furious. His arms were waving and his face was red as he knew he'd lost his prize.

We all watched the wild man swimming away, sometimes visible, sometimes covered by waves, sometimes holding up a hand, then disappearing below the surface. We watched and we watched as he got further away until he was quite gone.

And that might have been the last time I saw him, but it wasn't.

I was down on the shore at the end of a long day when the year was dying, watching the sun plunge into the sea to cool its toes after a day running across the sky. I looked out over the water. The sun was in my eyes, and there was a rock jutting up ahead of me. But it wasn't a rock. It was moving, and it was swimming towards me, scales shining in the last surviving sunlight. It was the wild man.

He looked happy. He was free. He recognised no cross, no rules, no men with chains and burning irons. He was smiling, because he knew they'd never catch him again.

Right up to me he swam, close enough to touch, and there in his hand was the magic shell he had showed Jack and me in the castle. I wondered at him giving it to me then, but of course he didn't need it, for the sound of the waves would never rest for him.

The wild man swam out and I watched the waves carry him, past the boundaries, past the reefs, to a place where the pointing finger of judgement would not rest on him. The tide rushed in over my feet and such a fullness, such a brightness came over me, it kept me standing there until night and familiar voices called me back to town.

Days and weeks passed by, with the same rules and the same narrow streets. But all this time later, when I hold my shell and hear the booming surf slamming against the clouds for joy, I still know that I'll never drown.

33

The Tale of Blanche Heriot

A Surrey Tale

In times of trouble bells have been used to sound the alarm. They've called forces to muster and rung out for celebration. We hear them at christenings, weddings, and funerals – they are part of the soundscape of the traditional cycle of life.

The ringing of the bell in the tale of Blanche Heriot means the difference between life and death, and it's an interesting one in the context of what we know about historic church clocks. It was possible for Blanche, the heroine of the story, to literally manipulate time to save her lover's life.

Although there is some doubt about whether the whole of the tale is true, its characters, Blanche Heriot, Neville Audley and Herrick Evenden, were likely real people, living at the time of the end of the Wars of the Roses. Edward IV of England had just won back the throne, so the domestic romance of Blanche and Neville has a political backdrop.

The Curfew Bell of Chertsey was the fifth bell in a ring of eight at the medieval parish Church of St Peter. It was recast several times. The bell is still rung on weekday evenings between Michaelmas and Lady Day, and there is also a bronze statue of Blanche Heriot clinging to the bell in Chertsey today.

EC

They say that time itself can't be altered, and maybe that's true, but as for the clock that tells the time – well, that's another story.

In Chertsey, there once lived a young woman whose name was Blanche Heriot. The meaning of 'blanche' is 'white' and I can't say that it was a name which suited her, for she had flaming red hair and courage to match it, and passion which burned like a beacon.

Whatever she did, she did with all the force of her being, so it made perfect sense that when she fell in love, she did it in a fierce, all-encompassing manner. Her lover's name was Neville Audley and he was every bit as fiery and feisty as Blanche. They were a well-matched pair indeed, and everybody had been saying that they should wed for as long as living memory.

Blanche and Neville themselves rather accepted their marriage as a done deal too, and in truth, their passionate natures meant that they had already consummated their betrothal under the light of a brilliant red harvest moon. They sneaked home at dawn, long after the curfew bell had sent less-bold folk to their beds.

Luckily, their families weren't at all opposed, and all were more or less primed for the happy day, whenever the couple should choose to name it. Blanche's mother had a dowry chest full of lavender-scented linen for her and Neville's father had a fat purse of money for him. They had even discussed where they might live, in an old weaver's house in the nicer part of town which was then for sale. Everything pointed towards Blanche and Neville living a long and happy life together, full of kisses, quarrels, and a tumbling brood of carrot-haired children.

That was until everything changed.

A great contention broke out between the two noble houses of York and Lancaster. Now, when contentions broke out in Chertsey, they were usually over something insulting said at a family gathering or a borrowed bucket which had mysteriously never been returned, but the houses of York and Lancaster were quarrelling about something much less tangible than a missing bucket – the right to sit on the throne of fair England.

Of course, these noble houses couldn't keep their disagreements to themselves. They needed armies, and so they needed to bring the people into their arguments. They brought in plenty of men from Chertsey, with swords and billhooks to make a point, and Neville Audley was among them. I've said that Blanche's name didn't suit her, and the colour white didn't suit her lover either, for he fought under the red rose banner of the house of Lancaster, red as his love's hair and red as blood.

Neville was eager to go, but Blanche made him promise that he'd ride back to her in one piece. He was practising his swordplay and his horse was stamping impatiently, for he suited his master in temperament and was keen to be galloping into battle alongside his brethren, hooves churning up the mud and eyes rolling back to strike fear into the hearts of the enemy. Off they rode, and that was the last anybody in Chertsey saw of either horse or man for a good long while.

Well, Blanche was just worried sick about Neville in her heart, though she never mentioned it out loud. Everybody who met her thought she was even more lively than usual, quick to laugh and bold with a comeback. Of course, those who knew her a bit better saw that her hot temper was quicker to flare up than it had been before, and plenty of her friends were on the receiving end of her too-sharp tongue. When they gossiped amongst themselves, they said that Blanche was missing Neville more than she could bear.

And it was quite true, she was. Every evening, she lit a candle in her window and burned some fragrant herbs in its flame, and she said a prayer to the Virgin Mary to bring Neville back safe and whole. Then she gazed in the direction she imagined him to be and sighed in a way she would have heartily mocked if anybody else had been doing it.

Neville was not fighting in the direction Blanche gazed, but in quite the opposite one, and the battles he was fighting in were all opposite too, for everything seemed topsy turvy. Although the Lancastrians threw themselves into the war with all the enthusiasm and conviction of their red rose standard, they were losing badly.

That wasn't Neville's fault at all, for he fought ferociously, whirling like a dancer with his bastard sword swinging as fast as light. He was like a smouldering coal in the hottest part of the battle and he killed many men. So much so, he became known as the scourge of the Yorkists and the House of Lancaster praised him as a hero despite the oncoming tide of success for the House of York.

That tide came in at last, however. Edward, son of Henry VI, was crowned King of all England. The Lancastrians kept fighting back, but it was really to little avail. At last, the two sides met at Hexham in as bloody a conflict as the whole war had seen.

Neville Audley acquitted himself well, sending many a Yorkist foe to the grave. He became separated from his fellows at a misty edge of the field, where he came upon a man in the enemy colours with the white rose badge on his chest. Neville saw an opportunity, until he realised that the man was unarmed and was kneeling to attend to the lame hoof of his horse.

Rather than stab him in the back without honour, Neville sheathed his bastard sword. The man turned and saw this act of charity, and he called down God's blessings on Neville's head.

They exchanged words for a moment, with the strange camaraderie of foes, and for that short space of time they were just two men, and neither could remember what they were really fighting for.

Well, it transpired that the man was one of King Edward's friends, and he knew the way the war was likely to go, so he slipped a garnet ring from his finger and gave it to Neville, as a token of thanks for sparing him. Neville put the ring on to his own finger, next to his love token from Blanche, and they wished each other well.

Ultimately, the House of Lancaster was crushed, of course, and Neville was forced to flee.

England was no safe harbour for him any more, what with the price on his head from having killed so many of the House of York's finest men. He knew he must flee to the Continent, to seek refuge in France, where they were sympathetic to the Lancastrian cause.

It would be dangerous, terribly dangerous, for Yorkist soldiers were out searching for him, but Neville knew he must see his love Blanche, if he could, and persuade her to come with him to France and start a new life with him. He was sure that their families would understand. Both Neville and Blanche spoke abominable French, but that wasn't the sort of thing that he paused to consider.

It was hard for him, travelling back to the county of his birth with men hunting for Lancastrian rebels. He travelled by night, and when he reached Reigate there was a fierce chase through the town and Neville had to hide in the old Baron's Tunnels to evade his pursuers.

But at last, he made it back to Chertsey and rode as fast as he could to Blanche's home as night clouded the sky.

She was gazing out of her window in the wrong direction when she heard the hoofbeats of Neville's horse. She jumped up and ran down to him in her nightdress and oh, they were glad to see each other! Such kisses and embraces and words half-angry and half-loving were exchanged! Stories of the war tumbled out of Neville, and he showed Blanche the garnet ring and told her about the man whose life he'd spared.

But then Neville mentioned that they needed to leave for France, as soon as ever they could. Blanche, being as impulsive as she was, was all for it and would have jumped up before him on his horse without pausing for clothes or money or even a piece of cheese to eat.

That was when Blanche's garden was surrounded by soldiers.

There were four of them and their dog barking furiously, and they all drew their swords on Neville. The fight which ensued was furious and farcical both, with the dog chasing Neville round the sundial while he hacked at the soldiers. Blanche climbed the apple tree and threw the hard, unripe fruit down at the soldiers' helmeted heads.

Well, the scuffle stopped when the soldiers managed to overpower Neville, but two of them were wounded badly and the dog lay dead in the raspberry bushes.

Blanche screamed and railed and called the soldiers all manner of terrible names, but they read a proclamation for Neville's capture and told him that he was sentenced to die at curfew the very next day. And then they took him away.

Some girls would have cried or fainted, but Blanche wasn't much of a one for either of those things. She'd tried them, of course, the same as anybody, but she'd found they rarely did her much good, so weren't worth bothering with. Instead, she walked up and down by the light of the moon, brushing her fingers against the sharp-smelling rosemary, and she thought.

By the time dawn painted the sky pink, Blanche was fully dressed – and she had a plan.

Now, the Heriots had a friend, Herrick Evenden, who visited them every few days. He was an amiable young man with no romantic interest whatever in Blanche, which was a profound relief to both of them and allowed them to be very good friends. When Herrick rode up to the Heriot house with the feather in his hat bobbing jauntily, Blanche met him in the garden and asked him if he had any plans for the day.

Nothing firm, said Herrick, who had been planning to see if she wanted to take a picnic into the forest or go boating.

Well, said Blanche, would he mind very much going to the town jail and seeing Neville, who had been arrested and was going to be executed, and getting from him a certain garnet ring?

Herrick was astonished to hear that Neville had been sentenced to death so soon after arriving home, but he recognised the determined look in Blanche's eyes, which told him to shut his mouth and keep listening. And when he had done that, Blanche continued, would he mind terribly taking the ferry to London as fast as he could and showing the ring to the new king to get his pardon for Neville?

Although this sounded like a near-impossible task to Herrick, who had never met a king and would have been quite happy spending all his days not meeting one or indeed drawing any undue attention to himself, he found himself being firmly propelled by the shoulders towards his horse, and Blanche pressing a bundle of bread and wine into his hands – 'for the journey,' she said – and before he knew it, he was carrying out her madcap scheme, just as he always did.

Well, the day drew on, and Blanche waited and waited. The sun travelled across the sky until it was high and hot and still no word came from Herrick or Neville. Blanche walked into the town and pretended to be shopping, while keeping an eye on the jail for any activity, but there was nothing.

London was not so very far, especially using the ferry, but Blanche worried as she had never worried in her life that Herrick would never make it back before the curfew bell. What if the king was away or wouldn't see him? What if? What if?

The sun continued its journey until it was late in the afternoon and Blanche began to be truly anxious. One of the soldiers outside the town jail was sharpening his sword, and Blanche began to fear that its keen edge would bite through Neville's neck if Herrick didn't come soon.

She waited on the path towards Laleham, where she would see the ferry as soon as it came, and spoke sharply to anyone who greeted her.

The sun plunged below the edge of the horizon.

At last, a long, painful time later, Blanche glimpsed the ferry in the distance. She couldn't tell if Herrick was on it or not, but she realised with horror that now the light had gone from the sky, the curfew bell would be rung. Even if Herrick were on the ferry, it was half a mile's walk from the landing and he would be too late.

Blanche had to take matters into her own hands.

Lifting up her skirt, she ran as fast as she could to the church at Chertsey Abbey. The bell tower was one of the older designs, with a separate door into the bell loft. Blanche wrenched it open and began to climb the ladder to the bell loft. It was dark and cobwebby and stank of bat leavings, but she climbed on.

When she reached the loft, she could see the great bell hanging in the darkness, with its inscription to the Virgin Mary. There was a narrow balcony around the long drop to the ground below. Without pausing to think, Blanche launched herself at the bell, taking a huge leap, and caught hold of the clapper. She swung there, muscles burning and screaming, but she knew she had silenced the bell.

Well, when the bellringers came to do their duty, they reached for the rope and tugged on it as usual, but no sound pealed forth from the church tower!

'Something wrong with the bell,' said one.

'A bad workman blames his tools,' said the other. 'Pull harder!'

And so, pull harder they did, and poor Blanche was dashed against the sides of the bell and the wooden frame around it and bruised terribly, but she still clung on, silencing that dreadful death knell with her own body. Her red hair streamed behind her as she swung and still the bell made no sound.

Down below, the bell ringers paused in their attempts and went to interrupt the sexton in his prayers to ask his opinion. The sexton, a dramatic sort of person, immediately assumed the worst and that the tower was haunted by malevolent ghosts. Armed with candle and Bible, he began the ascent to the bell tower to exorcise the spirits. This was somewhat slow and ponderous, as he had to keep changing hands with the candle and Bible. The bell ringers followed behind him, offering encouragement here and there.

Although the bell was no longer being rung, Blanche clung on regardless, just in case anybody were to try ringing it again and the soldiers at the jail take it for a sign to execute Neville. Her arms were begging her to let go, but Blanche told herself she must cling on a little longer if it would prevent Neville's head from rolling on the abbey mead.

Well, when the sexton found Blanche he was astonished, and was all for exorcising her anyway, until one of the bellringers recognised her.

Blanche explained herself, and the ringers were so sorry for her plight that they vowed they wouldn't ring the bells again today, not even if the new king paid them ten guineas himself and offered them a title. They helped Blanche climb down from the clapper, where she promptly collapsed in a heap like a quivering aspic pudding.

Well, you can probably imagine how the rest turned out. Herrick got off the ferry with the king's pardon and Neville was released with a hearty handshake and an apology, and he apologised in turn and vowed to buy a new dog to make up for the one he'd killed in the fury of his capture. When Blanche regained her strength, she climbed back down the bell tower and was reunited with her lover.

They feasted and they danced, and if I wasn't sitting here telling you this story I'd still be enjoying their hospitality, celebrating their wedding and the bravery of Blanche Heriot of Chertsey. Her legend goes on, and there's a statue of her, clinging to the bell, in Chertsey Abbey grounds to this very day, even though Blanche, Neville, and the old bell have all passed over into the record of time.

34

Cuthman of Steyning and the Devil

A Sussex Tale

All across England there are natural topographical features which have become inextricably tangled with legends. Devil's Dyke in Sussex is one such place, and in its story we meet the Devil as a personified figure who can be outwitted.

Within the folk tale canon there are plenty of examples of the Devil being deceived, usually by comical means. There is even an entire subsection of the Aarne-Thompson-Uther tale-type index devoted to 'deceiving the devil by breaking wind'. This kind of mockery of a symbol of fear was necessary in the past, when the Devil was an invisible and malign force thought to influence crops and sickness.

I find the association of the Devil with pre-Christian religions fascinating. An eleventh-century text called De Falsis Deis, *or* 'The False Gods', *connects the figures of Mercury and Odin to the Devil, implying that these figures were cunningly created by the Devil to lead souls astray. And there's lots of evidence of various charms against the Devil in Sussex today. Few pubs don't have a horse brass or two, and it's common to see lucky horseshoes pinned over people's doors.*

St Cuthman, in addition to confounding the Devil near Brighton, also pushed his mother in a wheelbarrow from Devon to Sussex, waiting for a sign from heaven to show him where to build a church. The shaft of his barrow broke at Steyning, and Cuthman built a timber church on that spot – all of which is pictured on the Steyning town sign.

EC

Many moons before the Bosham Bell was lost, and long before Bonnie Prince Charlie hid in a yew tree near St Leonard's, this tale of chalk and wave rippled over the downland. I know it's true, for a man my great-grandfather knew saw it all happen.

In that time, a tide was turning in the hearts and minds of the people of Sussex. The old faith had woven its tapestry of gods there for a while, but now the new faith had dyed the cloth.

The Devil was deeply angered by the Wealden folks' adoption of the new teachings, and he was trying every trick he could think of to sow doubt and confusion. You may have heard of the one he tried over in Mayfield against Archbishop Dunstan.

Dunstan was a man of the Church, but he was also a skilled metalworker and smith. One day, when he was hard at work making shoes for horses, the Devil came to tempt him, disguised as a lovely woman. She chatted and flirted with Dunstan, but as the talk grew ever more lewd and wild, he began to guess the truth. So, he kept on working at the forge, as the Devil sidled closer and closer, and stroked his arm and made all manner of suggestions.

But Dunstan snatched his red-hot tongs from right out of the fire and pinched the woman's nose between them. She shrieked and writhed and then she changed her shape – once, twice, thrice – each new shape more monstrous, until at last, the Devil stood before Dunstan in his own terrifying form. Then Dunstan released the tongs and the Devil flew away to Tunbridge Wells to bathe his blistering nose in the waters.

It wasn't the last time the Devil brushed with Dunstan, and it's a fair thing to say that he'd somewhat taken against the village of Mayfield, for on their next meeting he told Dunstan he intended to knock down every house there. But Dunstan was ahead of the Devil again – he'd nailed all those horseshoes he'd forged over the doors of all the houses, and that kept the old Adversary at bay.

Now, while the Devil was preoccupied with the malice of Mayfield, there was a shepherd by the name of Cuthman, who lived hard by the church in Steyning. Cuthman was no ordinary shepherd. In fact, he had built the church himself, from strong new timber, brighter than silver or gold. It's said that he performed all the labour himself, but he struggled to lift the great roof beam.

As he was heaving and dragging it up the ladder, a stranger appeared and took his load from him, helping him to finish the church.

Afterwards, when Cuthman asked his name, the stranger replied, 'I am he in whose name you are building this church'.

But ever since the church had been finished, Cuthman had lived a simple life in the fields, looking after sheep. Many was the hour he spent sitting on a wide stone, chewing on a straw and gazing down at the sea.

That stone can still be seen today, if you walk through Cuthman's Dell, and they do say that miracles happen there. I don't know, for I haven't seen, but I've been told that laying an afflicted limb across that stone will make it well and whole again.

One afternoon, as the light was beginning to die away from the sky and it was getting on for the set of the sun, Cuthman was sitting on his stone and watching the place where the sky met the sea. A magpie flew down into the field, then another, then another.

Cuthman saw a great dark shape like a cloud in the sky, but with huge leathery wings, and he felt a coldness take hold in his heart. It was a lonely feeling, like fear and grief mingled together.

When Cuthman tore his eyes from the shape in the sky, he saw seven magpies sitting in the field about his feet and he knew then the truth of what he could see in the clouds, for he remembered the old rhyme:

One for sorrow, two for mirth,
Three for a funeral, four for a birth,
Five for heaven, six for hell,
Seven for the Devil, his own sel'.

It was the Devil, right there in the sky, flying inland from the sea.

When Cuthman saw a huge dust cloud to the east of where he sat, and vast clods of earth begin to fly into the air, he knew that the old Adversary had his eye on an evil more grotesque than any yet seen in those parts. But what should Cuthman do? He couldn't leave his sheep to the mercies of snatchers or wild beasts.

So, he said his prayers and asked for help, and it seemed to him as though a warm, low voice came to him. It was all at once like the call of the geese flying overheard and like the voice of his mother singing him to sleep. And that voice told him exactly what to do.

So Cuthman took his shepherd's crook and he drew a wide circle all around his sheep, containing them within an invisible boundary.

Then he hastened away as fast as he could in the direction of the dust cloud to see what the trouble was.

Now, the Devil was in a fierce black fury after what had happened with Dunstan, and he was in no hurry to ever go back to Mayfield. The air around the Devil was blue with the insults he shouted about Dunstan and his burning tongs. But now he would show Dunstan, for he had a cunning scheme to punish all the people of Sussex, who no longer cared for him since their conversion to the new religion.

The Devil had decided that he would take his pronged shovel and dig a vast channel – a long, furrowed trench like a wound through the land – from Poynings, where he had landed with his hooked wings folded around him, right down to the shore. When the ditch reached the sea, it would let in its raging waters and drown every Christian in Sussex, washing away their churches and wood and stone and sinking every last iron horseshoe to the bottom of the ocean. Then their prayers and their bells would do them no good at all, for he would carry their souls away into his kingdom of fire and sulphur.

So the Devil grasped his pronged shovel, and he dug and he dug. The first clod of earth he turned up flew to the west and became Chanctonbury Hill, and the second flew to the east, where it became Mount Caburn. Yet another was Cissbury and a further was Rackham Hill.

Nobody could say that the Devil didn't go about his business with a fearsome will, which may be why we have the saying 'to work like the Devil'. He shovelled until his clawed hands burned and he felt an ache in his cloven hooves, and yet he kept shovelling.

While he was working, he felt weighed down by the heavy gold in his pockets, for it's well known that the Devil always carries glittering gold and salty soup about him to trade for hungry souls. So, he took his gold and hid it deep below Trundle Hill and left one of his golden calves to guard it from opportunistic thieves. And then he kept on digging his trench, doggedly determined to wash away Sussex and all its God-bothering girls and Bible-bashing boys.

Night came down dark and heavy while the Devil worked. The hedgerows were full of snuffling moles and shrieking foxes, frightened at what the Devil was doing to their homeland, and with no moon, the only light was the luminous eyes of the owls watching for prey.

By that time, Cuthman had walked the long miles from Steyning to Poynings and the site of the Devil's Big Dig. He saw at once what the

Devil was up to, and he felt that cold and grieving feeling about his heart once more, as though a red claw was choking the life from him. But he beat his shepherd's crook three times against the ground – once for father, once for son, and once for holy ghost – and that gave him the courage to tap the Devil on his burning-hot shoulder – so hot that it scorched the skin from Cuthman's fingertip.

'What are you digging there so busily, Devil?' said Cuthman, chewing on the end of a straw and trying for all the world to make it seem as though he was just passing the time of day.

'I'm digging a channel to let in the sea and carry thy soul away from thee,' said the Devil, wiping steaming sweat from his dripping brow.

'You'll be at it a long time,' said Cuthman, sounding as disdainful as he could, even though he was sore afraid to see how much the Devil had already dug of the great, deep valley.

'I'll be done before the dawn,' said the Devil, 'and the sun will bleach your bones when they wash up on Shoreham Beach.'

'I'm not so sure about that,' said Cuthman. 'It seems to me as though you've a long way to go yet. I tell you what, how about a wager?'

The Devil stook back from his digging and leaned on his spade, for as we all know, he cannot resist a wager, a trade, or a gamble of any sort.

'I'm listening,' said the Devil.

'I'll bet that you can't dig all the way to the sea by morning,' said Cuthman, pointing down in the direction of the coast.

'Done,' said the Devil right away, for he'd already dug a fair few metres along, and he knew that he had half a black sheep still left in his pocket, ready to gobble down to bolster his strength for a long night's work.

'You've not heard the rest of it yet,' said Cuthman. 'If you don't succeed, and you haven't dug all the way to the sea by morning, then you're to fly back to where you came from and not trouble us here again.'

The Devil laughed, a sound like the rumble of coals falling into the fireplace, for he knew it would be an easy task for him. The stars had only just begun to show their shapes against the blackness of the sky and there were many hours yet left of night.

'And if I do succeed,' said the Devil, 'I'll take your soul in payment too.'

Cuthman neither agreed nor disagreed to that directly, but he did point out that if the Devil succeeded then he and his soul would be washed away anyway.

'But never pray as you're being drowned,' said the Devil, 'or I won't have my sport at all.'

Cuthman made no promises about that. Instead, he said to the Devil that he would let him get on, as it wouldn't be a fair bargain to keep him talking all the night and waste his time.

The Devil thought this showed a far more reasonable spirit than he could have expected under the circumstances and made a few flattering comparisons between this mild-mannered young man and the tong-wielding Dunstan of Mayfield. Tipping his hat to Cuthman, he went back to his digging with a fresh will.

As soon as the Devil's back was turned, Cuthman started running across the fields to the east, in the direction the morning sun would rise. Soon enough, he came to a cottage, all shut up for the night, and knocked loudly on the door, pounding on it fit to break it down until a window opened and a young woman put her head out.

'What's the meaning of all this noise?' said she.

'Let me in,' said Cuthman. 'The Devil's digging a trench to drown us all and we've got to stop him.'

Now the young woman, whose name was Ursula, had not got where she had in the world by blindly trusting in the words of strangers. She had the freehold of her own home and twenty chickens besides, and she thought to herself that this was the oldest trick of all, a young man trying to gain entrance to her home in the most shameless way. But even as she thought this, it seemed to her that the cross hanging on her wall began to glow with a golden light, and out of the light came a voice. It was huge, like the sigh of the distant sea, and tiny, like the cry of a newborn chick, and it told her to trust the man at the door and let him in.

So, Ursula unfastened the door and let Cuthman in, and Cuthman explained his plan to her. On his signal, she was to light a candle and set it on her windowsill, then to hold a sieve up in front of it to make a dimly glowing globe of light.

Ursula took up a sieve and lit her candle from the low-burning fire and carried it over to the sill. While she held the sieve there, Cuthman went out into her yard to where the sleeping cockerel sat. He struck the cockerel a blow on his feathered neck, enough to knock him from his perch and startle him awake. As the cockerel fell, he crowed, loud and harsh.

Well, Cuthman said another prayer and it was as though he'd set a cheese in motion rolling down a hill, for all the cockerels across the length and breadth of the Weald set up a riotous crowing, even though it was still the middle of the night.

The noise was loud enough to startle the Devil into dropping his pronged shovel. When he looked around, he saw the pale, glowing light of Ursula's candle behind the sieve and he mistook it for the rising morning sun. That and the sound of the cockerels crowing all around him, echoing off the Downs, was enough to convince him that morning had come and he was nowhere near finishing the trench down to the sea which would drown all the God-fearing folk of Sussex.

But a bargain is a bargain, and once struck it cannot be wriggled out of, not even by the Devil himself. The Devil cursed and flailed, but he was bound by the wager and had to fly back to his own land, leaving his work half-done. As he flew off to the north, he met his wife coming in the opposite direction to see how he'd been getting along with turning the tide against Sussex. When she saw that the work was unfinished and that her husband was spitting and cursing and foaming at the mouth, she began at once to bawl at him and berate him using all the worst words she had picked up on her travels through the world.

The Devil swore and spat at her, but she took her great cudgel and beat him about the ears with it until he was quite giddy. The pair of them carried on for so long that way that neither noticed the sky wasn't light and day had not yet broken, and so Cuthman's trick passed without them noticing at all.

Eventually, they hounded each other so bitterly that both dived down into the crust of the earth to escape each other, flinging up huge clods of turf behind them. And those mounds are known as the Devil's Grave and the Devil's Wife's Grave to this very day.

As for Cuthman, he said goodbye to Ursula and went back to his home, and when he returned, he found that an invisible hand had kept his sheep within the circle he had drawn upon the ground and none had been lost to wandering or to wolves.

And that's the story of how the people of the Weald escaped being washed away into the waves, and how Devil's Dyke was dug in a single night.

35

The Legend of Guy of Warwick

A Warwickshire Tale

It's not enough to simply be a knight by title. The complex code of chivalry dictates that you must also complete various heroic deeds. At the heart of the tale of Guy of Warwick is the idea of proving yourself, which features in a lot of medieval romances.

There are multiple versions of the Guy of Warwick story, but it originates with the twelfth-century Anglo-Norman romance, Guy de Warewic, *in which our hero has many epic adventures spanning continents. It's resonant of other romances like* Sir Gawain and the Green Knight *and* Erec and Enide, *and the catalyst for a knight's quest in tales like these is often a beautiful woman.*

In Guy's story, Lady Felice isn't satisfied with just a knight's title *for her prospective lover – he has to make his fame. The tasks available to a knight-in-training varied widely. They usually featured some grand battle with a monster – in this case, the terrifying Dun Cow. And there is a supposed Dun Cow rib at Warwick Castle, although they're now claiming it's a narwhal tusk, which seems highly unlikely.*

Elsewhere, Guy of Warwick was included in a version of The Nine Worthies, nine historical figures of distinction who embodied the ideals of chivalry. Guy's deeds were celebrated through ballads and pageants right through history, and after the Second World War, he had a resurgence in popularity at patriotic local events.

EC

Since the time that God was born and Christendom was established, many adventures have taken place, not all of which are known about yet. When these adventures are recounted, we should learn from them so that we become wise ourselves and leave ignorance behind.

Closer to that time than we are now, there was once an English earl who controlled Warwick. He was rich in gold and silver, but also in friendship. He especially loved horses, and often made gifts of fine stallions to his closest friends. He was generous with rewards and well known as a fair and just ruler.

Now this earl had a daughter, and she was as fair as a flower in a meadow. Her eyes were the celestial blue of a summer sky and her hair was red gold like the sunset on a field of corn. Besides being exceedingly attractive, she was very clever and had studied with the finest tutors her father's money could buy. She was an expert in astronomy, anatomy, and arithmetic. Many men from many lands travelled to Warwick to win her hand in marriage but none were successful. She turned every last one down.

Her name was Felice, and she came to be called Felice the Beautiful, for her good looks surpassed those of all the other local maidens. Unfortunately, her great advantages in life had also given her a great and terrible pride. Nobody who came to woo her was ever good enough for her – not learned enough, not handsome enough, not rich enough, or had accomplished no great deeds – for Lady Felice had read all the romances, in French and English and Latin too, and she prized a hero above all else.

Now, the Earl of Warwick had a steward named Segward, who was his oldest friend. In their youth they had fought many battles together and ridden across many miles of country. But their exploits must sleep until another tale is told, for my story is about Segward's son.

A finer young man could not have been found anywhere. He was kind and strong and handsome, and everybody loved him. He was a good swordsman, but he was also very capable on horseback, which drew him to the Earl's attention for his excellent riding. The Earl asked this young man to be his cupbearer, and he gladly accepted.

At Whitsuntide it was the Earl's habit to hold a huge feast for all the nobles. The long tables groaned with civet of hare, gilded sugar plums, and peacocks stuffed with oysters. The knights sat in the great hall and the ladies were in another chamber. The Earl called to the steward's son, whose name was Guy, and instructed him to carry a fine goblet of wine to his daughter in the other room.

Well, the moment Guy saw Felice in her silk gown with her golden hairnet, his heart flew towards her like a swallow flying south. The love welling up inside him could not be measured. It seemed to him to be larger than the limit of the world. He did his best to please her, but his hands were trembling, and his words were falling over themselves, and he spilled the wine on the floor, despite his normally steady hands.

The other ladies in the chamber were having a good look at Guy, and sent plenty of amorous glances in his direction, but he had no eyes for any of them, for Felice the Beautiful had his heart.

After the feast, Guy shut himself up in his chambers in total misery. He closed his shutters and languished in darkness without lighting a single candle. None of his usual activities held any pleasure for him. There was only one star in the heavens for him now – the Lady Felice.

Eventually, he resolved to go and speak to her, even if it was the last thing he did. So, off he went to Lady Felice's garden, where she was tending her physick plants, and he proposed to her immediately, just like that.

Far from being pleased, Felice was furious.

'How dare you?' she said. 'You, the son of a mere steward? When I tell my father about this, he'll have you drawn and quartered. Get out of my sight at once, or you'll be dead before the next cock crow.'

Guy was so overwhelmed with sorrow at this rejection that he shut himself away again. He wouldn't eat and he couldn't sleep, and his father and friends were very worried about him. Eventually, after weeks of growing thin and pale, he decided that there was no point in living at all without Felice's love, so he returned to her garden.

'Lady Felice,' said Guy, 'you told me that if you saw me again, you would have me executed. I'm here to say that you must go ahead, since life without your love is no life to me at all.'

Then he threw himself on the ground in front of her and wept so hard he watered the sun-baked earth.

It was hard for Felice not to be a little flattered that this handsome young man would rather die than live without her, and she began to feel a bit sorry for him. But she tried to explain, reasonably this time, that because she had previously rejected knights and earls, she could hardly accept a person like him, with no title or good name. If she were to do so, her honour would be no better than mud. Of course, if he were a knight and had proved himself, then it would be easier for her to consider his proposal.

Well, Guy leapt up, his tears drying as fast as the hope was budding within him. He knew the Earl of Warwick favoured him, so the very next day he went along to ask the Earl to make him into a knight and vowed that he would serve him for as long as he lived. The Earl had no objection for he liked Guy, and soon after, in a great ceremony of purple silk and pearl garlands, Guy became a knight. The Earl presented him with a special gift: a great two-handed sword which he had once fought with himself.

'Look,' said Guy to Felice the Beautiful, after the feast which had been held in his honour. 'I am a knight! Now do as you promised.'

'Promised what?' said Felice. 'You may be a knight in name, but you've neither jousted nor fought with other good warriors. That two-handed sword of yours has never tasted blood or sweat from your grip. How can I give my love to an unproved knight?'

This was not great news for Guy. He did his best to joust with his new knightly fellows, but they were friendly matches and no real proof of glory. Felice remained aloof, and despite his father's pride and the many expressions of interest Guy received from the other ladies at the Earl's court, he was not satisfied.

Now, it came to pass that on Dunsmore Heath a ferocious beast was on the rampage. Sparks flew from its galloping hooves, its eyes were hot coals, it breathed flame, and it mashed its victims into paste with its huge blunt teeth. It was the dread Dun Cow, and it roamed the heath in search of prey, destroying farmland and brutalising any person it met.

Like so many monsters, the Dun Cow had once been kind, with a shining white hide and gilded horns. She was big as a house, with eighteen udders, but despite her great size she had once befriended the people of Shropshire and freely given a pail of milk to all who needed it. However, a local witch tricked the cow by milking her into a sieve. The sieve could never be filled and the Dun Cow's milk ran dry. This made her so angry that she ran from Shropshire into Warwickshire, destroying everything her giant hooves touched.

The Earl wanted to raise an army against the cow. But the newly knighted Sir Guy stepped forward and said that he alone would go against the monster. Lady Felice wanted a brave deed performed and this could be it. The Earl was reluctant, but he eventually agreed.

The Dun Cow led Guy on a madcap chase around the county, and even his masterful horsemanship scarcely allowed him to keep up with her. But he wounded her at Mickleton and slowed her down, then tracked the drips of her blood back to Dunsmore Heath, where he cornered her and killed her. In death, the Dun Cow's face was so sad and peaceful that Guy felt a stab of remorse.

A triumphant parade was held in Guy's honour and all in Warwick celebrated his bravery. All except Felice. When he presented her with one of the Dun Cow's curling horns, she put it aside disdainfully and told him that one sole deed was not enough to make a hero.

At that, Guy went into a kind of frenzy. If he ever heard of anyone being terrorised by a beast he rode off to dispatch it. He became known the length and breadth of Warwickshire as a monster killer. His fame and renown grew. The few remaining local monsters tacitly agreed to slink off and try their luck elsewhere. I heard of a wyvern who is still skulking in a cave below Gloucester to this day, worrying about Guy of Warwick. He slew the Boar of Birmingham and the Dragon of Draycote in a furious fiery battle which took off Guy's eyebrows and the dragon's head. He gave Felice a dragon's tooth set with a ruby on a golden chain, but she shut it away in her jewel casket and remarked that people had been slaying dragons since before the time of Brutus and it was no very special thing.

Guy began to despair that she would ever love him, and so he started to accept challenges further away from home in his desperate attempt to impress Felice the Beautiful.

It came to pass that King Anlaf of Denmark had been eyeing up England for many years, and he thought he would invade it. He descended with his army to seize it by force. King Athelstan of England, understandably piqued, mustered a huge force of dukes, earls, barons, and wealthy lords at Winchester, and all the priests and bishops assembled too, to pray against the invasion.

But Anlaf of Denmark had a secret weapon. He had brought with him a giant called Colbrand, immensely strong and merciless, more feared in battle than a hundred knights. Unless Athelstan agreed to pay tribute to Denmark every year, Colbrand would destroy England. That was, unless an English warrior could defeat him in single combat.

Well, Guy knew that this was the challenge meant to make his name and he rode to Winchester at once. They faced each other down, Guy

and Colbrand, and at first sight they seemed hopelessly outmatched. Colbrand had a huge amount of arms and armour with him, all piled on to a cart. He was thirteen feet tall and his battle axe had gruesome spikes protruding from it that would bite into steel like a knife sliding through butter.

The battle lasted for hours, with neither tiring. Several times Guy thought he nearly had Colbrand, except for that he couldn't reach the giant's head! His two-handed sword was long, but he still couldn't reach higher than the giant's shoulder. Dancing around Colbrand, Guy moved in circles as quickly as he could, bewildering the heavy giant.

As the sun set on the battle, Guy was able to get behind Colbrand and into his cart of spare weapons. He stole one of the giant's axes, putting all his strength into lifting it. It was much longer than Guy's sword, and with the axe he was able to reach up and give Colbrand such a massive blow on the back of his neck that his head fell off. With the last of the day's light, Guy thought he saw a look of lingering sorrow in the giant's dead eyes.

The Danes were mortified that their champion was dead, and King Anlaf and his men made their way in great sadness to their ships and sailed back home. King Athelstan was grateful enough to reward Guy with fine lands, and Guy of Warwick's fame spread throughout England.

By now, he was receiving all kinds of proposals of marriage and invitations to the best baronies in the land. But Guy had loyalty to none other than his first friend, the Earl of Warwick, and eyes for no woman but Felice.

'Surely now I have done everything you wanted,' said Guy, when he gave her the giant Colbrand's girdle.

Felice could see that he truly was the best and bravest of all knights and she finally relented. They were married, and Felice the Beautiful was smugly happy in the knowledge that she had the prize all England coveted for her own. The wedding feast lasted fourteen days and nights with minstrels singing beautifully and gifts for all the townsfolk from Sir Guy of Warwick and his self-satisfied bride.

But even amid all this celebration, and even after their bodies met under the bedsheets, Guy was not perfectly happy. Even as he looked at Felice, with her red-gold hair clothing her in light, he could not stop thinking about the creatures he had slain. Over the ensuing weeks, a single-minded conviction took hold of Guy – he had to make amends.

He told Felice that he was going to make a pilgrimage to the Holy Land. 'Take my two-handed sword,' he said. 'Keep it safe for my son.'

Felice was incandescent with rage. Her idea of life as the wife of the celebrated Guy of Warwick did not include a husband who was absent. She tried every tactic she could think of to change his mind, one moment screaming, the next crying, then smothering Guy with kisses, then insulting him. Guy resisted all these manoeuvres and prepared to depart for Jerusalem.

When it came to parting, Felice was sorrowful, regretting her hasty words. She gave him a golden ring with a secret inscription inside to remember her by, and Guy promised to return to her.

With that, he set off, speaking to nobody and travelling incognito so that nobody could ask him to slay anything. On his way to Jerusalem, he visited many other holy places where saints were honoured, as many as he could, for seven long years.

In Guy's absence, Felice became very charitable, building many abbeys and caring for the poor. She never laughed again, but she had a beautiful son who grew strong and courageous in his father's image.

Guy did eventually return to England, but by that time he was tired and ill, and his adventuring days were over. He made it almost as far as Warwick, to a place called Gibcliff, and there he rested in the cave of a hermit. While he was there, he had a dream that Saint Michael came to him, wearing his feathered armour and holding a two-handed sword which looked much like Guy's own. He told Guy that he had only eight days left to live. Guy was grateful to God's friend for the warning and sent the hermit to Felice with the gold lover's ring she had given him.

When the hermit presented Felice with the ring, she was glad and sad at the same time. She rode to Gibcliff as fast as she could with her young son and arrived only just in time. Guy was beyond words by this point, but he kissed her in farewell and put his hand on his son's head in blessing. And then he died.

When his soul had departed, it turned into a white dove and flew up to heaven on the shoulder of Saint Michael, for Guy had atoned for all his years of violence. His fame endures and his tale is still told.

As for Felice, she regretted that she had kept urging him on to further deeds and had so foregone many years of happiness which might have been.

36

The Witch of Westmoreland

A Westmoreland Tale

There are 197 tarns scattered across the Lake District. These mysterious bodies of water have been the subject of myth and legend across the ages. The word derives from the Old Norse tjörn, *which means 'small mountain lake'. From* Beowulf's *Grendel and his fearsome mother to the terrifying Jenny Greenteeth, the things that lurk in the depths of these waters have inspired any number of tales.*

The story of the Witch of Westmoreland actually comes from a folk song, rather than a local legend. However, it is inspired by a local myth about female centaurs in the Windermere area. Deer, swimming across the shallow ends of the lakes, would get water weed caught in their antlers. In the twilight, they resembled long-haired centaurs, giving rise to the myth.

Shape-shifting witches appear across cultures, but it is rare to encounter one who can transform into a horse or a centaur. Female centaurs, as an idea, first appear in Greek mythology as the Centaurides *and were frequently the subject of art.*

The story is a 'romance' in the true sense, neither tragic nor comic, but combining elements of both. It is also rich in symbols, inspired by medieval romance poems and songs. However, the original folk song ends with the lovers parting and the knight given a blessing which may just turn out to be a curse, as eternal life, for the knight, becomes something long and weary.

EC

In the darkest days of autumn, when the land was falling into slumber and leaves tumbled from the trees and flecks of ash from the bonfires tumbled up and the hearth was a safe haven from the bitter cold, and stories danced in the flickering candlelight and turned the shadows on the wall into leaping figures, time slept.

There was a soldier who fought in the warband of his king. He bore the blood-red rowan shield, and it had always kept him safe. Before the company had ridden out, the augur had blessed their shields with runecraft, so they would be protected in battle. But the leader of the warband they fought bitterly against had prayed to his gods for rain that would last two hundred days and would wash the rune words from the rowan shields.

The sky cracked and the rain howled, and the tide of the battle turned. The two sides met on an open moorland, wide as woe and open as a mouth to the pitiless sky. The battle was a horror of whirling axes, of lopped limbs and cries of agony. And in that battle the soldier took a terrible wound. He felt it rip through him, fire and ice and darkness all at once.

It could not be called desertion when he dragged himself away from the fight, fainting over the back of his horse, with his grey hawk and parcel of grey hounds following behind, for the fight was lost, the king run through and pinned to a tree, and the dead would fill many a waiting barrow. The soldier did not turn his horse for home, for home had already been burned, and there was nothing left for him but to die.

Cold was the crack of the crows' cries as they wheeled and circled around him as he rode, and he knew he would be their carrion soon, for they could smell the dark blood seeping from the wound in his chest. The forest was dark with the black skeletons of trees which latticed the windows of the sky. His horse's hoofprints showed his passing only for a moment before leaves hid them. Mirroring and repeating paths confused his dying sense. His blood fell like drops of cinnabar spilt from a nudged inkwell, spotting his horse's neck.

He was carried into a clearing where a huge black raven sat on the withered stump of a tree. It had a wicked beak and a bright, inquisitive gaze. The soldier tried to sit up in the saddle, for he knew it would take out his eyes with a vicious stab of its beak if it thought him dead. But his blood fell on to the tree stump and the raven dipped its head and put the tip of its beak into the blood, and it was given language:

Nor water, nor oil will clean your wound
Only the Witch of Westmoreland.

Dark spots swam before the soldier's eyes, but he asked the raven what it meant. The bird told him to ride on through the night, towards the brightest star which hung low over the hill they called Arnsbarrow, and there he would find the witch who could heal his wounds.

So, the soldier rode on, through the forest and towards the brightest star, sitting on the brow of Arnsbarrow like a coronet. His grey hawk kept the skies over his horse's head, until it suddenly dived down into the grass. The soldier heard a shrill cry and then the baying of his greyhounds as they eagerly loped to join the hawk.

He saw that they had captured a struggling mountain hare with a lily-white coat, which lay pinned beneath the hawk's talons. The soldier would not begrudge them a meal, but then the blood from his wound dripped down onto the hare's spotless pelt and it spoke as the raven had done:

Why do you ride in a hurry this way
When you'll be dead before break of day?

The soldier told the hare that he sought the witch who could heal his wounds. Gesturing with its long back leg towards the clump of trees below the bright star, the hare directed him towards a secret mere, hidden from sight by a thick forest, and told him that there he would find the witch.

Cold was the soldier, and tired and faint, but he kept his eyes open and his hand pressed over the piece of broken spear in his chest, even though he was losing blood fast. He reached the edge of the hidden tarn at last, and its surface glittered with the reflection of the bright star above it, making a mirror of the water. He saw no witch – he saw no soul at all, except for an owl, which sat in the branches of a willow tree and called its mournful sound.

The soldier could not reach the owl, but his faithful grey hawk touched its wings to his bloody hands and flew up, up towards the owl, where it brushed its feathers with the soldier's scarlet blood, until it too could speak.

'Where is she?' cried the soldier. 'Where is the witch who can heal my wound?'

And the owl hooted in reply:

Gather the goldenrod growing here
And throw its blooms into the mere.

The greyhounds helped the soldier to gather the bright fronds of goldenrod, bringing them to him in their mouths, and when they had enough he cast them into the sparkling mere as the owl had told him.

The flowers sank beneath the surface of the water, disturbing the reflection of the star in bright ripples. And from the very centre of the star, up rose the form of a beautiful woman with black hair all slick from the water. But as she emerged from the mere, the soldier saw that she was only a woman to the waist. Below was the body of an ebony-black mare, glistening wet and ready to run.

And run she did, faster than ever a horse had run before. The soldier took the horn from his belt and with almost his last breath he blew a blast on it. His horse and his hounds and his hawk knew well the signal, and they gave chase at once.

The horse carried him towards the woman who was a mare and the greyhounds shot off to tangle themselves around her hooves. High overhead his hawk flew, screeching directions as they gave chase to the witch who could heal the soldier's wound.

They dashed through the forest until, at last, the soldier's hounds and horse held the witch trapped against the trunk of a vast oak. But the woman who was a horse held out her hands towards the soldier.

'Stop,' she said. 'We are far from the battlefield, so now lay down your rowan shield.'

In wonder, the soldier lowered his shield, and he watched as the part of the witch that was a mare melted away, leaving behind a whole woman in a blue dress that shimmered and clung like the waters of the mere.

The soldier half-slid from his horse and into her waiting arms. The witch took a frond of the goldenrod twisted into her rippling black hair and packed it tightly into the wound in his chest. At first it burned like hellfire itself, but then a warmth spread through his pierced body, like the healing warmth of the sun.

Once she kissed his bloody lips, and twice, and thrice, and by the time the third kiss was finished his wound was healed.

The grey hawk hooded its head beneath its wing and the greyhounds lay down to rest, for all that night the soldier lay with the Witch of Westmoreland on a bed of crushed bracken.

The next morning, she gave him three kisses once again and whispered in his ear that he would never be sick or be slain, not so long as he lived, for he had spent the night with her. And then she changed again, her back lengthening out until she was part mare again, and she galloped back into the mere where she vanished below the water.

The soldier called to his hawk and hounds and spurred his horse, and away he rode, leaving behind the secret lake at the top of Arnsbarrow and the creatures who had guided him there, and the mysterious Witch of Westmoreland.

Long was his life and valiant, for he lived to fight for new warlords and proved himself a hundred times a hero. In all that while he was never sick, nor did he sustain a wound, even though he threw himself headlong into fights that others scorned as madness. But he had no family, no friends, no kin to call his own, and the years passed by until the soldier was an old man, still strong and hale, but grey-bearded and lonely as the solitary wind.

Age scarcely withered him, and he went on and on in this way until he was weary of life and had no hope of death. And so he vowed to return to the Witch of Westmoreland and ask her to lift the charm she had placed over him – the gift that was beginning to feel like a curse.

His horse and his hounds were gone to their graves and his hawk was long since freed to the wind, so he had no company on his journey. It was All Saint's Day when he set out for the west, to follow the light of the brightest star to the top of Arnsbarrow.

It seemed that even the star's light had waned to a dull and sickly gleam in the mere. With shaking fingers, the soldier bent to gather an armful of the withered goldenrod which grew around its banks and sprinkled it into the water.

The head that rose from the mere was no longer ebony black, but white as a winter sky, and the coat of the black mare was flecked with grey and silver, and the eyes of the Witch of Westmoreland were tired from many years resting below the lake.

'You can heal all wounds,' said the soldier. 'Can you heal the wound of loneliness and a too-long life?'

The witch stamped her hooves on the ground and swished her silver-streaked tail, and then she took the soldier in her arms and swung him up on to her back. And the soldier took the horn from his belt and with almost his last breath he blew a blast on it.

Over the rolling mists on the lake's surface a brace of ghostly greyhounds came running, kicking up enough ripples to make the reflection of the star in the water just as bright as it had ever been. Above the soldier's head, streaking through the foggy clouds, a ghostly hawk flew down like a silver arrow and perched on his shoulder.

Once the soldier kissed the witch of Westmoreland, and twice, and thrice, and by the time the third kiss was finished she was galloping away over the lake into the sky, fast enough to heal any wound.

In the darkest days of autumn, when the land was falling into slumber and leaves tumbled from the trees and flecks of ash from the bonfires tumbled up, and the hearth was a safe haven from the bitter cold and stories danced in the flickering candlelight and turned the shadows on the wall into leaping figures, time awoke, and spun its wheel once more.

37

A Cuckoo in Winter

A Wiltshire Tale

Avebury Henge is part of a very large Neolithic site which includes the largest stone circle in Britain. Built between approximately 2850 and 2200 BC, Avebury has caught the attention of archaeologists, historians, and folklorists alike.

In addition to producing some fascinating excavations, including discoveries of human remains buried with the particular tools of their trades, Avebury has given rise to a number of legends. The area is supposed to be very active for fairies, who have been heard or left evidence of their presence, including rings of growing mushrooms and flowers.

As for cuckoos, before we understood more about the migration of birds, it was a widely accepted piece of folklore that cuckoos went underground in winter, perhaps to holiday or rest with the fairies.

It is interesting how stone circles, barrows, and burial mounds have become associated with fairies and the Otherworld, too. I have always loved stories that include the mysteriously fast passage of time. From Urashima Tarō *to* Rip Van Winkle, *and of course, the English* King Herla, *the price of doing a favour for a fairy can be steep.*

Alexander Keiller was a real person who bought the Avebury site and attached manor in the 1930s. My narrator for this tale is his third wife, Doris Emerson Chapman, an artist who is sometimes credited with the beginnings of forensic imaging. She sketched skulls and began to create facial reconstructions.

EC

The tiny shape of the bird circling above me is a dark grey smudge against a lighter grey sky. I pause in my sketching, tearing my eyes away from my charcoals to the sky and trying to make out the bird, but it's too far away, too small, too indistinct, and I lose sight of it as it flutters high above the megaliths.

I'm sketching the shape of a skull, a broad standing stone at my back. I like being outside in the air, hearing the sounds of the dig around me, despite the biting breeze. I often joke to Alexander that I spend more time with the dead than the living, but he's just the same. We've both always been fascinated by the past.

Actually, it's how we met. Alexander had been an archaeologist for his whole career, while I was an artist first. I sometimes wish we'd met in Paris while I was exhibiting there, in a different world – a glamorous, champagne-coloured one – but Alexander and I met at an excavation, with soil beneath our fingernails and the excitement of discovery shining in our eyes.

Alexander had just founded the Morven Institute of Archaeological Research, which I joined to further my interest in trying to understand our ancestors. He likes nothing better than the dig itself, brushing dust and earth away to reveal buried secrets, and I help him to bring them back to life.

It started by accident, when I'd been drawing one of the skulls we found at Chippenham and had absently started to round out the face as we talked. Alexander had looked at what I'd done and asked me if I could create a full reconstruction of how the owner of the skull might have looked in life. Since then, I've been doing it for every new find.

We talk for hours about the lives people from the ancient past might have led: what they ate, what they wore, the tools they used. It's more than our work – it's our obsession. Alexander once brought bones to bed. Archaeology is the most dangerous sort of addiction, because you know that there will always be more to find. For me, it's an act of imagination, too. I can approximate bone structure and facial muscles and fat, but I choose hair and eye colour, add clothing, tell myself stories about the personalities and feelings these bare bones once possessed.

When Alexander found out about Avebury, the sale was completed almost before he told me where we'd be going. He had been married twice before, and I had my history too, but it was Avebury which decided us, and at the manor he'd bought to form the base of operations for the dig, I became his third wife.

The shout comes from further away down the two parallel lines of stones we call Kennet Avenue. They've found something. I run towards the shout, leaving my sketchbook behind, already able to catch Alexander's excited voice as it dances towards me on the breeze.

He's down in the pit, sleeves rolled up and forearms brown with mud. I can see the shape of the half-buried megalith, the one we call Stone 38, which Alexander and his team have been steadily excavating, and below it, the pearly sheen of old bone.

There is a peculiar excitement for me in uncovering human remains, in a way that I never feel for a pot or a hoard of coins. I suppose it's the feeling that this person, whoever they may have been, once breathed and talked and experienced all the trappings of life, just as I do. They laughed, they wept, they loved, they lost.

We'll have to excavate carefully to establish whether the skeleton is complete, which could take many long hours of work. But the first thing Alexander does when we make a discovery is always the same and has nothing to do with the mechanics of the dig. It's almost a superstition now, I think, but Alexander insists that it's important to record the local legends as we work.

I don't know where he found George Snelgrave, a man who seems so aged that his weathered face resembles one of the buried stones, but whenever we find something of note, Alexander wants Snelgrave there. I can understand why – and not just because Snelgrave looks old enough to remember some of the centuries-old legends he recounts as though they happened yesterday. But Alexander insists that we record everything he says. He has some idea of tying the folk legends to the facts when we eventually exhibit the finds.

There's a bit of bumbling around the stones while we wait for Snelgrave to be fetched from Avebury village. Alexander climbs out of the trench around Stone 38 and squeezes my hands excitedly. 'I hope he's complete,' he says, and I know he's talking about the skeleton. 'I wonder how he died.'

I wonder too, as I look down at the exposed sternum and protruding clavicle we can see below the stone. Will this find tell us something vital about the ritual practices of early man? Will it open a tantalising door into the distant past through which Alexander and I can step, walking the long road back until we lose ourselves?

The brother and sister who hang around the dig and run errands for us when we need soon return with George Snelgrave, leaning on a walking stick that looks as though it's been cut from a still-living tree. His eyes are a blue so light they remind me of the cold, flat sky above us. Alexander rushes forward and shakes his hand warmly, chattering nineteen to the dozen, filling Snelgrave in on the details of the discovery and asking him if he knows of any mythic significance concerning a man buried under a stone.

I can see some our colleagues rolling their eyes, but Alexander believes that the local legends have value, so nobody actively challenges it.

'Oh yes, I wondered when he'd turn up,' Snelgrave says, as though he has expected our vital find for weeks.

'He – who?' Alexander says, with the eagerness of a school boy for a half-holiday.

'Oh, you don't know that old story?' Snelgrave says, with the faint incredulity with which he always greets our ignorance about local hearsay. Alexander assures him that we do not, and the old man settles himself at the side of the trench, legs dangling down between the struts, lights the half-smoked and evil-smelling cigarette he keeps behind his ear, and begins.

It was somewhere in the middle of the fifteenth century, or thereabouts, that a new priest came to Avebury and began preaching against the stones. They were bad luck, said the holy man, and leftover relics from pagan days, when men talked to birds and rivers and mistook them for gods.

Stones like that had no place in the valley of God, and the only thing to do was to pull them down and break them up and bury them deep in the earth where pious folk might never see them. He thought the stones were haunted, you see, by ghostly guardians, demons of fog and air who would whisper dark and delightful words to the people of Avebury and turn their heads and hearts.

So, the word went out in Avebury that the stones were to be broken, and all the local men took hammers and picks and went about it. None was excepted, old or young, even those who thought in their private hearts that the ancient monuments were best left well alone.

Among them was John Dancey, the cordwainer, though his slim fingers were best suited to detailed work and not the rough task of stone-breaking. He had no appetite for it either, preferring to sit alone with his shoes and listen to the birds rather than shout and gossip with the other men. He was a lonely soul and had never found another to tell all his thoughts.

Still, he lent his strength, for he wanted no questions asked by the new priest or any other, and he heaved on the ropes with the rest when they were bringing the stones down. He was standing by when they were about to bring down that stone you now call number thirty-eight.

That was when he saw a tiny grey bird with a striped chest and golden feet, just below where the stone would come crashing down. It wasn't moving, but sat helpless, seeming unable to even hop, let alone fly. John Dancey could see, even from this distance, that it was a cuckoo, though winter had come. Everybody knows that cuckoos are never seen in winter because they go underground to stay warm.

John Dancey didn't pause to think. Within moments, the stone would be down, and the injured cuckoo would be crushed, so he darted in and carefully picked up the bird in his hands and stowed it in his jacket, hiding it away from the sight of others. If he'd been any slower, both he and the bird would have been ground to nothing more than blood and stone dust.

As soon as he could, he slipped away from the work party toppling the stones and went back to his own home, outside the main part of the village but close to the trees. When he took off his jacket and let the tiny cuckoo out on to the table, he soon saw why it hadn't been able to fly away. One of its wings was broken and it wasn't able to do any more than flap the other frantically. But John Dancey was careful with his hands, and he took his finest cut strips of leather and with time and coaxing, he managed to set the cuckoo's broken wing straight, so it might heal.

Well, a cordwainer's cottage was no place for a wild bird, so when night fell John Dancey said to himself that he would take the cuckoo back to the stone ring where he had found it and set it free. As he set out, black clouds knitted themselves together over his head, making the night sky appear darker than it was, and soon a heavy, dark rain fell down and a fierce storm battered Avebury.

John Dancey was on the point of turning back more than once, and he was less and less sure about leaving the cuckoo alone, but he reached the stones nonetheless. Many had been toppled already by the work of the village men, but there were some yet standing. John Dancey made his way to the tallest of the stones, so it might provide some shelter for the little bird. But as he nestled the bird in the hollow of grass beneath the stone, lightning sliced open the sky, leaving a jagged white scar.

John Dancey threw himself to the ground as the lightning struck it. When he thought it was safe to open his eyes again, he saw with amazement that a great space like the portal to a tomb had opened below the huge standing stone, just where the lightning had hit. In the entrance – for John Dancey could see that was what it was – the grey cuckoo, miraculously unscathed by the bolt of white fire, fluttered as though it were waiting for something. Its wing was whole and good as new.

He got slowly to his feet. Beyond the bird was a dark doorway into the space underneath the stone. John Dancey knew, though the cuckoo spoke no words, that it wanted him to follow it into that dark passage. And though he had no light and he was wet through from the rain, he did follow.

He walked and he walked, and it was too dark to see the cuckoo, but he heard its wingbeats ahead of him. He walked and he walked, until the darkness flowed away like poured water and stars drifted around John Dancey's head. In time, the stars gave way to flaming torches and braziers full of burning coals. Some of the flames were different colours – blues and greens and deep, vivid purples.

On he went, until the cave he was walking through began to resemble a gracious house of many centuries previous; a square villa with tall columns and a low, sunken pool in the centre. Within the pool a great table floated, held up seemingly by nothing. It was covered in a thick cloth the colour of the night sky, in whose folds and gathers fireflies seemed to hide and chase each other. Every available inch groaned under the weight of a strange and opulent hospitality. Ropes of pearls and diamonds decorated huge golden and silver platters displaying the heads of parrots and bursting with caviar, with fishes chasing each other in perpetual aspic, with jellies containing violets and roses. In the centre of the table, a sculpture in ice in the shape of two dragons swallowing each other whole bore a great glistening pile of fruit. Mysterious and beautiful perfumes floated around the table.

In the pool around the table nymphs and dolphins frolicked and splashed, their soft laughter a delicate harmony to the silvery chimes of a chorus of dulcimers. Above the table, strange birds with coloured plumage and bright red eyes soared and called to each other. Some of the birds were books, which flapped their pages like wings.

The cuckoo flew away behind one of the columns, and when John Dancey stopped to gaze in wonder at everything around him, a figure came round the other side of the column where the bird had vanished. He wore silk in all the colours of the sky and a crown of silver cuckoo feathers. Behind him, dancers dressed in flowers and shells began to move sinuously. He slid through the dancers like spilled oil and came to greet John Dancey.

He was long and slim, with legs and arms which seemed to give the impression of more legs and arms, although there were only two of each. There was something of the spider in the way he moved; sinuous, co-ordinated. His hair was the colour of smoke and ashes and changed in the light, so it looked light silver at times and darkest black at others. His mouth was so full of sharp teeth that a kiss would have cut his lover's lips to ribbons.

As the cuckoo prince came closer, John Dancey could see that his feet were bare. In all this magnificence, he had no shoes to warm his feet. 'You have given me passage back to my kingdom of mysteries,' said the cuckoo prince. 'Only one thing I ask of you. You are a cordwainer, a maker of new shoes. My toes are cold and my feet are bleeding from years of long wandering. Make me a pair of shoes, and in exchange I will give you all the gifts of my land.'

John Dancey said that he would make the shoes, for he was mesmerised by the sight of the shimmering fairy prince who had been the cuckoo he saved. But he said that he had no tools with him to make the shoes and would have to journey home to fetch them.

The pool beneath the banquet table began to bubble and steam, its clear waters changing to cloudy black and orange magma. Black tentacles began to crawl from the water. 'No need to leave,' said the cuckoo prince. 'I have everything here that you need.'

'Then I will stay,' said John Dancey.

The waters calmed and the tentacles vanished. The cuckoo prince lead John Dancey through his grotto. The walls were seamed with copper and gold, and here and there clusters of glow worms softly illuminated the juts and hollows of the black rock. Although they must be deep below the surface of the earth, there seemed to be open sky above them with subtly changing weather; comets shooting across the sky and the occasional light flurry of snow.

It seemed as though the cavern was unfurling before them, new rooms popping into existence as the cuckoo prince required them. He took John Dancey to an approximation of a cordwainer's workshop, though it was worlds away from the simple room in Avebury. Its walls were studded with pearlescent shells and the whole thing gleamed with a pale, greenish lustre. Monstrous oysters in the walls opened their mouths as Dancey passed, showing glorious, unnaturally huge pearls cushioned in their hearts. Some of the pearls' surfaces moved with wispy smoke. Some of them had eyes.

John Dancey took to the workbench and there he found leather of silver and gold and thread spun from glittering spider's silk. There was even a pot of boar bristles like those he used to guide the thread through the leather at home, but instead of black and coarse, they were white and as soft as clouds. John cut and measured and fitted the shapes of the shoes around the cuckoo prince's feet. His long toes flexed and unfurled, and sometimes they tapped on the floor, restless, and changed into bird's feet and then back again.

At last the shoes were made, and they were like no shoes John Dancey had ever made before. They were long-toed turnshoes of gold and silver, and they were held together with stitches as fine and invisible as gossamer. The cuckoo prince put on the shoes, and they fitted him as though they were a part of his feet.

'My wandering is finished,' he said. 'You have given me this gift, and now I will give you mine.'

From that moment, the strange and glorious world below the standing stones unfolded its wings and revealed itself to John Dancey. The cuckoo prince took his hand and brought him to the feasting table. They ate slices of a stuffed roast swan with three heads, and the cuckoo prince cut into a huge pie with a gleaming crust which seemed to tremble as though there were something alive inside it, and a flock of birds never seen in England's skies burst free and whirled around the table.

He handed John Dancey a twisted blue wine glass whose stem was a live snake which curled around his hand and hissed with a poet's tongue.

Three days John Dancey stayed in the house of the cuckoo prince. Three days passed in pleasure and wonder. Three nights passed too, curled in the cuckoo prince's bed, whose long posts were trees laden with fruit of every colour which burst open into silver-winged butterflies as they found delight there. Each kiss was bright as ice and left red marks lingering like petals.

But after three days and three nights, John Dancey sighed and said that he must go back to his village. There were those who would think him dead, and his old father was alone in the world without him. Although they rarely spoke to one another, John Dancey knew that he had responsibilities.

When he told the cuckoo prince that he must leave, an expression of sorrow painted the ageless face of the fairy, but he didn't argue. Instead, he reached into a silk-lined casket full of emeralds and took out a fragile green egg, which he handed to John Dancey.

'Keep it safe and never crack it,' said the prince, 'no matter how you are tempted.'

He took a wine goblet and spilled its contents on the floor of the grotto. The pool of wine seemed suddenly to deepen, widening out before them until it was a great dark lake. Then he gave the cordwainer an ice-cold kiss and pushed him into the pool.

John Dancey fell through the black waters without once becoming wet. Fish swam around him, silver and black. Each fish had the cuckoo prince's face, and while some smiled, the scaly features of others were split wide in screams.

John Dancey woke by the standing stone. There was no sign of a split in the ground or that lightning had struck at all. The ground was cold, but it was hard as though it hadn't rained for weeks. Over the three days and three nights, the cordwainer had become used to the heavy, scented air in the cuckoo prince's grotto, and the cold blast of Wiltshire wind knocked the breath from him.

He walked into the village in a daze. But where was the village? Where were the houses he remembered? There was the forge, but its front had changed almost beyond all recognition. There was a cottage that he knew, but next to it was a tall, new building, with a jauntily painted sign which proclaimed it The King's Arms, established 1747.

John Dancey thought he couldn't trust his eyes, so he went into the inn. All around him were people in the strangest clothes, more outlandish to his eyes than anything in the fairy's kingdom. He stared at them, and they stared at him too, out of place in his workman's clothes. Somehow, he found the voice to ask the nearest man for the date.

'Why, you fool,' said the man, flicking the strange, long skirts of his coat, 'it's the year 1770, in the reign of King George III.'

'1770!' John Dancey exclaimed, his voice trembling. 'Then my father–'

He stumbled from the inn and made his way to the churchyard, which was still where he remembered it to be. Tears blinded his eyes as he wandered those sorrowful aisles, and each time he saw a name of a person he had known, with their date of death three hundred years ago, he let out an anguished cry. Three hundred years! Three hundred years he had been below the earth, and yet it had felt like just three days.

At last, he found his father's name written on a humble cross in the far corner of the churchyard, under a holly bush, and he knew that allowing him to return had not been the cuckoo prince's gift, but his curse. There was nothing left for John Dancey in Avebury now.

Night was falling as he made his slow way back to the standing stones, his thoughts wild and disordered. Where had he to go except back below the earth? But the ground was whole and the night clear and bright with no sign of a coming storm which would open the passage to the barrow for him again. He shouted and called and drummed his hands against the stone, but it was stern and silent.

At last, in desperation, he took out the green egg the fairy prince had given him, and though he had been told not to, he crushed its shell in his fist and cracked it. As soon as the shell was broken, a cuckoo made of mist and stars shot out of the shards of eggshell and flew up into the sky. With the bird's release, John Dancey aged three hundred years all in an instant, for in the egg his old age had been curled.

He died on that spot, by the barred entrance to that other world, and when his body was found by the curious villagers of the eighteenth century, he was buried by the stone here, for nobody knew who he was, nor could they fathom why he should be wearing the clothes of long ago.

There's silence after Snelgrave finishes speaking, and then one of our archaeologists starts laughing.

'That's a fairy tale,' he says. 'That's nothing to do with any provable facts. You can't know that any of that actually happened.'

'Well, that's the story and you asked for it,' says Snelgrave, annoyed, and he stumps off soon after, leaning on his great staff.

Alexander is subdued after the old man's departure and I know that he's disappointed. 'It could be interesting once we can date the bones,' I say, sounding silly even to myself. 'Are they from the eighteenth century or the fifteenth? Let's see who emerges when I do the reconstruction – if the skull's intact.'

He squeezes my hand and nods, but both of us know that anything we come up with here will just be conjecture and Snelgrave's wild tale hasn't helped us with anything concrete.

'Buy Snelgrave a pint at the King's Arms, will you?' he says to one of the others. 'And perhaps our man here dates from the eighteenth century – that's still nearly two hundred years old. It's something. I know we were all hoping for an example of neolithic man, but there it is. I'm going back to the house to write up some notes. Carry on.'

He removes himself shortly after and I know it's to hide his annoyance from our colleagues.

Although I, too, am disappointed, Snelgrave's strange story stays with me as I return to my station at the back of the tall megalith and my charcoals and sketchbook. I find my hand idly tracing some of the images from his tale – peculiar fish and fantastical birds. When I next look up at the sky, there is a bird circling above me. I wonder if it's the same one as I saw earlier. I can't make out the markings on its breast, but I can't help thinking of the lost cuckoo which held all John Dancey's three hundred years of age, endlessly fluttering in the white winter sky and trying to get back underground.

38

The Legend of the Swan

A Worcestershire Tale

In folklore, swans are often associated with the spirit world. Able to fly between the earthly and supernatural realms, this links them to angels, too, and they are also powerful symbols of transformation.

The fairy tale 'The Ugly Duckling' is all about blossoming into beauty despite the expectations of others, and there are countless tales of humans cursed to be transformed into swans. One of the most beautiful associations swans have, however, is as a symbol of faithful love and constancy. They form monogamous pairs, and often mate for life. Their song is also the stuff of legend. A madrigal by Orlando Gibbons captures the idea that a swan only sings once, at its point of death.

Wolverley Court is a real place, and this story of reunited lovers supposedly really did happen there. In fact, there are still remnants of the tomb effigy of the knight in the local church.

As for the lovers' broken ring, which becomes whole when they are reunited, posy rings with engravings were popular love gifts from the Middle Ages onwards. Many examples have been found, particularly dating from the sixteenth and seventeenth centuries. They featured little rhyming inscriptions either inside or outside the ring's band, and the inscription I chose for this story was a romantic one, but some were a bit more cheeky. For example, 'Take thou this, give me a kiss' has absolutely nothing subtle about it at all!

EC

Wide are the wings of a swan, wide and white, as it swoops low over the water and trails rippling droplets behind it. Wide, too, is my tale, as wide and full as a loving heart, and if you sit a while, I'll tell it to you the way I remember it.

I saw a swan that morning, bright as a star streaking across the pale blue morning sky, from the little chip of a window in the attic I shared with the other maids. All our days were the same in the summer milking season, steady and predictable as the beat of a heart, so that one stands out in my memory.

The buttery and the kitchen were already hot and sticky with chatter and gossip and the smell of baking. It was a lively, happy home, Wolverley Court, although the lady of the house, Mistress Walter, was a silent and lonely woman. She'd never married or had children to fill the court with laughter. Nobody knew why.

As I went through the stillroom and out into the yard to collect my milking pails I was joined by Solomon, the old dog. He was a huge wolfhound, long-legged and shaggy, but it was difficult to imagine his days as a hunting dog. Sleepy and sweet-natured, he had been part of the Wolverley family for as long as anybody could remember. He followed after me, wagging his ragged tail, and put his nose into my hand as I walked.

The fluffy dawn clouds cleared away to leave behind a sky as blue as the Virgin's gown and the birds were clamouring for joy. Solomon and I went through the orchard, where clusters of sweet-smelling pear blossom cascaded down the branches.

It was too early for our sweet, dark pears yet, but I could see the bumps on the branches where they would grow. There's nothing like that taste, sweet and sharp. There's a sharpness to the sight of those pear trees, too, for we all remembered the men mustering under their spreading leaves when the king called for all able and willing to join his cause.

A strange thing happened as I reached the edge of the orchard, where it gave way to the Wolverley meadows. The herd of placid short-horn cows had never disturbed old Solomon before, but that day when he saw them he took off running as fast as his rickety legs would carry him. I was surprised because I had never seen him stir his stumps so fast. He liked to follow people and sit quietly by the hearth with his nose on his paws, but here he was, running and barking like a young puppy.

Well, I followed after him, thinking he'd seen something he wanted to chase at last, which would make a story for the others later. We all loved the dog, but accepted that his hunting days, if they'd ever existed, were over.

Solomon stopped suddenly and started sniffing and licking at something in the long grass. I made my way over towards him, thinking that perhaps one of the cows had been injured. We still had wolves in these parts and it was not unheard of for them to come out of the forest with their bright-gold eyes and hungry bellies.

Then I screamed, loud as the day of my birth, for a shape rose up in front of me like a ghost. It was a man, but he was all bedraggled, in clothes that were little more than scraps of rag and with a beard down to his waist. There were chains around his wrists and ankles of heavy rusted iron.

'Solomon, get away!' I yelled, but the foolish dog was waiting patiently by the ragged man's side, wagging his tail as if he'd found a long-lost friend. That's what Solomon was like. If he saw a fox eating our chickens, he'd nuzzle it and try to get it to play with him.

Well, I wasn't about to wait around for the dog to develop a sense of danger. I ran back to the court as fast as my legs would carry me, because I knew for certain that there should not be ghastly chained men in the cattle field on an ordinary milking day.

I made a huge clatter rushing back into the yard, which turned out to be an embarrassment to me for Mistress Walter was there, sitting astride her horse and about to set out to ride.

'Whatever is the matter?' said she.

So, between taking breathless gulps of air, for I hadn't run so fast since I was a very little girl, I told her about the man in the meadow and the dog's reckless behaviour. A couple of the men started for the meadow, and I expected that to be the end of it, but to my great surprise, Mistress Walter went as white as the milk in the churn and set her horse off at a canter, off in the direction of the meadow herself.

'I've missed something here,' I said to one of the grooms. 'What, in the name of all that's holy, is going on?

'I've no idea,' said he, with a broad grin, 'but don't you want to find out?'

Well, I did want to find out, of course, because not a lot happened most days and this was more excitement than we'd known for months. So, we all followed Mistress Walter's horse down to the meadows as fast as we could, and our mouths were soon agape at the scene which greeted us.

Mistress Walter and the ragged man were in each other's arms, kissing like young lovers, despite his forlorn appearance and her unmarried state. They embraced as if they didn't care who saw them, and that was just as well for we were all standing staring. Solomon the old dog was sitting on the ground beside them, his efforts exhausted for the day, but his tail was beating feebly to show his pleasure.

We watched as Mistress Walter reached into the neck of her dress for a little velvet bag which she wore. She opened it and tipped out a little fragment of gold, like half a moon. As she showed the strange man, he reached into his pocket and pulled out another crescent of gold, just the same. The two halves fit together perfectly, just as if they'd been made to do so, for that's what they were – two pieces of the same gold lovers' ring.

We none of us knew what to think, but we could only guess that the stranger was someone that our lady had known long, long ago.

Mistress Walter sent for the smith, and he came with his tools. While he was about his work, striking off the rusty old chains on the stranger's wrists and ankles, we heard the history of his life. It seemed he had once been betrothed to Mistress Walter, but holy zeal had taken hold of his spirit and he'd gone off on Crusade as a soldier of the cross. It was only meant to have been for a little while, and the knight had every intention of returning to marry Mistress Walter while they were both still young.

They had broken their lovers' ring in two, and each of them had vowed to keep the half until they should be reunited. Even the inscription carved inside the ring was a sign of their promise to each other – 'united hearts, death only parts'.

And would you believe, Solomon the old dog, as faithful if not as wise as his namesake in the holy Bible, he had belonged to the brave crusader all those years before. He'd been left with Mistress Walter for her to care for while he was away, and she had cared for him – and never married either.

But then the crusader's fortunes had changed. After a fierce and bloody battle, as close to Hell as a living man should ever have to go, he'd been taken prisoner by the enemy. Rather than kill him, they'd locked him in a dungeon for many years, where he'd never seen the light of the sun and had no way to get a message to his beloved. But his faith had stayed strong, where many men might have become desperate and wanted to give up on everything.

He never stopped praying, and one night an angel appeared before him in shining robes and cast him into a dream. He half awoke to find himself being carried through the air, many miles above the clouds, on the broad feathery back of a huge swan, which flew across the world to drop him in our meadow. The next thing he knew was the rough tongue and excited barking of his constant old dog. We all agreed that it was a miracle of love.

No less miraculous was the day of the wedding. All of us who lived and worked at the court were there, after days of preparation. There was a little private chapel attached to the court where we worshipped on Sundays, and that was where the ceremony was held. We were all invited to see it, for Mistress Walter and her knight had no wealthy friends or relatives.

She looked beautiful as she came into the chapel to marry her crusader, with a wreath of pear blossom and hazel leaves on her head. She met him where he was waiting at the altar, bathed in sunlight streaming through the open church door, with the old dog sitting behind him beating his tail on the floor.

The smith had melted down their old promise ring and forged it fresh into two new rings. Each bore the same inscription, but when they exchanged them to make them one at last, we all knew that not even death would part them.

At the very moment the rings were placed on their fingers, a swan came soaring low through the open chapel door and flew right up the aisle, where it landed just between the newly married couple. And the crusader knight thanked God, in his joy, for the wonder which had saved him and brought him back to the woman he had never stopped loving, even in that dark dungeon on the other side of the world.

We feasted long, and sang and danced, and it was a marvel to see the gentle white swan lying down in the orchard next to the old dog Solomon, looking for all the world as though they were exchanging words. It stayed for some time, until night began to fall, then it flapped its great wings and flew away into the darkening sky. We never saw it again, but Mistress Walter and her knight stayed true to each other until the end of their days, and we always called the meadow 'the Knight's Meadow' after that.

I was popular, of course, as a teller of the tale, and I was often called upon to recount how I had discovered the ragged knight. In time, I was dancing at my own wedding. No swan flew in to grace that day, but I've always smiled whenever I've seen one since then, whether floating on the water or flying overhead.

And so my tale is told.

And if there's another piece of cheese or a slice of black pear, you can fill my bowl next.

39

The Discovery of Supposed Witchcraft

A Yorkshire Tale

This story is linked to a wider phenomenon, whereby seemingly well-meaning, learned people wrote entire books explaining how charlatans performed illusory 'spells', the religious contexts of uncanny events, and demonic practices, in attempts to prove that witchcraft did not exist. The irony is that many people then used these texts as manuals of sorts, each offering a handy guide as to spells to try at home.

Published in 1584, a little over two decades after witchcraft was made a capital offence in England, The Discoverie of Witchcraft, *and the story from it that I have retold here, followed the infamous* Malleus Maleficarum *and predated (if not inspired) James I's* Daemonologie *and the seventeenth-century publication of* The Lesser Key of Solomon. *These books formed a bedrock in the English psyche in relation to witchcraft.*

So, although Yorkshire has such an abundance of folk tales that I really could have had my pick (not least the legend of 'Old Mother Shipton', emanating from her cave at Knaresborough), I wanted to highlight this little story and Reginald Scot's telling of it, which had such a huge impact. Its ripples were felt in hundreds of subsequent witch trials, including in Yorkshire in the cases of Ann Greene, Isabella Billington, and Janet Burniston, not to mention that of the the Timble Witches.

Part of what makes it so interesting is the logic of why the accused was found innocent, not to mention the ways in which it connects so matter-of-factly to beliefs in fairies and the Otherworld in Yorkshire at that time.

MV

To call me an authority on the subject of witchcraft would be an exaggeration. Though there's no denying people do call me John Hyphastes on account of my unmatched alchemical knowledge, as detailed in my famous book *The Metallographia*, I am in truth a humble cleric.

I prefer to go by my given name, John Webster, and though some call me a Seeker, meaning to belittle my endeavours, such a title is not wholly incorrect. My writings on a range of philosophical subjects have drawn to me a degree of what might be called undue attention, yet though my *Saints Guide* and *Academiarum Examen* were viewed by some as controversial, it seemed to be God's will that I write them. This is on account of my most firm belief that all men should learn the best truths and the truest rights. It's for this reason that I state with all assurance that I cannot be an expert in witchcraft as, to put it simply, witchcraft does not exist.

I could not be plainer on this point, and have shown, time and again, that the works of John Dee and Paracelsus are anything but heretical. As finely demonstrated by both Boyle and Bacon, Dee's practices were naught but natural magic. And in natural magic I am a firm believer, as ought all learned folk endeavour to be.

Certainly, I know of instances of so-called witches. I was at York Assizes for the trials of Alice Nutter and Jennet Preston, and I journeyed to Lancaster at my own expense to witness the prosecution of the other so-named 'Pendle Witches'. Yet all alleged witchcraft is but chicanery. There are a great many sorts of deceivers and imposters in this world, and diverse persons under passive delusions of melancholy and fancy. Yet, there is no corporeal league ever made betwixt the Devil and these persons. He does not suck on a witches' body or have carnal copulations with them. Nor do witches turn into cats or dogs or any such animals, or raise tempests or the like, which is what my most recent book sets out to prove.

To speak of books, you needn't read mine, for the Bible says it all. There is not one word in the Bible that signifies a familiar spirit or a witch in that sense that is vulgarly intended in the common parlance; likewise, unholy apparitions and the power of the Devil. Certainly, there is the Witch of Endor in those pages, but the word 'witch' is a mistranslation, for if she was a witch for raising up Samuel then Jesus Christ must be thought a witch just the same for raising up Lazarus, not to mention his most holy self. And forget not that our world is full of wonders that mankind has yet not come to understand. Diverse creatures and minerals, such as beryls and crystals, might look to be miraculous to the foolish, ignorant, and impious, but such things are natural and not diabolical, as can be proved by the sustained application of reason.

To take a fine example from the times just after the Pendle trials, less talked about perhaps by virtue of the man who drew the court's focus being vindicated. His name was, like mine, John, and he was a simpleton. He was known in York for being unlucky. He was tricked and cheated all through his life on account of being innocent to the dark hearts of men. And John, touched in his way, such as he was, was the last person who ought to face down a judge, let alone a prosecutor such as Durant Hotham, Magistrate of East Riding. But I was there to watch, and I saw justice done.

To describe John to you, when I knew him best he was a dirty fellow. His hair was lank and long, his long nails bedded with mud. He slept often under the open sky up on the moors, coming to town only when he'd gathered sufficient roots and berries to trade with folk for a hot meal and bed. Yet one day, John came to York with something new to trade – a sympathetic powder, he called it. One to cure all ailments. And he knew not to sell it for a low price, and clutched the wooden box in which he held it close to his heart to defend it from thieves and cutpurses.

It took some time for John to find customers, but find them he did. And lo and behold, the powder worked. I saw a sample of it later, in the court – it was white and fine as milled flower, emitting an aroma like the scent of honey. And it was on account of the success of this powder, which brought a long line of people to see John, all with coin to spend for a pinch of his curative dust, that he found himself accused.

Folk could not understand how the powder might help a woman with a headache who took it as snuff, and then resolve the aches in a cripple's legs when the dust was rubbed upon them. That a man with plague who rubbed it on his buboes would soon enough see them disappear, while a whole house with Stop Gallant were saved from an affliction all knew to be incurable.

This happened not all at once, of course, for John would visit town with his wooden box and sell his wares, and when the box was emptied he would again stride out to the moors in all kinds of weather, returning days later with his stocks replenished.

The truth of what was happening on those moors was only revealed when John was clapped in irons. By then, he was less thin or soiled in appearance, having bathed and eaten many fine meals and bought himself new clothes.

Though Mr Hotham made quite the statement on John's evils, reading a declaration in which John admitted his powder was magic, when John himself was invited to speak he explained himself completely. Slowly, too, I must say, for John never had a skill with words, but he enlightened the court and saved himself in doing so.

He said simply that one night, before day was gone, he was going home from his labours being very sad and full of heavy thoughts, not knowing how to get meat and drink. Only then he met a fair woman in fine clothes who asked him why he was so sad, and he told her that it was by reason of his poverty.

To this she said that if he would follow her counsel, she would help him to that which would serve to get him a good living. He consented with all his heart, provided it were not a means to profit by unlawful ways, and she told him that it should not be, by any such ways, but by the doing of good and the curing of sick people.

The woman warned him strictly to meet her at that spot the next night at the same time. She departed from him and he went home to the space beneath an outcrop where he used to lay his head. And the next night, at the time appointed, he duly waited and she, according to her promise, came and told him that it was well that he came so duly, otherwise he would have missed that benefit she intended to do him.

She bade him follow her and not be afraid and led him to a little hill. There she knocked three times, and the hill opened and they went in.

They came to a fairy hall, wherein was a queen sitting in great state and many people about her. The gentlewoman that had brought John there presented him to the queen, and she said he was welcome and she bid the gentlewoman give John some of the white powder and teach him how to use it. This she did, giving him the little wood box, bidding him to give grains of it to any who were sick, saying it would heal them.

She then brought him forth from the hill, and so they parted.

The court was silent as John told this tale, yet questions followed. John was asked by the judge whether the place within the hill, which John called a hall, were light or dark, and John said indifferent, as it is in twilight. Being asked how he got more powder, he said that when he wanted, he went back to that hill and knocked three times, whereupon it opened. On going in, he said he was conducted by the aforesaid woman to the queen and so had more powder given him.

This was the plain and simple story he told before the judge, the whole court and the jury, and there being no proof, save what cures he had done to very many, the jury did acquit him. Mr Hotham seemed to judge John rightly accused, for he had the white powder from some spirit, yet there was no contract with the Devil; neither was it ever proved that the Devil did any good, either real or apparent, but is the sworn enemy of all mankind, both in their souls and in their bodies. Yet John's powder wrought that which was really good, namely the curing of diseases, and therefore, rationally, it could not be thought to have been given him by an evil spirit.

As for the notion that John had the powder from those people we call fairies, there are many that do believe and affirm that there are such people. Paracelsus hath a treatise holding that the fae are not of the seed of Adam and therefore he calls them non-Adamicks, but he states that they have flesh and bones and so differ from spirits, yet they can glide through walls and rocks as easily as we through the air – a function which Paracelsus which called their chaos. Some call them silvestres, some gnomes, but the proof of their existence is entirely satisfactory.

I remember the judge said, when all the evidence was heard, that if he were to assign punishment then John might well have been whipped or worse, had his tale been a deceit or imposture – yet it was true, so John walked free.

It is my view, firmly held, that in all such cases of magic, there is an explanation such as this to be discovered. For if it can be proved that a person did murder another, the means should be shown. Elsewise, it's delusion to call folk witches. And elsewise, in the fashioning of charms and powders and tonics, if a person has skills as a healer, as do I, then they ought be praised and rewarded for it, not hanged from a noose until dead.

As for John, after the trial he was seen no more, having strode up into the wilds and vanished from view. If I were him, I would have gone to that fairy hall and stayed there. It seems their queen is at least a benevolent ruler, and though they say we must all now give praise to the latest Stuart to take the throne, I refuse. Some say it's a divinely ordained miracle, but I'll tell you this: miracles are no more real than witchcraft.

Praise for *The Three Ravens Folk Tales*:

'The ghosts of M.R. James and Terry Pratchett haunt these stories… an exuberant mix of folklore, legend, history and landscape, with shudders and chuckles served up in equal measure, underpinned by deep knowledge of the material.' *Hugh Lupton, award-winning storyteller, performer and author.*

' The Three Ravens banner is a guarantee of solid research, entertaining prose, and the perfect mix of fun and danger, putting the reader in mind of the best who came before: Roald Dahl, Angela Carter, and now … *Three Ravens.*' *Mark Norman, author of* Black Dog Folklore.

'This tour of the traditional tales of English counties demonstrates that folklore is the past, present and future rock'n'roll.' *James Wright, author of* Historic Building Mythbusting

'A veritable travelogue of folk tales and legends of England to shorten the road, filled with charm, fun, heartache & mischief.' *Taffy Thomas MBE, first UK Storyteller Laureate*

Eleanor and Martin are masters of the spoken word. Their popularity in storytelling is evident. But it is now apparent that their words are equally important in the pages of books. Whether you listen to their podcast or nor doesn't matter as their words will paint pictures in your mind of ghosts, dragons, mermaids and other realms.The stories are unlike anything I've read before. They are unique, historically jam-packed reimagining's of English folk tales. Some are in the style of Victorian ghost story masters like A.N.L Munby or M.R. James while others are in the style of Thomas Hardy or Emily Brontë. But they are all original and entertaining. This collection is vibrant, elegant and beautiful. I cannot recommend it highly enough. *Adam Bushnell, author*

'This book is a delight to read. Thirty-nine folktales from around England are retold with a touch of mischief and lots of love for the richness of the stories. Thankfully, each tale has a well-informed introduction to set the scene and inspire the imagination.' *Owen Davies, Vice President of the Folklore Society and author*

'Think of these folktales not as definitive legends, but rather cheeky remixes that draw from the full breadth of folklore around England. The provided commentary highlights where a motif from one tale appears in another, but the resulting tale will still manage to both entertain and delight you. Fabulous folklore, indeed!' *Icy Sedgwick, author, folklorist, researcher, and host of the Fabulous Folklore podcast.*